MW01119188

BEAUTIFUL DAMAGE

Reader comments:

"I am so in love with this book! Each chapter kept me glued to the pages. When I wasn't reading it, it was constantly on my mind. I wanted to hurry and get back to reading it. I found it just that good!!"

"All the twists and turns were wild, and I actually gasped in several spots."

"I had to read ahead to the end because I couldn't take it anymore, but [Raina] layered in so many twists and turns that I couldn't even find out all the things I wanted to know. Reading ahead brought up new mysteries. So I had to go back and actually just be patient!"

SERIES BY RAINA ASH

BEAUTIFUL DAMAGE

RAINA ASH

Pink Fox Publishing

This is a work of fiction. Names, characters, businesses, organizations, places, events and incidents are either the product of the author's imagination or are used fictitiously. Any resemblance to actual persons, living or dead, events, or locales is entirely coincidental or fictionalized.

BEAUTIFUL DAMAGE

Copyright © 2024 by Raina Ash.

All rights reserved.

No part of this book may be used or reproduced in any manner whatsoever or by any electronic or mechanical means, including information storage and retrieval systems, without written permission from the author, except for the use of brief quotations in critical articles or reviews.

All characters depicted are 18+

Published by Pink Fox Publishing.

First Edition: October 2024

Printed in the United States of America

10 9 8 7 6 5 4 3 2 1

ISBN 979-8-9860770-3-1 (paperback)

ASIN B0DG6YCJKF (e-book)

Art is not a mirror held up to reality, but a hammer with which to shape it.
—Berthold Brecht

Series Soundtrack
(Spotify)

CHAPTER 1

SIENNA

AS MY EYES SCAN THE ballroom of glittering gold and black, the mantra I picked for this evening plays out in my head: *One feather can tip the scale.*

My own scale has always tipped the wrong way through some incredibly bad life choices. Those choices haunt me, shred me to pieces, leave gaping holes that might someday swallow me.

But not this time. Choosing to come here tonight has to be something that will help me do some actual good in this world, something to balance out all the darkness I've created.

My eyes dart across the black masks that cover everyone's eyes, a fitting visual for this art gala's theme of 'Hidden Desires.' My insides are so shaky I feel like I might faint. But I can do this, dammit. I can schmooze one of these rich assholes and get some funding for the community art program I want to create.

And I'll do it all in a faded gold thrift store dress.

Clutching my champagne in one hand, I take a step toward a group of men in designer suits. One in particular, with shimmery gold pants, black jacket, and a gold feather resting in his chest pocket, has a relaxed posture and looks approachable. Of course, I don't really know what kind of man he is beneath his outward appearance, but he's wearing a smile at least.

When I'm close enough to introduce myself, an *old* woman beside him pins me with her eyes. Under her scrutinizing gaze, all words die in my throat. Maybe she's bitter toward everyone, but her stare makes me feel exposed.

Like she knows all my secrets.

After checking my black mask to make sure it's still hiding the top half of my face, I retreat, weaving through clusters of bodies. Now it seems like everyone's shadowy eyes are on me, and they're all collectively thinking: "Imposter."

I stop at the edge of the ballroom, grateful for the distance between me and all the masked people. I really hate crowds; they're great for escape yet also the perfect opportunity for a kidnapping.

I never know who might be watching me.

Glancing at the marble tile, I shake my head. Why did I think sneaking into this thing was a good idea? I'm an art student—an old college student—and these people are all successful artists or art collectors. They don't want to help with my dumb art program.

I tug at my dress, suddenly wanting it off.

Through the sea of black and gold attire, Jada catches my eye. Her dark skin is radiant against her crisp white server's uniform, and her blonde and crimson braids are pulled back into a low bun at the nape of her neck. She weaves through the crowd with a tray of caviar, her movements as graceful and precise as when she dances ballet.

She stops in front of me and flashes her practiced, professional lip curve. "Caviar, miss?" she asks with a fake British accent.

I stifle a laugh. She's never once been to England, and she also curses like a sailor. Her mouth can be so filthy that she even makes me blush sometimes.

And I've seen some terrifying shit in my life.

I guess we all have those adjacent, conflicting parts of Self. We all have the capacity to become someone different, for better or worse.

Jada leans in, her contacts making her soulful brown eyes green today. She whispers, "Try some. Fucking proper posh nosh."

I'm not sure how she said that without getting tongue-tied, but I have the feeling her British kick is going to last for a while this time.

I grab a cracker piled high with the glistening black pearls and then take a bite. It's salty and squishy, with a texture that makes me want to gag. I force myself to swallow, washing it down with a sip of champagne; the bubbles sting my nose until I grimace. Ugh, I detest drinking—this flute is only a prop to blend in—but getting that fish taste out of my mouth was an emergency.

"Oh god," I mutter under my breath.

Jada gives me an evil smirk. "Start talking to people or I'll make you eat another. I didn't sneak you in to stand in a corner."

I exhale, wiggling my toes inside my gold heels. There are some big names here from the art world. Even though everyone is wearing the same black mask, I recognize a few artists, mostly by their signature styles. Yet, here I am like a smudge of charcoal on the Mona Lisa—someone is going to discover I'm a blemish and quickly erase me.

Just last week, one of my teachers noticed the muddied colors and bleeding edges where I'd overworked the water-color paint, trying to cover up a mistake on my final canvas. He'd only frowned and said, "Rough edges. No control. Your layering is wrong. Are we still at basics, Sienna?"

God, that stung, especially since I'd poured everything I had into that painting.

"Miss," Jada says, reeling my attention back. She waves the tray of caviar near my face, forcing me to take a whiff. "Try another. I insist."

The skin on the bridge of my nose wrinkles like bunched fabric. I give her the side-eye and she smirks again. "Fine," I whisper. "I'll mingle."

"That's my bitch," she whispers back.

Taking a slow, calming breath, I adjust my purse strap on my shoulder and weave through the crowd. I decide it's time for another mental pep talk, so I repeat one of my go-to motivational mantras in my head: *In every challenge lies an opportunity.*

I can do this.

I am capable.

Focus on the end goal and my purpose for being here; the rest doesn't matter.

My hand is trembling, so I grip my champagne flute tighter. The stem feels flimsy in my fingers, like I'm going to snap it. But really, why am I so nervous? I've survived way worse situations in my life—all I have to do tonight is mingle and try to find someone interested enough in my goals to exchange contact info.

Way easier than fighting for my life.

I scan the ballroom once again, heart pounding. My eyes catch on a woman wearing a princess gown made of lace and embroidered with pearls. I watch the subtle sway of the fabric, the shadows shifting along her collarbone, the reflection of chandelier light off the crystals in her up-do. If only I could sit in a corner and paint her. Instead, I try to commit the woman to memory for a later sketch. My work tends to be macabre, so I'm imagining her delicate dress in a forest of black, twisted trees, two red glowing eyes watching her from the darkness.

There should definitely be red, watchful eyes.

As I'm passing by a group, I hear the name 'Soulages' and my ears perk up. We were just studying him in my art history class, so he's fresh in my mind. I casually float over to the clique of older attendees and linger on the outskirts.

A woman with bright mauve lipstick is saying, "Well, I saw the show at the Louvre. There were a few paintings reminiscent of Soulages."

The group falls into a momentary pause, so I cut in before I can overthink it. "I love his technique—creating different sheens and textures from only the color black."

"Honestly," the man beside me says, "I'm not a fan." The group erupts into a heated debate.

I do my best to keep up and add comments, but they barely acknowledge me. I'm about to admit defeat when *the* Josefina Montoya suddenly appears; I know for certain it's her because she's not wearing a mask. Her shock of red hair and cheekbones that could cut glass are jarring under the ballroom's warm, romantic lighting. Yet, she's undeniably captivating.

My heart stops for a second. Montoya is known for her mixed-media pieces that explore human emotion and trauma through found objects. Her work has been an inspiration for me since I started painting myself out of my own struggles.

She glances my way, lowers her sharp eyes over my dress, and then turns to the man beside me. "Soulages is a master, of course," she says. "But I find his work a bit…one-note, don't you think? Always black, black, black. Where's the range?"

A few in the group shrug, but there's a lull and my heart leaps. I feel sick and jittery all at once, but I say, "Isn't that the point? He's exploring the depth and complexity of a single color. It's a study in restraint and nuance."

Montoya's gaze snaps to mine, her perfectly shaped eyebrows peaking. Her mouth twitches down. "Restraint can easily become repetition. True artistry lies in pushing boundaries, not limiting oneself."

I feel a flush creep up my neck, but I forge ahead, barely understanding what flows out of my mouth; I'm only repeating things my art history teacher said during a lecture. "There's something to be said for fully exhausting a concept. Soulages has spent decades proving black isn't just a color, it's a universe unto itself."

Montoya gives me a painted-on smile that lacks contrast. "Decades? And what have you been doing for decades, dear? From the looks of that dress, I'd say haunting Goodwill."

The group laughs, and I feel my face burn. I glance down at the faded fabric squeezing my body, suddenly aware of every flaw, every sign that I'm not elegant, wealthy, or sophisticated. That my art is just simplistic watercolors and moody macabre scenes, lacking the labyrinth of meaning found in works by Soulages or Montoya.

When the laughter wanes, I lift my chin even as my insides are sinking. I try to laugh it off. "Busted," I say, forcing a smile, but I hate how tiny my voice sounds. "I'm actually a student. I'm studying—"

"Aren't we all?" Montoya cuts me off with a wave of her hand. "But study doesn't equal talent. It takes more than a few classes, dear, to understand the complexities of the art world." She angles away, shutting me out. "Now, Edward, I noticed you haven't…"

I stand there for a moment, frozen, with a dumb smile on my face. I take a fake sip of my champagne, pretending not to mind Montoya's comment as I try to focus on the conversation. But what's the point of lingering? Even if, by some miracle, I say something interesting, these people will always see me as an outsider.

No, I shouldn't keep standing here. When the group ripples with laughter again, I take one last glance at my idol, then slip away.

I just need some air.

As I'm making my way toward the patio doors, my cheeks still burning, a man steps on the stage across the room. There are a few speeches scheduled for tonight that I'm interested in, but I've lost the heart to listen.

The people outside start flowing in, and the room quickly becomes suffocating. I stop at a bar to abandon my drink, then a few minutes later I've escaped into the chilly night air. Thankfully, I'm alone in the garden.

A deep, cleansing breath helps the world feel stable again. I push my purse to one hip and lean against a railing overlooking the koi pond. My fingers twirl the silver locket around my neck as streaks of red, orange, and black fish twirl in the dark water below. Around me, the patio is a paradise of plants and flowers lit by ground lights. It's another scene I long to paint—feels appropriate to fill it with bloodthirsty wolves waiting to pounce, eyes watching from all sides.

"Study doesn't equal talent."

She's right. Practice doesn't equal talent either; some

artists never achieve that elusive *something* that makes a piece truly great. My pieces, according to my teachers, are all rough, uninspired, drab…

I stare up at the crescent moon and touch the tear trying to escape down my cheek. So dumb. Why am I crying over this? These people don't deserve my tears; Montoya doesn't. No one does.

So why have I always given away my tears so freely?

As I shiver from the cold air hitting my bare shoulders, I hear the clack of footsteps behind me on the concrete. When I glance to my left, a man has stopped beside me to lean on the railing and stare into the murky waters of the pond. I tense and lean away, knowing I'm out here alone with this stranger, but he acts like I'm not here. He watches the fish—dark masses swimming around, blending into the shadows.

Even something so colorful and innocent-looking contains darkness.

"Beautiful night," he says, finally glancing my way.

"Yes." I study him for a moment, trying to gauge what kind of man he might be.

It's hard to see his eyes because of the mask and the lighting, but he's smiling at the shadow fish. His temples are gray, but there are no fine lines around his mouth, his fingernails are perfectly trimmed and clean, and the cut of his torso suggests he's got a muscular build. It seems he takes care of himself.

That doesn't tell me how he treats others, though.

My eyes wander back to his smile and the mole below his bottom lip. Something about the smile's soft angle helps me relax some in his presence. And I like that he's not pressuring me for conversation; he only gave me an opening if I wanted to make small talk.

We rest in silence together, and I close my eyes for a heartbeat. I just need a second.

In every challenge lies an opportunity.

I have to believe that, because without the thin sliver of hope I've held on to my entire life, what's left except despair?

Once the heartbeat passes, I open my eyes and straighten. Maybe talking to this man is the opportunity I've been seeking tonight; that sliver of hope tells me I have to try.

"It was getting a bit stuffy inside," I comment.

The man chuckles. "I saw you talking to Montoya, so I can only imagine."

"An acquaintance?"

"I'm an art dealer, so I've bought a few of her pieces. Mostly, I've heard rumors."

Hope surges—he's an art dealer. He'd be a great connection because he might be able to direct me to people interested in funding my art program.

I take a huge risk, hoping this guy has a sense of humor, and respond, "The rumors are correct. She's a bitch."

The man laughs, a deep, genuine sound that eases more of the tension in my shoulders. "That's the art world for you," he says with a lazy shrug. "Talent and ego go hand in hand."

I nod; the sliver of hope is growing.

"I don't believe I caught your name," he says. He angles his face toward me, catching some light so the shadows around his mask disappear. He holds my gaze with warm, friendly brown eyes.

I'm finally comfortable enough to smile. I extend my hand, about to respond, when a deep, rumbling voice comes from behind us.

"You don't need her name."

Mr. Art Dealer blanches when he lays eyes on our brooding intruder. My breath catches, but I'm sure for a very different reason.

This interloper is somehow the epitome of everything this networking gala symbolizes—sophistication, intellect, wealth. Or maybe it's better to describe him as a walking art piece, a tan Michelangelo sculpture made real. Either way, he's a lot of exquisite masculinity in a custom three-piece black suit. The gold rose pin on his lapel, sparkling with diamonds, catches my eye for a moment before I'm distracted by his inky black hair, firmly etched mouth, and intensely blue eyes that pierce through the shadows of his mask.

"W-we were just having a friendly conversation," Mr. Art Dealer stutters, cowering in the man's presence. "Stop policing me."

"Someone has to."

I'm in a daze as I watch their exchange. Half of me is trying to piece together what's going on because it seems they know each other, while the other half is still mesmerized by Mr. Imposing.

His words are hard and final when he speaks again to the art dealer. "Your conversation is done."

Blinking out of my daze, my initial reaction quickly turns to irritation. The art dealer starts to leave, trying to escape the intruder's overpowering presence, but I can't let this opportunity slip away. I need the art dealer's contact info at least; I've been fighting an uphill battle with my art program for so long I *need* this break.

"Wai—" I begin to say, taking a step to follow, but Mr. Imposing blocks my path. I huff and try to sidestep him.

He sidesteps too, preventing me from following the art

dealer.

"Excuse me," I bite out, hoping he'll get the hint and take a hike.

"You're excused," he responds, "but not if you're following that man."

I huff again because who does this guy think he is? Stepping back to create an opportunity, I try to rush around him.

The jerk actually *puts his arm out*, forcing me to stop abruptly so I don't smack into his inner elbow.

"Wait," I call out to the art dealer in a last attempt to salvage the situation.

But he either doesn't hear or he ignores me, slipping inside to lose himself in a sea of people. Since he's wearing a generic mask and dressed identically to other men, it will be impossible to find him.

A red coal flares in my stomach as I cross my arms and stare up at the man who lost me an opportunity. "That was a bit rude. *What* is your problem?"

His eyes capture mine and something shifts between us. He's looking at me with such a scorching intensity, and the magnetism between us is so strong that I falter in my irritation and have to take a step back.

Then he asks something I'm not expecting, "Are you alright?"

It's a phrase I'm not used to—Jada was the first person in my life to ever ask.

I lick my dry lips before answering. "Yes. I'm fine. But it was rude to interrupt my conversation." I somehow pull myself away from this striking man's orbit and face the koi pond again. "I really needed to network with that guy."

Mr. Imposing moves to the railing, completely focused

on me, but I refuse to look in his direction. I can't believe I was so close to making an actual professional connection and this jerk ruined it. Sex appeal doesn't excuse rudeness.

"Why's that?" the man asks. Now that he's so close, I catch his sinful smell. It's not an overpowering cologne; it might just be sandalwood body wash or shampoo. Whatever it is, it's mouthwatering.

I grit my teeth. "Doesn't matter. I'm too pissed at you to say."

He laughs—deep and resonant—and the sound makes my stomach flutter. "Pissed? You should thank me."

Now it's my turn to laugh. I finally look at him from the corner of my eye. "For what? I've been trying so long to find funding for my art program, and that guy could've been a great connection. He's an art dealer, so I'm sure he has a robust network. And *you* ruined it. Actually"—I turn to face him, steeling myself before looking at those brilliant blue irises—"he seemed to know you. Are you acquaintances? Can I please have his contact info?"

Dismissing my question, he asks, "What art program?"

My arms cross again, anything to shield myself from this man's raw energy. "It's a program I want to start for struggling teens and young adults. It will be like art therapy and a safe place where they can go, twenty-four seven, to express themselves and escape for a few hours. Escape their home life or...anything." I look away—I have to. The man's gaze suddenly shifted when I mentioned escape; I caught something in his eyes that I recognize in myself.

An open wound.

Now I'm wondering what kind of man he is, and I'm annoyed at myself for not considering that before engaging in this conversation. His appearance and energy just caught me off-guard.

That's never good.

I move away from him an inch and hug myself tighter because it's suddenly more chilly in the garden. The man unbuttons his jacket after a shiver rattles through my shoulders. He wraps the warm garment around my torso, then tugs on the lapels, closing them but also pulling me a step closer.

His woodsy scent snakes through my lungs again and I breathe deep, unable to pull any part of myself away from his orbit.

He's not flustered at all; the man is completely self-possessed and confident in every word he speaks.

Still holding the lapels, he says, "That art dealer you were talking to has a nasty obsession with groping women, primarily artists and his receptionists. It's better to stay away. I'm glad you caught my eye earlier, and I saw him follow you out here."

My breath stalls, and I squeak out, "What if you're lying? I don't know you. I don't know that's true."

The corner of his mouth twitches in annoyance and he releases the jacket lapels. "I'm not a liar. If you need proof, fine." He pulls his phone from his pants pocket and taps on it. Finally, he shows me the screen.

There's a news article with a picture of the art dealer—I recognize the brown eyes and the mole under his bottom lip. In big, bold letters the headline reads, "Rising Artists Unite in Legal Battle Against Predatory Art Dealer." The first few lines of the article mention that at least ten women are involved in the lawsuit about sexual misconduct.

I shrink away from the phone, moving back until I hit the railing. Why do I have such awful instincts? Why can't I judge someone's character correctly? He seemed nice. I took time to observe him and his demeanor was putting me at ease…

A memory invades my mind: A tall, willowy teenage boy sitting next to me on the grass, a permanent crease between his eyebrows. He sat with me while I cried. Talked to me. Listened. He was the first person in my life to really listen.

He was friendly at first too.

A sick feeling swirls around my gut, my open wound festering.

I glance up at my rescuer, wondering what he might look like under his mask. "Thank you," I say softly, still processing what he just revealed. That art dealer was another wolf in sheep's clothing, hiding in the gloom, hungry and waiting to pounce. I've encountered too many people like that in my life. Too many. I hug my waist under the large tuxedo jacket, trying to protect my most vulnerable places. "I-I think I should go home."

My protector is no doubt noticing my sudden shift—the waver in my voice, the shrinking of my body. I'm not scared of him because he saved me from a creep…I just need to be alone. Forget this entire night.

He nods. "Did you drive here?" I shake my head, and he pulls his cell phone from his pocket. "Let me call you a ride."

I don't protest; I don't pull away when he places a light hand on my shoulder and guides me inside and to the exit. And I feel safe as he waits with me near the curb.

Is this safety just another illusion?

I stare up at a street light, letting it blind me. "Why did he say you were policing him?" I ask.

"Because I am."

"But what does that mean?"

He pushes a thick hand through his dark hair before shoving it in a pocket. "Well, I attend a lot of art and charity events. Somehow, he's at half of them, and I always find him in some corner talking to a beautiful woman. They're usually in their twenties. Usually alone. So I chase him off." He curves his mouth in a slight smirk, and I get the sense he may never fully smile. "Bastard should be going to jail soon."

"Why bother?"

He glances at me and his expression is hard to read under the mask, but his lips have curved down. "Why? You want more victims?"

"No, of course not. I mean, why you? You could simply ignore it. Other people have read the articles, right? Gossip spreads. No one else is watching that man and keeping tabs on what he's doing."

"That's why I have to."

Through the dim light, I see those piercing blue eyes filled with conviction.

I don't know why, but I long to stand here all night just gazing into them.

Get away from him, Sienna.

A sleek black SUV arrives, and the driver hops out to open my door.

My rescuer is staring at me now like I'm a puzzle he wants to figure out, and I think I'm staring at him the same way. I'm drawn to his sense of justice, the straightforward way he talks. I want to trust that he's a good guy, but considering my instincts are always so, so wrong…

"Thank you," I tell my protector again, touching his arm without thinking. His biceps are large, unyielding.

He glances down to where our bodies are meeting, and

his forehead wrinkles, like he's quirking an eyebrow under the mask. He covers my hand with his; it's warm. Inviting. "I'm glad you're alright."

I yank my hand away from his heat.

"Here." He slides a business card from his pocket and holds it out. "If you need connections, I can help you find some for your program."

I run my thumb over the embossed name on the card: Declan Conte. There's only a name and a phone number, so I have no idea what this man does for work or who his connections might be. Regardless, there's a major problem with accepting his offer: a conflict of interest.

"Sorry," I say, returning the card. "I'm attracted to you, and the last thing I want is to get involved with a man I can't trust myself around."

Blunt? Yes. But I've been through too much shit in my life to walk on eggshells.

I think I hear a soft groan in his throat as his eyes burn with interest. His gaze sweeps down my body.

I clearly wasn't wrong in thinking the attraction might be mutual. Though *why* he's attracted to me when my thrift store dress is so obvious, I don't know.

He opens his mouth to speak, but I cut in. "I am grateful for your offer to help. Really. And for everything else. Thank you. But, um, good night." I slip into the SUV and the driver closes the door.

Once the driver is inside, I give him my address. I buckle up as the vehicle pulls away, then I sag into the plush leather seat. That's when I realize I'm still wearing Declan's jacket.

I feel a shard of guilt, but I wrap the garment tighter around myself, a cocoon of masculine scent and warmth and safety. I finger the gold and diamond rose pin on the front.

"I'm glad you caught my eye."

I'm wondering if he noticed me because I was so clearly out of place—some poor, Midwestern, almost thirty-year-old woman who thought she could mingle with the elites.

Well, whatever momentary insanity and chemistry we just experienced, I know it's not right for me to keep his jacket, especially since it feels so damn expensive. I pull my phone from my purse, then add Declan as a contact, punching in his phone number before I forget it. Once I'm recovered from this whirlwind night, I'll reach out to return the jacket.

With that settled, I let Jada know I'm heading home, then I lean my head against the cool tinted glass window. The Golden Gate bridge appears in the distance whenever the SUV crests a hill. It's lit up and shimmering in a sea of black.

I've painted that bridge so many times, yet I've never once captured its beauty—there are too many blemishes on my soul for me to do that.

I'm flattered that a man like Declan noticed me, saw me as someone worth rescuing. But I'm sure he didn't notice the shadows that follow me wherever I go. The secrets, wounds, scars.

If he knew how dark my past was, he'd want nothing to do with me.

CHAPTER 2

DECLAN

I'M BARELY AWARE OF THE jet engine's hum throughout the cabin as I stare out the window at the blue sky. It truly looks endless, blue melting into blue in every direction.

These trips are the only moments I feel any kind of peace.

Up here in the sky, there's a hollowness. A void. I'm far away from every annoyance going on below, away from anything familiar that brings familiar memories.

I can stare out at the blue abyss for hours and not think a goddamn thought.

April 10th doesn't exist up here in the clouds.

Neither do any of my failures.

I'm simply empty, as empty as the universe will be. One day, when the last dying star fades out.

The hum of the engines pulls me back and I realize that Davis, the VP of my security company, NexaProtect, is no longer talking. I check my phone, making sure we're still connected, then I rest it on my thigh.

"You were saying?" I ask, leaning back in my leather seat.

His sigh is loud through the speaker. "You're not listening again, are you?"

"I only spaced out for a moment."

"I thought those new sleeping pills were helping. Is it more insomnia?"

I turn my head to gaze out the window again, a dull ache behind my eyes. I'd rather not talk about myself—a topic I hate. "Is the demo ready for Halliwell and his team?" I ask, bringing the focus back to business.

"Yup. We're going to highlight the security breach they had last year. We'll simulate the vulnerability to show how our detection system would've stopped the hackers before..."

I close my eyes as Davis continues on, only half listening because my head is now pounding. This entire week has been nonstop flights to meet with clients or potential ones, and I'm finally flying home to San Francisco. Last night's dinner with Mr. Halliwell, the pretentious CEO of a hotel group, was especially annoying. God, that guy was the worst. He kept trying to hit on the server instead of fucking focusing on our conversation. If a partnership with the asshole wasn't so important for my company's expansion goals, I wouldn't even bother.

"Our tech team is working on the case studies for the pitch," Davis is saying. "Marketing wants to..."

Dammit, why is it so hard to pay attention? I'm not trying to disrespect Davis—he's a sharp, strategic man who does amazing things for my company—but I think I've been pushing myself too hard with all these expansions and partnerships.

Davis is right—I'm having insomnia again because the fucking pills stopped doing their job. I suppose I can't really blame the medicine. Endless work is how I've designed my life; the constant dull aches and pains in my body are a deserved torment.

April 10th is only three weeks away.

Resting my head back on the seat, eyes still closed, the

dark behind my eyelids is a welcome embrace. I think of the sky, endless, and how I want to dissolve into it…

"Declan? Hello?"

My eyes snap open and I inhale sharply. Fuck, did I nod off? I clear my throat. "Yeah? Sorry. You were talking about the simulation for the hack."

I can sense Davis' amused grin through the speaker. "I was. About five minutes ago. What are you doing? Deciding which woman you'll take to bed tonight?"

I snort. "Not exactly. I nodded off."

Davis knows about my sleeping problems and pretty much every other awful thing about my life, and when it's clear I don't want to discuss something, he tries a different approach: humor.

I don't mind. He's the only person I have any kind of friendship with—besides Sean—and Davis is good at getting me to laugh. It helps me survive nowadays, so I owe the man a lot.

"Ah," he says, his tone light. "You're napping now so you'll have the stamina to entertain multiple women tonight. Got it."

I laugh. "Fuck off."

His warm chuckle carries through the phone speaker as I stifle a yawn. "Well," he says, "we can discuss more of the pitch on Monday. Honestly, I can't fathom Halliwell saying no to a partnership. They're desperate and our track record is spotless."

"True. But I never half-ass anything."

"Oh, I'm *very* aware of that. The word 'anal' comes to mind."

I smirk and shake my head. "I'm hanging up now."

"Bye. Try not to spend the entire night entertaining

yourself. Maybe actually sleep for once."

I grunt, then rest my phone on the tray beside me. My next yawn is so prolonged that it brings moisture to my eyes.

I glance across the jet's cabin to Sean, my bodyguard, as he's reading a book. He's been working with me for about five years, and I take him on every trip. The man is shorter than me, but he's ex-military and trained in a lot of combat styles. Even though he's not bulky, you can tell just by looking at him that he can cause a lot of damage. His lean muscles always look coiled to strike.

I've hired a lot of bodyguards over the years, and Sean is the only one I trust completely with my life. Still, it's good to have a few around, so I usually hire at least one more to accompany Sean.

When I glance at him, his sixth sense kicks in and he immediately looks up, trying to gauge if I need something.

My eyes dart toward the bathroom near the back of the jet, then back to Sean.

He shrugs and says, "Jeremy's still in there." He drops his gaze back to his book. "Told him not to eat that Mexican food."

He's reading a self-help book about productivity habits, his black side-swept hair falling over his eyes. Honestly, I'm not sure how he sees because his hair is always in his face. I'm not sure why he doesn't cut it—he's half-Korean and people sometimes comment about his hair looking 'K-pop.'

That comment is the number one way to piss him off.

"What's your take on Jeremy?" I ask. He's the new bodyguard I've been trying out.

Sean shrugs again, a quick and controlled motion, then he flips a page in his book. "He's only been here a few months, so we'll see. So far, he's doing what he's supposed to, following directions. He asks good questions. Don't think he likes you, though."

"Why?"

"Just the vibe I'm getting. He makes a lot of comments about 'rich assholes ruining the country.' Seems to have a chip on his shoulder." He glances up. "You do happen to be rich and, well…"

"An asshole?"

"Hey, I didn't say it." He flashes a crooked smirk that tells me he's joking.

With the exorbitant salary I'm paying him, he better be joking.

I roll my eyes back to the window. "Well, I don't care if he likes me as long as he does his job."

"Yeah, he's doing his job and seems committed to good work."

A few seconds later, Jeremy appears, still buckling the belt on his black slacks. He's bulkier than Sean, but also a lot slower.

"Hey, boss," he says, flashing his gapped teeth.

I look him over, like seeing him for the first time. So this guy doesn't like me? He's usually smiling and saying something goofy. I glance at Sean, as if for confirmation of Jeremy's true feelings.

Sean nods and then goes back to reading.

I yawn again, deciding it's a topic I'll revisit later.

A nap would probably be a good idea, but I think I'd rather push through. I prefer to fill every waking hour of my life with either work or charity endeavors, entertaining a few women as I go. Sometimes, that entertainment is more about my date shopping to her heart's content, but I don't mind. If my dates are distracted by getting spoiled financially or in the bedroom, then they don't pry into my life and we can remain casual.

My eyes are drooping again, so I open my laptop to skim through emails—anything to keep me awake until I'm at least back home in Presidio Heights. A chat message pops up on-screen. Then another. In my sleep-deprived haze, I forgot to mark myself as offline. Since I've been MIA all week, a few of the women I casually date are messaging.

Hi, Daddy, Vanessa sends. The other woman, Martina, opens with: *Guess what I'm wearing tonight when I come over? The dress you said makes my ass "impeccable."*

I smirk. Impeccable? God, that makes me sound pretentious.

I can't help responding to Martina first: *Is that so?*

Martina: *Here's a preview.*

A second later, an image pops up of her caramel-colored ass in lacy white panties. The lace doesn't leave much to the imagination.

Me: *I think you forgot the dress.*

She sends a laughing emoji.

Vanessa must not like that I'm taking a few minutes to respond to her because she bombards me with messages:

I'd love to come over if you want some company.

Can I cook you a nice dinner?

I've been missing you all week thinking of how you've been all alone in those hotel rooms doing all your important work. No one to cuddle with.

I click my tongue as I consider my response carefully. Vanessa has really been pushing for a relationship even though I've repeatedly told her I don't do attachments. I'll need to have a tough talk with her soon so we can go our separate ways.

I'm not a man any woman can have a future with.

Me: *You know I don't cuddle.*

Vanessa: *Just offering! So you want me on my knees taking that dick like a good girl? I want to choke tonight, Daddy.*

I blink. That escalated quickly.

Me: *Unfortunately, I'm busy this evening. Use my account to treat yourself. Let's talk later.*

She sends a sad emoji followed by a kissing face. *Miss you, but thank you, Daddy.*

I tell Martina the same thing, then set my status to offline.

I read a few emails, respond to one, then I close my laptop, deciding to just stare out the window at the horizon of blue again.

As Vanessa put it, I am always alone in hotel rooms, at home, in life. That's how it should be. No woman will ever suffer again from being in my presence.

The most I'll ever allow myself is a casual hookup, as long as the woman herself is entertained and happy. And I prefer to avoid any fantasies. Though lately, I've been plagued with images involving someone very specific I met near a koi pond.

It's a torment I'm not enjoying.

Why in the hell do I keep replaying our entire interaction at the gala?

The moment I noticed her, she had stood out from the

crowd in that gold vintage dress. It hugged her petite frame perfectly; one long slit up the side to reveal an enticing tan leg. She was a classic beauty with a grace that conjured images of Audrey Hepburn in my mind. But something about her was edgy. Her angled black bob, the steel in her shoulders…she wasn't some obnoxious artist or an annoying socialite. She was a flash of reality among gala masks that only covered the ones people wore for a living.

Of course, I wasn't going to let Neville Fucking Hanson linger around her. That man is a predator. But my mistake was lingering myself once I had chased him off, like flying too close to the sun and getting blinded. The way her natural, light pink lips formed around words, the watchfulness in her dark brown eyes. That phoenix tattoo on her inner wrist, the one she tried to hide with a chunky faux-pearl bracelet. Why a phoenix? Why was such a stunning woman acting so unsure of herself? I had craved to talk with her and learn everything.

A huge mistake; now I can't shake her from my thoughts. Learning that she harbors an attraction for me certainly made it worse.

Yes, lingering was a very bad idea. I'm a possessive man when triggered, though also the worst kind—one who fails at protecting his possessions.

"I know you never loved me, so I saved you the trouble of ending things."

The silence of the cabin envelops me. I clench my jaw, my fingers tightening on the armrest as my chest caves in.

I won't go there. I won't allow myself to remember that letter.

Instead, I focus on what's around me—the soft brown leather beneath my hands, the gentle whir of the engines, the faint scent of my cologne. Slowly, gradually, I feel the memory recede. The tightness in my chest eases, my breathing evens out. I am here, in this moment. I am in control.

I'm high above everything, in the clouds, where I can escape.

With a heavy sigh, I run a hand through my chaotic hair. I need a cut and a shave. A punch to the face to give me some physical pain to focus on. I still box as a hobby for that very reason—physical pain is always a good distraction.

Glancing at my watch, I note the time. Thank God we'll be landing soon. I need a shower, some brandy, a night of poring over details about that pitch in a few weeks…

My phone vibrates on the tray beside me, and I wonder if it's Vanessa or Martina again. I pick it up for a quick check and find a text from an unknown number, but it has a San Francisco area code. It reads: ***Sorry I still have your jacket. Where can I deliver it?***

My jacket? Did I leave something at the dry cleaners? What—

A sudden rush of adrenaline makes my fingers tingle as I stare at the screen. Could it be her? The woman from the gala?

I blink, trying to stay grounded in reality. As much as my pulse is trying to pick up, I'm also wary. If it is her and she remembered my number, why is she reaching out now, weeks later? If she's trying to use the jacket as an excuse to talk about networking for her art program, I'd rather she lead with that. I'm happy to help, but I don't like games, don't like being caught off guard.

Well, it might not be her. Could be a wrong number and a coincidence.

Dammit, I should just respond and kill the suspense.

Me: *Who is this?*

Mystery Woman: *We met at the gala a few weeks ago. I accidentally left with your jacket. I'm sorry.*

It's pathetic how much my heart rate spikes. Why the hell am I so affected by this woman? We met one time for only a matter of minutes.

I stare at the phone, running my tongue over my teeth. I should give a simple response of either telling her to keep the jacket—honestly, I don't care—or give her an address if she's adamant about returning it. No need to instigate anything.

Just like her, I'm not interested in getting tangled up in someone I can't trust myself around. I prefer to keep things casual, and this strange attraction to her is…mind-numbing.

A simple response is the better choice.

Yet, another part of me, a part I thought I had locked away long ago, is feeling reckless.

Me: *The gorgeous woman in the vintage dress. I remember. I didn't catch your name…?*

Mystery Woman: *Thank you for calling it vintage. I know it looked cheap.*

Me: *Not cheap. It's a classic style. Feminine. Graceful.*

Mystery Woman: *Thrift store.*

Me: *Shows confidence.*

Mystery Woman: *No. Used up and should be thrown out.*

I smirk, liking our banter. Why is she so insistent on waging war over this dress? I'm a competitive man.

Me: *If it was such a cheap dress, why haven't I been*

able to stop thinking about you in it? Thoughts I probably shouldn't reveal.

That text may have been too bold, because the minutes tick by and she doesn't respond. Well, I had to say it. Her refusal to listen to my opinion about the dress struck a chord—I'm not a liar. Also, she's been in my mind so much that those words came out naturally.

Rather, they forced their way out, pushing past my barriers.

Despite the rumble of the jet engines and the sound of Sean flipping pages and Jeremy snickering at some video on his phone, the feeling of stillness settles on my shoulders.

The mystery woman doesn't respond, so I set my phone down. Well, that's that. I'm not a subtle man, so if my words were too straightforward for her, then it's better we don't continue.

I'm not trying to date her, anyway, so I shouldn't have gotten flirty. I only wish she didn't intrigue me so much. I wish she'd never told me about her art program. It's clear that she's determined, self-possessed, caring. Not just anyone has the compassion and drive to start a venture like that.

Her aspirations mixed with her exquisite beauty and edginess is a dangerous cocktail I really want to taste.

A stewardess appears to tell me we're starting our descent, and I decide to force the raven-haired mystery woman from my thoughts. I slide my laptop into my satchel and then tidy up my area, even though it will be another hour before the jet lands. I grab a notepad to jot down some thoughts about the damn Halliwell pitch meeting. If we're going to—

Buzz. Buzz.

I frown at my phone and then check the screen.

Mystery Woman: *What kind of thoughts?*

My abs tighten. Fuck, that's a dangerous question.

My thumbs hover over the screen as words scroll through my head. The best course of action would be to tell her exactly what I'm thinking so I scare her off. Most women find me too straightforward and honest.

If I rub her the wrong way, then good. We won't risk getting tangled in each other.

My thumbs quickly tap out the truth: ***Mostly fucking you in it.***

I hit send.

I'm about to drop my phone and be done with this when the damn thing buzzes.

M.W.: *Missed opportunity. I wasn't wearing panties at the gala.*

I stare at the message for a long time. Then I glance at my bodyguards, who aren't paying attention. I quickly adjust myself as a slow smirk spreads across my face. Every neuron in my brain sparks in a way I haven't felt in years.

Me: *Too bad you didn't tell me. I would've fucked you in the garden. You haven't done anything dirty with my jacket, have you? Strange you kept it so long.*

M.W.: *I'll make sure it's dry cleaned before returning it.*

My cock is now digging painfully against my zipper.

Me: *Don't. I'd rather smell you on it.*

Jesus, what is this woman doing to me? It's time for a

different plan: fucking this spitfire out of my system. I just need one night, one chance to indulge.

I don't deserve anything more.

Just one night…

Me: *Care to meet me at Fairmont Heritage Place this evening? Show me what you've done to my jacket. Just know that I'm a man with particular tastes.*

Blood pounds through my veins and groin as I wait for her response.

Mystery Woman goes silent.

Eventually, I set my phone down.

The jet lands, and the stewardess appears to see if I need anything before I disembark. With a shake of my head, I gather my belongings and exit the jet, Jeremy and Sean leading the way. Each footstep down the stairs is heavier than the last.

During the drive to my house, I keep thinking of her, each thought falling into a blank, endless void where once I felt the mystery woman's presence.

When I reach my destination, I dump my luggage in my bedroom, then go for a run. Later, after a quick shower, I bury myself in emails and contract details about the upcoming pitch meeting.

Mystery Woman is still clinging to my thoughts, so I start sifting through my contacts, compiling a list for her. By the time midnight rolls around, I'm exhausted—physically and mentally. Her lack of response is a bitter taste on my tongue, and I regret being so blunt. I should've been professional and changed the topic to her wonderful art program. I decide to message her, to try to salvage what I can.

Me: *I apologize for my earlier messages. I'll keep*

things professional. Attached is a list of contacts to help with your art program. I gave each one a heads up so they know you may be reaching out. Truly, I admire your commitment to building something for troubled teens; it's a great cause. Let me know if there are other ways I can help.

With that done, I swallow some sleeping pills and lay in the darkness of my bedroom. The bed's too big for one person; these satin sheets are suffocating. Of course, when I close my eyes, I'm only flooded with images of the mystery woman. In the morning, I'll replay her flirtatious texts in my mind, then feel guilty about jerking off to her in the shower.

But tonight, this moment, I'll allow myself to indulge in fantasies without that gnawing shame.

The funny thing is, my fantasies don't even involve fucking her. She's merely haunting my bed, resting in the space another woman once filled so long ago.

CHAPTER 3

SIENNA

WE FILE INTO THE ART room quietly, a flurry of shuffling bags, sketchbooks, and squeaky sneakers. I walk to one of the large wooden easels that circle the middle of the room and drop my backpack on the tile. Then I pull out my box of charcoal sticks and flip to a clean sheet on my giant pad of newsprint.

It's the second Monday of the month, so my classmates and I all know the drill: we'll be sketching a live nude model today. I don't care who this morning's model is as long as it's not the old guy who always falls asleep. His snoring irritates me.

As everyone prepares, our teacher starts wandering and observing, stroking the long end of his lavender and yellow scarf. His eyes dart around the room like a hawk.

I try to ignore his presence, but the hairs on the back of my neck stand up when he glances my way. I pray he doesn't look too much at my easel when I start sketching.

Shifting focus, I shake out some vine charcoal sticks onto the easel's painting tray. I hate using them because they break easily and make a mess on my hands and clothes, but I'll make do. Next, I select a few graphite pencils I'll use when the model does a long pose at the end. I almost grab my set of watercolor paints, but they're high quality and expensive, like fine china—only for special occasions.

A male model, probably in his mid-twenties, strides

in wearing a satin white robe. He has a mop of curly dark hair and his eyes are trained on the wall, ignoring everyone. We all snap to attention as he drops his robe and enters the middle of the classroom. There are a few giggles and whispers from some of the less mature students, but most of us just pick up our charcoal and get to work.

I mean, I understand *why* there are giggles. The man is, um, very endowed. And fit.

While I'm sure his sexual partners are extremely happy, I'm excited about his body for a different reason. My skills with capturing the correct bend and curve of human muscles are lacking—I drape my figures with a lot of fabric to hide my weakness—so having a model with such a sculpted physique will help me see how everything connects.

The man takes his first 2-minute pose, standing on one leg and bending like he's suspended in the middle of a run. I scratch the charcoal across the paper like my life depends on it. When the man switches to his next 2-minute pose, my fingers are black and itchy, but I continue on, flipping quickly to a clean sheet. My charcoal stick snaps, so I grab one of the pieces and scratch out the curve of a shoulder.

For the next fifteen minutes, the model moves through more poses, including two 5-minute ones. At the halfway mark, I'm preparing for him to take the longer 30-minute pose, but instead, he grabs a water bottle as the teacher walks over to him.

After a sip, he asks my teacher, "Maggie is still coming, right?"

My fingers clamp over a charcoal stick as my breath catches at the name. The stick snaps, pieces falling to the tile, and I grip the edge of my stool so I don't fall off.

The world is suddenly wobbly.

Maggie. Margaret. I haven't heard either one in forever. Margaret was my name once, a lifetime ago.

The teacher nods as he grabs two folding chairs and sets them up for the models. I exhale a slow breath, my hand shaky as I reach up to finger my silver locket. Most everyone from my old life called me Margaret, but my grandfather always called me Maggie. I liked 'Maggie' and the way his warm, weathered voice always said it through a grin.

He died when I was twelve, and for a few years I could still hear his voice saying to me softly, "Why, there's my Maggie. My little Maggie girl with sunshine in her smile."

I stopped hearing his voice after I turned 21. That's when Margaret Diane Ariti officially died.

Someday, if I'm brave—or stupid—enough, I'll visit my grandfather's grave in Chicago. Legally, I'm not allowed to go back to that city, but I want to introduce grandpa to who I am now: Sienna Bishop.

"Here she is," the male model says when a tall, blonde woman walks in.

She drops her robe, revealing a lean, fit body of pale skin, and sits on a folding chair next to him. The two models then drape their bodies into one another in an elegant, romantic embrace.

"Thirty minutes," the teacher speaks up. "Make it count. Focus on capturing the essence of the form, the play of light and shadow. Don't get bogged down in the details at first. Only see the shapes."

A realization hits suddenly, and my gaze snaps down to my locket. The engraved flowers and swirls are now covered in black charcoal.

No...I touched it with dirty hands? A loud broken noise slips from my throat and a few classmates glance over.

The teacher does an exaggerated "ahem," reminding me to shut the fuck up.

I wrap part of my T-shirt collar around the locket to clean the mess, but I think it's too late—black has invaded the tiny hinge and crevices. I don't dare open it, afraid I might dirty the only picture of my grandpa that's left.

My nose stings as I release my stretched-out shirt collar, but I certainly can't start crying in the middle of class. I cycle a few positive mantras through my head, pinching my nostrils.

Mistakes are human.

I give myself permission to be human.

The biggest mistake is never admitting you made one.

Sniffing, I release my nostrils and grab a graphite pencil so I can sketch something before time runs out. Later, I'll figure out a way to carefully clean the locket, my only memento from my old life. I'll fix this mistake, just like I fixed all the previous ones.

I make the first mark on a clean sheet of paper, my hand shaky at first and then smoothing into a rhythm. Listening to the scratch of pastels, pencils, fingers across pages in the classroom, I allow myself to get lost in my drawing with no judgments. Just pure expression. I need to work through the emotions the name Maggie just brought to the surface.

My graphite seems to move with its own consciousness, capturing the couple loosely on three-fourths of the paper, then shifting to the surrounding white. Their romance bleeds into mounds of bones, a twisted black staircase, a doorway with menacing, watchful eyes peering out from the shadows.

Then, almost without realizing it, I sketch a male

figure on the top step. A rose blooms from behind him and obscures one of the ominous eyes. The man, gazing down at the embracing couple, isn't the usual sinister presence that appears in my work, but something different. Something... protective. He's blocking the eyes, creating a barrier with his body to shield the couple from everything threatening to rip them apart.

As I work on the finer details of the naked couple, a flush creeps up my neck. My mind flashes to the text exchange with Declan last Friday. He certainly didn't hold back, his words filthy and charged, sparking heat in my core. I haven't felt that kind of heat, well, maybe ever.

I knew messaging him would be a conflict of interest. I just really wanted to return his jacket. It's been nagging at me.

But seriously, I just *had* to ask, "What thoughts?"

The last thing I wanted was to lead him on, to start something I couldn't finish. Yet that's exactly what I did. Even after I ghosted him when I realized I was getting in too deep, the man still had the decency to apologize for his part and send me contacts that might actually get my art program off the ground. The contacts are phenomenal—a mix of local arts organizations, community leaders, and potential funding sources.

Declan must've spent a few hours curating that list, and then to tell them all to watch out for my email...just me, some unknown student who doesn't even fit in the art world...

I'm still speechless.

"That's time," the teacher says, jarring me back to this cold, stuffy classroom.

The models put on their robes as the teacher wanders,

glancing at easels and offering comments. Normally, this is the point where I scramble to grab my shit and bolt before he has a chance to make some cruel but honest assessment of my work. He has never liked anything I've done, saying that my pieces are "too illustrative and surface-level in a program meant for serious arts."

Today, though, I'm too drained to move, as if this drawing took more out of me than I realized. I also feel good as I gaze at what I've drawn. This came out of me?

The teacher's shadow falls over my easel and my stomach tightens, preparing for the worst. He strokes the end of his lavender and yellow scarf, then his goatee, as he studies my creation.

"Hmm," he finally says. "Inspired. Good work, Sienna." With that, he walks off.

With a slack jaw, I stare at his retreating figure. My eyes then scan the room, noting the pads of dense sketching paper around me, the heaps of quality compressed charcoal sticks, the top-tier paints and brushes and portfolio cases of other students. Clothes that are name brands. Skin that's supple and sun-kissed, barely older than twenty.

Then there's my station: broken charcoal, nubby pencils, inexpensive flimsy newsprint, paint that took an entire semester to save for...

My fingertips are stained black, skin freckled and dry and blotchy from the sun. I'll be thirty soon, practically an old lady in this college environment.

Yet my arms prickle with goosebumps as I grin. Inspired?

He's right.

AFTER AN AFTERNOON SHIFT AT one of my three jobs—this one as a beauty consultant at a retail store, though I rarely wear more than mascara—I come home to find Jada and Mystical on the couch eating popcorn. The space is completely Jada's style—vintage mismatched furniture, vibrant throw pillows, colorful artwork of street scenes, and an assortment of potted plants scattered *everywhere*. I often trip over them.

Jada hops up to give me a hug, looking too comfy in a pair of pink booty shorts and a tank. Today's eye color is violet, which I'm happy about—she tried white contacts yesterday and they freaked me out.

"Cheers, babe," she says. "Left yah pizza in the fridge." She smacks my hip playfully. "Now get your jim-jams on cuz we're doing an 80s movie marathon."

Mystical, who's a music major and changes his name every month to reflect his inner child's journey, lifts his hand to acknowledge my presence. His bald head is new, along with the red robes and rosary beads.

Jada notices me giving him a confused look. "There's a note on the fridge about his month-long vow of silence," she comments. Her voice and faux British accent lower. "But I heard the twat singin' in the shower this morning."

With a laugh, I finally drop my backpack next to the sectional couch, taking a moment for some daily gratitude. Every time I come home, I give myself a second to just feel so overwhelmingly thankful. Regardless of everything, I'm lucky to be here, with Jada and Mystical, with food to eat and a cozy bed.

Safety. I'm thankful for safety.

San Francisco wasn't where I was supposed to end up. The authorities first dropped me off in Utah to start a new life. Then they got shady and someone started stalking me, so I fled. I knew San Francisco was expensive; I also loved the art scene. I arrived with pretty much nothing except some idealistic dreams and enough money to live in a motel for a month.

Thankfully, before I ended up on the streets, I met Jada. She was at a bar celebrating her 21st birthday alone. She looked so sad and hopeless that it struck a nerve, and I just couldn't live with myself unless I tried to cheer her up. We started talking, I bought her a drink, and we hit it off.

For the last five years, we've been besties. I completely lucked out, not only because she's an amazing friend, but because her parents bought this house in the 80s and gave it to Jada when they moved to Seattle.

My rent is so low, people would literally kill for it.

"I'd love a movie marathon," I tell her, "but I have an evening shift at the record store. Can I show you something?"

She plops down on the back of the couch, her crimson and blonde braids bouncing with the movement. "Always."

"Okay, well"—I flip through my large sketching pad and peel back the tissue that's protecting my drawing—"I got my first compliment today. Teacher said it was 'inspired.'" I carefully turn the pad to show Jada and Mystical my work, biting my lip in anticipation.

Jada inhales slowly, her violet eyes lighting up as she takes in the sketch. "Oh, babe, that's beautiful."

Mystical glances over and gives me a "not bad" head bob.

I feel like hugging my sketch pad, but I resist—I need to spray my drawing with fixative so the charcoal doesn't smudge. "Thanks. I can't believe it. I actually made something decent."

Jada frowns and tips her head to the side like trying to shake off my comment. "No, you *always* make amazing shit. I love your paintings. This is just…" Smile lines spread around her eyes as she studies my drawing again.

"The best?"

"Crackin."

I'm not exactly sure what that means, but it sounds good, so I'll take it. "Kay, well, I'm going to spray this and get ready for work. Thanks for saving me pizza. I'm… knackered?"

Jada shakes her head. "Proper hungry. Need some nosh."

I laugh and escape to my room, the hardwood floors creaking as I navigate the narrow hallway. Jada follows, watching me lay my sketch pad on the worn wooden floorboards. I grab the fixative off my cluttered desk. I should probably do this outside, but…it's San Francisco. We're lucky to live in an actual house, so asking for a backyard is too demanding.

Jada pops open the window, letting in a breath of cool, foggy air. It's a challenge, but I squat in my constrictive beauty consultant pantsuit and spray a thin coat over the paper, preserving every inspired line and shadow. The next step is to buy a small canvas and do a color study; I'm definitely turning this into a larger watercolor painting.

"Hey, what's this?" Jada asks, so I glance behind me.

Crap. I left the jacket out, hanging on a hook near the closet.

I haven't told her about Declan and I'm not sure I want to—I don't want to make him real in my life. I haven't even Internet-stalked him. He's just…a fun dream.

I try to pretend the jacket is nothing important by waving my hand before capping the fixative. "Oh, uh, I was at the thrift store an—"

"Sienna," Jada says, dropping the British accent and turning to me with a hard look that weirds me out. "Where did you get this?"

"Uh...thrift store."

"You did not get this at the thrift store." She opens the jacket and begins searching the seams and pockets for any clues. Then she touches the gold rose pin on the lapel. "Don't bullshit me. Explain."

I straighten, still feeling weirded out by her reaction to a simple garment. I ditch the fixative on my desk, then move to the closet, kicking a pile of dirty laundry out of the way. The record store doesn't care what I wear, so I grab a pair of ripped jeans, an oversized beige sweater, and vintage black boots. Calling the boots 'vintage' is a nice way of saying the soles are barely clinging to life.

I start undressing, happy to get this scratchy pantsuit off. "You're acting like it's a big deal. It's just a jacket."

Her expression eases a little, and the accent creeps back in. "Not trying to freak yah out, babe, but I know this pin. I've worked their galas for the past two years." She pauses until I slip the sweater over my head and adjust it. As if watching me has decided something, she begins taking the pin off the lapel. "You know what? Ride or die. Yah don't have to tell me. I'll just return it, no harm—"

"Stop," I say as I cross the room. I grab for the pin that's now in her grasp, like she suddenly ripped out my lung and I need it before I collapse on the floor.

She jerks back, holding what I want out of reach, then she presses a palm against my chest to keep me away. "You don't have to explain, babe. Maybe it was a shit mix up at the coat check, or if you took it on purpose, doesn't matter. They take these pins very seriously and only a few of the top donors have one. I mean *millions* in donations." She glances at the back of it. "But it's okay, babe. I'll sneak it back in during an event next week. Leave it on my supervisor's desk and she'll take care of it. It'll be—"

Stretching my arm, I manage to snatch the pin, able to inhale fully again. I glance at the back, noticing the 'D.C.' engraving that Jada read. Then I press the diamond encrusted pin to my heart. My voice is tight when I ask, "You think I stole this?"

Is she seeing Margaret right now? After all these years, all my attempts to be better, give back, start an art program to help people…is Margaret still so easy to see?

Jada freezes, her chest rising and falling with shallow breaths. I can almost see her thoughts churning while her mouth hangs open for several beats. The words spill out. "It doesn't matter. I'll return it an—"

My nostrils flare. "I did *not* steal. I might be some broke bitch, and a shitty artist on top of that, but I am not a fucking thief. A guy gave this to me. He…" Clutching the pin, I search the dirty floorboards like they can back me up, but I'm already crumbling under the half-truth of my own words.

Declan didn't *give* me the jacket. He lent it to me so I could find warmth for a few moments, then I walked off clinging to it like a child.

My chest squeezes and collapses all at once.

I did steal.

Stealing is something Margaret did; Sienna is supposed to be someone better.

Jada steps forward. "Babe—"

"I have to get ready for work." My words are a hard warning as I turn away to face the window.

"Sienna—"

"Work," I bite out.

Jada lingers for a moment, then the floor creaks under her shifting weight. "I'm sorry," she says. "I'm really sorry. I don't know what I was thinking. That was shitty of me." She leaves, closing my bedroom door.

Quickly, I secure the pin back to the jacket lapel. My hands are shaking, but I get it done. Then I smooth out the fabric with my palms. Good as new. It's fine. I'm not a thief. I didn't mean to take the jacket. It was only an accident.

I'm not the person I used to be. I'm not Margaret.

Margaret's dead.

I'm Sienna now, who never steals or lies or hurts people. Sienna, who has at least one person who cares about her, a bestie who thinks Sienna had a golden childhood. Sienna has hopes and aspirations to become a better artist while also creating an art program one day to help change lives.

Sienna will do good in this world. She's resilient and pure and doesn't need anything from anyone, confident in her own worth.

I need to return this jacket and prove all of that.

The moment I think of texting Declan, though, of demanding a drop off location so I can free myself of this accidentally borrowed garment, my body seizes up. With a mind of its own, my hand reaches out, fingers grazing the soft fabric. Almost in a daze, I snatch the jacket off its hanger and swing it around my shoulders. As I slip my arms through the generous sleeves, I'm engulfed by Declan's scent—a mix of sandalwood, citrus, and something uniquely masculine. It's intoxicating, comforting, and utterly wrong all at once.

The jacket settles on my frame. It's too large but somehow perfect. I lean against the wall, wrapping the front around my waist tightly. I imagine Declan's arms around me and how that might feel. Warm, comforting, a sense of belonging...

Things I've always craved; things I once gave up my autonomy for.

I don't even know Declan, don't even know his full face. So this is all pretend and completely foolish. I'm taking his few kind gestures and turning them into something more—a shield, the illusion of a safe place where the darkest parts of myself are forgotten.

My tendency to romanticize men I don't truly know is exactly why talking to him is so dangerous—I will too easily give myself to a man I'm drawn to.

Margaret did and being with that man took everything from her; I'm determined not to let Sienna make the same stupid mistake.

Besides, if Declan is so esteemed that he gets a coveted gala pin, he'd choose better than the broken pieces of a girl still struggling to put herself back together.

With a shaky breath, I force myself to remove the false safety of the jacket, to hang it back in its place. My body feels cold, exposed without its warmth, but I ignore the loss and focus on lacing my boots.

I'm Sienna. Strong, independent, solitary Sienna. This is how it has to be, for my own safety; for the safety of everyone around me.

CHAPTER 4

SIENNA

I GET HOME FROM MY record store shift around ten, which is two hours earlier than normal. The place closed early because the damn looters attacked the department store across the street. I understand closing the store was for safety, but looters are usually after designer brands or household goods; I can't imagine they'd care about dusty old records.

To top it off, one of the criminals bipped my fucking car even though I didn't have anything in the back seat. There was nothing for them to steal, yet now I have to get my passenger side window replaced. As if my insurance isn't already sky high. It also might rain tonight, and I doubt the plastic bag I taped over the window will hold.

I'm grumbly and tired by the time I reach the front door, kicking off my boots before I even step over the threshold. Despite my annoying evening, I'm ready to hash things out with Jada.

No one is home. The note on the fridge tells me that she and Mystical just went 'out.' And they must be planning to stay 'out' into the wee hours of the morning since they thought I'd be coming home around midnight.

Guess I'm alone with the jungle of plants.

After eating some cold pizza and taking a quick shower, I change into some thin cotton pants and a baggy shirt. Then I secure my locket around my neck. At work, I cleaned the outside with a cotton swab, but I'm still nervous about opening it. The picture is probably okay, but I worry I've tainted it. For now, I just press it against my heart, leaving it closed.

I flop onto my bed, my pink salt lamp providing some much-needed moody ambiance amidst the clutter. I sneeze. My room still smells like chemicals even though the window has been cracked.

When I roll onto my side, I gaze down at the 'inspired' drawing laying on the floor near my desk. I study the protective figure at the top of the stairs—the firm line of his shoulders, the relaxed tilt of his hips. It wasn't intentional, but my frantic charcoal strokes make it seem as if light is spilling across his face, covering everything in shadow except a slight smile. I move to the floor, squatting to get a better look. Yeah. Definitely a smile.

I'm always amazed at what spontaneous, beautiful mistakes can appear in my work. That smile may have been from a slip of my finger, the edge of a nail grazing the page. But I love it.

A sudden urge to shred the entire thing bubbles up, so I scoot away, pressing my back against my bed. I've never seen Declan's smile, yet now I'm putting it on a pedestal?

But…the figure in the drawing isn't him; I need to erase that from my head.

I need to erase his presence from my life, aka the jacket. I don't want to get tangled with anyone, even in make-believe.

More determined than ever, I get off the floor and snatch my phone off the bed. I send Declan a message: *I'm sorry I didn't tell you thank you for the contacts. Thank you. I really appreciate the work that went into that list, but I don't know if I can use them. Please tell me how to return your jacket. I'd like to get it back to you tomorrow.*

There. It's done. No more jacket. No more obsessive thoughts about this stranger. No more connection with him, not even through people he knows.

My phone vibrates and I glance at the screen.

Declan: *Are the contacts not helpful? I have more I can provide. Are you looking for traditional investors? Philanthropists? Tell me what direction to take and I'll send another list.*

I want to tell him, "No, please stop helping me. I don't want to owe you anything. I can't have any connection to you because it's dangerous to keep feeling this pull, to have you inspire my work. It's dangerous when I allow myself to get lost in a man."

Instead, I glance at the time, chewing my thumbnail. It's almost midnight, so I figured he wouldn't see the message until morning. I hope I didn't disturb him.

Mistake after mistake after…

Me: *I'm really sorry if I woke you.*

Declan: *I was awake.*

My shoulders relax from that info, and I lay back on my bed, knees hanging over the side and feet flat on the floor. I'm debating how to respond and ask about returning the jacket again, when he texts: *What is your name?*

Pressing my phone to my stomach, I shake my head. This is why I don't get involved with anyone—too many questions. Jada and I work as besties because she doesn't get curious. She lives in the moment, taking me as I am now, and never digs deeper.

One day, when I first learned that her parents live in Seattle, she casually asked about mine. I just said, "My childhood was good. Yours?" And she replied, "Good."

That was the one major lie I ever told her, and it worked because I've always sensed she's hiding secrets about her past, too. Neither of us cares what happened before the day we met and so our friendship is perfect.

But this man, I feel it in my bones that he'll ask questions.

Me: *No names.*

Declan: *But you know mine.*

Me: *You gave it to me. I prefer no names.*

A minute later, he writes: *My assistant can retrieve the jacket. Just let me know where he can meet you.*

I stare at the message, suddenly curious about what Declan might do for work. He's clearly rich if he can afford millions in donations and has an assistant. Maybe several of them.

Regardless, this is good. Good. I could probably have the assistant meet me at school or a coffee shop, somewhere simple. It's a clear, concise way to sever this unexpected connection, to return Declan's jacket and with it, any lingering trace of him in my life.

As my thumb hovers over the screen, ready to reply with a meeting location, I feel a strange hollowness in my chest, a sense of something slipping away before I even get a chance to understand it.

I remember the way he touched my hand outside the gala, protecting it from the cold like it was second nature.

"I'm glad you're alright."

My gaze drifts to the jacket hanging on a hook. In the soft glow of the salt lamp, it looks almost ethereal. Dream-like. The gold rose pin glints in the light, the diamonds along the petals sparkling.

I know it's ridiculous—it's just a jacket, a piece of clothing that doesn't belong to me and never did—but I want it. I want it desperately. It's all I've ever wanted my entire life.

All I've never been able to possess, no matter how much of myself I've given away as trade.

The reasonable part of me switches off as I send a risky message to Declan: *What did you mean when you said you were a man with particular tastes?*

My heart is thrumming wildly as I anticipate his response. Part of me wants to power down my phone, delete his number, so I'm never tempted to ask something like that again. But the demanding, curious part of me keeps waiting.

Finally: *I like to be in control. I set the rules and expect to be obeyed.*

My entire body is buzzing as I ask: *What if someone doesn't like your rules?*

Declan: *Then I stop. Being in control doesn't mean disrespect, harm, or breaking a boundary. If something isn't pleasurable, I stop immediately. You can always say no, and I'll listen. But unless you utter that refusal, you listen to me.*

My breath hitches. That wasn't a subtle invitation, and I'm not sure how to respond. Heat is already burning in my core because even through text, he's such an overpowering force. An act of nature. Can I handle him? It sounds like he's requesting every ounce of my submission.

I've really never been in a situation like this. My previous experiences with a man were more animalistic. He focused on his own needs first, and it was usually quick and powerful. There wasn't room for 'play,' which is what I think Declan is hinting at.

What would sex with him even look like? Are there toys involved? Silk ropes? Cages? Any references I've ever seen about one person being in control while the other obeys are usually on the more extreme side of 'play.'

Except for saying no, I can't speak up at all? Can't initiate a kiss? Would I just lay down and let him do whatever he wants with my body?

My core pulses.

Well…letting him do what he wants doesn't sound completely bad. Though certainly not something I'm used to.

While my head is reeling, a new message pops up:

Would you like me to call?

I'm jittery, aching, hot and cold…fuck.

Me: *I don't know what to expect.*

I thought, considering how much scary shit I've seen in my life, that nothing could ever faze me. This conversation proves that assumption wrong.

Declan: *If you're unhappy and I'm not pleasing you, hang up.*

That makes sense, but…why am I even *thinking* of going down this path? I don't want to get mixed up with this man.

I don't, but…I'm curious.

And he has my body feeling unbearably flushed.

And it's only a phone call.

I type "yes" before I convince myself not to.

Me: *Yes. But no video.*

He's never seen my face without a mask and it needs to stay that way.

A split second later, my phone jingles. I tap the green button, sealing my fate.

I open my mouth to say a wimpy "hello," but he speaks first.

"Don't say anything yet," his voice rumbles, washing over me with the force of a dam breaking. "Just listen."

"Mmm-hmm."

"I want you wearing my jacket, so strip naked and wrap yourself in it."

Well, he's certainly not wasting any time.

"Okay," I say. Then I wince. "Sorry. Was that disobeying you?"

His light chuckle eases my nerves. "Yes. But I'll permit it."

"What if I slip up again?"

His voice is still holding bits of amusement. "Are you trying to test me? Put on the jacket."

I start to say "yes" but catch myself, snapping my mouth closed. It's a little freeing having him direct me. And a lot hotter than I anticipated.

Air cools my warm skin as I slip out of my PJs. Declan can't even see me, and yet I feel exposed, raw. A thrill shoots up my spine, making me shiver.

The floorboards creak as I pad over to the jacket, then I ease the soft, luxurious fabric over my bare skin, loving the caress of the silky smooth texture. It's so large that the hem almost touches my knees, and the scent leaves me delirious.

Since he's giving me permission and wants me to wear it, I let myself fall into the jacket's comfort and safety. Just for tonight.

After returning to the bed, I press my phone to my ear again and release a soft hum to let him know I'm back.

"Now tell me if you're wearing my jacket," he says. His tone is as firm and fluid as ever.

"I'm wearing it."

"Tell me how it feels."

"Um, nice?"

"You don't sound very confident. Try again."

I swallow, a little uncomfortable at how wet I'm becoming from his demands. He sounds so relaxed and certain about every word he's speaking; my body is responding with pure trust.

"How does the fabric feel against your skin?" he says a little softer, trying to prompt me.

I ease back on the bed, propping my head on a pillow as my finger circles a jacket button. This isn't what I had been expecting, but it's way better. When he had used words like 'obey' and 'rules,' I had immediately pictured something rigid and unpleasant. But the slight gentleness in his tone, the care he's taking to help me relax into this…it's not unnoticed. It seems there may be a certain ebb and flow to this kind of play, and I'm really starting to like it.

Still, the part of me that swore to be more careful around men is resisting the idea of giving him so much control.

Just enjoy the moment.

It's only a phone call.

I have the power to hang up, and he can't take that away.

Closing my eyes, I try to think of the words to describe what I feel; I'm definitely better at expressing myself through art than I am speaking. "It's, um, soft. A little heavy. My…" I touch my chest, feeling my hard, pebbled nipples.

"Tell me," he says in a tone that leaves no room for refusal and yet holds care.

"I…I like how it feels against my breasts."

I hear a very slight exhale come through the phone. It was so slight that it was probably my imagination, but it was like noticing the first frayed edge on a brush. Instead of smooth paint, there's now a small, rough imperfection on the canvas.

"Rub my jacket against your nipples," he says.

I press my palm over a lapel and make gentle circles, focusing on the silky fabric moving along my skin. My nipples are aching now, so I pinch one, pulling slightly. I wish I had both hands free to do more.

"Can I put you on speaker?"

"Good girl, asking for permission. Yes. Put me on speaker."

I smirk at the 'good girl' because it's a little silly. Yet, why does it also feel so damn satisfying? Any lingering hesitation fades, and I'm ready to do whatever this man asks of me.

Which is scary. I shouldn't be willing to do whatever a man asks. Ever. Though I did feel safe with him at the gala, why am I so ready to give myself to a stranger?

That's always been a dangerous part of my personality.

I shove the worries aside because he's not actually here; this phone is my barrier. This is only a fun, fleeting game. That's how it needs to stay; a man will never get all of me.

Never again.

Now on speaker, I lay my phone near my head and touch my chest with both hands. I fall silent, just enjoying the sensations.

"Describe what you're doing," Declan says.

My words are flowing easier now. "Enjoying the feeling of the jacket on my nipples. I really like it. I'm wet and I want more." I squirm as I fondle myself, my senses enhanced by Declan's scent that's now all over me.

How would it feel to have the real Declan over me? I close my eyes and let my imagination run wild. I'm sure his body is a masterpiece—strong, symmetrical, every movement done with skillful intention. I bet he'd fill me so completely that I…

A moan escapes me, and I hear another frayed edge in Declan's breath.

I want more. He's the one in control, but that doesn't mean I can't unravel him.

When I give him another moan, he responds with a slight grunt.

His voice has dropped and taken on a gritty tone when he says, "No more talking. Just listen." I think I hear fabric shifting.

My core clenches and I squirm again from the anticipation of what he's going to tell me.

"The jacket you're wearing is custom tailored from imported fabric. It cost eight grand. Right now, I want nothing more than for you to ruin it."

I squeeze my thighs together, desperate to touch myself but trying to do my best to wait until he commands me. Before I blurt out "How?" I bite my lip to keep quiet.

His voice is a dark, throaty rumble that moves through every vein. "Since you like the feel of my jacket so much, rub yourself on it. Make a mess. The next time I see it, there should be evidence of what you did. And don't hold back. I'm going to jerk off to every moan and sound you make."

I barely manage an exhale because this man has stolen all my breath. The heat under my skin is so intense that I moan like he's penetrated me as soon as I press the jacket sleeve against my pussy. I pull the fabric along my crease, moaning again and savoring the satisfaction of hearing Declan's heavy, ragged breathing.

Imagining how he might be stroking himself to only my voice is driving me nuts. I wish he was here. I wish it wasn't his jacket getting messy from my wetness, but his hands, his mouth, his...

I moan, pushing two fingers inside myself while my other hand continues to wreck every inch of jacket I can press between my shaky thighs.

Thankfully, my moans are preventing me from saying something stupid, like giving him my address, begging him to come fuck me in any way he pleases—I bet he'd be here in a heartbeat.

What a strange kind of comfort...it feels like I could ask him anything and he'd comply. So really, who has the control? I smile at the wicked thought.

His heavy, completely erratic breathing through the phone wraps around me, and I cry out as the tension builds. I rub faster and harder against the ache, my hips bucking. When a groan comes through my phone—a sound that's unraveled yet strained, as if Declan was trying to hide it—I crumble inside his jacket.

Another groan from him causes a second wave of electricity to pulse through my body. I tremble and inhale his scent and continue to rub myself with the most luxurious, expensive fabric I've ever worn.

It's ecstasy.

But when I come down, I crash hard.

I bolt upright, swinging my legs over the edge of the bed to ground myself and find my breath. The bottom of the jacket is crumpled and damp against my thighs, the sleeves stretched out and wrinkled and messy. So very messy.

Declan's heavy breath drifts through the speaker, adding to the knot that all my swirling emotions are weaving. He wanted the jacket ruined, but I shouldn't have ruined it. It's not my jacket; I don't belong in it. I shouldn't be claiming it with my own scent.

What might he expect now? To meet in person? Date? I didn't establish any boundaries for what we're doing, I only let myself fall into it.

Stupid. What I'm doing is stupid and dangerous.

I let a man invade my thoughts, 'inspire' my art, then I willingly opened myself to him, let him command me, hear me, know me in an intimate way…

The last time I stupidly gave myself to a man without thinking, I became someone I hated.

I lost myself.

I hurt people.

Even though Declan hasn't shown me any red flags, I can't be doing this. Sienna doesn't do this stupid shit. She's cautious and a loner and focused solely on living a good, uneventful life. She's a decent person and I won't let her slide backwards.

"Tell me your name," Declan says, sounding more composed again. "Please."

It's the 'please' that makes me hang up on him.

It's an awful thing to do.

I'm awful.

But that 'please' is a request for information.

A request to know me.

He wants me to open doors I've sealed shut, and I just can't. I won't.

When I lose myself in another, bad things happen.

I'm sorry, I message him, tears already streaking my cheeks, but fuck me, I wipe them away and don't let more fall.

No more tears for anyone.

CHAPTER 5

DECLAN

THERE ARE MANY DARK EMPTY rooms in my house—a house that was never meant for a solo habitant. In one of those dark rooms on the second floor, I pour another glass of scotch, the amber liquid sloshing against the sides as my hand shakes. It's a telltale sign that I've already had too much, but tonight, I don't care. I need the numbness, the blissful oblivion that only alcohol can provide.

My head is already in such a fog I'm not sure what room I'm in. I got home from a long day of irritating meetings and started with two shots in the kitchen. Then I began wandering. This house is so large, with winding hallways and connecting rooms, that I enter another universe when the lights are off.

On days like this, part of me hopes I never find my way out of this maze of polished wooden floors, bare walls, and marble surfaces. That I can wander forever and never circle back to the light where every memory is illuminated.

So, I might be in the library or my office. The second story den. Several of these dark rooms have at least a small bar or a shelf dedicated to spirits, so they all blur together in the dim light. After getting my next drink, I move toward the window and bump into a couch. Guess I'm in the den.

I peel back the curtains to gaze down at the tiered garden. She made me build that garden when we moved in; she spent nearly every day tending to the flowers, teaching me the names of each kind. Under her care, the garden burst with colors and smells, roses from pink to dark crimson, tulips, rows of irises in every shade of blue. The stone pathways wove through lavender beds, wisteria draped over arches.

She adored that garden. Guess that's why I found her letter right there, resting on the stone of the fountain's edge, held down by the tiny white shoes I bought the day I found out she was pregnant.

"It's all for the best. You and I know I wouldn't have made a good mother."

I let the entire garden die after that letter—I didn't have the heart to see it bursting with so much life. It's now only dirt and sticks and abandoned pathways, a few stubborn roses clinging to life. I tore down the fountain myself—took a sledgehammer and smashed the entire thing, leaving the rubble as a visceral reminder that all I bring to women is destruction.

Turning from the window, I down the rest of my scotch, welcoming the burn in my throat. Anything to distract from the gaping hole in my chest.

Eight years. Today, April 10th, is the eighth anniversary of the day I read that letter.

A chime echoes around me, the sound trying to pull me from the darkness I'd prefer to fall into. With a sigh, I pull out my phone to check the video feed from my security app. My assistant is waiting in his car outside the gate.

My jaw tenses. Why the fuck is he here? He knows what today is.

He stares into the camera, looking a mix of friendly and terrified. "Mr. Conte," he says, brushing a blond bang off his forehead with twitchy fingers. "Um, you said to bring the jacket as soon as I got it. I met with her just a bit ago. I'm sorry. I know not to disturb you now, but you also said this was important. I wasn't sure."

So, the mystery woman resurfaced.

With a sigh, I hit the speak button on my NexaProtect app and tell him, "Leave it by the front door." Then I open the gate and close the app.

It takes a few minutes for me to stumble out of the room and make my way to the stairs. After crossing the vast, echoing spaces of this damn house, I finally reach the front door.

My assistant is driving away by the time I open the door and pick up the garment bag he hung on the doorknob. The chill of the evening seeps into my skin and I shake. But instead of retreating, I stand in the open doorway for a moment, my eyes unfocused.

Perhaps I should've asked my assistant to describe the mystery woman's face since I'm yearning to see it. I've imagined so many versions of her in my head—bushy eyebrows, thin and straight ones, a wide nose, a crooked one. The yearning to simply know has been growing, especially since she keeps running away.

Stepping back into my house, I close the front door, finally turning my attention to the white plastic bag draped over my arm. Inside, I'll find my jacket soaked in her scent.

I think back to our phone call, to the way her breathy moans and gasps set my blood on fire. The way she surrendered to my commands. It was intoxicating, addictive. A high I never wanted to come down from.

I hate to admit it, but she made me feel something. I became lost in her voice and actually felt excitement. A flicker of joy.

She seemed to enjoy herself as much as I had, so why run? Why hit me with a jab and end the call? Either I pushed her too far, too fast, or she's playing a game. I really don't know the woman beyond her ambitions and the way her presence affects me. She might be the kind of woman who enjoys the game of cat and mouse.

I don't.

The thought of her toying with me intentionally is like nails on a chalkboard.

One minute she's hot, the next she's cold. Responsive and eager, then distant and closed off. This is a cycle I'm all too familiar with—push, pull, love, hate. Over and over until I don't know what's up and what's down. What to believe or not believe. When to give space. When to cling desperately.

I fucking hate that game and I refuse to play it again.

My mind shifts to the garden, the letter, the…

I swallow hard and walk to the kitchen, laying the garment bag across the marble counter. My fingers grab the plastic in the middle and tear it open, ignoring the zipper. Inside, there's my jacket. But not soaked in her scent.

Cleaned.

She cleaned my jacket when I told her not to.

With one quick movement, I sweep the garment onto the tile. Then I stalk to the cabinet and grab a bottle to pour another drink, my vision blurring at the edges. I know I should stop, should go to bed and try to sleep. But I can't. Not when my mind is racing, my body thrumming with restless energy.

After hanging up on me, she merely messaged: *I'm sorry.*

For what? For playing a game? She doesn't want to use my contacts so clearly something is going on, and I keep letting myself get mixed up in it. I need her *out* of my head, out of my system.

I set my glass of scotch down by the sink without drinking. Fuck, I need to calm myself, but that's impossible to do in this house where memories are practically dripping from the ceiling. I decide to call a driver and go somewhere that always makes my problems feel smaller.

THE COLD SAND OF BAKER BEACH fills the cracks between my toes. A bitter wind stabs at my blazer and whips hair around my face. There's only one other person on the beach at this hour—a shadowed figure sitting on a rock and staring at the ocean.

I step forward until the waves lap at my bare feet, the water thick with the briny scent of the bay, and I take a breath. In the distance, the Golden Gate Bridge is illuminated in long strands of lights. Beyond the lights, pure darkness. The moon is a sliver and the ocean an inky black void. If not for the lighted boats and the sounds of water crashing against rocks, it would be pure nothingness.

Exactly what I need; this spot always helps me clear my head. Except, it's failing that duty tonight. The vastness of the water, the scale of the bridge—it should all put my problems into perspective. Yet I can't get one single, irritating thought out of my head: *She cleaned the fucking jacket.*

I curl my toes into the muddy sand until a sharp rock shifts under the waves and jabs me. I shouldn't care. I normally don't. After one woman in particular wrecked me, I thought I had learned my lesson about letting people in, about opening myself up to the possibility of pain. But here I am again, standing on the precipice of more anguish.

Fuck this.

Before I can think better of it, I pull out my phone and type a message: **Why did you clean it?**

I hit send. Part of me hopes she won't respond, that she'll just let this thing between us fade, becoming another ghost in my past.

Another part of me, the part that can't seem to stop obsessing, craves an answer.

Minutes tick by, each one an eternity. I'm about to put my phone away, to finally throw in the towel and write this woman off, when the phone buzzes in my hand.

M.W.: *Cleaning it seemed like the right thing to do. I enjoyed what we did, but I don't want attachments. I'm sorry.*

Me: *Same here. I don't want attachments. But I thought I made it clear; I like to be in control. You can't just disregard that.*

Her response is quicker this time: **You told me to hang up if I didn't like something. So I did.**

I stare at the screen. Guess I didn't satisfy her, didn't help her find pleasure. That's a tough pill to swallow, a thought that sits heavy in my gut.

Me: *I'm sorry you didn't enjoy what we did.*

M.W.: *I enjoyed it. But I said no names. You ignored that.*

I rake a hand through my hair, tugging at the strands. She's right, of course. I did ask for her name, did push for more when she'd already set a boundary. Is that why she cleaned the jacket?

I smirk. Seems I've met a woman as stubborn as I am. And yet, even though I have answers now, I still can't seem to let this go, even though every part of my logical brain says I need to.

I have plenty of women to keep me company, so why the hell am I so stuck on this one? She's a woman without a name whose face I haven't fully seen.

I've lost my mind.

An idea starts to form in my head, hazy at first, then it sharpens. It's reckless, impulsive, completely unlike me. But the alcohol buzzing in my veins, the raw ache of what today is, pushes me forward.

I type out the words rapidly: *I'm leaving for a conference in a few weeks. Hawaii. Come with me. I need to fuck you out of my system.*

M.W.: *Wow. Are you always this brutally honest?*

Me: *Yes. I hate games.*

I never deny how blunt I can be, and it has scared plenty of women off. The ones who stay, though, are the ones who can handle me and my strict boundaries.

My mystery woman doesn't respond, so I add: *You said you felt the attraction, so give us one night. I'll take you on a date, then back to my hotel room. In the morning, enjoy yourself in Hawaii, all expenses paid. We'll go our separate ways, no strings attached.*

I wait, staring at the black ocean. The weight of the night presses in—tomorrow will be a gray, foggy day.

Finally, my phone lights up with her response: *I can't. Sorry. I don't like owing anyone anything, especially not a man. I can't owe you for a trip. Please, don't text me again.*

With that, the guillotine falls. I honestly don't know

what the hell I was thinking; a moment of pure insanity.

I pocket my phone and start trudging through the icy sand back to where my driver is waiting. But I'm not going home. What I need is to pound my fists against the hard, unyielding surface of a punching bag. There's a 24-hour gym I frequent with exactly what I need, and if I'm lucky, there will be a few people interested in sparring.

My body craves the physical ache of getting pummeled.

As I walk, I close my eyes, letting the wind smack my face, letting the chill seep into my bones. I think I'm relieved my mystery woman said no, because I'm a tainted man, poisoned. Everything I touch turns to ash, so she's better off escaping.

I don't need another woman leaving me a letter and a pair of tiny white shoes.

CHAPTER 6

SIENNA

"I'M GOING TO FAIL," I mutter, staring at my reflection in my bedroom mirror. I look like a still portrait frozen in perpetual dismay.

"Oh, bullshit," Jada says, messing with my short curls. I told her my black bob wouldn't curl well, but she forced it into submission. She mists my hair with hairspray and I cough from the particles stinging my nose.

"You're perfect for the job," she continues. "You'll make a great receptionist, and they'll fucking love you. If they don't, they're little bitches and you'll find somewhere better."

I frown. Her British accent has been slipping this past week, and I've been missing the fun slang. 'Twat' is just more colorful than 'little bitches.'

"I don't care about the work environment," I say, smoothing the front of my crisp white blouse. "I have to get a job *now* or I'm screwed."

And I mean it. This past week has been a nightmare, a perfect storm of bad luck and bad timing. First, the record store let me go because they needed to downsize. I'm bummed because it was my favorite job—no dress code, super chill, plenty of time to work on schoolwork or just scroll through social media. But it's not like I didn't see it coming; the owner had been talking about financial troubles for months while trying to come up with creative ways to market the store. He sells records though—not a big demand for those nowadays.

So, I got fired from that job and thought, *Well, I still have two jobs and I'll find something else soon.*

The next day, my supervisor at the beauty counter said, "We need to talk." That's never good. Apparently, a coworker had been caught doing drugs in the bathroom and dropped my name. I never liked her and she knew it. I just didn't expect her to be so petty. Of course, I'd never do drugs at work, or at all.

The supervisor didn't believe me and demanded my nametag. I'll get a deposit soon for my last paycheck, but it won't be much.

Now, here I am, down to one measly part-time gig waiting tables on the weekends. It's barely enough to cover the exorbitant grocery prices in San Francisco, let alone rent, bills, and my crushing student loans. Oh, and all the extra art supplies I need for my final semester project, which is due in about two weeks. Things have been so chaotic lately that I haven't even started it, which is so dumb.

Jada holds me firmly by the shoulders, staring into my eyes with her red ones. Another pair of colored contacts I don't like. They're too creepy and make me think she's a vampire. "You got this. You're professional as fuck and they'll love you. Everyone else does."

I relax a little and smirk. "Thanks, but that 'everyone' is just you."

"And my opinion is gospel."

I give her a quick hug because she always has my back. She even said she'd let my rent slide until I find more work.

I hate the idea of being a burden, though, of not pulling my own weight. I absolutely need to nail this job interview this morning.

With a fragile sigh, I adjust my blouse for the thousandth time. As I slip into my flats, I say, "Well, wish me luck." My voice is only mildly shaky.

"You don't need it cuz the job's already yours. Hey—"

I glance at her. She's looking as comfy as ever in a yellow romper. "Yeah?"

She's eyeing my bedroom door, picking at her chewed fingernails. "Um, did you return that…" Her words fade into air because I know she doesn't want to say 'jacket' and risk another fight.

Of course, we made up and talked everything out. But knowing she even *thought* I stole something, even for a second before she regretted it, still stings. It makes me worry that people will always be able to sense my criminal past, no matter how far I distance myself from it.

I grab my purse, knocking some clutter off my desk that I'll pick up later. "I returned it."

"You never told me how you met Declan at the gala."

I freeze. "How do you know his name?"

Giving me a guilty but devilish grin, she responds, "The initials on the pin. After some serious digging, I found a very small mention in a very obscure article on the Internet. It was about a recognition dinner, and it mentioned a few benefactors that received pins for their support of nonprofits and the art community. I connected the name to the initials cuz I'm a fucking detective." I laugh as her eyebrows arch and she smacks her lips. "You know," she continues, "If you're having money troubles, this guy can—"

"No," I cut in sharply, forcing my mind not to slip back to thoughts of him. It's been a struggle these past few weeks, ever since I told him not to text. "I need backers for my art program, but it's just not going to work with Declan."

I'm too willing to give myself to that man.

"But this is the chance you've been waiting for, babe. You have an *in*. Sienna, listen, the guy is—"

"No, don't tell me. I haven't looked him up. I don't want to know." The less I know, the better; I really can't keep going on like this with my insides feeling so jittery and jumbled every time he crosses my mind. He needs to stay a stranger.

Jada is slack-jawed but doesn't say anything as I slip out of my bedroom. She follows, the floorboards creaking beneath us.

When I reach the front door, she gives me a quick hug, her floral perfume hugging me too. "I have a ton of errands to run, but when I get home later, we'll have a celebration dinner. Sound good?"

I grab my car keys off a hook. "Sure, but first I have to get the job. And I'll celebrate if it's, like, two-dollar tacos because that's all I can afford. Ramen and cheap tacos. Or I'll just drink flavored water. Losing a few pounds won't hurt."

"Stop it," Jada says, nudging me with her elbow as she laughs. "I'm paying. Now go get it done so you can stop worrying."

With a nod and a wave, I'm off to the interview.

As I navigate the morning traffic, I cling tightly to the steering wheel. I try to calm myself with deep breaths and by mentally rehearsing some possible interview answers, but my mind keeps wandering to this past week's biggest knife to the gut: the gallery rejection.

I tried. I really gave it my all and poured my heart into a series of paintings I called 'Broken.' Five paintings all depicting broken things associated with my childhood:

broken barbies, a broken swing set, broken lamps. Cracked dishes and ashtrays. A broken bathroom mirror. Not one set of ominous watchful eyes, which my teachers still insist are 'trite.'

I thought, maybe naively, that this could be some kind of break, some tiny step forward. The art show is in a renowned gallery, and they were specifically looking to showcase student work in an upcoming show. Being able to say I was accepted into the show would give me something amazing to put on my CV, which currently has nothing art-related on it. I know I don't need to be an amazing artist to start an art program, since it's a non-profit venture that requires more business skills, but it matters to me. I want to start a program *and* be an artist.

I want my art to mean something to others. Make them feel seen, inspired, moved...

After losing two jobs, I held out hope for a positive response from the gallery. But I've always been allergic to good luck. The rejection email was polite, but the subtext very clear—my work isn't good enough.

Everything is crumbling around me and soon there will be nothing left for me to stand on.

I blink back the sudden sting of tears, refusing to let my mascara run. *Stay focused.* If I nail this job interview, it'll give me the hope I desperately need.

Maybe an affirmation will—

My phone buzzes, so I fish it out of my purse on the passenger seat while keeping my eyes on the road. It's an unknown number. I don't like using my phone while driving, but something tells me to answer. I tap the speaker button.

"Hello?"

"Hello, Sienna?" a crisp female voice greets me.

"Uh-huh."

"This is Miranda from By the Bay Property Management. I'm glad I caught you before you arrived. I'm afraid we've had to put a freeze on all new hires for now. I'm so sorry, but we won't be able to move forward with your interview today. As soon as we open the position back up, I'll let you know."

My heart is unraveling, but I force my voice to sound cheerful. "Oh, okay. Thanks for letting me know. Um, when do you think the position will open again?"

"At least six months. We've had to do some restructuring. It came from corporate this morning."

I want to laugh because the owner of the record store used the same business-speak: "Sorry, Sienna. I need to restructure the store and figure out how to secure the bottom line for future growth."

Honestly, I think he Googled those phrases five minutes before I arrived for my shift, but regardless, 'restructure' is just a stupid way of saying "we're firing a bunch of people to save money."

"Okay," I tell Miranda. "Thanks."

"Take care."

Instead of turning around and heading home, I drive until I hit a beach parking lot, one of the few free places to park in this overpriced city. Then I gaze at the peaceful ocean and give myself permission to mess up my mascara.

I wipe my tears with the inside of my white blouse because I have zero fucks to give right now. What is *wrong* with this week? I'm used to hitting walls in my life—massive ones—but why so many all at once? I've needed just one tiny win for so long that it's getting harder and harder to hold on to hope.

With my mascara thoroughly ruined, I wilt into my seat, exhausted. Maybe Jada is right and I should see Declan as an 'in.' I just don't like the thought of owing him something or creating a connection. I was too willing to play along during phone sex. To have him control me, take over.

If I let him, would he take over my life?

I let a man do that once and nearly died, so why am I still like this? Why am I so needy for belonging that I want to give up myself? I don't know Declan, so trusting him this quickly is stupid. And dangerous.

I let out a frustrated sigh. Those contacts of his are pretty amazing…

Dammit, I don't know what to do about that man.

I can't keep sitting here in limbo—at least I know that. Since I've allowed myself a few moments to feel pathetic, I should get back to job hunting. I'll worry about Declan and my art program later. First, I need some income.

And I need a good mantra to get me moving. I decide on: *Life is designed to knock you down. What matters is getting back up.*

I repeat that mantra even though I feel my nose stinging and my eyes ready to spill more tears.

What matters is getting back up.

Just get back up.

I just need to—

My phone buzzes again, but only once. A text? For a brief, foolish moment, I want it to be Declan. I wish I would stop thinking about that man. I asked him not to text, so if he did, that would be disrespecting me.

I'm sure it's not him.

I hate that I hope it is.

I pick up my phone to read the message.

And step right into a nightmare.

Every vein in my body turns to ice.

Unknown Number: *Found you. Missed you, Magpie.*

No. No no no no no.

I can't breathe. Can't think. All I can do is stare at the words on the screen, my hands shaking so badly I nearly drop my phone. Only one person has ever called me 'Magpie' and I got him out of my life seven years ago.

I finally did the right thing and turned myself in, got a plea deal in exchange for evidence they could use against my ex and his boss. He's supposed to be in jail right now with a 30-year sentence.

This isn't happening. I was careful. I did everything Witness Protection told me to do, even after they abandoned me.

Buzz.

Another text from the number that has a Chicago area code: ***You been enjoying the ocean?***

I toss my phone on the passenger seat and whip my head around, searching. He couldn't be here, right? In the parking lot? *Now?*

Doesn't fucking matter. He found me.

I turn the key until my car rumbles to life, then I shift gears and slam on the gas. Tires squeal as I back up. They squeal again after I shift to drive and zoom out of the parking lot. A car narrowly misses hitting me as I steer onto the street without stopping. Thankfully, San Francisco is a lawless city in many ways—the streets are so narrow and cramped that people do whatever the fuck they want while driving, and cops usually don't care.

I run a few red lights, skid down a few hills, and I'm

home way too fast. But I need to be. I need to pack. I need to run.

My entire body is shaking as I throw open the front door, my heart hammering so fast it's hard to swallow. My sudden appearance startles Mystical, who is sitting on the couch. He yelps and whips his head to stare at me like I'm a robber.

"Sorry," I say quickly, darting past him to my room.

The first thing I do is yank open a drawer on my desk and grab a small journal inside. I flip to the front page, which is a packing list I made for emergencies after the last time I tried unsuccessfully to contact my WITSEC handler. The man disappeared off the face of the earth.

I knew if shit went down, I'd have zero help and I'd struggle to think, so I'm grateful I had the foresight to make this list. All I need to do is go through the steps and get out of here.

Maybe I'll drive to Mexico. Canada? Everyone flees to Mexico when they're on the run, so maybe Canada is a better option.

I'm getting ahead of myself. Pack first.

Taking a breath that's not very calming, I grab a plastic bag hidden in the back of my desk drawer. It has all of Sienna's credentials: her fake birth certificate, passport, an extra ID from a different state. Her fake history. It also has a slip of paper with the protocol I'm supposed to follow:

1. Do not engage or respond to the contact.

2. Immediately inform a WITSEC handler of the threat.

3. Avoid locations or routines the contact may know about.

4. Be prepared for possible relocation.

5. Follow all additional instructions given by a handler.

Well, it would be a great plan *if* WITSEC was still an option.

Two years after they moved me to Utah, my handler stopped calling to check in. Shortly after that, I swore someone was stalking me. The same hooded figure kept popping up everywhere, and I kept having nightmares of a pair of watchful red eyes observing my every move.

I followed protocol and called my handler to report it. The woman who answered said my handler wasn't available, and she took a message. Someone was supposed to call back ASAP.

They never did.

When I tried again, they said my handler didn't exist—no one by that name was a marshal—and they couldn't find my case file. I was continually told they were looking into the error and that someone would call, but all I got was silence.

That's when I knew something shady was happening and I was on my own.

I no longer felt safe in Utah, so I packed up a bag and fled to San Francisco; luckily, my stalker didn't follow.

I slip the paper with the protocol back into the baggie, then grab my luggage from the closet. I start going down the list.

Clothes. I change clothes; stuff some in the luggage. Toiletries. Laptop. An extra pair of shoes. A few favorite books. All of my emergency cash, which is only three hundred. A keepsake box from my years here living with Jada.

I choke back a sob.

Jada.

I'm never going to see her again. How did I not know this morning was goodbye forever?

No.

Focus on packing; cry later.

When I get to the end of the list, I grab my cherished watercolor paints and some brushes, along with two sketchbooks and a journal. I pause when I notice the small color study painting I did of my 'inspired' charcoal drawing. I wanted to do a large painting of it and make that my final semester project.

Well, my semester is clearly over—I'll miss finals, fail, and get stuck paying back the loans with nothing to show for it.

I grab the color study. It's not on the list, but I can't leave it. It's a small canvas, so I stuff it, along with the folded charcoal drawing, into my luggage, zipping it shut.

I touch my collarbone, ensuring my silver locket is where it belongs. Finally, I take a moment to survey my room. My home. This has been Sienna's only home, here with Jada. We've gone through a few temporary roommates, including Mystical, but it's mostly just been us.

I cycle through the memories: Me and Jada hanging out at the beach, flirting with guys at bars and then leaving without them, watching movies late into the night, complaining about work or life and then making ourselves feel better with chocolate. Borrowing each other's clothes and just…just being dumb single twenty-year-olds having fun, even though we're broke as fuck.

I love this cluttered, creaky old room and all the bad paintings spilling out of the closet.

I love this home that's choking on plants.

I love my best friend.

My hand shakes as I wipe away a few thick, hot tears and curse under my breath. I really don't want to do this. But I have to. Anthony already knows I'm in San Francisco, so I can't wait around for him to show up at the door.

He'll hurt Jada and Mystical.

I need to lead him away from here. Far away.

Breaking protocol number one so I can try to get him to leave San Francisco, I send the bastard a text: *Thanks for the warning. I'm already leaving the city.*

His response comes a second later: *Go ahead, baby. You know I'll find you.*

Fuck. Him.

With one last gut-wrenching look, I turn and exit my bedroom.

Mystical immediately stands when he sees the luggage. Breaking his vow of silence, he asks, "What's going on?"

I walk to the front door, already feeling washed out. Like someone is slowly removing me from the canvas of this living room.

I shake my head at Mystical. "Um, I can't…it's…"

He moves closer, red robes swishing around him as he gives me a concerned look. "Seriously, what's up? You okay?"

I inhale sharply to force the grittiness from my voice. "Tell Jada I love her please. I have to leave and I can't explain. But tell her I'm so thankful for everything and I love her. I'll miss her. She's the only person who's ever cared about me and—" My voice cracks, so I clear my throat. "I probably can't text, but if I can one day, I will. Tell her that please."

His eyes widen. "Wait. What—"

"I have to go. I'll miss you, too." I pull him into a firm hug, my stomach churning like I'm going to throw up. "I've loved getting to know you. You're a fun roommate. I want both of you to have a great life. Just be happy and…Tell Jada I love her so much please. Tell her that." I open the door quickly.

"No. Hey, what—"

I shut the door and hurry down the stairs to the sidewalk. He opens it to call after me, but I'm already gone.

CHAPTER 7

DECLAN

I'M SITTING AT THE END of the long tan conference table. There's a stunning ocean view behind me, visible through the floor-to-ceiling windows of the hotel's executive boardroom. The sun is setting, filling the sky with orange and pink, but as much as I'd like to appreciate the beauty, business comes first.

Halliwell and his team flew out this morning, so Davis is standing across the room giving our pitch. Back straight, shoulders square, he's every bit the cool, confident business-man. Though he's overly tan, in my opinion—he was out at the beach last weekend with his family and got sunburned. It has darkened since then into a deep golden hue, highlight-ing his cheekbones.

Every eye is on him. He just has one of those voices that captures attention—I often tell him he should've become a voice actor, skipping his MBA in favor of going into enter-tainment. But then he wouldn't be my VP.

He's so persuasive as he outlines the benefits of a partnership with our company that even I start nodding my head, completely sold.

I glance around. The hotel group's CEO, Halliwell, sits at the head of the table, flanked by his board members. Some look intrigued, leaning forward and jotting notes. Others look skeptical, their expressions guarded.

We'll find out in a few minutes if our months of

schmoozing these men were worth it.

Amelia, our head of product development, is beside me. Her sleek black hair is styled in a professional bun, and her eyes are focused on Davis. She nudges my elbow, then gives me a thumbs up under the table.

I lean closer to whisper, "Let's hope."

She smiles and then turns her attention back to Davis, ready to field any technical questions the hotel group might have once the presentation ends. She's one of the sharpest minds on my team, and I'm glad to have her here.

Davis clicks to the final slide, a summary of our proposal. "Any questions?"

The room is quiet for a moment. Then Halliwell leans back in his leather chair. He's a middle-aged man with slicked-back hair and a grin that irritates me—his teeth are too unnaturally bleach-white.

"Impressive," he says, his dark eyes sliding from Davis to me. "Your technology beats what we currently use."

I incline my head slightly, acknowledging the compliment but not returning his smile. Every time I interact with this guy, he rubs me the wrong way. He flirts with female staff no matter where we are. He's boisterous, disturbing others around him. And today, his gaze keeps drifting to Amelia, lingering just a little too long to be professional.

I lean forward, my broad shoulders blocking his view of Amelia, and try to get his focus only on me. "We're happy to clarify any points or provide additional information," I say, my tone level. "Our team is at your disposal."

Halliwell nods, then he leans further back in his chair, the hinges squeaking. He's not looking at me anymore. He's staring openly at Amelia, smirking. "I do have one question," he says. "For Ms. Chen, was it?"

Amelia straightens, her expression neutral, but I can see the discomfort in her eyes from the sleazy way Halliwell said her name. "Yes. How can I help?"

Halliwell folds his hands in his lap, his gold Rolex glinting under the boardroom lights. "I was wondering if you'd like to join us for a celebratory dinner tonight. I think we will be signing with NexaProtect, and I'd like to thoroughly go over the technical aspects of your proposal." He glances at his watch. "But it is running late and I'm starving. Davis, Declan, Amelia…you should all join me for dinner." His smile widens, showing too many teeth as his eyes dip to Amelia's chest for a second.

A hot spark ignites in my chest, my jaw clenching so hard my teeth ache. Out of the corner of my eye, I see Davis shoot me a warning look not to blow this.

I'm trying. I do my best to keep my cool, taking a deep breath and hoping to end this meeting quickly so we can start moving forward with this strategic partnership. The hotel group would bring in a lot of cash for my company and help with our expansion plans; I'm *really* trying to grit my way through dealing with this lecherous fucker for the sake of my hardworking employees.

I clear my throat, keeping my tone flat and emotionless. "We appreciate your offer, but we'll have to decline. Perhaps we can address any questions you may have now. We're happy to go over the technology again, so you feel fully informed before signing any contracts."

Halliwell thinks for a second, smoothing a hand over his oily brown hair. His shoulders drop, and he sighs as if I inconvenienced him. "I suppose. Ms. Chen, would you please go over how your system integrates with our existing network again? I'd like to understand more about the potential downtime when we switch over."

Amelia glances at me, and I nod. I'm relieved the asshole is finally focusing on business so we can finish this meeting and get the hell out of here. Crossing my arms, I relax into my chair as Amelia gathers a few papers and then stands.

As she walks toward the front of the room to use the laptop and go over a few slides, she passes by Halliwell. The bastard tries to move quickly, but he's not quick enough—I see his hand dart out, grazing Amelia's thigh, his fingers brushing against the hem of her skirt and lifting it half an inch.

Amelia inhales slightly, but she keeps walking, maintaining her composure. She's probably thinking she imagined it or accidentally brushed against the side of an armrest.

But I had a ringside view and know it was Halliwell. And that's the final fucking straw.

I'm on my feet in an instant, my chair scraping loudly against the polished floor. In two swift strides, I'm behind the CEO. Gripping the back of his expensive leather chair, I yank it away from the table, nearly tipping him out of it. He gasps.

Then I spin his chair to face me. I lean down, caging him in as my hands grip the sides of the chair. His eyes are wide as they meet my icy expression.

"My team is here in a professional capacity," I bite out, my voice low and dangerous, "and I expect them to be treated with respect. So here's what's going to happen. You're going to face Ms. Chen, lower your head, and apologize for invading her personal space. Then you're going to apologize to me and the rest of my team for wasting months of our valuable time. There's no way in hell we're partnering with a scumbag like you."

His initial shock quickly turns to outrage, his face flushing an ugly shade of red. His nostrils flare as he opens his mouth, no doubt ready to spit some indignant retort back at me.

But I don't give him the chance.

"Let me remind you," I say, cutting him off. I lean in so only he can hear. "My team learned a lot about your company during our thorough audits. Unless you want the feds on your back for the piss-poor way you're handling customer data, I suggest you keep your mouth shut and follow directions."

When I straighten, I take him with me, fisting his shirt and yanking him to his feet. Everyone in the room is staring at me like I've lost my damn mind. Well, except for Davis. He's frowning and shaking his head because he's seen me throw business deals out the window before.

I never do it without a good reason.

A tense silence follows my words. Halliwell's face flushes an even deeper shade of red, his mouth pressing into a thin line. For a moment, I think he might argue, might try to assert his authority or bullshit me. But he faces Amelia and bows.

"I'm sorry if I've offended you, Ms. Chen," he bites out, the words sounding like they're being pulled from him against his will. He turns to the rest of my team. "My apologies. I meant no disrespect. Perhaps we should table this discussion, give my board and I some time to review your proposal in—"

"No, we're done," I say. I nod at my team, signaling for them to pack up. "Gather your things. We're leaving."

"Mr. Conte, you're being completely—"

"What? Sensible in expecting a business meeting to be about business? You don't get to harass my employees simply because you have wealth." I button my suit jacket with a sharp tug, smoothing down the expensive fabric. "Since this is the way you conduct business, I don't believe a partnership between our companies would be productive. You would only tarnish my company's reputation. We'll take our proposal elsewhere. Perhaps to your biggest competitor."

My team is quick to follow my lead, packing up their laptops and folders while the hotel board members start whisper-yelling at their CEO.

I lead the way out of the suffocating boardroom, Davis, Amelia, and my three other employees falling into step behind me.

In the hallway, Amelia touches my arm. "Declan," she says softly. "You didn't have to do that. I can handle a little unwanted attention."

"I know you can. But at work, you shouldn't have to." I jab my chin toward the room we left. "Besides, that asshole was a pain. It's better none of us have to deal with him again."

She smiles. "Well, thank you. I appreciate you standing up for me."

I nod, then glance at Davis. He's giving me that look, the one that says, "I can't believe you acted like a caveman again."

I smirk, cocking my head at him like a curious dog. "Something to say?"

"Quite a lot, but nothing that'll matter now."

We all ride the elevator down in silence. When we reach the lobby, Davis and I wave goodbye to our team, watching them disappear out the entrance. The two of us linger in the hotel lobby.

Davis finally sighs, like he's trying to clear all the air from his lungs. "I know the guy was an ass, but that partnership was a big deal. You sure it was wise to walk away?"

I run a hand through my dense hair, feeling less certain now that the adrenaline is wearing off. "I don't know," I admit. "But I won't do business with someone who doesn't respect our team. His behavior was a red flag. Even if we closed the deal, he'd be a nightmare to work with long-term."

Davis adjusts the satchel strap over his large shoulder. "I guess." His eyes scan the people in the lobby, all dressed in business attire. "Any ideas about what partnership to go after now?"

"I'm sure you'll figure out some prospects."

He walks toward the exit with a knowing smirk. "So you ruined the pitch, yet I have to pick up the pieces?"

"It's what I pay you for," I say, following.

He laughs, walking through a glass door that I hold open for him. "Pay me? I own thirty percent of the company as one of the founding members."

"I'm still the majority shareholder."

"True. But how important is that really, when you consider that NexaProtect would fall apart without me?"

Outside, I stuff my hands in my pockets. "You're right about that."

"Damn right I am."

I pause on the sidewalk as I wrestle with my thoughts. The workday is over, and my employees are all heading home to their families. But for me, whether I go home or not, I'll just find more work to bury myself in, sifting through emails and documents late into the night to avoid the oppressive silence of my empty house.

Davis pauses beside me, giving me a curious look. If he's free, maybe we could grab a drink. I need distraction from the thoughts that never seem to leave me alone. Or I could text one of the women I casually date. Martina has been trying to meet up since I haven't seen her in over a month.

But no, I'd rather hang out with Davis tonight. I haven't had the heart for hookups lately, haven't been able to muster the energy to pretend they make me happy.

"Your wife and kids still out of town?" I ask Davis.

He studies me, then ignores my question. "You've been…off these past few weeks. Anything on your mind? Anything about…"

He stops short of saying her name, and I'm grateful. It's too painful to hear, even after all this time. She's simply an enigma from my past. My ghost. A fleeting reminder of a happier time in my life before everything fell apart.

I level my shoulders. "There's a lot on my mind, but nothing I can put into words. Thanks for asking, though."

He pats my back. "Well, if you can put it into words, I'm happy to listen."

"I know. Things would definitely fall apart without you, me included."

"Good to know I'm so appreciated," he says with a cocky grin, making me regret giving him a compliment. "And I am still flying solo. They'll be in Oregon visiting Betty's parents for a few more days. Happy hour?"

I nod, relief washing over me. A drink with a friend, a chance to forget, even if just for a little while—I need that. I follow him to the curb, pulling out my phone to call a car.

But as I do, it starts to ring. "Hold on," I mutter to Davis, glancing at the screen.

My body goes rigid. I blink and stare, not sure I'm seeing correctly. The caller ID reads: *Mystery Woman*.

It's been weeks of silence between us, ever since she asked me to stop messaging. I respected her wishes, as much as it pained me. Now suddenly a call?

Part of me wants to ignore her, to press decline and continue on with my night. But something stops me, a tug in my gut that I can't explain.

She's never called, so something feels wrong.

Stepping into an alley where there's less noise, I answer with a clipped "Hi."

"Hi," she replies, her voice so frail the tiniest wind might break it.

Silence stretches between us, heavy and thick. I wait, but she doesn't continue.

"You called me," I finally bite out. I don't know what to think of this woman. She draws me in, then pushes me away. And I'm conflicted about my own cravings to know her when I don't want attachments.

I thought everything was done, yet now she's pulling me back in.

"Yeah," she says, her breath coming a little too fast. "Is, um…Are you still going to Hawaii?"

I clench my jaw, the muscles pulsing under my skin. This is a game to her, isn't it? "Yes. The conference is next week."

I hear her exhale. "Okay. Well, I'd like to take you up on your offer."

I lean against the rough brick wall of the alley, my eyes falling to a dried puddle of vomit at my feet. I'm at a complete loss. What is this? Push, pull; hot, cold. What is with this woman? She clearly doesn't know what she wants, and

I'm letting myself get dragged into it.

I'm silent so long that she asks, "Um…You still there?" Her voice is shaky, unstable. Almost on the verge of tears.

I clench my hand, rubbing my thumb along my knuckles. If this were any other woman, if her voice held any other tone…I would hang up. But there's something there, a desperate edge that nags at me.

I'm not the kind of man who can turn away when a woman sounds like she's in trouble.

I take a deep breath, forcing myself to soften my tone. "It's strange, isn't it? That you told me to stop messaging, yet now you want to hop on a jet with me to Hawaii."

"I-I know. It's, um, I've just been thinking about what you said. Maybe you're right, we could explore our chemistry and…" Her voice breaks with a heavy breath. It's the sound of someone fighting back tears. I hear a faint sniffle.

My senses immediately heighten. She really better not be playing a game because my protector instincts are kicking in. "What's wrong?"

"I-I'm sorry. Why did I even call you? This is…I'm sorry." The line goes dead.

I groan. *God dammit.* I'm caught in her web again, but I'm too concerned to care. I hit redial, my foot tapping on the concrete as I listen to the ringing.

She picks up and I say, "Don't hang up on me again. Now, what's wrong?"

"I…I've just been under a lot of stress from…work. School. I actually don't know if I want to, um, explore anything with you. Sorry for saying that." Her breath hitches, the sound making my chest tighten. "I just…need to escape the city as soon as possible. For, um…to just get a break. Mental health reasons, you know? I'm asking a lot and we don't know each other. I know that. I'm sorry. You just offered and…I really need to leave. Please."

Mental health reasons?

Escape?

Her voice is dripping in desperation. I can tell she's at a breaking point, and it pulls a memory to the surface. I can hear the pleas from the woman who still haunts the house we picked out together.

"What am I turning into? Please, stop me. You have to get me help, Declan. Please, you have to!"

Mystery Woman's request has me too raw. My muscles tense in preparation to fight whatever's distressing her this much. There's no way I can say anything except, "We'll leave tonight. I'll text you the address to the private airport. Meet me there at seven thirty."

"Thank you. Thank you, Declan." The relief in her tone is so profound it makes my chest swell.

I also like the sound of my name on her lips. Too much.

"Sure," I tell her.

I don't know what else to say, so I end the call.

My next thought is: *What the fuck am I doing?*

This woman won't even give me her name, show me her face, and she doesn't want me to know much about her. She also seems confused about what she *does* want, which is a mutual feeling.

Two confused, guarded people don't work well together.

But even as the doubts cloud my head, I won't back out. Not when she sounded so nervous and desperate.

I have to remind myself, though, that I've been tricked before.

"Please, Declan. I just need you. Get me out of here. I

promise I'm okay now."

I shake off the whispers from my ghost and walk out of the alley. I have calls to make, especially to Sean and Jeremy, so they can accompany me.

First, I need to tell Davis that happy hour will have to wait; there's a mystery woman in my life I can't seem to walk away from.

CHAPTER 8

SIENNA

DECLAN IS SITTING ACROSS FROM me on the jet—his private jet, no less. And the man is…beyond words. When I had imagined what he might look like without the gala mask, I never thought he'd be *this* striking.

He's wearing a brilliant white button up tucked into black slacks. The simplicity of the outfit makes his blue irises pop—irises no longer hidden in shadows. Those blue eyes are framed by angular cheekbones, a sturdy nose, and thick dark eyebrows. I can now see his Italian ancestry.

The cherry on top of this smoldering cake is his hair, somehow darker, longer, and more wavy than I recall from the gala.

But regardless of his sex appeal, there are storm clouds in his gaze.

He's reclined on a tan leather seat, one ankle crossed over his knee, clicking a pen in one hand.

Click. Click. Click.

He's been studying me the entire half hour we've been on this jet, his mouth shifting from smirking to frowning in a repetitive dance.

I keep glancing over at his two bodyguards in the corner, Jeremy and Sean, because I'm trying to ignore Declan. My eyes always wander back to him. I like watching that strong jaw flex, and my fingers ache to feel the stubble along his tanned cheeks. That night on the phone, I loved hearing how his voice unraveled more each time I moaned; now I'm longing to witness him unravel in front of me.

Here I am running for my life, terrified I'll never truly escape Anthony, yet Declan's sex appeal is strong enough to overpower that.

Shifting in my seat because I'm feeling flushed, I adjust the large black sunglasses covering the upper half of my face. I'm also wearing a gigantic sunhat so I can hide under the generous brim.

I lucked out because Sean was the one to greet me outside the private airport. I had shown my ID to security inside, away from prying eyes, then quickly put my sunglasses and hat back on before meeting Declan and Sean near the jet. I was relieved that neither Declan nor Sean had to know my name. The airport officials and flight crew now know, of course, but they said they'd be discreet.

Declan frowned when he saw me but otherwise didn't say anything about the accessories

Well, he hasn't said anything at all besides "hi." Then he gave me a grunt when I said, "Thank you for letting me come."

I don't care that Sean saw what I look like, but for Declan, I need this barrier. I know it's silly—some might say irrational—but hiding my full face keeps him at a distance, reminds me to remain detached when the pull between us is so strong.

These sunglasses and hat are a statement: we don't need to know each other.

I glance at his bodyguards again. It's a little strange to have them around, but I guess it's normal when you're rich. They're both doing their own thing—Jeremy is on his phone and Sean is reading, his long angled black bangs falling into his face. I talked to them both a little and Jeremy is very chatty while Sean is…I don't know. He seems like a guarded, slightly secretive person.

My eyes shift back to Declan as he clicks that damn pen.

Click. Click. Click.

Instead of focusing on that intense gaze of his, I need to start thinking about my next steps. Hawai'i is just a temporary fix. Though I'm excited about seeing the main island for the first time, I'm not planning on sight-seeing. I need to disappear. Maybe I could live on one of the smaller islands. Find a job catering to tourists, save up some money.

I should have enough time to do that. Since I already smashed and then ditched my phone in a random trashcan back in San Francisco, Anthony shouldn't be able to find me, especially if I pay for things with cash. I don't know how he tracked me after all these years, but he's not a wizard. Once I save enough money, I can fly to another country, get as far away from the States as possible. Disappear in some tiny European town that's off the map. Anthony might have connections in the U.S., but I can't see how he'd find me in another country.

I run my trembling thumb over the small phoenix tattoo on my inner wrist. It's the only tattoo I have, and I got it to remind me of everything I've survived. That I can survive tough shit. I *will* get through this.

Still…I feel on the verge of a panic attack from merely thinking of Anthony—thinking of the lonely 17-year-old boy with a rough childhood, the boy I met when I was 16, more than a decade ago. The boy I watched turn into a man filled only with venom.

I close my eyes and try to focus on the hum of the jet

engines.

Anthony isn't here.

I'm thousands of miles away from him in the air.

Just focus on my breath, the hum, the—

Click. Click. Click.

That sound is grating on my nerves, so I open my eyes and frown at Declan. "Can you *please* stop?"

He stops immediately, twirling the silver metal pen along his fingers. He finally drops it onto the seat next to him.

The night we met at the gala flashes through my mind.

"I'm glad you caught my eye."

I can't imagine him saying that to me now. All I'm doing is taking advantage of his sense of justice in protecting women—something made clear at the gala.

Margaret was good at taking advantage of men. Not that I was flirting with Declan because I had an agenda, but Anthony taught Margaret how to do that. Then he sent her to 'accidentally' bump into rival dealers and flirt until she was trusted. She'd find secrets, weaknesses, then Anthony would use that to take them down.

Sometimes, all the way down.

Yes, they were criminals involved in a dangerous world. But they still had families.

"Sorry," I say. I'm speaking to Declan and to all the people that Margaret hurt.

Declan's gaze tries unsuccessfully to pierce through my sunglasses before dropping. While massaging the back of his neck, he scowls at the floor. Then he undoes his cufflinks and rolls up the sleeves of his shirt.

My reaction is involuntary—a slight intake of air once his veiny forearms are exposed. A thin layer of dark hair blankets his skin.

He catches my reaction and studies me some more, his face a hard mask. With a swallow, I tuck a strand of hair behind my ear and turn to look out the window at the night sky. I wish he would stop looking at me so damn intensely. It's…unnerving. And also doing things to my body I'd rather not acknowledge.

To my relief, he stands and crosses the jet, putting more space between us. At the small bar tucked along one wall, he begins making a drink. Ice clinks into a frosted glass. The top of a decanter makes a sharp *pop*. Amber liquid is poured.

"Would you like something?" he asks, his back to me.

"Oh, um, no thanks. I don't like drinking."

He corks the decanter. "There's tea or soda."

"Tea, I guess. Thank you."

"Iced or hot?"

"Hot?" I don't know why I phrased it as a question, but I'm a little surprised at how accommodating he's being. I'm using him for a free trip to Hawai'i and he knows that, so he could've just left me to fend for myself, escaping to the room in the back.

Instead, he's lingering.

He disappears around a corner, where I think there's a small kitchenette. Five minutes later, he reappears, carrying a mug in one hand and his glass in the other.

He hands me the mug and I get a generous inhale of his scent—the same delicious scent I wrapped myself in when I had his jacket.

My mind slips to that night again, to images of him stroking himself while commanding me to rub the silky jacket between my thighs.

Dammit, do not think about that.

I sip the tea, hoping it will burn my mouth and distract my brain; unfortunately, it's the perfect temperature.

"There was only green," he says before returning to his seat across from me.

"That's fine. Thank you." I take another sip, letting the warmth soothe my stomach.

Ice clinks in his glass as he sips his whiskey, or whatever it is. "So…classes have been stressful?" he asks.

My stomach knots. I was afraid he might initiate small talk. I only nod, trying to return to our awkward silence.

"What are you studying?"

"Art," I say.

"What kind of art?"

I stare into my tea, watching the pale green liquid swirl. "Doesn't matter."

He sighs and fixes his gaze into the blackness of night.

God, I feel like the shittiest person ever. I steal this man's expensive jacket, agree to phone sex but then hang up, reject his offer for more fun even though I would *really* like him to 'fuck me out of his system,' tell him to stop messaging, then call out of nowhere and beg to go to Hawai'i under his expense. Plus, I do all of this when we're not dating, he barely knows me, and I have no intentions of hooking up.

I can't imagine why he's still being so patient and accommodating, or trying to talk to me.

I'm clearly a mess and a really awful person.

I set my tea on a tray and then take off my boots. I'm wearing my go-to outfit of black leggings, clunky boots, and an oversized sweater. It's comfortable for the jet trip, but Hawai'i is a lot warmer than San Francisco. Stupidly, I packed a lot of sweaters and only two T-shirts. I can't spare the cash to buy new tops, so maybe I'll just cut off the sleeves.

But I change positions so my feet are tucked under my hip, then I lift my chin. Yes, I'm a mess and being awful, but I need to focus on today's mantra: *What matters is getting back up.*

I can fix this.

"I'm sorry," I say, and his eyes focus on me again. He doesn't respond, just waits, so I add, "I'm sorry for everything. And for being crazy. I'll pay you back."

The first whisper of a smirk lifts his full lips. He sips his drink. "Will you?"

I hold myself firm as I nod. "Yes. My funds are lacking at the moment, but I want to pay you back. I'm not trying to get a free ride, I just needed an escape. I appreciate you being so accommodating."

His face is emotionless as he turns to his bodyguards.

Sean seems to immediately sense that Declan needs something. He glances up and asks, "Yeah?"

"Can you give us some privacy, please? Hang out in the bedroom."

Jeremy lowers his phone. "Together?"

Declan's eye twitches. "Yes. Watch a movie."

"A movie? There's only the bed to sit on and it's barely a full."

Sean pulls him to his feet before he can protest more. Then he says evenly, "Come on. You don't wanna cuddle with me? I'm good at it."

Jeremy rolls his eyes. "Whatever, man. I'm picking the movie."

Silence descends as they disappear down a short hallway. Now I'm alone with Declan. I cast him a wary glance.

He reclines further into his seat, letting his legs stretch

out into a wide V, and my gaze traces the outline of his muscular thighs through his dress pants. "I wasn't expecting you to pay me back," he replies, "but if you insist." He sips his drink, drawing out the suspense. "The hotel room is about seven hundred per night, and we'll be there for ten nights. This jet is about thirty thousand one-way."

I swallow hard as I do the math in my head. That's... too much. But when he gave me the address to a private airport, I expected as much.

"Okay," I tell him, keeping my voice steady and forcing myself not to flinch. "My half for the jet is fifteen. I can make that work. Eventually. I once paid off a car that cost that much. So...it's doable." *Most expensive fucking flight of my life.* It will take me years to pay off that debt, but it'll prove that I'm not just being selfish and repeating things Margaret did. I meant what I said—I'll figure out a way to find the money. I always have.

"It's a two-way trip," he comments.

"I only need it one-way." His brow furrows and I know he's about to probe into my response, so I quickly add, "And I appreciate your offer for a hotel room, but once we land, I'll find a cheaper place for myself. I'm sure there's a budget motel." Or I'll sleep on the beach. I was homeless for a year after I turned 15.

I touch my phoenix tattoo. I'll make this work. I have to.

Declan continues to look confused, but there's something else in his stare—rigid steel. Leaning to his left, he reaches for an intercom button.

After a second, a man's voice crackles over the speaker. "Yes, Mr. Conte?"

"I may need to turn around and go back. Just a heads

up. I'll let you know shortly."

"Copy that."

I drop my feet to the floor and dig my fingernails into the armrests, needing something to cling to. Adrenaline spikes my heart rate. "What? No, we can't turn around. We have to go to Hawaii."

Declan is the definition of cool confidence, and no matter how stormy his gaze gets, the rest of him is always poised and in control. He merely leans forward, resting his thick forearms on his knees. Then, a single word: "Why?"

"I-I told you. I'm stressed from school and work. I just needed a break."

"No. You wanted a one-way ticket, so you can ditch me at the airport."

My mouth stays shut; I don't have any excuse for that.

He leans an inch closer, continuing to pin me with his gaze. "How much longer are you going to keep lying to me, whatever your name is?"

I still can't figure out how to respond because I certainly can't tell him the truth, and anything else would be more lies.

"What's going on?" he asks, his tone a little softer. "Bad breakup? Trouble with the IRS? Did you commit a crime?"

That last one hits too hard, so I jump to my feet, pushing my sunglasses up my nose because they feel loose; any minute they could fall, exposing how I really am. "I'm not a fucking criminal."

Not anymore.

Margaret was. Not me. Not Sienna.

The woman I used to be is dead and buried. There's even a gravesite for her back in Chicago.

Declan takes a breath and then says, "I'm sorry. I'm not

trying to accuse you of something. But considering you're on my jet, I'd only like some *truthful* indication of why you don't want to return to San Francisco."

I shake my head, feeling like I'm collapsing in on myself. "You have to stop asking. Please stop asking things about my life. I only need to get to Hawaii, and it's very important. That's all I can tell you. Please, I can't go back right now." I fall into my seat, feeling like I've hit a new low. It's hard for me to plead with anyone like this, especially a man I've already asked too much of, but it's my life on the line. Telling him the truth might also put him in danger.

Though I don't think WITSEC is looking out for me anymore—something crooked happened in their system—their number one rule was to never reveal your true identity. No matter what, never tell anyone you're in WITSEC.

I shake my head again. "I'm sorry I can't tell you. If you want me to drop to my knees and beg, I will. Just please don't turn the jet around."

With a groan, he scrubs a hand through his wavy hair and turns his confused and concerned expression to the ceiling. Then he hits the intercom button with a fist. "Stay on course for the Big Island."

"Copy that."

I sag into my seat. *Thank God.*

Declan directs his exasperation at me. "Fine. I can respect your reasons for keeping things to yourself. But don't insult my integrity. There's no fucking way I'm letting you stay in some budget motel. I invited you, so while I'm in Hawaii, you'll be staying with me in a hotel room. One that I pay for. You're also insane if you think I'd charge you for this jet trip. Keep your money." He stands and storms toward the bar. Over his shoulder, he adds, "That's not up for discussion, or I'll tell the pilot to turn around. Understand?"

I nod weakly, feeling a little uneasy about what he means about me staying *with* him. I don't like being trapped by a man—been there, done that, not doing it again. Though I'm here voluntarily, demanding that I stay in his room is pushing some boundaries.

I really don't want him to turn the jet around, but I have to clarify a few things. "Is there only one bed?"

"No. It's a suite with two rooms."

I exhale. *Good.*

"I might only stay one night," I say.

He sighs loudly. "As I said, while I'm in Hawaii for the next ten days, I would prefer you stay with me so I can ensure your safety."

Oh. That's…actually sweet. "What if I only stay one night, though?"

Another sigh. "I really can't stop you, but it would irritate me."

I chew my bottom lip as I watch him prepare another drink for himself. My next question is the most important: "But you wouldn't stop me?"

He pauses what he's doing at the bar and glances over his shoulder. "Of course not. You're my guest, not…" He doesn't finish his sentence, but he looks concerned as he returns his focus to the bar.

Okay.

Okay. I'm just his guest; he's not trying to trap me.

He's not another man like Anthony. I hope.

There's just one more detail left to clarify. "Your original invitation was about…well, fucking me and then cutting me loose while you go to your conference. If I let you pay for everything, is that what you're expecting?"

He slams the bottom of his glass against the bar top as he mutters, "Jesus fucking—" Whipping around, his eyes are ablaze. "You think I can't possibly be trying to help without an ulterior motive?"

I open and close my mouth a few times, trying to find the right words. Finally, I say, "You seem noble and patient, but really…I don't know you. I don't know you well enough."

One side of his mouth caves in and he grabs the decanter to finish pouring his drink. "Not personally, but I'm sure you know *of* me."

"No."

After his drink is ready, he returns to his seat, taking a heavy gulp of whatever's in the glass. "Don't lie about any Internet searches you did. Every woman I'm with looks me up."

My body is drained, and I have a headache. This has been such an awful day; I just want to sleep. I even sound exhausted when I respond, "I don't want you prying into my past, so it's only fair I don't pry into yours. I know nothing about you except that you're rich enough to afford a private jet and you like art galas." I lower my voice to mumble, "You're also bossy."

He must've heard that last part because he huffs out a light chuckle. The ice in his glass clinks as he swirls it. "You really didn't research me?"

"No. Why would I lie about that? We're just two people who only know each other…temporarily." Once we get to Hawaii, once I get a full night's sleep, I'll start figuring out my new life.

I hope I don't have to kill Sienna and create a new identity. I like her.

Declan has fallen strangely quiet, his gaze unfocused as he stares at the empty air in front of him. For the first time since we met, I wonder what I would find if I looked him up. Does he also have a past he doesn't like people knowing? Or is he bitter about gold diggers—women only dating him for all the fancy things he can buy?

Well, I already know he's rich and I don't want any of that. I couldn't care less if I live the rest of my life dirt poor. All I've ever wanted is to make art and have a good, simple life. As Sienna, I also want to make a difference and do something to help others.

Those are my desires. Even if I flee to another country, I'm promising myself right now that I won't give up on my art program for troubled youth. I didn't have help when I was struggling as a teen, so now I want to be that support for someone.

If I live long enough.

Declan finally snaps out of his thoughts, his face still a dark storm, and gulps the rest of his drink. His eyes dip to my locket, which I'm currently clutching, and he answers my previous question. "The only thing I expect during this trip is for you to stop being so stubborn about how I spend my own money, which includes how I choose to spend it on you. That's all." His gaze captures mine again, and it's back to its normal molten intensity. His voice is raw and layered as he says, "If you change your mind about sex, you'll have to beg for it."

The sudden ache between my thighs is unwanted, but it's not like I have control over my body. It's apparently a traitor. So are my thoughts, because I get a flash of Declan towering above me, stroking himself, while I'm on my knees begging. It's incredibly hot and I'm irritated he put that in my head.

I lift my chin defiantly. "Sorry to disappoint, but I won't change my mind."

The smirk that lifts his mouth makes him irritatingly more handsome.

Damn this man.

I stand and adjust my sweater. "If it's okay, I'd like to rest in the bedroom until we land."

"Of course." He presses a different button on the intercom. "Our guest would like to use the room, so please return to the cabin."

Jeremy's voice crackles through the speaker: "Aww, what? No. We just go to the part w—" It cuts out suddenly.

A second later, Sean's voice says, "Yes, boss. Be right there."

Declan shakes his head at the floor, then tells me, "I'll have the stewardess let you know when we're making the descent."

"Thanks."

Once Sean and Jeremy appear, I retreat to the private bedroom in the back of the jet. I shut the door, then collapse on the bed. The weight of the past twelve hours presses down on me, and I almost can't breathe.

What I'm doing is crazy. I'm going off to Hawaii with a man I barely know, who clearly has some control issues, and I'm hoping he doesn't turn rotten the way Anthony did.

I'm insane. But what choice did I have? It was either take a chance with Declan so I could hop on a jet out of town ASAP, or escape by car, a much slower mode of transportation. The jet seemed like the better choice.

I only hope it was the right one.

This entire day sucks. I just want to go home; I want to

be in my bed listening to Mystical snoring or Jada watching TV too loud in her room.

I grab a feather pillow and sob into it.

Jada would've gotten home a few hours ago; Mystical would've told her about my frantic departure. She'd have cried and sent me a thousand texts that will remain unanswered. Then she would've called and called and called, every attempt going straight to voicemail while my smashed phone sits in a trash can near Hayes and Webster.

Now, Jada is probably sobbing herself to sleep, confused and angry and hurt that her best friend abandoned her with no explanation.

She hates me, I just know it. That thought has turned my insides into strips of shredded veins and muscles and bone.

We swore never to do that to each other.

CHAPTER 9

DECLAN

WHO KNEW MY MYSTERY WOMAN snored? She's across the living room in the suite's second bedroom, but the builders must've cut corners because the walls are thin. It's three in the morning, and I'm lying awake, staring at the ceiling, listening to that woman snore.

I smile in the dark.

Giving up on sleep for the night, I fling the covers off. I grab my laptop and busy myself with work for about an hour. My body is still tense from the jet, so I dress in work-out clothes and decide to go for an early jog on the beach. I send the snoring woman a quick text to let her know I stepped out—in the unlikely event she wakes while I'm gone—then I lace my sneakers and grab my backpack.

"Want me to go with?" Sean asks when I step out of the suite. His eyes are still glued to a book. I swear, he reads one or two a day, all self-help or biographies.

I'm sure he's been in the hallway all night, but he looks completely awake and energetic. I always tell him he doesn't need to literally guard the door, just accompany me to places, but he never listens. He and Jeremy are across the hall, and that's good enough for me, but Sean is stubborn. Mostly paranoid. Someone broke into my room one time during a work trip; Sean has been extra diligent ever since.

That is why he's the best.

"No," I tell him. "I'll be back soon. Besides, I'm still

irritated you got to see her face, and I didn't."

He flips a page and smirks. "You're missing out."

Grumbling, I leave down the hallway.

A handful of minutes later, my sneakers are in my backpack and my bare feet are pounding the sand. The resistance challenges my muscles to work harder. I usually run on the beaches near home a few times a week, but the ocean around the Big Island is more serene. There's less trash, no people. Just sand, water, and fading stars.

After ten miles, I'm sweaty and my thighs ache, so I sit along the water's edge, letting the waves caress my feet. I chug from my water bottle as I gaze at the ocean. The sun is starting to crest the horizon, replacing the darkness in the sky with orange and red.

I lean back on my hands and watch. It's been a while since I saw the sunrise. Even though I struggle with insomnia, I always keep the curtains closed until the sun is up.

For good reason.

Tiffany loved the sunrise; she said it was a new beginning every twenty-four hours, like everything before it didn't have to matter. Her obsession meant she was awake before I was, and she always got me up early on the weekends.

I would trudge up to the rooftop patio with her, half asleep, then we'd hold each other and watch the horizon. When the sky was finally lit up, she'd tip her head back to grin at me.

"Welcome to a fresh start," she'd say.

That was during the early years when she still smiled.

My chest feels hollow now, and I realize sitting down to watch the sunrise was a stupid idea. I start the jog back to the hotel.

Along the way, thoughts of my mystery woman creep in.

What the hell am I going to do about her?

The woman is…infuriating.

She's clearly running away from something. It's not that I want to get involved, but she is involving me since I was her means out of California. Despite that, she won't give me any answers. A name. Won't even show me her entire face.

I don't like the dynamic.

I've also never met a woman so ridiculous as to offer to pay me for the use of *my* private jet. The women I date are always eager to spend my money—which has never bothered me—yet this one is trying to split the bill?

It's half insulting, half bewildering.

Mystery Woman isn't just a fascinating puzzle, she makes me feel out of control.

A feeling I absolutely hate.

So the question remains: What do I do about her? Set her free? Or keep trying to peel back the layers so I can further help?

She seems to need it.

I reach the hotel elevators and jam my finger against the button. I'm so on edge even after the run that I feel ready to jog up the stairs to the suite. Instead, I lean against the wall and try to have some patience.

The sensible part of me says to let my mystery woman go. Since she just wanted to use me for a one-way ticket to Hawaii, fine. See ya. Have fun.

But the damn protector in me can't turn his back on a woman; I know I won't rest until I feel more in control of the situation.

Selfish, I know. Like I'm trying to redeem myself.

The elevator finally arrives, so I ride it up. As I approach the suite, I nod at Sean.

He breaks into a wide yawn.

"Get some sleep," I tell him. "I don't need you out here in the hallway."

He flips a page of his book, something with 'zen' in the title. "The point of security is to be there for the unexpected."

"Then at least get Jeremy to switch out."

"I will soon."

I'm about to open the door when a thought stops me. Since Sean is here, I tell it to him; maybe I just need to say it out loud since I'm struggling to make sense of it.

"She didn't look me up."

Sean lowers his book. "A lot of people have heard of you."

"She hasn't. Yet she didn't research my name."

"Is that a bad thing? You've said you hate people knowing about…you know."

"I do." I wrap my hand around the door handle. "But I'm so used to people knowing that it feels strange she doesn't."

When people learn my name and that I have money, they immediately hit the search button. They find stories about my wealth, my company, exposés on the endless stream of women I date, articles about my 'heart wrenching and tragic' personal life. Then they come to me with their admiration, greed, judgment, lust, or pity. Often, all five.

Yet, not the woman in my suite.

"You gonna tell her then?" Sean asks.

"I don't think so. She doesn't want to stick around anyway, and it's actually a relief to have a clean slate."

I can understand why she doesn't want to reveal her own history. When others don't know your past, there's a sense of freedom. A fresh start.

As I enter the suite, I'm thinking about a long, hot shower and some black coffee. That's why I'm startled to find my mystery woman pacing in the living room while wringing her hands.

No sunglasses.

Jesus, she's beautiful.

"Declan," she gasps when she notices I'm here. Maybe I'm imagining it, but she looks relieved to see me. "Where were you?"

"Out for a run."

"Oh…"

"Everything okay?" I ask, dropping my backpack near the door and stepping closer.

She nods sharply, glancing at my sandy calves.

I can't take my eyes off her. After weeks, finally I can see the full color of her dark brown irises, the slender curves of her eyebrows, the slight upturn of her petite nose. She has a few freckles just around her eyes.

"You're stunning," I say.

Her eyes bulge and she touches her cheek. She spins around. "Dammit."

"There's no reason to hide. I've already seen you."

With a sigh, she faces me again, her cheeks flushed pink.

I can't help the animal in me, whose gaze wanders down her body, taking in the black boy shorts and the outline of her puckered nipples beneath her thin sleeping shirt. "I really like what I see."

Her ivory cheeks turn a deeper shade of pink and she

crosses her arms, possibly just realizing she's not wearing a bra.

A thought occurs to me, and I stalk closer. "You looked a bit…scattered when I walked in. Were you worried about me?"

She scoffs and rolls her eyes. "As if. I just woke up, and you weren't here so—"

"You were worried."

Her disdain is over-exaggerated, her voice rising in pitch. "No. I wasn't worried so stop putting words in my mouth. I woke up early, and I was only curious why you weren't here. It was, like, four in the morning and you were gone for two hours. It was only noticeable, that's all."

"Sean was in the hallway the entire time. You could've asked him."

She crosses her arms. "Well, I didn't know that."

I stalk closer, expecting her to back up. She doesn't. When she wets her lower lip, it takes every ounce of self control not to wrap an arm around her waist and devour her. It's important for her to come to me first. She needs to show me, without a doubt, that she's interested because I refuse to play any games.

However, I allow myself one light touch, running my knuckle gently over the curve of her flushed cheek. "Thank you for showing me your beautiful face."

Her lips part and I can tell she's flustered, breathless. *Wonderful.*

"I-I didn't do it on purpose," she says. "I forgot."

"Because you were so concerned about where I went."

This time, she doesn't argue, only steps away from my reach.

I think I've pushed too much, so I walk toward my

bedroom. "I sent you a text that I was going for a run."

She only nods absentmindedly.

The thrill of seeing her react so strongly to my absence and then to my presence is coursing through me. I can't resist saying, "I'm taking a shower. Join me."

She makes a disgusted sound, followed by a snarl. "No thanks. You always this cocky?"

"You can find out." I flash her a smirk before disappearing into the bedroom.

CHAPTER 10

SIENNA

I ADMIT, I ALMOST FOLLOWED Declan to the shower. Almost. Then I looked at my surroundings again to give myself a big dose of reality.

Here I am, in a 5-star hotel, a tropical paradise, with a ridiculously handsome man who can afford to drop 30K on a five-hour flight. Whatever insanity I'm experiencing, it's temporary.

I should pack my bags right now. After getting a good night's sleep, I was supposed to make a plan for my new life and figure out a way to tell Declan 'adios.' I shouldn't be here, relaxing on the patio of this suite while gazing at the unbelievably blue ocean.

Why am I hesitating to leave?

I adjust my bra strap underneath my T-shirt, garments I changed into so Declan won't get more fuel for his dirty thoughts. I try to focus on the birds and the stunning view instead of the sound of the shower running inside.

This suite is a dream. It's the size of a small house. There's an enormous living room with cream-colored couches and wooden floors. The kitchen is decked out in marble, the bathrooms too. Every room has floor-to-ceiling windows, so no matter where you are, the ocean is in plain sight. I can even see the translucent water from the enormous tub in my bathroom. This place is like something out of a movie.

I'm completely drowning in my own guilt—guilt from using Declan as a means for escape, guilt from abandoning Jada. Throw in gradients of anger at myself for still being here. Since Anthony is looking for me, I shouldn't be lounging around like I'm on vacation.

I need to leave. Just pack my shit and...

The shower turns off, and I can't stop myself from imagining Declan stepping out, grabbing a white towel off the rack as steam swirls around his tan skin. His muscular body glistening with water, damp hair falling into his eyes as he dries off. If that man walked out onto this patio, right now, wearing nothing but a towel and a smile, I might give in. Might beg.

I'd beg him to fuck me as I stare at the endless ocean.

I wish I hadn't been so stupidly concerned about where he was earlier.

But when he was gone, when I thought, I don't know, that he'd had enough of me and left, or that something bad had happened, that he just wasn't coming back, I felt the loss.

The man makes me feel safe.

If he leaves, or if I step outside this hotel room without him, I'm no longer safe.

But really...I'll never be safe. The world can't promise that. As long as Anthony is out there, he'll look for me; anywhere I go is only a temporary sanctuary, not true freedom.

As long as he's alive, I'm trapped.

So what if I just surrendered to Declan and to this entire Hawaii fever dream? For nine more days, I can live in a fantasy where a rich, hot guy wants to fuck me, and I can pretend life is perfect. I can be happy, even if it's all make-believe.

Is temporary happiness better than none at all?

The heavy stone in my stomach says no—I shouldn't let myself get mixed up with any man. Instead, I should focus on starting over. Again.

This temptation to ignore the truth must be part of Margaret trying to bubble up to the surface, to break the locked door I sealed her behind.

Margaret hid behind men and excuses. She didn't have self-respect and let a man control her, possess her, trap her. She wanted to belong so badly that she fell for Anthony and let him pull her deep into his world. Then she committed crimes for him, watched him do horrible things. She infiltrated rival groups, stole, committed fraud, cleaned his bloody clothes, hid evidence of his evils. And so much more.

He never physically hurt Margaret, but he trampled everyone else to maintain his way of life and satisfy his boss; Margaret never tried to stop him. She was only complicit, believing that his special mix of possession and manipulation was love.

Sienna is nothing like her. At least, she's trying to be the opposite. Declan has been testing her resolve to stay away from men who like control.

What if I only get myself in trouble again?

I should just go. I'm confident Anthony can't find me here—at least not for several months—but me being with Declan is still dangerous for him. I think I just attract danger.

Closing my eyes, I inhale a deep breath of the salty ocean air. Being homeless on the streets of Hawaii for a while won't be so bad. At least it'll be a paradise around me.

Just get back up.

Today. I'll pack my shit today and just leave to start my

new life. No more excuses.

I hear footsteps through the living room behind me, then the fridge opens. Though he's several feet away across the suite, I sense Declan as if he's mere inches away, breathing hot air along my skin, giving my entire body goosebumps. My resolve starts to crack.

Quickly, I stand and move to the patio railing, wrapping my fingers around it with a death grip. I can't let go, because if I turn around, if Declan is half naked in a towel, it's over.

His footsteps travel across the floorboards, getting closer.

"You hungry?" he asks, only a few feet away now on the patio.

I can smell the tropical shampoo he used to wash his hair. It must still be damp, so my fingers would glide right through, twisting the strands so easily…

I angle my head down, staring at the buildings below. He's probably clothed, but I'm not going to risk it. "Um, no, I'm okay for now."

"When you get hungry, feel free to call room service."

"Yup. Thank you."

"Don't be stubborn and starve yourself," he grumbles, and it's such a sexy sound. "I don't want to come back to find you passed out from not eating."

My chest tightens. *He's leaving?* My head involuntarily starts to swivel in his direction, but I stop myself from looking at the last second, staring down at my feet instead. "Oh, um, you're going somewhere?"

"Yeah."

I wait, giving him an opening to tell me where he's going, but he doesn't. His conference, whatever it's about, doesn't start for a few days, so I don't know what he might be doing now. I guess he could have friends who live here, or business contacts.

Women.

I hate how that thought makes me sad. We don't have any ties to each other, so he can do what he wants.

I don't respond, so he walks back into the living room through the open French doors. "If you need something, call me. Sean will be across the hall, so don't feel bad about bothering him if you need something. That's what I pay him for."

Call him? That'll be hard to do since I don't have a phone. I don't remember his number, so I can't even use the suite's phone.

I just nod.

My fingers tap restlessly along the railing until I hear the front door open. That's when I whip around. He's wearing slacks and a black button up, damp hair somehow looking styled.

"How long will you be gone?" I call out.

He pauses in the doorway, glancing at me over his shoulder. "Not sure." He looks so passive it's irritating.

Why do I care so much?

"Where, um...where are you going again?"

He turns around, letting the door close on its own behind him. The loud *click* echoes through the suite. He moves into the living room, the warm morning light hitting the angles of his face perfectly.

I'm mesmerized. This man is definitely a work of art, and I'm craving to paint him.

Putting a casual hand in his pocket, he asks, "Would you rather I stay? I'm happy to give you...company." His voice dips lower at the end, and my body does not miss the subtext.

I'm instantly flushed.

"I could paint you," I blurt out. But dammit, I didn't really mean to say that. I should pack and leave while he's gone.

This is an opportunity to slip away without any questions.

Declan leans against the couch and crosses his arms, the shirt fabric straining against pure muscle. "Naked?"

"No," I say quickly. "Clothed."

Dammit, why am I continuing this conversation?

"Do you need supplies?"

"Only a canvas." *Shut your mouth, Sienna!*

He rubs the stubble on his chin, glancing up at the ceiling as he considers it. "Well, I was going to set up a few business meetings to make my VP happy, but this sounds a lot more interesting."

Business. Not women.

Just some business meetings.

I hate how relieved that makes me.

He pulls out his phone. "Let me make a call, and I'll get that canvas for you."

A BLANK CANVAS SITS ON a wooden easel in front of me. We're in my room because I like the angle of my window as it faces the ocean. Declan is sitting on my bed, probably getting his scent all over the sheets.

This was a bad idea.

Declan on a bed is sending my mind into some wild

fantasies.

At least he's fully clothed; there's no way I'd get through this if he wasn't.

His black button up is open at the top and he's on the edge of the mattress, leaning forward, his elbows resting on his knees. The ocean is framed through the floor-to-ceiling windows behind him; his eyes match the water.

My hand trembles slightly as I grab a pencil. It's going to be hard to focus on anything except his piercing gaze. The way he's looking at me…It's like he can see every shadowed corner.

I want to run.

No, I can do this. It was my idea to paint this ridicu-lously intense man, and I'm not going to chicken out now.

One stroke at a time.

I start by sketching the basic lines of his form. The broad shoulders, strong jawline, the crisp folds of his suit. The slight weight and hunch in his posture that people might not notice.

The more I study him and pay attention to every detail, the more I notice the subtle things. There's a faint scar on his left outer wrist, a long thin line, as if from a sharp blade. I notice another scar like that on his neck, just under his left ear.

His eyes are a mesmerizing, deep, aquatic blue, but also…tired. There's a slight puffiness around each one, and his gaze…there's something deeper behind the intensity. It might be that open wound I sensed when we first met. And there are no laugh lines or creases edging his features.

I have yet to see him fully smile. Does he ever smile? Right now, his lips are set impassively in what could be a practiced position. He's objectively striking and handsome, but a closer look shows he really only has three expressions—intense, neutral, slightly amused.

My heart aches the more I discover those little signs that he's troubled in some way. Maybe he's simply a stressed businessman, working himself to the bone. Still, my heart is aching for him.

I finish the sketch and reach for my paints and palette. As I grab some tubes to mix a cream color for the bed, my hands hesitate. When I saw him from a distance in the living room, I was struck by his beauty, thinking only of that. I had intended to paint a classically composed scene, focusing on his sculpture-like features.

After a closer study of him, I can't. Maybe he'll hate me for it, but I have to follow my gut. A new vision is blossoming in my mind, and I simply can't paint anything else. Instead of adding any tans, greens, or browns to my palette, I add only three colors: white, black, aquamarine. Then I mix several shades of grays and a range of light and dark blues.

Brush in hand, I get to work.

Since I've been painting for almost a decade and I've taken several studio classes, my body has built a certain amount of stamina for this. Painting is draining. I'm often sitting or standing in the same position for extended periods, and my arms and wrists certainly get tired. But repetition has trained me to handle a few hours.

For a model, though, which is Declan today, holding a position longer than 45 minutes is tough. I had told Declan he could ask for breaks, but he hasn't. For two hours, he's been a statue, with his elbows propped on his knees, hands clasped. Staring at me. He hasn't flinched, spoken, and he's barely blinked.

The painting is nowhere near finished, but the foundation is set. After setting my brush and palette down, I grab my sketchbook, making some quick notes and drawings about details I'll add to the painting later.

Finally, I step away from the canvas. "Okay," I tell him.

"Done?" he asks, still not moving.

"No. It will take several more hours, but I'm done for now. I have everything I need to finish the finer details later."

Nodding, he starts to straighten but winces. He moves his arms slowly with a groan, then rubs his neck, groaning some more.

I bite back a smile. "Sorry. I told you to ask for breaks."

He returns my smile with a smirk that makes my stomach flutter.

Finally straightening fully and stretching his back, he says, "I didn't want to interrupt. You turn into a different person when you paint. It's captivating." He rolls his neck and then stares right into me again. "You're beautiful."

My face warms as I look at my hands, dirty from graphite and paint splatter. "I doubt that," I say softly.

He steps toward the easel. "Can I take a look?"

I block his path. "Oh, it's not ready yet. And you don't really want to see my poor techniques."

"Of course I want to see it. How long will it take to finish?"

"Maybe…twenty hours."

He smirks. "Guess you have something to do while I'm at the conference."

My nod is filled with guilt because I plan on leaving before his conference starts.

He rubs his wrist, right above the scar, and I'm so curious about it. Before I can ask, he points near my luggage in the corner. "Will you let me see that one?"

He's pointing at my small color study, the one I couldn't leave behind. It's propped up next to my luggage, facing the wall so only the wooden frame is showing.

I hurry to pick it up, shaking my head. "Oh, you don't want to see this. It's just a rough version of a larger painting I want to do. It's very unfinished and doesn't look good."

Undeterred, he walks over, holding out his hand. "May I?"

"You're going to think I'm an awful painter because it's very messy."

He only waits.

Sighing, I hand it over, rambling about details he probably doesn't care about. "I came up with a charcoal sketch in class. My teacher actually thought it was okay, so I'm trying my best to turn it into a painting. I want to do a large canvas though, so I'm practicing first and figuring out the best colors. I have a tendency to mess up when painting final pieces so..."

I'm not entirely sure if Declan is listening because he looks like he's blocked out the entire world while staring at the color study. Pressing my back against the wall awkwardly, I wait.

He only keeps looking at it, brow furrowed, eyes shifting around the canvas to things they've already seen.

"That bad?" I finally ask, even though I'm not sure I actually want to know. My teachers have always been harsh critics of my work, but I care about Declan's opinion more than all of theirs.

He shakes his head slightly. "How much?"

"How...much what?"

"How much do you want for the finished painting?"

I laugh, breaking the tension that had coiled in my stomach. He lifts his eyes from the canvas, not looking amused, so I stop laughing. "You're serious?"

"Of course."

No one has ever wanted to buy one of my dumb paintings, even when I've tried to list them for dirt cheap online. Trying to keep things light, I shrug and say with a smirk, "I don't know. Ten bucks? Maybe a hundred to cover the materials I'll use. I know that's a lot—"

"Be serious."

I swallow because he has moved closer, making my body hum. "Well, I've never sold a painting, so I have no idea. I'm hoping to put it on a thirty by forty canvas. Maybe bigger if I can afford it."

His eyes drop back down to the color study. "Make it bigger. I have a Marlene Dumas hanging in my living room. I paid five hundred for that, but this is better." Gripping the small canvas like he doesn't want to let go, he says, "This will replace the Dumas, so I'll give you seven hundred and buy the canvas and paints you'll need."

My mind must be glitching because I know who Dumas is and how much her paintings are worth, so I don't understand how he got one of her pieces for only five hundred dollars. Still, seven hundred plus the materials I'll need is beyond anything I could've hoped for.

I'm about to say yes when reality smacks me in the face.

I can't paint anything for him. I can't even show him the finished painting I started today. I'll be disappearing soon.

Since I'm taking too long to gather my thoughts, Declan adds, "Just to be clear, I mean seven hundred thousand."

The sound I make next is some mix of laughter and

shock. "That's...No...I...I'm a student. My paintings are nothing."

His eye twitches. "I'm an avid art collector who is well known in the SF community, yet you're suggesting my tastes are bad?"

He moves an inch closer, and I struggle to get words out as he pins me with those blue, serious eyes. Pressing my palms against the wall behind me for support, I say, "Of course not, but...how could you like my painting that much? That's just a practice canvas, so I could completely fuck up the final piece."

The rough edges around him smooth out and he's back to staring at my sloppy watercolors. "It strikes a chord, I guess you could say. The couple embracing at the bottom are in their own world, while the male figure at the top of the stairs can only watch. He's lonely. He's an outsider. He'll never be able to touch them, get close to their experience, yet he's stuck watching. The door behind him is open, but he'll never walk through it. He'll never look away; he'll never get close."

That ache in my heart for him flares, so I gently take the canvas from his grip. "That's interesting, because I see the man on the stairs as a protector. See?" I point to the figure's little accidental smirk. "He has a smile. The couple is embracing in a dangerous world, but he's there to protect them and ensure the darkness on the edges of the canvas never hurts them."

His voice wavers. "A protector?"

I nod, then admit something I probably shouldn't. "I, um...I was thinking of you when I drew this."

A look of broken inhibition flashes across his eyes. Pressing his palm on the wall next to my head, he leans dangerously close. "Tell me your name. You've withheld it long enough."

The canvas slips from my hands to the floorboards. That same broken inhibition courses through me too.

I can't stand this anymore, the way he makes my pulse race and my body hum. The way my heart aches to hold him while also yearning for him to take control and tell me every dirty thought he's had about us.

I can't go on this way.

"Declan?"

A smirk tugs at his lips, his gaze intense and hungry. "That's my name. Funny if we have the same one."

I shake my head. "I'm ready to beg for…"

He groans and lowers his head, his mouth hovering inches from mine, daring me to bridge the gap. "I don't like games. I have to know you truly want this."

"Want isn't the right word. It's more about need."

"Then fucking kiss me."

My mind is screaming at me to run away, but my body eagerly obeys his command.

CHAPTER 11

SIENNA

AS SOON AS I PRESS my lips against Declan's, a switch is flipped. His arm snakes around my waist, pulling me flush against his unyielding torso. I gasp against his mouth because he's ravenous. Then I taste his minty tongue, full lips, the groan he releases as he explores. My knees feel like they're going to buckle any second, but his arm around my waist keeps me standing.

Breaking the kiss, he watches my lips part on a gasp, my chest rising and falling rapidly. He chuckles, completely satisfied with how he's affecting me. "Seems I've left you breathless."

Trying to maintain some composure, I respond, "Don't get cocky."

"Oh, it's too late for that."

His hips roll into my stomach, pressing his full, hard girth against me.

My throat releases a traitorous moan, and I reach down, gripping his length through his slacks. Since we've been teasing each other for so long—or maybe it was only me doing the teasing—a burning need has completely taken over. I hastily undo his belt, top button, zipper. In seconds, I've freed him, eagerly running my fingers up and down his silky, warm, pulsing hardness.

He's completely in control and level-headed as he reaches down to grab my wrist. "Keep your hands to yourself until I tell you not to, got it?"

I nod, and he secures my hands behind my back.

Moving his mouth to my ear, he whispers, "You're going to be good and do everything I say, aren't you?"

I let out an 'mmm' or maybe it's a moan because I can't quite find the breath to say, "God yes."

"Good," he rumbles. Then he nips my ear. "I'm going to savor every fucking second of this."

An involuntary shudder wracks through me. I love it and I hate it. I want to fully let go and surrender, yet I'm terrified.

Doesn't matter because I'm in too deep now to stop; I'm sure my body won't let me.

My eyes drop to his erection. Keeping my hands to myself might be impossible. All I want is to stroke him, run my tongue along his thickness, force him inside me because he's going to stretch me past my limits.

Right now, he's only holding my wrists together with one hand and touching my shoulders with the other, but I moan from my own dirty thoughts.

"You're going to make this difficult, aren't you?" he asks, running a thumb over my burning cheek.

I nod, and he chuckles.

"Should've known." His lips find mine again.

The kisses this time are slow, teasing. Though my hands remain pinned behind my back, my body arches toward him. He only said to keep my hands to myself, not anything else. I lift my leg, running my thigh against his hip, trying to urge him closer.

Breaking the kiss, he steps back, one eyebrow raised. "Do I need to tie you up?"

"Maybe," I whisper, sounding bolder than I feel. Getting

tied up isn't something I've tried, but I'm open to the idea. Especially with him.

"I'll remember that for next time."

There's a flutter in my chest. *Next time?* There shouldn't be a—

He takes my hand, forcing me to stay in the present, and then leads me out of my bedroom. We cross the suite to his room. I glance around because it's a little different from mine. The bed and ocean view are similar, but the punching bag is noticeably out of place.

I must look confused or I'm glancing around at everything too long, because Declan holds my chin firmly, forcing my attention back to him. "I had the punching bag brought in. The suites don't come with one."

I'm about to ask for more details, which I know is silly considering what we're doing, when his kiss silences me. His hands thoroughly roam my body for the first time, gliding down my chest and erect nipples, my stomach, thighs. He runs a single finger over my crease, pressing the fabric of my leggings in and making them wet.

His hands reach around to cup my ass, and his low voice rumbles, "Face the mirror and undress for me. Slowly."

"Mirror?"

He turns me to face a large vanity mirror that points right at his bed.

Satisfied with the command he just gave, he unbuttons his shirt and peels it from his body.

My core clenches and my leggings become more helplessly wet.

Oh. My. God.

I'm captivated by every flex and bend of his muscles through the mirror's reflection; he might be more sculpted than any male figure ever carved from stone.

I can't stop watching as he sits on the edge of the bed, leans back to prop himself up with one hand, and begins stroking himself.

Slowly up and slowly down.

I want to break the rules and touch him desperately.

"I thought I told you to undress," he says with a level tone, completely composed and at ease with himself. He strokes his cock like it's the most normal and natural thing to do.

His tip is glistening with pre-cum, hand stroking slowly up, slowly down.

I bite my bottom lip and moan.

He only meets my gaze through the mirror's reflection, challenging me while also teasing me beyond my sanity with what he's doing.

Finally willing my shaky hands to move, I grasp the hem of my sweater and pull it over my head.

Declan keeps watching, almost impassively. It's strange to see both him and myself at the same time in the mirror. I see what he's seeing, what's turning him on. And all it's doing is adding fuel to the fire that's erupted underneath my skin.

Next, I shimmy out of my leggings. I notice his eyes dip to my ass. I'm not wearing sexy underwear at the moment, just plain black hipsters, but they are riding up, revealing the bottom curve of my cheeks. Declan seems particularly fascinated with it, so I pull the underwear up more, turning them into a makeshift thong.

I feel very satisfied when his strokes become a little faster.

"Take them off," he commands. "The bra too."

"Why don't you take off your pants?"

His gaze slides up to meet mine in the reflection. "Are you disobeying? Because that means punishment."

Struggling to keep my breath steady, I hold Declan's smoldering gaze in the mirror as I reach behind me and unhook my bra. Slowly, I let it slide down my arms before dropping it to the floor. His eyes rake over my exposed skin and my nipples harden into tight peaks under his intense scrutiny. Finally, I hook my thumbs into my underwear and wiggle my hips as I peel them down my legs, bending at the waist to give him a good view.

For several long minutes, I stand here, naked and facing the mirror, while he just strokes himself and enjoys the view. He didn't tell me to do anything else, so I just wait.

In agony, I wait, feeling uncomfortably wet.

After an eternity, he stands and grabs his discarded button down off the bed. Then he drapes it over my shoulders.

"Put this on," he commands.

I do as he requests, then look in the mirror at how large his shirt is on my torso.

"Same as last time," he adds, guiding one of my hands between my thighs. "Only now, you won't be able to clean it."

"Is this one of your particular tastes?" I ask. "Making me dirty your clothes."

One corner of his mouth floats up in a smirk. "One of them, but I have many." His hands grip my waist and he prods my back with his firm length. "Ruining expensive clothing through fucking is another."

The way he says 'fucking' is so primal and gritty that I immediately start rubbing between my thighs.

He lets out an appreciative groan and returns to reclining on the bed, stroking himself lazily.

Just as I did with his jacket, I press the fabric of his shirt against my core, let it flutter over my clit, get messy with my wetness. It's not as silky as the jacket, but it's dense and soft. Expensive feeling. Luxurious. And I'm enjoying how I'm ruining it, as Declan commanded.

When I'm close to reaching ecstasy, my moans more frequent, Declan stands again. He stalks toward me. Finally, he sheds his pants and briefs on the floorboards, then grips my hips and pulls me roughly against his warm, bare skin. My back hits his hard chest, flooding me with so much heat I feel like I'm about to melt.

"Look how beautiful you are," he says.

And I do look. I watch as this large man trails a finger from my collarbone, between my breasts, over my quivering stomach. I suck in a sharp breath as he grazes my sensitive folds. Then he plucks my nipples, runs his thumbs over the hard peaks.

His body makes mine look so small in comparison that I'm almost engulfed. Or rather, I'm cocooned, held safe from the world's darkness.

He's the man at the top of the stairs protecting me.

And also the one on the floor embracing me.

His name escapes my lips like it's so natural for me to say. "Declan."

He meets my gaze with those aquamarine eyes, and I say it again, a bit needier.

"Declan."

Abruptly, he spins me to face him. I gasp, my breasts pressing into his warm, demanding, comforting torso.

"You do make things terribly difficult," he says before kissing me.

My hands graze his chest hair as his mouth explores

mine with so much pressure it's almost uncomfortable. But I don't mind the pressure or the way he's forcing my lips to match his rhythm, how he bites and sucks and takes.

I've missed feeling wanted and craved like this. Missed a man needing to possess me.

But it is different this time.

Before, I was possessed without a second thought, used for physical gratification. It was always quick and sometimes I was left without an orgasm.

But Declan waited for me to give myself willingly; I'm possessed by him through my own free will. And I have a feeling he won't be happy until I orgasm.

"Stop," I whisper.

He stops immediately, pulling back, his body motionless. "What's wrong?"

I shake my head. "Nothing. I…I just needed to check." Wrapping my arms around his neck, I say, "Keep going. Please keep going. Tell me what to do. Do whatever you like. I'll obey everything."

He swallows hard before dipping his head. "God, what am I going to do with you?"

His mouth claims mine again; I surrender completely.

After kisses that are more gentle but still mind-numbing, our bodies break apart. He walks to the nightstand and opens it, pulling out a foil.

"Oh, I'm on birth control," I say. "Tested and negative."

He hesitates, fingers tightening and crinkling the wrapper.

He rolls on the condom anyway.

I decide to unpack what that might mean later.

When he returns, he crushes his body against mine, kisses me until I'm faint, then turns me to face the mirror.

Silently, he sits on the bed.

"Now straddle me," he demands, "but keep watching yourself."

I obey, backing up and climbing on top of him in a reverse cowgirl. His hands roughly position me into a squatting position, and damned if I don't look like some porn star trying to give the camera a clear angle of all the best parts.

He palms my breasts through the open shirt, kissing along my shoulder. "You have my permission to touch me now."

Not wasting a second, I reach down and grip his cock that's between my legs, revel in the thickness and feel. I push down on the condom so it strains against the swollen head, then my thumb grazes the tip. His cock twitches in my hand.

In the mirror, I can see his chest rising and falling in heavy bursts; I watch the calm and collected expression on his face start to crack.

I want him to unravel.

I want all of him to unravel under my touch.

Lifting himself, he says, "Now satisfy me."

I almost fall off the cliff from just those words.

Raising my hips, I grip him firmly. Then I lower myself, guiding him deeper, inch by inch. It's a little painful as he stretches me open, but once I'm at the base, the full, pleasurable sensation masks any sharp pinch.

For the first time, he releases a long, reverberating moan. The ache it causes between my thighs is more than my body can handle, so I bounce and grind on him. My head lolls back and my eyes close as his cock pounds against my restraints.

"Don't stop watching," he says, smoothing his hand up my inner thigh to my center.

It's like I'm watching a porno; I barely recognize myself. My cheeks are pink, my body flushed, and I'm like a wild woman milking every inch of his cock.

Declan stares into my eyes as his fingers circle my clit. "So fucking gorgeous."

I cry out, approaching my climax. The ache is unbearable, and his fingers are relentless and my entire body shudders and tenses and releases as the wave hits. Heat pulses between my thighs and ripples through my senses and I can't stop moaning. My voice quickly rises in pitch to a scream as I bear down hard on his cock, trying to milk more pleasure from him.

While I'm losing control of my body and mind, Declan keeps rubbing me while his other hand wraps around my stomach so I don't tumble onto the floor. When I finally stop screaming, but before I fully come down from the high, he flips me onto my stomach and fucks me.

He's a caveman, curling one hand into my hip and pinning my shoulders with the other, owning me completely. His grunts rise in aggression until he's almost snarling.

My body decides a second orgasm is a good response, and I start trembling again from another release.

Declan lets out several cuss words and his moans intensify as he thrusts hard and fast, filling me. Finally, his thrusts soften and he slows, catching his breath. His hands release me and he bends forward to kiss my back through the shirt I'm still wearing. I'm sure it's plenty wrecked now.

"Fuck," he exhales, pulling out of me. He yanks off the condom and tosses it in a bin.

"Uh-huh," is all I can say because I'm completely spent, sprawled out on my stomach. I don't even have words to describe how incredible that was. I only know I yearn for more.

More of his commands in the bedroom.

More of him inside me.

More of him.

I can barely move, but I manage to glance up as he sits on the edge of the bed. He's staring vacantly at my back, caressing my skin. He places a soft kiss on my shoulder and then walks across the room, slipping into the bathroom. A moment later, the shower turns on.

His departure makes my body hollow, cold. But it's good he didn't try to cuddle or have pillow talk. His absence is a reminder that I shouldn't crave more with him.

Why did I even let things escalate this far?

What a bad lapse in judgment.

Needy. I let needy Margaret take control instead of resisting and standing by my desire not to get involved with men.

I groan and cover my head with a pillow.

Just smother me now.

But now it's done. I had my fun, and I hope Declan fucked me out of his system.

As soon as he's asleep tonight, I'm leaving.

CHAPTER 12

DECLAN

THE GARDEN IS BLOOMING. SO many colors. I walk along the familiar stone pathway to the fountain, and there's Tiffany—radiant, beaming. I remember that smile, so bright on her good days.

I can sense our son nearby. But where…oh. She's holding him.

They're no longer in the garden. It's dark.

She's holding him in the dark, and now I can't figure out where they are.

Suddenly, there are flashing lights. I hear the roar of the crowd, the *ding ding* as the match starts. My opponent punches me square in the jaw and I'm knocked out. Blood spills from my nose onto the mat.

Ding ding.

Ding ding.

Where did Tiffany go?

"You're better off without me, Declan. I know you tried, but there's no saving me."

Where is our son?

Ding ding.

I jolt awake in bed, my heart pounding, my skin slick with sweat. I grab at my chest, willing my heart to slow down. While I'm trying to catch my breath, I wipe my cheek. My fingers are damp. It's not sweat, though. I was crying in my sleep.

Buzz. Buzz.

I glance around the room, blinking moisture from my eyes. For a second, I'm disoriented because nothing is familiar in the dim moonlight that's streaming through the window.

Where the hell…

Right. I'm in a suite, not at home.

This is a hotel suite.

Buzz. Buzz.

My damn phone is rattling on the nightstand, so I slap a hand over it. The digital clock next to it reads 2:03 AM. Who the hell is calling at this hour? I unlock the screen, squinting at the sudden flash of light that hits my eyes. Blinking until my vision is no longer blurry, I see Sean's name.

I rub my tongue along the roof of my mouth, suddenly feeling how dry my throat is as I answer. "What's going on?"

"M.W. left the suite with her luggage." Sean's voice is calm and professional, but I catch a hint of concern. "She didn't notice me because I was around the corner. I followed her."

Still trying to shake sleep from my brain, I throw my covers off and sit up.

M.W.

My mystery woman.

So…she decided to leave after all.

Hunching forward, I rest my elbows on my knees and release a heavy exhale. I don't know why her leaving gives me such a hollow ache. But after finally deciding to fuck, I guess I thought…

Doesn't matter. She has her own life; she doesn't want my help.

I'm of no use to her, the same way I was no use to

Tiffany in the end.

Why do I always fail the ones I want to protect the most?

My throat is even drier now, so I swallow painfully. "You followed her where?"

"She's been in the lobby for the past fifteen minutes," Sean says. "She's just sitting in a chair near the window. Seems to be lost in thought."

I close my eyes, trying to settle the churning in my gut. A thought occurred to me yesterday in the shower, after I left her weak and satisfied in my bed: did she sleep with me because she felt I was 'owed'? She was definitely concerned on the jet about paying her share of the expenses.

I ignored that thought yesterday, and when I got out of the shower, we shared dinner together on the patio. God, she was gorgeous in the light from the sunset—her short black hair pinned back to frame her elegant cheekbones, bottom lip permanently caught between her teeth. Brown, soulful eyes stealing glances at me, then darting away. I had wanted to kiss her, but she looked tense, like she didn't want to be touched.

Everything seemed okay when we said goodnight, and I had looked forward to seeing her beautiful face again in the morning.

Now that she decided to leave—without saying good-bye, no less—I'm left wondering if she only instigated sex as 'repayment.'

It's a sickening thought because I'd never want that.

"If she leaves the hotel, do you want me to follow?" Sean asks after I fall silent.

Fuck, this situation feels like I've been pummeled in the ring. Do I want to track her down, to demand answers? A part of me screams yes.

But the rational side, the side that's been hurt before, knows better. She hopped onto my jet because she's running from something, not because she wants to be with me. I've also learned in my life that the more you cling to a woman, the more she'll beg to leave.

This is what Mystery Woman wants, so I'll respect that. Besides, I'll always be the one left behind.

Avoiding all attachments is best.

"No," I say, my voice raspy. "Your job is security, not investigation. Let her go. I'm not her jailer. She's free to do what she wants."

"Under—"

"Wait." I scrub a hand over my face, thinking about her wandering the streets alone. "If she leaves, just make sure she gets somewhere safe. Maybe she'll head to a motel or she could have friends here. Wherever she goes, she needs to arrive safely. It's late, and she'll be a woman out wandering around with luggage."

"Understood."

I end the call, staring at my reflection in the mirror facing my bed. Hours ago, my mystery woman was riding me, her sexy legs wrapped around my body. Now she's another woman who has vanished from my life.

I deserve nothing less. As I've known for a long time, I'm terrible at protecting my possessions.

Not that my mystery woman ever let me get close enough to call her mine.

Not that I should want that.

I need a drink.

I leave my bedroom to grab a bottle of wine off the pressure plate in the fridge. After uncorking it and pouring a glass, I realize I've lost the will to drink. I dump the glass in the sink, dump the bottle in the trash. When I can't even find comfort in alcohol, I know I'm fucked.

Still restless, I walk to my mystery woman's room as if I'll discover her there, but there's no trace, not even the portrait of me she had started. The bed is impeccably made, like it was never slept in. The only hint anyone was ever in this space is one single used towel in a heap on the bathroom tile.

My body is heavy and my feet hard to drag across the suite as I walk back to the living room. I open the double French doors to let the breeze in, then sink into the couch, staring at where the ocean should be. Can't see it though— it's completely black in the distance. An ink stain.

I want to see it, need to know I *can* still see it, so I sit on this damn couch for three hours, getting up only once to use the bathroom. Eventually, the dark sky lightens to gray, and the first arc of an orange sun peeks above the horizon.

Funny how I've avoided the sunrise ever since Tiffany left, yet now I've seen it two days in a row.

Funny.

The door clicks.

Opens.

I don't look because I figure it must be Sean. Possibly Jeremy. Then I hear the familiar squeak of some particular luggage before the door clicks shut.

My heart jumps into my throat, but I still don't turn around. What if I'm imagining this?

A soft voice clears behind me, then, "I went for a walk."

It is her. She came back?

Why?

Gripping the edge of a couch cushion, I play along and

ask, "Did you have a pleasant walk?"

"Um…yeah," she responds, her words monotone. "I went…for a walk. But I'm tired now. I'm going to bed."

"Let me know if you need anything."

The squeaky luggage rolls across the suite in the wrong direction. She enters my bedroom and closes the door.

The room doesn't matter.

She came back.

CHAPTER 13

SIENNA

I BUNDLE DECLAN'S SATIN SHEETS around my body, rolling until I'm completely cocooned. His wonderful scent envelopes me—citrus, sandalwood, sweat. It's soothing and intoxicating, and I can't get enough. Burying my face in his pillow, I breathe it all in while the early morning light warms my shoulders.

Then I make fists and groan loudly into the pillow. What the fuck am I doing?

I've barricaded myself in his room for the past 24 hours; I can't stay in here forever. Eventually, I need to leave and face the man in the living room.

Declan has been surprisingly patient about my hibernation. He hasn't tried to kick me out, hasn't said anything really. He's been bringing me room service, checking in periodically with light taps on the door, asking, "Need anything?"

And if I'm feeling too frozen and guilty to answer, he simply taps gently again and repeats the question, only leaving once I give some muffled response. He hasn't sounded angry or annoyed. Just lets me know he's here.

It's sweet, but every time I realize he's hovering outside the door, making sure I'm okay, I only feel shittier.

To top it all off, I was a very nosey bitch yesterday.

I spent hours exploring every nook and cranny of his room, learning the little details that make up the man who has so thoroughly captivated me.

His closet is organized, filled with expensive suits and a few gym clothes. I ran my fingers along the fine fabrics, imagining how they would feel against my skin.

I wore one of his jackets to bed, loving the safety it wrapped me in.

Then I made a few jabs at his punching bag in the corner, which looked worn. I wondered, is it his personal bag he stows on his jet? I imagined when he might punch it—when he's frustrated after a long day, looking for a quick workout on a Sunday morning, out of boredom.

His watch was resting on his nightstand, facing the window and catching the light. I slipped it onto my wrist, the gold band too large for me. But I loved the feeling of wearing something that belonged to him, something he carries with him everywhere.

In the bathroom, I examined his toiletries, the high-end products that contribute to his gorgeous appearance. I put a dab of his hair gel in my palm; misted his cologne along my neck, the scent mingling with my own in a way that felt intimate and erotic.

Now, this morning, I've been rolling around in his bed, avoiding the fact that I need to fucking leave. I know I owe him an explanation, or at least an attempt at one. I just don't understand why it's been so difficult to open the door.

Every time I've reached for the knob, thinking of facing the questions he must have, I'm gripped by a paralyzing panic. My heart races, my body shakes, and a cold sweat breaks out along my skin. So I retreat back to the bed, back to his scent, to safety, until the fear subsides.

Now the sun is rising on Day 3 in Hawaii. I'm determined to face him—his frustration, disappointment, confusion…all of it. I know we agreed to no attachments, but that doesn't mean I should've snuck away in the middle of the night. I essentially 'hit it and quit it' so I deserve any wrath he wants to give.

Closing my eyes, I take a deep breath and search my brain for a mantra that might help. I come up with: *I am not my past. I am not my mistakes. I am worthy of love and happiness.* But that's too hard to swallow; I feel like a liar every time I say it. So I switch to: *"Fear is the path to the Dark Side."*

It's a quote from Yoda, but it somehow fits. Margaret is my dark side, and I don't want to become her again.

Sienna is a boss bitch who accepts responsibility.

It's time to be a boss.

I dress in a pair of clean purple leggings and a sweater—I've already worn the two T-shirts I brought. Slowly, tentatively, I walk to the door, my legs shaky but holding me up. My hand hovers over the handle and I feel my heart picking up speed.

Whatever. I'm going to do this, even if I step out into the living room with a full-blown panic attack.

An intense feeling of doom and dread washes over me—like I'm about to drop dead—but I turn the knob and fling the door open. Feeling flushed and shaky, I glance around the empty room, finally noticing Declan sitting on the patio. He hasn't noticed me yet, though; I don't think. His back is facing me as he gazes out at the ocean.

I need to calm my racing heart and my trembling body, so I take my time to just breathe slowly and deeply, staring at the back of his messy, dark hair. When my heart feels steady enough, the panic only a strong nervousness now, I walk through the living room.

Before I can even try to speak or step through the open doorway to the patio, Declan says in his deep voice, "Good morning." He doesn't turn around, but continues speaking. "I just ordered room service. Would you like to join me for breakfast?"

I can't see his expression, but his tone doesn't sound angry. It's a little flat, but not disappointed or upset.

Maybe he's unaffected by me sneaking away in the night? That thought actually doesn't relieve me the way it should.

He doesn't care if I leave?

God, stop being so needy.

"Okay," I whisper, not even sure if he heard me.

I sit beside him at the square table so I can gaze out at the ocean, sunlight hitting my face. I glance over. Declan is wearing a white tank top, showing off his muscular arms, and a pair of boxer-briefs, showing off those muscular, hairy legs. Since I've been holding his clothes hostage, I think he's been wearing that outfit this entire time.

He also looks tired—puffy, bloodshot eyes that need rest.

He finally glances back. Our eyes lock and his intense blue gaze sends a spark up my spine, like it often does. But still, no anger or irritation on his face. He actually gives me a soft smile.

He's smiling.

It's the first time I've seen him smile, the first time he's looked anywhere close to happy. The sight steals my breath for a moment.

Then his gaze drops to my sweater, his eyes widening slightly. Next, his brows lower into a heavy concern, so I glance at myself, wondering if there's some giant stain on my top. But no, just a plain maroon sweater.

He looks away but still seems very worried. "Are you… cold?"

"No."

The fractured lines on his face deepen, like his skin is clay and someone is pushing their thumbs throughout it.

What's wrong with my sweater? It's like he hates it.

I try to give him more info in case that will help. "I, well…I stupidly packed a lot of sweaters by mistake. I'm used to San Francisco weather, so I didn't think about Hawaii being so warm. I've already gone through the two T-shirts I brought. Might have to cut the sleeves off of this if it gets hotter today."

His forehead softens, but not the tension around his eyes. "Why don't you roll the sleeves up? For now."

"Uh…sure. I guess I could." I don't think the sleeves will stay above my elbows, since the sweater is baggy, but I do my best to fold and scrunch the fabric until my forearms are exposed.

Declan studies the newly exposed areas of my skin, the tension in his expression finally fading.

So strange.

His attention returns to the ocean. "We'll go shopping today, so you can get new clothes." I open my mouth to protest, but he stops me with a firm stare. "You agreed not to argue about how I want to spend my money."

Pressing my lips together, I pick at the hem of my sweater. He's right—I did agree. That doesn't mean I deserve him buying me things. Even if he's rich and a fifty-dollar top is like pennies to him…I don't deserve such treatment.

"Fine," I say. "We'll go shopping." I stare at my feet, two words heavy on my tongue. Two words I've been needing to tell him. "I'm sorry."

I hope he understands that I'm apologizing for hiding in his room, for everything.

He only gazes at the ocean, his eyes flitting to a bird that lands on the patio railing. "You have nothing to apologize for."

Someone knocks, so Declan gets up to answer. He returns with a cart of food, setting a silver serving plate in front of me. We eat our waffles and poached eggs in silence.

Not complete silence—there are waves crashing against the shore and birds chirping, our forks and knives scraping against ceramic plates.

And cycling through my head, all the reasons he's wrong.

CHAPTER 14

SIENNA

WE STEP INTO A SMALL boutique on the west side of the island. It's a quaint little shop with some bohemian vibes, and the interior is a kaleidoscope of colors and textures. I'm half assaulted by the sheer volume of garments and accessories crammed onto shelves and racks, half hypnotized. My artist's soul simply wants to explore everything, touch every woven beach hat and study the dyes on each dress. The scent of coconut and hibiscus draws me deeper into the madness.

I glance over my shoulder once I'm halfway into the shop. Declan lingers near the entrance, his arms crossed over his broad chest as he stares out the window like a soldier guarding the entrance. He's wearing dress pants, because that seems to be all he ever wears, and the most "vacation-y" thing he might own: a black button down with black embroidered palm trees you can only see with a close inspection.

There's a fragmentation in his posture, a distance in his gaze.

I glance away. Things definitely aren't the same between us now, and that silent breakfast didn't help.

Since I know he'll refuse to leave unless I pick something to replace my sweater, I ignore my uneasiness and start sifting through racks. I select a few items—a pair of black bootcut leggings, a floral crop top, and a dusty rose romper—but as I head toward the two tiny changing rooms,

Declan's voice stops me.

"Is that all you're getting?" His tone is rigid and my stomach flutters. The rigidness isn't mean, it's reminiscent of the way he commanded me in the bedroom.

I glance down at the bundle in my arms. "Um...yeah?"

Since Declan is still near the entrance and we're talking loudly at each other from across the shop, the middle-aged woman near the cash register glances up and watches our exchange with interest. No one else is in the shop, so maybe it's a slow day.

Declan sighs, uncrossing his arms. "Get enough outfits for the rest of the week."

"I only have so much room in my luggage."

"Then I'll buy you a bigger luggage."

My lips tighten. I want to argue because I don't know why he's hell-bent on buying me so much stuff. Art supplies, food, clothing, luggage. But the unyielding intensity in his eyes stops me from responding.

Stubborn man.

Reluctantly, I turn back to the racks, grabbing a few dresses, some linen pants, and a couple more tops.

In the changing room, I try on each item mechanically, and they all fit just fine. Some aren't really my style, but it's good to stretch outside my comfort zone. Try something different. As I spin and review the floral dress, I'd like to leave the store wearing, it almost feels like I'm watching a movie starring someone else.

It's a film about a woman on vacation with her man, and neither of them has a care in the world. They have an easy, simple life together. He showers her with gifts; she basks in the attention, and they live out their days in euphoria. Perfection.

Fantasy.

Not my life at all.

I'm about to take the dress off, but I know Declan will say something if I try to leave the store wearing my sweater. I let the dress fabric fall around me with a sigh.

This isn't some movie; I'm not Declan's girl. I'm taking too much from him.

My stomach feels awful now, churning and eating itself.

Coming back was a mistake. Why the hell didn't I leave?

Leaning against the wall, I close my eyes and clutch my stomach. I can't get a handle on any of this, and I can feel myself becoming obsessive; I've done it in the past. I became obsessed with being wanted, cared for. Obsessed with belonging and being with someone broken like me. I gave myself up to satisfy each one of my insecurities. And that obsession led me down a dark path, made me blind to the corrosive attention from my ex.

Is that what's happening again?

What if I'm missing something important about Declan? Something that will cause me harm in the end?

I try to clear the lump in my throat. I *need* there to be something wrong with him. Every attempt I've made to put distance between us has failed. Both of us keep pushing things farther and farther.

Because the way he fucked me was too good; the safety I feel around him is too comforting.

All of it terrifies me.

My presence in his life only puts him in danger. A lot of danger. Because what if Anthony somehow followed me?

I sit on the tiny wall bench in the changing room, the flimsy wood groaning under my weight. Holding my stomach, I sob silently. I don't want Declan to get hurt. Because the more I hope to find some fault in him, the more I see that he's a good man.

I shouldn't have come back; I shouldn't have gotten him mixed up in my problems.

What I'm doing is reckless. I'm acting from pure lust and neediness.

So stupid and…

Tap. Tap.

I gasp, glancing at the turquoise-colored door.

"Miss? How is everything fitting?" It's the woman who works here.

Rubbing my wet eyes furiously with the heels of my hands, I stand. Then I wipe my face with my sweater. I gather the clothing and my purse.

Finally, I open the door with a bright smile. "It's all perfect. Thank you."

She must notice my face is pink and splotchy because she stares at me for a moment. Then she smiles warmly, her brown skin crinkling around her eyes. She touches my arm. "I'll be up front when you're ready, dear, or if you need anything."

I nod, and she walks away. With my purse and a heavy bundle of clothes in my arms, I pretend to look at hats and sunglasses, trying to give my skin enough time to change color, so it's not so obvious I was crying. Before leaving the little corner of the store, I grab a pair of dark sunglasses and put them on, just to cover my red eyes. Then I meet Declan at the register.

As I wait while the woman rings everything up, a glint of opal catches my eye. There's a pair of dangle earrings on a rack, the stones shimmering with iridescent hues. I reach out, my fingers grazing the smooth surface. They're really cute.

Declan plucks the earrings off the spinning rack. He also grabs the matching necklace and adds them to the pile of clothes without a word.

I feel a flush creep up my neck.

I shouldn't have touched them.

When the woman is finally done, she flashes Declan a bright smile. "That'll be eleven-oh-five-ninety-eight."

I almost have another panic attack. Over a thousand dollars for a few outfits??

"Oh, I should put some things back," I say, reaching for a dress on the top of the neatly folded pile.

Declan grabs my wrist, his expression unreadable. "We'll take all of it," he tells the woman, handing her his black credit card.

I yank my hand away and stare at my feet.

Declan won't let me carry any bags as we leave, so I follow him out. The floral dress I'm wearing feels foreign on my skin. It definitely doesn't match my black combat boots. I mean, the dress is beautiful, but it's not me. None of this is. The dress, the earrings, the lavish spending, it's…

I hold my stomach again. What *am* I doing?

I should be busking on a street corner somewhere to earn enough money for a plane ticket out of this country. India might be a good pick since it's densely populated. I can disappear into a small town where my ex will never think to look for me.

Instead, I'm here in Hawaii, wearing a dress that's too pricey, hanging around Declan and being a coward.

"Thank you," I murmur as we walk to the car, where Sean is waiting. "For the clothes."

Declan pulls the earrings and necklace from a bag before handing the rest to Sean. As Sean pops the trunk, Declan turns to me, staring into my sunglasses.

"Worth it to see how beautiful you look," he says. Then he points at my boots. "I like the contrast."

I smirk through my blush. "I'm always ready for a fight."

"I believe it." He moves closer, slipping the earring hooks into my lobes. Then he moves behind me to fasten the necklace. His fingers graze my locket, adjusting where it lies beside its new opal companion. He lingers and I sense he wants to ask about it. Thankfully, he doesn't. I have yet to open my locket since the day I dirtied it in art class.

Maybe I'll never open it again, leaving my grandpa completely untarnished.

Declan's attention shifts, and he traces a finger along the exposed skin of my shoulder and upper back. Then he smooths his fingers down my arms.

The feathery touches send a shiver up my spine, but it seems like he's searching for something. He has been trans-fixed on my skin this morning. Does he think I got injured, and he's looking for bruises?

He finally stops examining me and steps around to my front. Hooking a finger under my chin, he tips my head back so I have to look up at him. "Truly stunning."

I try to lower my chin and look away, but he doesn't let me.

"Do you hear me?"

My knees have gone weak, so I nod only so he'll let me step away. I don't feel beautiful; only like a fraud.

"Join me for a walk near the beach," he says.

"Sure."

Sean waits in the car as we start strolling. After walking

a block in silence, we reach a wooden boardwalk along the edge of the sandy beach. The warm breeze envelopes us in a comfortable silence, and I take a deep breath, trying to stay in the moment and out of my head.

Declan's voice shatters that attempt when he asks, "Why did you come back?"

"If only I knew that myself," I want to tell him. Instead, I watch a seagull rip open the belly of a crab. His friend plucks out the watchful, blank eye of a dead fish.

I felt so sure of myself when I left the suite two nights ago. But when I reached the lobby, my feet just froze. My body refused to move out of the entrance into the night, my head feeling light and dizzy. I finally sat in a chair until I stopped feeling so faint.

As my head cleared, so did my resolve.

I know it's bad to hang around Declan so much, but I thought…Anthony can't *really* find me here, right?

I don't have a phone. I didn't buy a plane ticket or use my credit card. I'm untraceable. So…I have a little time.

Not a lot, but some.

Why not enjoy this paradise for a few more days? Why not allow myself this brief escape into a fantasy life before facing reality again?

Of course, when I returned to the suite, hoping to slip in unnoticed, Declan had been awake. Waiting. That completely threw off my confidence because I really didn't want him knowing I had even *thought* of leaving without saying goodbye, especially after that mind-blowing sex.

Since then, I've been a mess of conflicted thoughts, going back and forth about whether or not I made the right decision in coming back.

Declan continues to wait patiently for my response

as we stroll along the boardwalk. I know I owe him some kind of explanation, but I don't even know where to begin. I certainly don't want him knowing about my past, getting dragged deeper into it.

Instead of revealing the full truth, I give him half of it. "I thought we both needed more time to…to fuck each other out of our systems."

He remains stone-faced, but nods. "I think you're right. I'm craving more of your body. I haven't yet been able to taste you."

A sensation like warm honey drips through my torso and pools in my lower belly. I wasn't really expecting that admission, but I should have—I know he's a direct man.

Time for me to be direct, too, so we're completely clear about what we're doing and the boundaries. "Having a deadline will help," I say. "You're here seven more days, right? That's plenty of time to just…do whatever we want with no pressure. When the days are up, we go back to our separate lives, keeping a fond memory of our time in Hawaii."

Declan stops walking, turning to face me with a gaze that seems to peer through my dark sunglasses. "Seven days," he repeats, his voice low. "Then we walk away. No strings, no regrets."

I nod, my core clenching from just how much we can enjoy each other in a week.

He slips off my sunglasses with slow, purposeful movements, then hooks them on my dress collar. "Anything I want?"

"Everything."

He cups the side of my neck, his thumb trailing the vulnerable center of my throat. "How could I possibly say no?" His lips press against mine in a kiss that's both tender and electrifying.

I melt into him, my hands fisting his shirt and pulling him closer.

As I'm moaning into his open mouth while his tongue explores, a voice interrupts us.

"Hey," the male voice says, getting closer.

Declan and I break apart to look at the man in a tropical Hawaiian shirt and swim shorts.

He lowers his sunglasses. "Hey, yeah, you're...uh, Brass Knuckles, right? 'Brass Knuckles' Conte?" The guy stops a few feet away, grinning ear to ear, his pale skin nice and pink from the sun exposure. "Yeah, it's you. Hey, man!" He tries to bro shake with Declan, but Declan remains unmoving, staring at the man with a tight frown.

The guy is undeterred, pulling his phone from his pocket. "Can I get a picture?"

"No," Declan says sharply. "But I'll do an autograph."

The man is a little flustered by Declan's sour attitude, but he pulls a napkin from his pocket and, miraculously, a pen.

As Declan tries to sign the thin paper without tearing it, the guy rattles on, "Man, I saw your fight against Martinez back in...fuck, wasn't that like fifteen years ago? You were incredible! The way you took him down in the fourth round...legendary, man."

Declan only grunts, finishing the sloppy, jagged autograph and handing it back.

The man grins at the napkin. Then his face suddenly drops, and he steps closer, lowering his voice. "Hey, listen, man, when I heard about your wife, I was just so—"

"If you'll excuse us," Declan cuts in, grabbing my elbow and pulling me away.

"Thanks, man!" the guy calls after us. "Miss seeing you in the ring!"

Declan continues to pull me away until there's significant distance between us and the stranger.

My mind is racing, questions burning on my tongue as I stare up at his hardened profile. The chasm of what I don't know about this man is so vast, so intimidating.

When he finally slows down and releases my elbow, I can't hold back any longer. "You were a boxer?"

Declan nods, his gaze fixed on the horizon. "A long time ago."

"Are…are you married?" *Please don't tell me I'm a fucking mistress.* I'd be so pissed.

"A long time ago," he echoes.

I want more details, to know about this part of his life, but I also don't want to unlock that door. My past is hidden for a reason; his might be too. Besides, his vacant stare and the rigid set of his shoulders make it clear the subject is off-limits.

Suddenly, I glimpse it again: the similarity that connects us.

We're two people with an open wound, and we desperately want it covered up.

He's been doing so many kind, generous things for me without knowing anything about what I'm running from. Finally, there's something I can do for him.

Entwining my fingers with his, I squeeze his hand and give him a big smile.

He looks startled, glancing down at our hands wrapped together. Then he gives me a questioning stare.

I only smile wider. "You know, it's a beautiful day. The water here is the deepest turquoise-blue I've ever seen. The beach is one of my favorite places, so let's keep walking and forget about that man. Let's forget about everything except our little vacation."

He glances at the sand, then the corner of his mouth turns up. He tightens his grip on my hand. "It's one of my favorite places, too."

With a temporary bandage for our wounds, we keep strolling along, hand in hand.

CHAPTER 15

DECLAN

WE RETURN TO THE SUITE and my mystery woman mumbles something about a bath, taking her shopping bags to the bedroom that was originally hers. A moment later, I hear the water running, filling the tub.

Otherwise, the suite is thick with silence.

I sit on the couch for a moment, replaying the day. After shopping and strolling along the beach, we had lunch, then I gave Sean the afternoon off and drove Sienna around the island myself. I didn't ask since she doesn't like questions, but her wide-eyed sense of wonder told me this might be her first visit to Hawaii.

Driving was difficult because I couldn't stop glancing at how happy she looked.

My mind also snagged on the beach incident. I don't get stopped by fans much anymore, and that was certainly bad timing. My mystery woman could've easily probed me for details about Tiffany. Most people do. Yet she did something far worse: she held my hand.

Such a simple gesture that people always miss. They offer shoulder pats and "I'm so sorry" and "It wasn't your fault." They send cards and give sympathetic looks as if they can possibly fathom what I went through. When they've vomited enough condolences and feel satisfied by their efforts, they leave.

But a simple, silent hand wrapped around mine? It's

more comforting than all of that other bullshit. A hand means someone is staying to bear witness to the hard times and pain.

To share a burden.

My mystery woman really messed up my head by doing that. Especially since I know she has the capacity to disappear in an instant.

I'm all-in for this fling she wants, but I hope she's going to stick it out. I really need these remaining seven days to prepare for her departure. Maybe a fling will only make goodbye harder, but fuck it. I want this time with her.

While she's still in the bathroom, I order room service and decide to do a quick workout. Of course, it's the first time I'm seeing my room since she's been hibernating in it.

The room is a beautiful disaster.

I smirk at the pillows and sheets tossed around, some on the floor. Her sketchbooks and drawing pencils are also scattered haphazardly, along with a few pieces of clothing. The bathroom isn't much better—makeup and towels everywhere.

My smirk grows as I take off my shirt and walk to my punching bag. I'm a man who prefers order, but I don't actually mind her mess. It means she's inhabited my room, been in my space. I like that a little too much.

After wrapping tape around my hands, I get to work, slamming my fists against the stiff material. I think of my fight with Martinez, the match the guy on the beach mentioned. Martinez was a lifetime ago, and it was the match that launched me into the spotlight. Fuck, that bastard was tough.

Martinez was a southpaw, which always threw me off. His stance was unorthodox, and he had a right hook that could come out of nowhere. He was a counterpuncher, always waiting for me to make the first move so he could capitalize on my mistakes.

Honestly, my technique wasn't the best back then, but I had stamina. I knew I just needed to keep applying pressure, never letting him settle into his rhythm. I worked the jab, keeping him back, and then I'd follow up with a combo, mixing in some body shots to wear him down.

Finally, in the fourth round, I saw an opening and my glove connected with his jaw. Knockout.

After that, I kept getting knockouts, usually a few rounds in. During one interview, the reporter talking to me made the comment, "You have any brass knuckles under those gloves? You come out with punches they never see coming!" That earned me the nickname.

Distracted from the memories, I hit the bag a little too hard and sloppy, a jolt traveling up my arm. I shake it off, rubbing my wrist.

Martinez—that fight was the beginning of the end, the start of a high in my life, followed by a sharp downward spiral.

It was the night I met Tiffany.

Sweat is pouring into my eyes, so I try to wipe it away, but my arm is also covered in sweat. Need a towel.

When I turn toward the bathroom, my mystery woman is standing across the room in a fluffy white robe, her hair wrapped up. She gasps and then bites her bottom lip, looking a bit flustered now that I've caught her spying.

"Uh, just getting my things," she says, grabbing a sketchbook off the bed.

All I can think is: *She took my hand.*

I'm also amped from endorphins and a good dose of

testosterone, so it's no question what I'm about to do.

I cross the space quickly, pulling her against me and kissing her hard. She gasps into my mouth and my only response is to work my tongue around hers. Her fingers dig into my biceps, holding on as I spin her back onto the bed and cover her with my body, never breaking the kiss.

Finally, she turns her head. "You're kind of sweaty and gross."

I chuckle. "And?"

She squirms under me, glancing at me like I'm pure sin. "It's really hot. Watching you punch that bag was hot."

I tear her robe open. "Good. Because I'm not stopping until I'm buried inside you." My lips suction onto a nipple and I bite gently, savoring her moan and the way she's still squirming beneath me.

I'm usually more patient than this—I like to play and tease, getting my desserts only after my woman has gotten several of hers. But I have zero patience now; I just crave to be inside her like it's my dying wish.

Guess tasting her will have to wait for next time.

Or perhaps there's a compromise.

My hand dips between her legs, feeling that she's more than ready for me. Then I move my fingers to my lips, tasting. I do it again, savoring her blush as she watches me.

"Something you like?" I ask, doing it a third time.

She only squirms in response, her chest arching up into mine.

I am aching to fuck her, but that look in her eyes makes it impossible not to play a little.

Quickly, I grab a silk tie from my closet. Her eyes widen in surprise as I approach.

"Lose the robe and stand up," I say.

She doesn't miss a beat, following my commands as I take off my pants. Once she's naked in front of me, her skin pink and breath heavy, I spin her around, securing her hands behind her back.

My knuckles trace the delicate curve of her shoulders, then I say into her ear, "On your knees."

She sucks in air, but doesn't protest; she faces me and lowers herself to the floor.

With her hands tied and shoulders curved back, her tits are shoved out just for me. Each nipple is hard and pointed. Eager. When I bend down to taste her lips, my palms cup those soft, warm tits. I take my time, enjoying the way they give under my touch and roll through my hands. Then I twist a nipple until she moans.

"Good?" I ask, making sure I'm not taking things too far.

She nods. I lower my hand for more confirmation—she's so wet it's spreading down her thighs.

I smile. Seems my mystery woman enjoys being tied up and teased.

"Open," I say as I straighten, gripping the base of my cock.

She swallows and then her eyes fixate on my length, her gorgeous mouth falling open, ready to take in all of me. Holding the back of her head, I guide her forward. She gags, but I keep pushing until I've hit the back of her throat. Her muscles constrict and it's pure heaven. A moan rumbles from my chest.

I pull out, letting her gasp for air.

"Good?" I ask again.

"Yes," she says breathlessly. Then she takes my cock back into her mouth without guidance.

I give her control for a moment, allowing her to pleasure me however she likes.

Her throat, tongue, lips…are exquisite. Her head bobs back and forth like she's starved, her tongue repeatedly hitting a pleasurable spot below my tip. Before I'm aware of it, my balls tighten and I'm ready to release down her throat.

I grab her hair and pull her away quickly, not wanting the fun to end just yet.

"Get on the bed. Stay on your knees," I tell her.

She does, and then I help her lower her torso, her shoulders pressing into the bed as I raise her hips higher.

Fuck. She's on complete display for me, glistening and puffy. I smack her ass, leaving a light red mark, and she cries out.

"Good?"

"More than good," she says with a muffled voice, since her face is buried in the sheets.

"I can see that." I press my mouth between her thighs from behind, my hands kneading her luscious ass. My tongue revels in her wetness as I smack her again, harder. Then I spread her slit open with eager fingers. She moans and it's the most wonderful sound.

Changing my position, I lay on my back, pulling her hips down until she smothers my face. With two fingers hooked inside her, I suck on her clit, bringing her close to the edge. I need her close because once I'm fucking her, I won't last long. I feel on the verge of coming just from eating her this way.

Before I send her off the cliff, though, I move away, eliciting an angry groan of protest from my delicious mystery woman.

I search the nightstand.

Fuck, where are the condoms?

Then it hits me: I only brought one.

That was stupid.

I was originally thinking I'd enjoy only one night with her if she was interested. And I knew I could always go to the store. What I didn't anticipate was being so hungry for her I lost the capacity to think—we could've bought more foils earlier today.

She rolls over, peering at me with hooded eyes as my hand squeezes the edge of the nightstand. "What's wrong?" she asks, and I turn to gaze at her messy damp hair, those flushed cheeks, and the 'come fuck me' look.

My cock twitches.

"I'm out of condoms, so change of plans." I return to her, covering her petite frame with my body and pressing our lips together. She smells like tropical soap, her entire body fresh and clean, waiting for me to dirty it more.

She pushes against my chest, urging me to stop. After brushing her fingers over my cheek in a way that's too tender, something I normally object to, she says, "I'm on birth control. I promise."

I'm tempted, so very close to thrusting inside her, bareback.

But that 'promise' hits too close to home. I don't know this woman well enough. Don't know her name. And promises are too important, especially when it comes to creating an innocent life.

Moving her hand from my cheek, I kiss her fingers. Then her beautiful mouth. Then my teeth find her nipples, pulling more gorgeous moans from her throat. As soon as I get more condoms, I'm going to fuck her until she screams. For now, we'll both need patience.

She's on her back now, so I move to her head, holding my cock out until she understands and starts pleasuring me. As I'm debating whether to spill down her throat or on her chest, she pauses.

"Touch me," she whimpers. "I'm so close."

I slide my hand between her thighs. "I didn't forget about you, my dirty little princess."

Her eyes dart to mine, flashing wide for a second, then she bites her bottom lip and moans.

Hmm, did she like that name? Note taken.

My fingers hook inside her again, thumb working circles around her clit, as we chase our mutual release. It doesn't take either of us long—her pussy is soon pulsing around my fingers as I pull free of her mouth and come on her tits.

She's eager to take me in again, though, running her mouth up and down my length while moaning softly, making my body tense and twitch every time she licks my tip.

I finally stop her movements. "Good girl. But save some for later."

We're both breathing heavily, trying to catch our breaths, and she's staring at my mouth with a lot of anticipation. I normally don't linger after sex for a make-out session, but what the hell. I untie her hands and then lie beside her, exploring and savoring her lips until mine are raw.

Finally breaking away, I take a quick shower and then go out for those damn condoms.

Dinner from room service is cold when I get back, so my mystery woman warms it in the oven. We watch a movie on the couch and eat, then she goes to my room to pack up her stuff, preparing to vacate.

That bugs the hell out of me.

I follow her to the room, peel her hands away from her luggage as she tries to stuff a pair of jeans inside, then I roll on a condom. Soon, I'm fucking her against the dresser. Watching her tits bounce in the mirror makes me come so hard I get dizzy for a second.

When I'm done and she makes another attempt to pack up her shit, I push her back onto the bed and eat her out. I'm too spent to come again, but I make her climax several more times. When I'm finally done pleasuring and enjoying her body, she's too boneless to even lift a finger.

Good.

I kick her luggage toward my closet, then I wrap her up in my sheets, turn off the light, and climb into bed next to her. We face opposite directions, but I can feel her body heat warming my back.

The sound of her snores fills my room. I stare at the curtains and smile to myself. I forgot to take my sleeping pills, but there's a possibility I might get a full, restful night of sleep for once.

I had grown tired of her merely haunting my bed; better to have her in it.

CHAPTER 16

SIENNA

DAY FIVE. THE HALFWAY POINT.

I feel the weight of every minute passing, every second ticking by. I'll have to leave Declan soon, leave my life as Sienna behind. I'm still undecided, but I'll likely find some shady person to make me a new identity. Probably safest.

But that's a future problem. For now, all I need to do is focus on what I'm painting.

I'm out on the patio in the midday sun, the ocean sounds lulling me into a trance. After swiping my brush over a gray shade on my palette, I blend the color into the shadows under Declan's feet. I'm determined to get the portrait of him finished before we say goodbye. I don't know how he'll react to it, but it's something I want to give him. A parting gift.

It's Sunday, and Declan's conference started yesterday. He completely missed the first day because we were too busy in bed. It was the best sex of my life—multiple times—but I'm happy to get a reprieve today since he left for the conference this morning. I'm sore all over my body from the positions we tried, and there's a sweet ache between my legs from his thickness.

I'm not complaining.

Never.

Hovering my brush over the canvas, I pause before making another stroke. Unable to stop myself from smiling,

I gaze into Declan's watercolor eyes. Even though I drew those eyes and then painted them a brilliant blue, they're still giving me an electric buzz. Guess I should feel proud that I captured his intensity.

My smile widens. I do feel proud, and I really hope he keeps this painting. Even if he shoves it in a closet, I can live happily under a new identity if I know he has something from Sienna close by.

Too bad I don't have enough time to paint what he requested—a larger version of that 'inspired' painting. Chewing on the end of my paintbrush, I wonder: would he really give me seven *hundred* thousand for it? I mean, fuck, how rich is he? I can't even fathom seeing that number in my bank account, so it's too bad I'll never find out.

But if my life ever gets out of the danger zone, maybe I'll look him up and see if he's still interested.

Or…what am I thinking?

My shoulders hunch, carrying the weight of only five remaining days, as I dab my brush in some black and create a darker edge along a crease in Declan's suit. I shouldn't be thinking of contacting him in the future. I can't. I can't contact him or Jada.

God, now I'm back to thinking about Jada feeling so hurt and sad and betrayed…abandoned.

My chest is aching too much to continue working on the painting, so I move it to my room, where Declan won't see it. Then I grab my sketch book and start drawing the flowering plants tucked along the edges of the patio. Just something pretty and carefree. My mind needs a break.

The front door opens, so I glance over my shoulder, expecting to see Sean sneaking to the fridge for a snack.

But it's Declan.

He loves his three-piece suits, even in warm Hawaii, so of course that's what he wore to the conference. I wonder if it makes him stand out, or if a lot of other people at the conference wear business attire. I've been wondering so much about him lately—what he does for a living, if he has any hobbies, his favorite color.

Anything and everything. But this little obsession is bad, so I push it down deep inside me and lock it away.

I grin as he enters and sets a paper bag on the kitchen counter. After running a hand through his loose, sexy dark hair, he grins back. His blue eyes light up and look mischievous.

My stomach flips. *So ridiculously handsome.*

I turn back to my sketch so he doesn't see me blushing. "You're back early," I say, adding shade to a flower petal. "Or are you just breaking for lunch?"

I hear the soft tap of his oxfords along the floorboards as he approaches. "I sent you a few texts, but they went unread."

Swallowing, I try to brush it off. "Strange. So what do you—"

"I also called," he continues, clearly not ready to drop the subject. "Straight to voicemail." He's behind me now, so he rubs my shoulders with those thick, skilled fingers of his. "I asked Sean, and he said you were in here painting. I gave it some more thought and realized I haven't seen you with a phone at all during this trip." He doesn't sound angry, only curious, as he leans down to kiss the side of my head. "Any comment about that?"

I worried he might notice eventually, because who goes days without looking at a phone in this modern world? "It, uh, broke."

"It broke between you calling me and meeting at the airport?"

I try to keep my voice from rising in pitch because I'm usually an awful liar. "Yup. Crazy, huh? The screen just went black and it wouldn't turn on. Some defect my model is known for." I start sketching another flower to try to act casual. "I figured I'd deal with it later."

"We can take it to a repair shop."

My heart jumps. *Dammit.* That sounds reasonable, and any reasonable person would try to get their phone fixed before throwing it away. Could I claim to simply be unreasonable?

Instead, I continue to sketch a flower like everything is fine. "Oh no, that's okay. I need to look into the warranty and it's a big hassle I just don't want to think about right now. I'm not expecting any calls, so I'll get a phone later. Thanks though."

"Hmm," is his response. I don't think he's buying my excuse, but thankfully, he changes the subject. "Well," he says, rubbing his hands over my arms, "I'm done with the conference for today, and I brought something we can play with."

My hand pauses over the page. "Play with? What do you mean?"

Pressing his cheek against my hair, he inhales deeply. Then his hands run down the length of my arms, coming back up to trail along my collarbone. I'm wearing one of those sleeveless tropical dresses he bought me at the boutique, so my shoulders are bare. He takes full advantage of it, burning trails in my skin with his fiery touch.

"I'll show you soon. But first, are you done sketching your pretty little flowers?"

I laugh. "Oh, you think they're pretty?"

"Mmm. But they don't suit you."

"Why's that?"

He caresses my earlobe. "I like your edgier work. It's evocative. Moody."

"So I'm moody?"

His chuckle warms my chest; I love hearing him laugh, which he's doing more often. "Moody isn't a bad thing. I enjoy your moody paintings." He touches my sketchbook. "Make these flowers moody and we'll hang it on the fridge."

"Oh, do I get a gold star too?"

"Absolutely."

We both laugh and I reach up to touch his hand that's on my shoulder. I love our little moments like this.

I tip my head, exposing the side of my neck so he can press his lips against it. His tongue darts out to taste me, and I feel flushed all over. "I could be done sketching," I say, "depending on what you have in mind."

"I'm sure you know exactly what I have in mind." He sucks gently on my earlobe, and I bite back a moan.

His fingers trace my collarbone again before both hands dip into the front of my dress and discover I'm not wearing a bra. Instinctively, I arch into his touch as he palms my breasts, kneading them with slow, purposeful movements.

I don't restrain my moan this time, my head dropping back as he pinches my sore, hardened nipples. His hands have explored so much of them these past few days, giving me the sweetest satisfied ache every time he brushes them with a thumb. It's pain and pleasure and need and agony all mixed together.

Moving his mouth close to my ear, he says in a gruff tone, "I've spent the entire morning not listening to a damn thing at that conference. All I could think about was your beautiful mouth sucking my cock."

His words send a spark down my spine. It ignites in my very center, one strong muscle contraction making me squeeze my thighs. My body is already pulsing to have this man between my legs again, as if that already didn't happen over and over yesterday.

I'm really struggling to get my fill of him.

"Are you ready to get on your knees?" he asks, completely composed, completely in control.

I don't mind a damn bit.

I nod.

He walks around my chair to face me, waiting. I dropped my pencil and sketchbook, then I slide off the chair. My knees meet the warm, smooth concrete of the patio. It's an uncomfortable hard surface, but I don't care; at this angle, I can see how hard he's been for me.

I glance up through my eyelashes. His eyes, so dark and hungry and intense, are trained on mine. "That's my dirty little princess," he says softly, caressing my cheek. "Now unzip me."

Doing as I'm told, I undo his belt and top button, then drag the zipper down slowly, inch by inch. Blood is whooshing through my ears and I salivate, so eager to have him in my mouth, to satisfy him; I know he'll give it back tenfold. Every ounce of attention and pleasure I give, he pours right back into me. I've never experienced such a give and take during sex, like the two of us are an infinity loop, moving between moments of selfishness and generosity in an endless dance.

Well, until Friday.

This loop has an end. The connection will be severed.

But thinking about that makes me too sad, so I focus instead on what I have now.

Right now, I have Declan.

His body. His attention. His dominance over me that I've let myself surrender to.

Well, I've only surrendered my body; the rest is locked away.

I pull down the band of his boxer briefs. His erection springs free, twitching as if beckoning me closer. He's so hard and bulbous, pre-cum dripping from the tip, that it almost looks painful.

I reach up to run my hands over his silky length, but he grabs my wrist. "Just your mouth."

I take him fully into my mouth, his tip hitting the back of my throat. He releases a loud groan and heat engulfs me. I close my eyes as I savor his hardness, the taste that's salty, tangy, him. His hands thread through my hair, guiding me up and down, guiding the pace. I take him in again fully until I'm choking on every inch. He grips the back of my head, holding me in place, stealing my air.

When we first started playing these games that night on the phone, I wasn't sure if I should ever give in like this. Anthony had accepted what I gave him carelessly, controlling my life, my sanity, breaking off pieces of me bit by bit.

But Declan seems to cherish everything, never taking too much, pulling back when I've reached my limits. He might have some control issues, but they're not destructive like Anthony's.

He actually takes the time to satisfy me in bed; Anthony was never one to 'play.' Too impatient.

Either way, Declan has shown me that real control is tender. It guides and supports; it doesn't just take until there's nothing left.

I trust him.

Now, I can't think of wanting anything else than to feel his powerful gaze on me.

When I glance up, I find those deep blue eyes watching like I'm doing the most fascinating thing in the world. There's tension in the lines etched above his brows, but the slight curve of his lips softens his expression.

He looks pleased with the pain of being so close to coming.

Holding my breath, I'm content to keep him in my mouth as long as I can handle, to feel his release spilling down my throat, but he grips the back of my hair and pulls me off.

There's another rumbling groan.

"Fuck, you're too good at that," he says. "It's dangerous."

I smirk, giving him a sassy look. "How cheesy. It's not dangerous."

He chuckles and caresses my cheek. "I'm not sure how else to describe what you do to me." After helping me to my feet, he adds, "I can't get enough of you."

We kiss, and I cling to him. "*Same,*" I want to say.

And I want to ask, "*Can I belong to you?*"

I've craved it since the moment he laid his jacket over my shoulders.

I could surrender completely to this man—body, heart, essence.

But that's a dumb thought. The two of us have an expiration date.

He breaks the kiss and takes my hand, guiding me off the patio. "Let me show you what I brought for us to play with."

CHAPTER 17

SIENNA

HE LEADS ME INTO THE kitchen and then rifles through the paper bag on the counter.

I laugh as he hands me a box of edible body paint. "Well, this looks like fun."

"I'm glad you agree. Now, let's get you out of that dress."

"Only if we get you out of that suit first."

His gaze turns devilish, and he picks me up, making me yelp as he cradles me against his solid chest. "Do you always have to fight me?"

I stroke his red silk tie as he carries me to the bedroom. "I think that's what you like most about me."

"It is refreshing."

I tuck my feet so they don't bump the doorframe, then I start to undo the knot in his tie. "So, your other women are just quiet all the time, doing everything they're told?"

As soon as I ask, I regret it, because I don't want to think about all the other women he's been with. Since he's a man who doesn't like attachments, he probably dates often. Maybe he's even talked to his other women during this trip. Maybe he messaged one this morning, said something dirty or…

He drops me on the bed, and I bounce, breaking my train of thought. Good, because I was on the edge of spiraling.

Pressing his hips between my legs, spreading them

open and exposing the fact that I'm not wearing panties, he teases my opening with the head of his cock. I'm breathless because he's not yet wearing a condom, and I know that's important to him.

Has he finally decided I'm not a liar? That I'm really on birth control?

Placing his hands on either side of my head, he lowers himself and asks, "What are you talking about? Other women? I'm not sure they exist. I can only think of you. You're the only one I want."

That admission shocks him more than it does me—I see it in the slight widening of his eyes and the way his body becomes deathly still. We gaze at each other for a moment as my heart thunders.

Only me?

Thankfully, he moves off of me to stand beside the bed, changing focus.

I'm sure he didn't really mean that. He shouldn't.

Regaining his composure, he finishes loosening his tie and then takes off his jacket. "I'll humor you and undress first. But don't get used to commanding me around."

I just nod, still trying to push his earlier statement from my mind. He strips for me, kicking off his shoes, peeling off his button down, then his pants. He finally drops the boxers, standing naked in all his muscular glory, stroking himself as I watch.

I'm already so wet and needy it feels like a slight breeze could push me over the edge.

"Your turn," he says, completely composed with every angle of his body solid and level.

I sit up and whip the dress over my head. Now I'm completely naked, exposed. Eager to have him do whatever he pleases. He could fuck me with a paintbrush and I wouldn't even bat an eye—I crave this man's satisfaction that much.

He stares at my pussy as he strokes himself in a languid rhythm, then his gaze travels up my body. This intoxicating man makes me blush by saying, "What an exquisite canvas I have."

I bite my lip as he grabs the box of body paints and pops it open. He makes me feel like a supermodel, but that's definitely not what I see in the mirror—only a Plain Jane. A woman not deserving of all this attention. I mean, come on…he's rich, and I'm sure he's dated *actual* models.

His momentary interest—or lapse in sanity—would never survive past our expiration date. I have nothing to offer a man like him.

He bites my nipple and I gasp, turning my alarmed gaze on him.

Hovering over me, he says, "Don't know what you're thinking about, but eyes on me." He kisses me, pressing his mouth against mine like he's starving.

Only a momentary lapse in sanity.

After raising himself, he settles between my thighs again, sitting back on his heels. He pops the top on a small jar—blue. Before dipping the brush into the liquid, he hesitates. "Do you have a favorite color?"

I lick my lips, debating whether I should lie. I go with the truth: "Burnt sienna."

"Hmm. Our colors are limited. Would you prefer something close? Red instead of blue?"

"Blue is fine. What's your favorite color?"

He dips a finger into my wetness, making me twitch. "Pink. Your entire body is my favorite."

I purse my lips. "I'm not all pink."

Still teasing my wetness, he licks the pebbled surfaces of my breasts, then my lips. "The best parts are."

"Are you going to paint me?" I say, squirming under him as my core aches. All his teasing is too much. "Or do I have to take over and ride you?"

He smiles so wide he shows his teeth, and the little worry lines around his eyes become joyful crinkles.

That sweet ache in my chest comes back. I love his smile. It's like he only shows it to me.

"As if I'd let you," he says. "I want to have my fun first."

His fingers pluck a nipple, and he kisses me to swallow my soft moan.

Finally, *finally*, he returns to sitting back on his heels and dips the brush in the blue paint. When he makes a stroke along my stomach, I gasp from the coldness, then I giggle like a dumb schoolgirl.

It's not like all of this isn't sexy—it definitely is—but in just twenty-four hours of us fucking like rabbits, something in him has shifted dramatically. He's still dark and brooding most of the time, but there are these little glimpses of a playful side. It has relaxed me, turning me into a giggly mess sometimes.

A coolness spreads over my flushed skin everywhere he makes a brush stroke. I watch his gaze shift as he works, his brow furrowing in concentration. Whatever he's painting captures his complete attention for several minutes, so I wait patiently until he's done. He finally lifts the brush to admire his work on my torso.

I glance down and smile—he drew a rose. A really good one. "That's beautiful. I didn't know you could draw."

"I doodled in high school to keep myself awake in

class."

"So, you were a bad student?" I tease.

Smirking, he runs the brush over my sensitive nipples, making me suck in a sharp breath. As my skin cools under the paint, he dips his head to cover me with heat from his tongue. I shiver and moan, running my hands through his unruly hair, pulling him closer.

He adds more paint along my skin, then eagerly licks it up. His hands caress me as he moves downward, painting designs as he travels. I'm riddled with goosebumps and my veins are lava by the time he reaches the juncture of my thighs. It's all I can do not to buck against him as he spreads me with two fingers, then swirls the brush over my clit.

I must look desperate because he only grins and asks innocently, "What?"

I moan a light protest. *He knows what.*

"Oh, you want me to clean up the paint?"

This time I groan.

"Or just add more?" He runs the brush up and down my crease.

"Your mouth," I finally pant out. "Stop teasing me."

"Well, you should've asked...such a dirty princess."

The muscles between my thighs pulse.

Damn him. I don't know why I like that nickname so much, but he's weaponized it.

I'm ready to pull his hair out when he finally presses his lips around my swollen clit and sucks hard. I cry out, then gasp his name. It's the first time I've called out 'Declan' like this, so his eyes snap to mine as he licks and probes. His gaze is laser-focused, as if he's branding me with his dark stare. There's so much emotion in that look I can't decipher. But I know I want to be branded.

I want to be his.

He dips two fingers inside me, stretching and teasing. My hands grip his hair and I rock into his mouth.

If I was his, we could run away together. I wouldn't have to disappear alone.

I wouldn't be alone.

Such a dangerous, naïve feeling.

As he thrusts his fingers in and out, the tension in my core builds. "I want you," I pant out, twisting my fingers so deep in his hair I'm probably hurting him.

He doesn't seem to care; he only keeps pinning me with stormy eyes while his mouth and fingers push me toward breaking.

"Fuck…I want…you…Dec—"

Heat shreds through me, my core pulsing and aching as my body falls apart. I grind against his mouth, milking every drop of pleasure from his tongue that I can. But even as I'm coming down and my core stops pulsing, an ache remains.

Someone to disappear with me. What a beautiful, dumb thought.

Declan doesn't want a broken woman. He has his own life—a business, obligations, friends. He wouldn't drop everything for a woman he's barely known for two months. Also, I'd have to explain to him *why* I need to run away, explain my past.

He wouldn't like me if I revealed the truth.

Our little fling is fun, but this life could never be mine; my burdens are too heavy.

I'm also starting to have feelings for Declan, so I'd rather not see the look of shock and disgust in his eyes when I explain I'm a criminal.

That I hurt people.

That he might be in danger just from knowing me.

He lifts my chin with his finger, pulling my unfocused gaze back to the moment. "You're slipping away again," he says. "Thought I said eyes on me?"

I nod weakly.

He studies my sad expression, and those versatile lines around his eyes deepen with worry. "It wasn't good?"

"It was. I loved it." I pull him into a kiss, tasting a mix of raspberry paint and my own essence on his tongue.

Why am I getting lost in the past? In realities I can't have? Declan doesn't know my dark parts, and we only have five days left. I need to enjoy them.

Shaking away my depressing thoughts, I give him a smile and poke the worry line between his brows. "I want to paint you now."

He rolls, pulling me with him until I'm on top. I shift my hips to straddle him, his cock jutting upward in front of my pelvis. His hands gently caress my thighs as I lean over to grab a jar of orange body paint from the nightstand.

Once I have a loaded brush in my hand, I can't think of anything to paint. He's already so finely chiseled, a work of art, that I simply add shadow and contours to his muscles— accentuating the curves of his six-pack, shading the edges of his pecs so they pop even more.

The entire time, he observes and kneads the parts of my body he can reach. Then his thumb slips between my thighs to dance around my clit. I can't concentrate and don't want to, so I return the paint and brush to the nightstand.

I run my palms up his torso. The orange mixes with his tan skin, making a mess.

After Declan rolls on a condom, he licks the paint off my fingers, twists his hands roughly in my hair. He lifts himself and rumbles in my ear, "Take what you want."

I don't hesitate, lifting my hips and then impaling myself on his rigid cock. We both moan. Then he fucks me, holding my waist and thrusting up ruthlessly until my entire body is trembling and burning.

As I'm screaming out another orgasm, I'm sure I hear him say against my ear, "I want you too. Fuck, I want you." Then he crumbles with me, moaning and grunting as he shakes and pulls my hips down hard against his.

When we're both limp, I move to lie on my back, giving our bodies a few inches of space since he told me he doesn't cuddle. Fine with me because cuddling is too intimate. We need to avoid that; this fling is purely sex.

I probably shouldn't sleep in his room again tonight. He keeps finding ways to stop me from packing up my stuff, but tonight I should be firm and sleep in a separate room.

I should do that.

As he's still catching his breath and staring up at the ceiling, he says, "I'd like to take you out to dinner this evening. After we get you a new phone."

My skin is sweaty and sticky, so I'm craving a long soak in the tub. Something to wash away the paint and the guilt. "I appreciate the offer, but you don't need to do that. You know I'm uncomfortable with you buying me so much stuff. It's bad enough you're paying for the suite and the food and won't let me pay my share."

"If I can't spend my money on others, what's the point?"

His comment reminds me of something Jada had said before, that only top donors to the museum and arts foundation get rose pins like the one Declan has. I roll onto my side to face him. "You don't like just going overboard with whatever you want? Buying houses around the world. Yachts. I don't know how much you make, but I can barely fathom what it would be like to earn more than a hundred thousand a year."

He cradles the back of his head with his hands, broadening his chest. His body looks so comfortable, I wish I could crawl closer to snuggle, run my fingers through that chest hair.

The corners of his mouth twitch. "I'm not into collecting houses or boats. I have everything I could possibly need and then some. Scaling my business has taken a good chunk of my assets lately, but I still have too much. I'm not a man who wants to hoard money, especially when it can benefit others."

The sharp contrast of our lives isn't lost on me; there's a casualty in the way he discusses money and privilege that feels almost alien.

"Why do you work so hard if you don't need more money?" I ask, genuinely curious about what drives a man who seems to have zero financial struggle and doesn't care about building wealth.

His gaze becomes unfocused, his blue eyes dimming. "I don't have much else besides work. I'm also responsible for my employees—they depend on my company to support their lives. I don't take that for granted. So, I like to see growth—in my business, in my people. Success in business is one way I can measure my ability to make an impact. To give back for—" His words cut off suddenly and his mouth seals shut.

I smooth my finger over a wrinkle in the sheets. "To give back for what?"

"Just to give back."

BEAUTIFUL DAMAGE | 185

I sense there's something more, but I don't ask. I'm already prying too much, and it's only resulting in my mood dropping. The more I know about him, the larger the divide between us grows. His world is about legacy and impact; mine is purely survival.

I trace the scar on his neck with the pad of my finger, something I've done a few times mindlessly.

He stops me, capturing my hand and turning to face me. "I'm surprised you haven't asked," he says, tapping the scar. "Others do. I know it's noticeable."

"It's not really my business."

"You're not curious?"

"I am but…" *But we shouldn't be asking each other those questions.*

He caresses my cheek, his eyes vacant like he has hollowed himself out. "Tell me something about yourself, anything, and I'll tell you how I got the scars."

My mind is screaming at me: *Do not tell him anything. You don't want to know.*

Why get close to a man I have to leave?

Unfortunately, I'm delirious in the afterglow of sex, and my lips part. "I grew up in Chicago," I find myself saying. "I was an accident. My parents never wanted kids, but their families pressured them not to get an abortion. My grandpa on my mother's side told her that once she held me in her arms, her heart would change."

Declan's gaze becomes less hollow as a crease deepens between his brows.

Now I'm the empty one, my body turning rigid. Is this the first time I've said this out loud? I swallow down pain from the memories, trying to focus only on the facts as I continue. "My mother's heart never changed. Growing up, it was clear they didn't want me. They took care of me out of obligation and because of the pressure from my grandparents, but there wasn't any love or affection. I was left alone a lot. Given food and clothes, then left to take care of myself."

The memories bite harder than I expected, the soft spot in my chest aching terribly. I think about what that alone time led to, how I started drinking at age 12, seeking validation from much older boys. How I met Anthony when I was 16 and thought I was in love, that he loved me. That doing whatever he asked me to do, no matter how wrong it was, only proved my devotion. Made me belong to him. He said I was his 'ride or die' and I was too young to understand at the time that he meant it literally.

"If you're not with me, you'll die," he once told me. And I laughed.

I fucking laughed.

I didn't know it was a threat.

"My grandpa was there," I add, almost in a whisper. "When I was a kid. He loved me and cared for me when he could visit. But he was eighty, with poor health. He died when I was twelve. That's who I have in my locket." I touch the silver metal as it rests near my collarbone. Then I try to clear my throat several times and stop what's trying to come up. I'm unsuccessful because a stupid tear slips down my cheek.

Declan kisses it—he doesn't merely brush it away. He moves closer to press his soft, warm lips against my trembling cheek.

It's the first time anyone has shown me such intimate tenderness.

"That's terrible," he says. "You didn't deserve such awful parents."

He tries to hold me and wrap me in his comfort and scent, but I push away, wiping my face and dropping my gaze. "Well, that's my sob story," I try to joke, but my voice is too rough around the edges for light-heartedness. "Guess it's your turn."

He rolls onto his back again and closes his eyes, like he doesn't want me to see what might pass through his gaze. "Alright," he says through a heavy sigh. His tone is level, business-like. "I got the scars from my...my wife, Tiffany."

A jolt races up my spine and my lips part in a gasp. I was expecting the scars to be from an accident or some disgruntled boxing opponent. But *wife*?

After another dark sigh, every muscle on his face relaxes, eyes still closed. He's blank—a lot better at hiding heavy emotions than I am. "She struggled with bipolar disorder. She...hurt herself on multiple occasions. One day, I came home to find blood in the kitchen and followed the trail to the bathroom. The door was locked, so I broke it down."

"Oh my god," I whisper, bracing for the worst. I grab his hand, holding on like he's going to slip away.

He finally opens his eyes to glance down at our inter-twined fingers, almost impassively. I see what he was trying to hide: a light shimmer of moisture along his lashes. "It's hard to explain how she was during bad days. Not her nor-mal self. Like someone else had taken her over and there was no getting my wife back, no pulling her out of it. She was okay when I found her that day, bleeding from a few cuts, but okay. But she was threatening to do more, and I wasn't going to let that happen. I tried to grab the utility knife. In the struggle, she caught me with it a few times."

Even though it's his traumatic memory, he's a lot more

composed than I am. I'm shaking and the tears are flowing. I want to ask if she's okay now, if she found help, if she moved on after the divorce, but I'm too much of a wreck.

"Declan," is all I manage, pulling him into an embrace. I know I pushed him away when he offered comfort, so I won't blame him if he does the same, but I can't do anything else right now except try to hold him.

He accepts it. He wraps his arms around my back and presses his forehead into the crook of my neck, breathing deep. He clears his throat, the tiniest indication that his mask has cracked.

Neither of us speaks. We simply embrace, which soon shifts to a form of cuddling. Our legs tangle and we relax into a more comfortable position, still pressed close to one another. I scoot down, my head tucked under his chin. Then I listen to his heartbeat as tears dry on my face.

I fall asleep in his arms, resting in the silence between our damaged parts.

From the blissful darkness, he kisses my forehead, waking me gently. "Join me in the shower."

I nod, following him in a daze, holding his hand as he leads.

Without speaking, we soap each other's bodies. We kiss passionately while hot water streams down our cleansed skin, but it's not from lust or desire. Each kiss is comfort, care, our attempt at mending the rips in our pasts that never stay sutured.

Finally, we return to the bed to cuddle and watch a movie, lost in domestic bliss.

We fall asleep in each other's arms.

CHAPTER 18

DECLAN

FOUR DAYS REMAINING.

I can't stop gazing at my mystery woman as she eats dinner across the table. The restaurant is a low rabble around us because all I can focus on is her. The candlelight flickers across her face, casting shadows that only highlight her beauty.

Of course, my eyes keep dipping to that low V on her dress. She picked it out earlier—reluctantly—when I told her I wanted to buy her a dress for our date. Even though she protested like always, she spent a few hours trying on different styles, as if she wanted to pick the right one.

She did. She's a vision in deep blue silk, and I'm mesmerized by every movement she makes.

I don't seem to be the only one who is distracted; her eyes keep scanning my suit. Seems I made a good outfit pick as well.

She chews a bite of her salmon, then sips her Merlot, her eyes surveying my plate. "You haven't eaten much. Is the lobster bad?"

I focus on her generous cleavage again. She's not wearing a bra and I'm picturing the way my hands are going to slip into that V later, parting the fabric to reveal her tits. I'm thinking I might fasten her hands behind her back again, giving myself complete, unrestricted access.

Smirking to myself about the fun we'll have soon, I sip

my wine. "No, the food here is delicious. Just saving room for dessert."

Her bottom lip puckers as her brows lower in thought. "Which dessert? I've been eyeing the crème brûlée at the next table."

I grin against the rim of my glass at her innocent reaction. It's amusing because she's anything but innocent in bed. "Oh, just something sweet that'll drip down my chin and make a mess."

She gives me an almost disgusted look, half of her top lip twitching as if pulled by a string. "What dessert is—" Her beautiful cheeks turn crimson as her eyes become delicate saucers when she realizes I'm not talking about food. Lowering her head, she whispers, "Declan," like everyone around us is suddenly staring.

The way her teeth have captured her bottom lip, the way she shifts in her chair, shows that my words had the intended effect.

I'm enjoying her reaction too much and want to push a little, so I say, "I'm tempted to crawl under this table and have my dessert now."

Her voice lifts. "Oh my god, I would die of embarrassment."

"As long as I get you to come first."

Her sudden laugh is loud and robust, so she covers her mouth, giggling to herself. I join in her laughter, letting it shake my shoulders before another sip of wine.

When she's done giggling, she leans forward, her eyes dancing with a lightness this date has brought us both.

"What?" I ask, because she's staring at me.

"I don't think I've seen you laugh like that before. I like it."

It may be my turn to blush because my cheeks are warm. But she's right; I don't remember when I've laughed so freely. Likely years.

It's this woman across the table—being with her smoothes some of my jagged edges. I only crave more of her, all of her.

I need her to be mine.

Shifting focus to my food, I take a few bites, chewing slowly as thoughts circulate. I crave her in a way I never thought I'd crave a woman again. Tiffany left a deep chasm I've been lost in for so many years. And I swore off all relationships, not wanting to fail someone so horribly ever again.

Then my mystery woman comes along and I find myself with new thoughts about my future. A future that could include her. A future where my evenings aren't consumed with work, casual hookups, or drinking and wandering the labyrinth of my empty home.

I set my fork down and wipe my mouth roughly with a cloth napkin. *What the hell am I thinking?* I can't allow myself to have such a…meaningful future.

My life is designed the way it is for a reason—less heartache, less opportunity to fail someone, fail at keeping them safe…even from themselves.

Four days. She can't be mine because I only get her for a few remaining days.

But I need something; if she can't fully be mine, I at least need a few pieces.

"So," I say, "tell me more about your grandfather. He sounded like a caring man."

My words are a mistake because her body instantly seizes up, the lightness fading from her gaze. With shoulders that are high and almost touching her ears, she plays with her silver locket. "I…I know we shared some things last night, but I really prefer not to talk about my past."

My walls raise in reaction to hers, though I still crave to have a few pieces of her to take with me when our trip ends. "You're right. I apologize for bringing it up. How about this—what do you love about painting?"

Her eyes are unfocused as she twirls her locket.

I try to give her a little nudge by adding, "Besides, we need something to talk about. We've already exhausted the topic of which season of CSI was the best."

Some of that lightness returns and her shoulders lower. "Well, painting for me is…almost like breathing, I guess. When I'm in front of a canvas, I feel like my real self again. It's how I cope, how I process my emotions. The way my parents treated me…I just needed an outlet, so I started drawing when I was young. In high school, there was an art teacher who…" She releases a tight sigh while shaking her head. "How do you always get me into talking about my past?"

"Maybe you really want to tell someone. And I want to listen."

My words seem to disturb her—her shoulders curve and tighten again, making her collarbone pronounced, and her forehead becomes a valley of ridges, like she's bracing for a blow.

I search my mind for a new topic to put her at ease; we might talk about spin-offs for CSI since we share a common interest in that show.

Before I can speak, she shakes her head like deciding something—or surrendering to something—and says, "My, uh, art teacher encouraged me to try different media. She was really supportive and brought in extra supplies just for me. After trying a lot of things—textiles, pastels, clay, acrylics—I discovered I loved how watercolor isn't something you can tame."

I watch as her spine slowly straightens, and her lips soften into a smile as she talks. Her eyes ignite, something fierce burning in their depths. It's the same energy I observed when she was painting me. She comes alive when talking about art.

But she doesn't continue, so I lean back in my chair, spread my legs out, and swirl my wine. "Tell me more than that. You've got me curious."

She offers a tiny smirk. "Well, when you make a mistake with watercolor, it's less forgiving. The colors are transparent, so everything underneath informs the top layer. Other types of paint can be covered up. You can take an acrylic painting, for example, cover the entire image with white, and no one will ever see what's underneath. Watercolor always shows what's underneath. I like its honesty." She fiddles with her napkin. "But…I'm also not very good. It takes a lot of skill to use it correctly and the things I paint aren't really 'fine art.' My teachers tell me I'm not reaching the intellectual levels true art achieves. They say my colors are muddied."

A primal flare ignites in my chest; I can't stand the thought of someone speaking ill of my mystery woman. "They're idiots," I say in a biting tone. "Your work could easily be in a museum or at auction. The depth of emotion, the insight…it's extraordinary."

A blush creeps up her neck, and she ducks her head. "So, um, why did you get into boxing?"

The corners of my lips tighten. Why does my mystery

woman seem to hate praise? She deserves it.

But I go along with the topic change. Though…she picked a difficult subject. The truth is complex, rooted in a childhood of emotional neglect. I was an only child. My mother died when I was young, leaving me with a distant, workaholic father. I left before finishing senior year of high school, figuring I could get my GED later. I had been spending time at a boxing gym, enjoying the physical release, and a trainer there said I had potential. So I went along and let him train me. I didn't have any life goals to speak of; I simply wanted to be away from my father and start a life of my own.

My father didn't end up caring about my departure. We kept in touch for a few years. He came to my wedding later on, then he faded. He eventually passed away from cancer, and when I attended the funeral, I realized I really knew nothing about the man.

Sienna is waiting for my response, picking at her food. I know she doesn't like delving into the past, and a part of me understands. The more we share, the harder it will be to let go when our time is up.

Even if, deep down, I know it's already too late for me.

"I needed an escape," I say finally, opting for a simpler version of the truth. "I loved the thrill of training, the satisfaction of winning. It made me feel powerful at a time when I didn't have much control over my life. Dominating opponents was intoxicating."

She nods. "And why did you stop—" she begins, then catches herself. "Uh, never mind. That's probably telling me too much."

She's right. I stopped because of Tiffany's mental health, and once we go deeper down that rabbit hole, my mystery woman will know the most important parts of me; primarily, how I'm a failure.

I know she's already leaving when our time is up, but if there's any chance she might stay, knowing my darkest secrets will make her run, regardless.

Not talking about our pasts…it's for the best.

We lapse into silence. The only sounds are the clink of silverware against plates around us and the murmurs of nearby conversations. I watch her, noting the way her eyes dart around the table like she's wrestling with something internally. It's a push and pull I've become familiar with— one moment she's open, the next closed off and distant.

I think back to yesterday, to the way we held each other. The comfort she offered was unlike anything I've experienced. Most people who meet me already know about Tiffany, thanks to all the fucking news articles. So the women I'm with treat me like a lost puppy looking for shelter.

That pity pisses me off.

But this woman across the table, she seems to understand, though she doesn't yet know the full story. She hasn't pitied me or treated me like a wounded bird needing to be mended. She's simply been…here.

Like she understands that life's cruelty is a given; all we can do is desperately cling to each other, hoping to survive.

But we each still have our walls. We're both fighting against the current, trying to keep our heads above water even as we're drawn deeper into whatever this is between us.

Realizing we both need a reprieve, I decide to steer us back to safer waters. "So, CSI: Cyber. Did you waste your time watching it?"

My unexpected comment earns me a laugh, and she's looking more comfortable again.

We spend the rest of dinner on lighter topics, then she

enjoys some of that crème brûlée. Afterward, we walk along the beach. The sound of the waves and the warmth of her beside me create a sense of peace I wish I could hold on to.

Back in our suite, I finally get to enjoy my dessert, tying her hands as I had envisioned. I make her leave the dress on as she comes all over my mouth. Then I fuck her—there's something I enjoy about dirtying expensive garments with sex. And as I pound her against the wall, tearing a slit in her dress while doing so, I imagine what it would be like if she were truly mine, if I could wake up to her smile every morning, fall asleep to the sound of her earth-shattering snores every night.

It's a future I crave, yet I'm terrified of pursuing. I might fail her again, like I failed Tiffany.

My mystery woman deserves better than that.

CHAPTER 19

DECLAN

THREE DAYS REMAINING.

The thought echoes through my mind as I stare at my reflection in the steamy bathroom mirror.

With heavy limbs—even though I've been sleeping better and feeling rested with M.W. in my bed beside me—I give myself a quick shave and then comb gel through my damp hair. I don't want to leave her today since the minutes are counting down, but I also have work responsibilities and need to attend at least some of the damn conference.

I run my thumb over the scar on my wrist, tracing the raised line of tissue. I hate looking at my scars; they only conjure images of blood on the tile and Tiffany's horrified brown eyes.

After our struggle that day, after I had the utility knife away from her, she had suddenly snapped back to herself like she'd been sucker punched. She gaped at the gashes she'd made on my body, tried to give me first aid even though I wanted to tend to her wounds first.

The way she had clung to me, sobbing and shaking, is still too vivid.

"Please…take me somewhere," she begged. "I'm so sorry. Take me…have me committed. I need help. I can't… can't do this…"

Our bodies were bloody from superficial wounds we needed to clean, but I sat on the edge of the tub, in the house we'd bought together just two years prior, holding her, rocking her, telling her it would all be okay. Touching her stomach where our son was growing, I told her we'd get through everything. I wouldn't leave. I would keep her safe. NexaProtect had taken off. We had money to pay for her care. All she needed to do was focus on feeling better and I would take care of everything else.

I took her to the best mental hospital money could buy, held her hand as she checked herself in. I visited every day, brought her favorite garden and fashion magazines, told her how proud I was of her for getting help.

It felt like a fresh start; I had dreams of Tiffany returning to her vibrant, bubbly self. She'd birth our son, and she'd be happy. We'd both be happy. She had always wanted to be a mother, so I thought our son would heal everything.

After one month into the three-month program, she begged me to come home. "I miss you," she told me during one of my visits, her face pale and drawn. "I can't stand being away from you. I don't like this place. There are too many people talking all the time and I'm exhausted. I'm already feeling so much better. My head is clear again, and I just want to be home and tend to my garden. This environment isn't good for the baby."

My gut told me not to listen—she needed intensive therapy and someone making sure she took her medications.

I should have said no.

But I was weak. I missed her too, missed our life together. I thought I could handle it, could be there for her in a way the doctors couldn't.

I was wrong. And it cost me everything.

I grip the edge of the marble bathroom counter and hunch forward, pain splitting my head open. Those memories are something I keep locked away, trying only to think of them only once a year on the anniversary of when Tiffany left. But my mystery woman has compromised so much inside me. I've been craving to know everything about her, and my scars were a bargaining chip. I wasn't sure she'd take the bait, if she'd be vulnerable in return, and now I've sunk even deeper into her.

Regardless, should she ever become mine, she'd end up another possession I fail to keep safe. I couldn't protect Tiffany from her own demons. What makes me think I could do any better with M.W.? She's clearly running from something. If I let her in, let myself care, how long before whatever she's fleeing catches up to her? When it does, will I be powerless yet again, watching as someone I care for slips away, knowing I should have done more, been more?

Or she could choose to simply leave me behind. Leave me in an empty house with questions that have no answers.

With a retching sigh, I release the bathroom counter. I need to stop letting these repetitive thoughts cycle in my head. I need to focus on getting ready for the day.

I walk to the closet and start picking out clothes. M.W. stirs on the bed after I'm mostly dressed and buttoning my gray shirt. I try to move quietly, but as I grab my watch off the nightstand, she groans. She's laying on her stomach, her bare back exposed while sheets cover the rest of her, and her eyes flutter to give me a half-awake glance and a slight curve of her lips.

"Have a good day," she mumbles.

The simple phrase, the casual domesticity, is a profound pang through my chest. It's been so long since I had this, since someone saw me off in the morning with a smile.

I walk to the bed, brushing a strand of hair off her

shoulder. Her skin is warm, and it's hard to resist the urge to climb back in beside her, to lose myself in her softness for yet another day.

I want to take her back to San Francisco with me. Want to ask her why she's so determined to stay in Hawaii, what she's running from. I want to be the one she runs to, the one who protects her.

At the same time I yearn for that, I know I'm too fucked up, too haunted by my ghosts. It's too selfish to try to make her mine.

I press a gentle kiss to her forehead. "I'll see you this afternoon," I whisper, my lips lingering on her skin. Then I tap the new cell phone on the nightstand, the one I bought her yesterday. I still don't believe her story about what happened to her old one, but what matters is that I have a way to contact her again, something I may need more than she does. "Text me if anything comes up or just to say hi."

She nods, pulling the sheets up to cocoon herself in my bed.

My bed—I'd rather she never sleeps anywhere else.

With a heaviness in my gut, I force myself to pull away, to walk out the door before I can change my mind. The door clicks shut behind me as I enter the hallway; it's a hollow, echoing sound.

"You want me here?" Sean asks, sitting in a chair and reading like always. He flicks a long black bang from his eyes.

Jeremy is down the hall looking bored, like he's tired of hanging out in his and Sean's suite.

I adjust my watch, trying to shift my mind to business and away from the woman sleeping in my bed. "Yeah. Both of you should stay here with M.W. I'll be fine."

"Got it."

I SETTLE INTO MY SEAT, just one among a sea of people. I'm attending a panel that's discussing global security challenges, sipping a coffee I picked up near the entrance of the convention center. Hope it'll help me focus because my mind is not into this today.

As a man steps up to a podium and starts introducing the panelists, I scan the room. I met with a lot of founders from startups today. They're always a gamble to partner with but can sometimes pay off big. Regardless, I'm hunting someone more elusive: John Nakamura, the CEO of a casino group with a lot of Vegas properties. Davis heard from a contact that Nakamura would be here. His properties had a huge security breach recently, which shut down operations for an entire three days, costing hundreds of millions. He's likely antsy for better security services—something my company is more than happy to provide. But he's a hard man to reach. Davis thought I might 'bump' into him here. It's a longshot, but worth a try.

As one panelist answers a question about GDPR compliance, my mind wanders to the woman I hope is still naked in my bed. This coffee is useless. I take another sip and give up on trying to focus.

Completely distracted now, I pull out my phone and shoot her a quick text, telling myself it's only so I can check that she's using the phone I bought her.

Me: *Morning again.*

I roll my eyes at my bland message. As I'm trying to

think of something to add, she responds with a picture that gets my heart pumping.

It's a simple shot of her laying in my bed, her arms stretched high to give me a bird's-eye view of her gorgeous face and smile. Her short black hair is splayed around her head, looking adorably messy, and she's still a little sleepy-eyed. I brush my thumb over the soft freckles that are only under her eyes.

I completely forget where I am for a moment; the world becomes a dull hum around me. She's my singular focus, an all-consuming beacon, a magnetic pull that I'm powerless to resist.

In a move that's not like me at all, I snap a selfie and hit send. I follow it with: **Thought you might like to see how much you made me smile.**

Then I rub my chin, wondering how I suddenly developed a glass jaw. But I think I'm enjoying it; my cheeks hurt from grinning so wide.

When's the last time I felt so…giddy?

The crowd around me laughs at something, snapping me back to this stuffy conference room. When I think about staying here in search of a unicorn versus going back to the suite to be with my mystery woman, I feel like an idiot for even wasting a moment debating it.

There's no question what I want.

I stand and hurry through the rows of chairs to the exit. Once I'm outside the room, I turn left toward the entrance of the convention center.

My phone buzzes, and I'm hoping she sent another picture. But it's not her; it's Davis.

I have a few minutes of walking until I'm outside, so I answer.

"Hey," I say, moving closer to the walls where there are fewer people.

"Any sightings of Nakamura?"

"Nope."

He sighs, and his voice is tighter and edgier than normal. "Well, that's disappointing. But, hey, do you have a few minutes? There's a situation." Davis is normally a cheerful guy who always looks at the glass half-full, so the serious tone of his voice makes me stop.

"Yeah, one second." I move to a small outside balcony, away from the people and chatter. The sun is blinding after being inside for so long, so I step into a shaded area, glancing down at the street below, which doesn't have much traffic. "Okay. What is it?"

Another heavy sigh, which he rarely does. He's not one to waste sighs on small matters, so my concern is peaking.

"What?" I ask again, my stomach coiling tight.

"We've, uh…we've been getting some strange emails over the past couple of days. Threatening ones."

My grip tightens on the railing around the balcony. "What kind of threats?"

"At first, we thought it was just your run-of-the-mill scammer or troll. Some college kid trying to be funny by getting access to our internal messaging system. Like some kind of 'fuck you' to big business. You know, just a dumb kid. Because the emails weren't threatening at first. They were literally just bad knock-knock jokes."

"And?" Sometimes Davis doesn't get to the point fast enough for my liking.

"And, well, yesterday they started flooding in non-stop. Employees are getting swamped with the same emails and they're struggling to weed through them all to find important ones from clients. We've set up filters and adjusted the server settings to mitigate the flood, but it's been only partially effective." Yet another sigh. "But there's"—he clears his throat—"About the email we started getting yesterday… well…"

I make a fist, digging my fingernails hard into my palm. "Will you just tell me? You know I hate when you tiptoe around shit." I don't enjoy sounding so gruff, but he's got me concerned with how he's hesitating to say what's so damn threatening about these emails.

He clears his throat. "Um, I'm just going to send it to you. Before you read, though, just know that we're tracing the source, and we already set up a temporary server for employees to use. We're monitoring the new server, and so far, the flood hasn't replicated there. One second. Okay. Sent you a screenshot."

I lower my phone to check the image. As I read the single sentence, my blood runs cold, a sick feeling rising in my throat. There's no question what the email is about.

Does the world know about the baby?

Fury crashes over me like a relentless wave, so intense it nearly takes my breath away. How dare they. How dare they fucking bring up my son.

And how the fuck do they know? I hid every last record so the vultures in the press wouldn't speak about him. The only person who knew was Davis, and I'm completely certain he'd never betray me.

"Find them," I grit out, my voice pulling zero punches as I try to contain my rage. "I don't care what the hell it takes, Davis. Fucking find them."

"I know. I know. We're working on it. And"—his voice

lowers—"no one understands the message. They just think the hacker is talking nonsense. I don't think anyone will link it to you."

"Doesn't matter because this asshole knows. What if they send something to the press?" My pulse is hammering now. It would devastate Tiffany's family, bring the wrong attention to NexaProtect. "Fuck. Who could…"

"I don't know, but I promise I'm throwing every resource I can into this. I've got our team working overtime. I know you're not due back until Sunday, but you might want to scrap the hunt for Nakamura and return ASAP."

I drum my fingers on the railing, too many thoughts flooding me all at once. "That would be best," I tell Davis.

What about the remaining days I thought I had with *her*? I want those days because they're all I get.

Three entire days of my enigmatic mystery woman just…gone?

I might murder this asshole hacker when we find them.

I shove a hand through my hair, pulling on the roots. Davis doesn't exactly know I'm here with a woman. "I don't know yet," I say. "I trust our team to find the source, but I know my presence can help. I'll be here at least one more day and then…" Then she's gone from my life forever. Unless I convince her to finally tell me what she's running from—ask her to return home with me and make this more than just a fling.

That's a risky step because if I ask for a relationship, she'll eventually learn about my past. My failures. I have a lot of baggage and ghosts; I can't ask her to take that on with whatever she's dealing with.

"There's one more thing," Davis says.

I close my eyes, trying to brace myself as I'm still

processing the last blow. What kind of fucking asshole would flood my company with an email like that? I've made a lot of people unhappy over the years, but I can't think of any true enemies, not someone who would do something like this. "What else?"

Thankfully, he doesn't tiptoe around the issue this time. "Halliwell has been trying to get in touch with you. Insistently. He says it's extremely urgent."

"I thought I made myself clear—we're done with him."

"I know, but he's insisting on speaking with you directly. He says he won't stop calling until you contact him."

I rub a hand over my face, suddenly feeling like all the strength has drained from my muscles. All I want is to go back to the suite, lose myself in the woman who is waiting for me, and escape the rest of the world.

Maybe that's impossible.

"Just ignore him," I tell Davis. "He struck me as a whiny man who doesn't like losing, so he's probably trying to throw some clout around to get us to partner with him. Just focus on the emails because I want to personally murder whoever sent them."

Davis laughs nervously. "I know you don't really mean that."

I stay silent. Ultimately, it wouldn't be good for my company's reputation if I did something so reckless. Doesn't mean I don't *really* want to.

"Right," Davis says. "I'll keep you updated."

"Thanks for handling this. It's…I appreciate everything you do. Thanks for always being in the trenches with me."

I hear a smile in his voice. "Of course. You'd be useless without me."

He's damn right about that.

I hang up, slipping the phone back into my pocket. My head is spinning, my gut churning, and I really do need to punch something. Before I get to the suite, I'll stop by a gym. I don't even care about changing. I just need to smash my fists against a bag.

Does the world know about the baby?

Moisture pools at the corners of my eyes. I can't think about that fucking email or my son right now. If my time here has been cut short, if I can only allow myself one more day before reality comes crashing in, then I'm going to make the most of it. I want to be completely consumed by M.W. and forget everything else.

I take a breath, walking back inside and turning again toward the convention center's exit. A quick stop at the gym to get my head straight, then I can return to my mystery woman. Once I'm back, I'm not leaving the suite again until our time is up.

That's the plan. Of course, once I'm near the exit, I see my unicorn: John Nakamura. I yank off my tie because it's too tight around my neck. Then I stuff it in my pocket. *The fucking timing.* I'd really be an idiot not to talk with him, and I have responsibilities to my company and the people I employ.

What an irritating day this is turning out to be. Quickly, I pull out my phone, seeing that M.W. sent a heart emoji to my previous text, along with: *You make me smile a lot, too, handsome.*

Her words relax some of my tension, and she's really tempting me to say 'fuck it' and return to her right now. But the more sensible part of me responds: *Give me two hours. Then I'll come back to you and we'll be the only two people in the world.*

Straightening and plastering on a polite expression, I walk toward Nakamura.

CHAPTER 20

SIENNA

FACES WEREN'T DESIGNED TO SMILE this much. It's like my mouth is permanently stuck in a goofy grin.

For a solid ten minutes, I've been on the patio, distracted from my painting because I keep staring at Declan's selfie. I study each sharp curve of his features, the luminous light in those blue eyes as he smiles, the loose hair brushing his forehead. When I first met Mr. Intense, Overpowering, And Chiseled, I never imagined he could ever look so…cute. I see a tenderness in him now, behind all that brooding.

It's doing all kinds of things to my heart.

We'll be the only two people in the world.

God, those are the kind of words that might make me stay.

I want to.

I want to do much.

Just the two of us forever…what an amazing thought.

After dinner yesterday, we walked along the beach just being happy together. It was so normal. So wonderfully, blissfully normal.

We held hands, stealing kisses and smiles from each other. He even grabbed my waist and playfully suggested we go swimming since I said I'd never actually swam in the ocean.

"But we have clothes on," I told him.

"Why does that matter?" he shot back. "It'll be the first

time either of us has done it. A memory together."

I convinced him not to carry me into the waves, but it was a side of him I'd never seen—carefree and utterly adorable. And the way he looked at me was like I was the only person in the world who mattered. Like I was precious, cherished. Perfect, just as myself.

My heart cracked a little, both from wanting to wrap my arms around him and never let go, and because he only knows one part of me.

He'd never look at Margaret that way.

I finally close his picture and set my phone on the patio table beside me. Then I pick up a brush to add the final finishing touches to Declan's portrait. As I gaze at his likeness on the canvas, I can't help but wonder: What if this wasn't just a temporary escape? A fling?

What if this could be real?

Hope blooms in my chest even as terror bleeds in. Wanting something, really wanting it…that's when there's the most to lose.

But God, I want this. I want him.

I want lazy mornings tangled in sheets. I want deep conversations about everything and nothing and comfortable silences.

I want a love that feels like coming home.

With Declan, I can almost see it, taste it, touch it.

He doesn't have to learn about Margaret, does he? I can just tell him I have a crazy ex—like *extra* crazy—and then see what he thinks. I know he couldn't disappear with me since he has a business to run, but maybe we could do a long distance thing? I would flee to another country and he'd visit me on the weekends. He has a private jet.

Shaking my head, I laugh at myself because it all sounds

ridiculous. Who wants a long distance relationship? No matter what, I have to disappear, so that's all I could offer Declan—me at a distance.

My gaze falls on the long scars I've painted on his neck and wrist, the ones he usually keeps hidden beneath crisp dress shirts and expensive watches. His eyes held so much raw pain when he spoke about his ex-wife. I'm wondering if this portrait is a terrible mistake.

Sometimes I get too absorbed in a painting and continue purely on instinct. But it doesn't always work out; the failure of my past paintings has shown me I may have a really shitty artists' intuition. When I first started blocking out this portrait, it felt powerful to highlight his scars, making them blue like his eyes and the ocean in the background. Now I'm sick with doubts.

What if seeing the scars, even in paint, is too much for him? What if it reopens old wounds?

I set down my brush, chewing my lip as I study the canvas. Maybe I can change it. Paint over the scars, blend them into shadows and highlights. It feels wrong, like I'm erasing a part of him, a part of his story. I also don't want to cause him any hurt.

While I'm staring at the painting and trying to decide, I hear the suite door open. I turn to find Sean poking his head in, black hair covering his eyes so much I wonder how he sees sometimes.

When his head swivels toward the patio, he points his chin at me. "Did you order room service?"

I'm about to say no when I realize Declan must've sent it as a surprise. He's done that a few times, and I am a little hungry. "Yes. Thank you."

Sean opens the door wider and Jeremy wheels in the

cart.

Jeremy flashes a cheesy smile with his crooked teeth. "Working hard, huh?" he asks, leaving the cart in the middle of the room.

"Yeah. Almost done, though."

His eyes scan the room lazily as he backs his bulky frame toward the door. "Cool. Cool. Well, enjoy!" He and Sean leave.

I laugh to myself—I haven't talked to Jeremy much, but he's usually smiling and being goofy.

I hop off my stool and hurry to the cart. Last time, Declan sent fish and chips, which I had told him was a favorite dish of mine. I wonder what I'm getting today. The same thing or something new?

I lift the silver plate cover.

I drop it and the world around me instantly shatters. Metal clangs on the floorboards, echoing in my ears, but I can barely hear it through the rush of blood in my skull. I don't even gasp, just stagger back with a slack jaw and wide eyes and a haunting stillness in my body that only my racing heart challenges.

There's no food on the plate, only a white folded note next to an old flip phone.

And a crimson and blonde braid.

The stillness in me fractures—one hand clutches my stomach, the other covers my mouth and each shaky inhale.

Fuck, I can't breathe.

Jada's braid.

"No, no, no," I whisper, like I'm trying to cast a counterspell. I reach out a trembling hand, but I can't bring myself to touch the note or the braid.

My eyes dart around the room like Anthony is here,

watching me, but I'm alone. Sean and Jeremy are just outside the door. There's no way Anthony could be here, though I wouldn't rule out the possibility of him scaling a building.

Who delivered this? Sean must've accepted the cart from someone—an innocent server or someone pretending to work here?

Is Anthony here on the island or stalking me through his many contacts?

What if Sean or Jeremy are part of this?

What if Declan…?

Thoughts tangle in my head and I feel like I'm on the verge of trembling apart. I sit on the edge of the couch to force myself to take deeper breaths. Spiraling into 'what ifs' won't help. I need to calm the fuck down and think rationally. Trying to look at evidence and strategize is what helped me survive all these years, so I can't just have a freak out.

I take a breath. When I look at the evidence, Declan can't be part of this. Meeting him was random, and Anthony is very territorial. He likes to play games, so he'd never want me to be with another man.

Somehow, though, Anthony found me.

He found my friends.

Jada.

I choke out a sob, my breath coming in shallow bursts again. What if he hurt Jada or Mystical?

I've been so stupid—I shouldn't have made any friends. I got careless. I trusted my new life too much, felt too safe. I don't know how Anthony got out of jail so many years early, but that's exactly what he always does. He always gets what he wants, no matter the cost.

Wiping my face, a patchwork of hot currents burn through me, and I return to the serving cart. I grab the note and read it.

> *Why did you run from me, baby? I miss you. But you know I love our little games, so I'll give you this one single pass. Run again and I'll slit more than just your friend's hair. Call me. Can't wait to hear your voice, Magpie.*

He signed it with a heart.

I shred the note into pieces and let them fall on the tray.

Jada.

What did he do to her?

Since he already knows I'm here, I have to call her. I need to know she's okay, even if she hates me for bringing such a violent man into her life.

God, she must hate me so much.

I walk to the patio on trembling legs to grab my phone, then fear squeezes my heart so tight that I can't bring myself to actually call.

I'm nothing but a coward.

Instead, I send her a text, thankful that I memorized her number: ***Please tell me you're okay. ~S***

She replies instantly: ***Sienna??? Where are you??? I'm okay. Are you okay???***

I exhale. Safe. She's safe.

Before I can respond, she messages again: ***There was a prick who came to our house a few days ago looking for you. Complete fucking psycho. Pulled a gun and took some of my hair...??? I fucking called the cops but they're useless. Are you okay? He was wearing a mask but I saw his arms. A Black guy with a tattoo of a bleeding rose. Know anyone with that tattoo? He wouldn't tell me his name. But he had a gun and kept demanding I tell him where you were. I***

*didn't know. I told him about Declan. I'm sorry. I was so
scared.*

A tear hits my phone screen. A Black man with a rose
tattoo? That wasn't Anthony then. Must be one of his men.

Me: *It's okay. Don't apologize for that. I'm so glad
you're okay. Mystical is okay?*

Jada: *Yes, but where are you? ARE YOU OKAY??*

Counting my heartbeats, I consider my response carefully. I can't tell her anything because I've already put her in
too much danger. The more she knows, the more she'll be
pulled deeper into Anthony's twisted games.

At least…at least I get to say goodbye.

The tears continue to flow as I type, making it hard to
see: *I'm so sorry for involving you in this mess. I can't tell
you more. I'm just so, so sorry. I love you. You've been the
best friend I've ever had. The only person who has cared
about me so much and made me feel like family. You're
like my sister and I want you to have the best possible life.
One day, I'm going to see your name listed in a Broadway
play or as a choreographer for someone famous, and I'm
going to smile and feel so proud of you. I'm already proud.
You're such an amazing dancer. I know this is all confusing
and scary, but you have to forget about me. For your own
safety, just forget. I want you to be safe and far, far away
from my mess. I'm sorry but I can't ever contact you again.
Tell Mystical he was a great roomie and I'll miss him too.
I wish him the best. Thank you for everything, Jada. I love
you.*

I don't know how else to end, so I just hit send.

She starts blowing up my phone:

What???

What U talking about?

Talk to me! What—

I block her number, then fall into sobs, tossing the phone on a patio chair and just crouching. I crouch and hug my knees as sobs rip from my throat. It's like I've fallen off a cliff, falling and falling, and I keep waiting to splatter on the ground, but I don't. I only keep falling.

During this trip, I thought I was finally getting to a place where I could forget Sienna's life and move on. But talking to Jada brought every ounce of agony back.

The flip phone vibrates, clattering against the plate on the serving cart. My eyes dart to it as I suck in a breath. Every fiber in my body wants to toss that phone over the patio railing, but Anthony will only make good on his promise to hurt Jada.

He's not a man who likes to be kept waiting.

Forcing myself to move, I scurry to the cart and grab the phone. The negative space of the room swallows me. There's no more running; he has me cornered.

I flip open the phone and press the green answer button.

"Well, hey, Magpie," he says, his voice like barbed wire pricking my old scabs to create new wounds.

Until now, he only existed in my memories as a silhouette. Now the blackness is bleeding away, giving him highlights and detail. I picture him as I last saw him—a towering shadow, his dark hair slicked back in that meticulously neat style he favored. Piercing black eyes. A tarnished smirk playing on his thin lips.

The day I left for good, he had been in his apartment

talking with some men. He'd been wearing a fitted wool jacket over a dark gray shirt that clung to his frame. His pants were deep navy and perfectly tailored, not a crease out of place, and his boots, black and polished like they had just been unboxed. A single gold chain with a cross hung around his neck. I always thought that was ironic—a man like him wasn't going to heaven.

I heard the name Londyn Seever, some actress that Anthony's boss, Victor, had been focused on. I didn't know what any of their conversation was about because I'd done my best not to get involved with 'business,' only business Anthony wanted me part of.

But that day, I was done—no more dirty work, no more hurting people. That night, I ran to the safe house the authorities had promised me. That night Margaret died.

Now Anthony wants to resurrect her.

I can't find my voice, but I let out a few soft whimpers.

"Aww, what's wrong, baby?" Anthony coos, trying to sound caring. His voice is too sharp for that.

I don't even know what to say because he's caught me and I already know what he wants. I finally croak out, "I'm here."

His chuckle is like broken glass. "Oh, I know, baby. I know exactly where you are. How'd you bag a guy that rich? Declan Conte. Didn't finish high school. Started as a boxer and had some success. Got married to a ring girl then made a career shift and started a tech company. I don't know how someone without an education created a multi-million-dollar company, but I guess some bastards are lucky." He laughs to himself. "Or maybe not since he drove his wife to kill herself."

I suck in a sharp breath. *What?* I thought they got

divorced. I thought…

Oh god no. Poor Declan.

That's why he didn't want to keep talking about his wife, because she…

I squeeze out more tears as a thousand-pound boulder seems to crush my heart. "He didn't…he didn't do that. She was struggling. She had bipolar disorder and…" What do I care what Anthony thinks? I don't. I just don't like anyone accusing Declan, such a caring man, of 'driving her' to that. When he told me about his scars, it was clear how much he loved her and fought to get her help.

"Don't be so blind, baby," Anthony says. "The media always lies. You're with a dangerous man and you don't even know it." His voice gets tight and he snaps, "You could show me some *fucking* gratitude for coming to rescue you."

I want to scream at him, tell him to fuck off, but that would only result in terrible consequences. So I ball my hand into a fist and swallow my bitter words.

He makes a smacking sound like he's cleaning his teeth with his tongue. He sighs long and deep. "You get twenty-four hours to leave that man, or I'll start killing off your friends. You know I'm not lying."

"I know." I choke back a sob; Margaret watched him hurt plenty of people.

"Twenty-four hours. See? I care, baby. I do. I'm not *trying* to hurt others, so don't force me to do it. I know I've been gone a long time. You got lonely. That's okay, baby. But if you want your friends and that man alive, then you need to leave in a way that's natural, so he won't follow. Got it?"

I swallow. "Yes."

"That's my girl. And I'm sure you already know this, but don't do anything stupid. I paid off his bodyguard. Fuck this up and the rich guy dies while you watch."

The call ends.

I'm so wrecked, so shocked, that I can't even let out my sob.

He'd make me watch?

Of course he would.

My next thought is, *Which bodyguard?*

Then a protective shell hardens around my heart. Nothing matters right now except keeping my loved ones safe. I won't let my friends or Declan get hurt.

I wipe my wet cheeks. No more crying. Sienna doesn't run, she faces the storm. Shuffling through all the inspirational quotes I've filed away in my brain, I pick one to get me through the next 24 hours: *"Strength grows in the moments when you think you can't go on but keep going anyway."*

I have to keep going, especially since lives are on the line. It was naïve of me to even think I could have a future with Declan; anyone who gets close to me gets hurt. My focus now is keeping him safe.

If I'm honest with myself, though, I've already fallen for him. He fills me with the warmest, most pigmented feelings I've ever known. I feel safe with him; he's protective, generous. And he's been through so much, yet kept going for the sake of his company, for the sake of donating his money and…

Yes, I have strong feelings.

Whatever I have to do to keep Anthony away from him, I'll do it. I'll need to break Declan's heart in a cruel, messy way. I'll have to destroy him, so there's no chance he'll follow.

I'll tear him down, as much as it will kill my soul to do that.

By the end of today, he needs to hate me.

I just have to find the strength to do it, because every time he's near me, he pulls me into his orbit and I never want to leave his arms…

I have to be strong about this.

Then, to ensure his safety and the safety of my friends, I'll give Anthony what he's always wanted: me. No more running. No hiding. I'll get his attention off the people I care about.

After that…I don't know.

One step at a time.

I gather the torn note and burn the pieces in a small metal bowl, dumping the ash when I'm done. Then I stuff Jada's braid and the flip phone in my luggage.

When I'm done cleaning up, I place the silver plate cover back in place and wheel the cart into the hallway. Jeremy is down the hall in the middle of a yawn. He glances at me, then looks down at his phone, uninterested.

Sean is the only one who makes eye contact, lowering his book. Through his thick, deceptive bangs, his gaze follows me as I slip back into the suite.

CHAPTER 21

DECLAN

WHEN THE ELEVATOR DOORS FINALLY open, I jog through the hallway toward the suite. Thankfully, talking to Nakamura didn't take long—he was very interested—and we scheduled a time for me to fly out to Vegas for an official meeting. Then I only spent a half hour at the gym letting out my anger and frustration with a sparring partner. My head is clearer, I'm back at the hotel, and I'm ready to burrow myself in a bubble with M.W. for the next twenty-four hours.

I pass Jeremy with a quick wave and then can't hide my smile from Sean as I approach the door.

He smiles back. "You look more upbeat than when you left."

"Happy to be here. There's a shit show at work, so we'll have to cut this trip short and leave tomorrow."

"Got it"—he nods his head at the door—"Will she be joining us?"

Same question I have. It's clear she doesn't want anything serious, and even if she does, she'll likely hate the weight of my baggage.

I've been going back and forth about it. Ultimately, it seems we might be two people on separate paths, no matter how much I want it otherwise.

I'll offer her a trip home, but even if she takes it, ending things with our fling might be best.

It's a crushing thought.

I bypass Sean's question and ask, "Anything eventful happen while I was gone?"

"Nope. She's just been painting."

I enter the suite. Despite the situation at work still weighing on me, some of the burden lifts when I see M.W. sitting on the couch facing the open French doors. It's a warm, bright day, the living room bathed in welcoming sunlight. I cross the space, running my fingers through her black strands when I'm close enough.

"Hi," she says softly, still gazing out at the ocean.

"Hi, beautiful." I move around to the front of the couch, ready to pull her into my arms, but it's like I hit an invisible fist.

My body tenses. Something feels…off about her expression, her posture. Everything about her is strained and artificial.

I sit beside her, caressing her knee. "Something wrong?"

Her eyes dart to mine, flashing wide with alarm, then she gives me a plastic smile. The next second, the smile drops and her brows become weights, crushing shadows over her eyes. I blink and she's smiling again.

It's like she can't get her face under control—a jumble of dueling expressions.

"Oh, uh…no. It's…" She pulls me into a hug. "How was the conference?"

I press my palms against her back, feeling the rigid muscles, the jutting of her shoulder blades. She's not melting against me like she has been these past few days. "I couldn't concentrate," I say. "And there's a situation at work we should talk about later." I pull back. She's still fighting with her smile. "What's wrong?"

She attempts to relax the unyielding grooves in her forehead, then she grabs my lapels and pulls me into a kiss.

It feels too good to kiss her after such an irritating day, so I indulge for a moment, cupping her cheek and sighing my pleasure. Her rigid posture finally softens, and she exhales against my lips, letting my tongue explore her mouth.

Fuck, this is too good, too intoxicating.

I have to pull away because my gut knows something is off. My chest constricts when I notice the tear sliding down her cheek. "Tell me what's wrong," I say, brushing the moisture away with my thumb. "I don't enjoy seeing you upset."

Somehow, my words only fill her expression with more sadness, her gaze withering downward. All I want is to fix whatever the problem is so I can see her happy again. Whatever is causing her pain, I'm ready to burn the world down to stop it.

"I know," she says. "That's why you're so wonderful, Declan."

Bringing her hand to my mouth, I kiss each knuckle. "I appreciate that vote of confidence. Now tell me what happened."

She studies the ocean as if hoping to find something out there. Finally, she says, "I finished the portrait, but I'm worried you might not like it."

"That's all?" The knot loosens in my gut, and I encourage her to stand with me. "I can't imagine not liking it. Show me."

"It might trigger you."

She's really piquing my curiosity with that comment. What did she paint? "It'll be fine. Show me."

She leads me to her bedroom. The easel is near the

window and a towel covers the canvas. My fingers are itching to uncover it and see what she's so concerned about. I know she has insecurities about her art, but I find her pieces magnetic.

"I'm sorry," she says as we stop in front of the easel.

"Don't apologize before I've even seen it. And don't apologize after. Never feel remorseful for self-expression, no matter how anyone else feels. Art is meant to evoke a range of emotions; the stronger, the better."

I don't think my words are comforting because her shoulders are still drooped as she grabs the edge of the towel. "Well, hate was not what I was going for. I got lost in the concept and…I just don't know. You'll see." She hesitates to reveal the portrait, so I do it for her, tugging the towel off and tossing it aside.

I inhale slowly.

The portrait is an assault—mesmerizing, provocative, putting me in a clinch and not backing down.

I'm speechless. Frozen.

There I sit on the canvas, off center on the bed and gazing at the viewer with an expression that's a mixture of so many emotions. I sense grief, longing, hope, a kindness that's also jagged and commanding. How did she possibly capture all that in a few brush strokes? My gaze is guarded, vulnerable, warm yet icy. The entire painting is black and white except for bold blue eyes, the faint blue of the ocean framed in the windows, and…

I lean closer to take in the details. The scars on my body are blue. What a perfect parallel to make—the history of those scars connected to the raw emotion in my eyes, while the rest of my body is polished and in control.

But that gaze isn't in control. Nor the scars. And the

ocean is…a loss of certainty with a longing for freedom. There's a tiny boat on that ocean, and I interpret it as my thoughts seeking escape from everything else in the painting.

Escape from the past. Myself.

True escape.

However, to be on that boat, I have to give up control and face the chaotic ocean.

She's studying me as I'm staring at the painting in a daze. Her voice is shallow. "Say something. Please."

"There are no words."

She sniffs, her voice straining against her throat. "Then you do hate it. I'm so sorry. I know I should've taken the scars out. It wasn't a good decision to leave them. I never make good decisions."

"I don't hate it. This painting is—" My eyes finally fall to the bottom corner of the canvas, where there are faint letters almost hidden around the edge of the bed. A signature.

Sienna.

I find her gaze and suddenly, she's no longer a mystery. My entire world just expanded. "Perfect," I say, her name ringing in my head. "This painting is a perfect portrait of me. Your name is perfect." After moving closer, slowly, since she looks on-edge, I caress her cheek. "Sienna. Why does it feel like I knew that?"

This captivating woman…how has she appeared in my life for such a short time, and yet seen me so completely?

Her bottom lip is pinched between her teeth, and she won't meet my gaze. "You really think it—"

My mouth crashes against hers, savoring her gasp. Since words are too much of a struggle, this is a better way to express myself.

CHAPTER 22

DECLAN

I NEED THIS WOMAN.

I crave every inch of her, every smile, every heartbeat, every broken piece she's afraid to show.

Sienna.

She has to be mine.

I've been too conflicted and insecure up to this point. Full of so many doubts. But I've decided. Whatever it takes, I can't let her fucking walk out of my life, no matter how undeserving I am.

I'll find a way to become deserving. Though I failed in the past and lost Tiffany, that doesn't mean I'll fail again.

I have to try.

I've fallen in love, so there's no other option but to try.

Her hands clutch the front of my shirt, fingers twisting the fabric like she's afraid of falling if she lets go. I wrap my arms around her waist to keep her upright, then I hold her tight.

My mouth presses harder into hers and she lets out a soft whimper, pushing on my chest. I pull back, realizing I may be coming on too forcefully.

She's breathless, with burning pink cheeks and fluttering eyelashes, gazing up at me with worry twisting her brow.

I'm not sure why she's looking at me that way, but I try to give us both a moment to breathe by saying, "You're a magnificent painter. I don't know how you saw...everything.

That portrait is completely me."

After hesitating, she reaches up to touch the light stubble along my jaw. "You let me see everything. I only captured it."

I press our foreheads together. She's right. She created cracks in my walls, and now I'm ready to fall to my knees before her. "Tell me I can be inside you."

She weakens against me, lowering slightly as her knees bend, but I hold her steady in my arms. "Declan…"

"God, I need it."

"I thought…I thought you liked to make the demands. Be the one in control."

"Tell me, Sienna." Rolling my hips, I press my hardness against her and she moans. I'm ready to give up all control for this woman. "Don't fucking leave me in agony. Tell me."

"Yes."

In an instant, I lift her off the ground, walking forward until I can toss her back onto the bed. This isn't the time for play or buildup or patience. My need is too strong. I'm already shredding off my clothes, yanking my shirt over-head. She helps me with my buckle, and then my pants and briefs are on the floor. Thankfully, she's wearing a summer dress, and it's easy to remove. Finally, her bra and panties, the last barriers, are gone, and I press my naked, rigid form against her softness.

Her essence and grace envelopes me as I brace my hands on either side of her head and explore her mouth some more. She's clawing at me, squirming, meeting my tongue with hers in a messy dance. It's the sloppiest we've ever kissed, and I only crave more.

"You're staying with me," I rumble as I graze her neck with my teeth.

"What?"

"San Francisco. You're flying back with me and we're going to fix whatever you're running from."

Her eyes are round with surprise as she shakes her head.

I don't care—I won't accept no this time. I'll do everything possible to convince her that 'yes' is the only answer.

Raising myself, I grip her knees and spread her legs wide, gazing down at all of that glistening pink I'll do anything for. I want to bury my face in her beautiful pussy, but other needs are simply too strong at the moment. As a compromise with myself, I shove two fingers inside her so she gasps and bucks, clenching deliciously around my knuckles. Then I bring the fingers to my mouth, sucking and licking off her taste.

Her expression is a war between shock and lust, her eyes wide but her tongue running over her bottom lip. I grin, dipping my fingers in once more, then feasting on her essence. Grabbing her hips, I yank her closer, my cock prodding her delicious entrance.

"But," she says quickly, "a condom."

"I'm going to come in you."

Her cheeks deepen into an even lovelier shade of pink. "But you always…"

"Tell me, Sienna. Tell me I can."

Her mouth snaps shut, and she nods, bending forward and reaching for my shoulder, yanking me back down on top of her as I thrust deep into her wetness. "Come in me," she says through a moan. She wraps her legs around my hips and squeezes me closer.

A condom feels like nothing; the absence of sensation. There's only a numbing heat. But with that damn barrier gone, I can feel all of her—every varying depth and shifting pressure in a warm, slick embrace.

It's my soul connecting to hers, our bodies uniting as one.

My thrusts are hard and purposeful, each one stealing more of her breath until she's gasping and moaning. Gasping and moaning.

"I'm not letting you go," I say into her neck. "Sienna, you're staying with me."

I can't get enough of her name on my tongue. Can't get enough of her body, her primal gasps of pleasure and fingernails leaving marks on my back. The way she clenches around my cock, holding me, welcoming me home.

Can't get enough of the way she nibbles her lower lip when nervous and becomes an enigma while painting. Her giggles and push-back; her hand reaching out to clasp mine. The snores that shake the walls; the mess of her clothes and art supplies around my room. Her ambitions, playfulness, empathy.

Her. I'll never get enough of her.

"You have to stay," I whisper before a kiss.

Feeling all of her puts me in a trance. I'm completely inside her; she's completely enveloping me.

"You have to."

Each moan from her throat and buck of her hips becomes more frantic. Her body is tensing and writhing, urging me to thrust harder, deeper, faster. My balls tighten, but I hold out until I feel her body surrender. Until she's trembling and screaming and grinding me harder.

While her thighs shake, I finally spill inside her, cursing from the intensity, burying my face in her sweet-smelling neck and matching her moans and shaking limbs. Her scent, a mix of vanilla and sex, makes me drunk.

As the shudders of pleasure finally subside, I rest my forehead against her shoulder, both of us breathing heavily. With effort, I break our sweaty, flushed bodies apart and roll over to collapse on the bed. As I do, I bring her with me, cuddling her so she can rest her head against my chest.

Instead of us basking in the afterglow, however, the warm feelings coursing through me shatter when I hear her weeping.

I try to lift her chin and get her to look at me, but she dips her head, refusing.

"Sienna, what is it? Did I hurt—"

"No," she croaks. She clings to me as if her life depended on it.

I'm at a loss for words because I have no clue what's going through her head. The way her body opened up to me just now and matched my intensity told me she's feeling something. But whether it's lust or the feelings I have, I can't say.

Though she finally gave me her name, I know she's not one to open up easily when something is bothering her. It was hard enough just to get her to say she had fears about the painting.

I'm not the best with my emotions either, so I just wrap my arms around her, holding her close and safe. My lips brush her sweaty forehead, her hair. I nuzzle my cheek against her head, sighing deeply. And I stay silent, letting her weep if that's what she needs to do right now.

Through the silence and rhythms of our breathing, comes a question I wasn't prepared for: "What happened to your wife?"

An insatiable hollowness creeps into my chest, and I

stare up at the spinning ceiling fan. The hollowness spreads until my entire body is numb. This is a moment I've been avoiding and fearing for years. I've kept every woman at a distance, setting rules and boundaries for casual dating and hookups, and buried the day my life changed forever. Though there are a few news articles out there with surface-level details about Tiffany's death, the full truth is only known to a handful of people—needed medical examiners, a few authorities, one doctor, and Davis.

I always envisioned myself growing old alone—anything to avoid a situation like this. Yet, Sienna is in my life now and…and if I want her to stay, she should know the heavy baggage I carry. A relationship can't be built on lies and secrets. Not one I want to be in, anyway. Tiffany kept so much from me, and if I'm going to move forward with Sienna, honesty should be our foundation.

Or maybe I'll simply scare her away—she'll decide my demons aren't worth the hassle. My experiences with Tiffany do affect my need for control, something Sienna has often challenged.

I stroke her soft hair, gathering my thoughts. She asked, so I'm not going to skirt around the topic—I'll tell her every last painful detail. This is going to hurt, so why not just rip the Band-Aid off?

"Tiffany killed herself," I say, the fucking emotions already clawing at my voice and giving it frayed edges.

Sienna gasps, probably both at the truth and my blunt admission of it, but she's been with me long enough to know I'm straightforward.

Her palm presses into my chest. "I'm…so sorry. That's…unimaginable."

I wait, giving her time to ask for more details. I know

it's human nature to be curious. Because of the news stories, which reported on her suicide but nothing else, I've been asked one question too much in my life: *Why? Why would she do that?*

I've never known what to say because I don't have an answer. I've struggled for years to understand what Tiffany was thinking. All I know is that she was never herself in those depressive episodes. Like something took over her mind, convincing her to do things my Tiffany would never want.

"What happened?" Sienna finally asks.

For the first time, instead of deflecting or giving some minor detail so I can change the subject, I talk about it. "She...well, I mentioned she struggled with BD. It was something she'd been struggling with her entire life. She told me once she attempted suicide as a child. I couldn't fathom a child feeling so depressed that they could think to..." I clear my throat, trying to keep my voice from cracking. The more I talk, it's like I'm wandering deeper down a dark tunnel. What if I can't find my way out?

"She was happy around the time we met," I continue, trying to focus on the motion of the ceiling fan so I don't collapse into myself. "She found some helpful therapies, the right mix of medication. She was happy. We were happy. But she still had moments that made work difficult, so I wanted to support her. My boxing career was taking off, but she was more important to me, and I knew boxing would wear on my body eventually. It's not a career that's easy to do once you hit thirty. So I made a pivot. I'd met some people getting into tech and lucked out with those connections. They gave me a boost in the tech company I wanted to start. I actually didn't know shit about it, but I met Davis, who is now my

VP—" I glance down at Sienna, who is gazing at me with a softness that wraps around my heart.

I kiss her forehead and refocus—she doesn't need so much backstory. "Regardless, my company did well. Tiffany and I moved from a small apartment into a large house, and she was free to spend her days at home taking care of her mental health. She liked to hang out with friends, host small parties. That was a good time for both of us. Well... two major things happened in the span of two months—her brother died in an accident, and she became pregnant with our son." My damn voice cracks on the last word, so I clear my throat as hard as I can.

Sienna chews her bottom lip and looks like she's going to sob, so I train my eyes on the fan again, forcing myself to continue. What I tell her is something I've already relived over and over in my head for years. Inside, outside—it's the same pain.

"While she was trying to mourn the loss of her brother, her body was also changing rapidly from the pregnancy. It made all of her symptoms worse. Suddenly, her medicine wasn't working, or she stopped taking it. I never found out. Everything spiraled. My VP began managing the company while I stayed home with Tiffany. But nothing I did helped. She found no comfort in me. I was useless to her."

I pause because I'm fighting too much emotion clogging my throat; I need a moment to beat it back. Closing my eyes, I focus on the darkness. My mind is flashing through snippets of volatile days—Tiffany's manic pacing and clawing at her hair. Those bursts of energy that made her spend an entire day cleaning a house that wasn't dirty. The razors and bloodstains and talks about her life meaning nothing, that existence meant nothing because we're all doomed to die. Even the universe. She would always take things as far as possible—she would die, then all humans would die, then the sun, then the universe. And, in her mind, because everything had an end that meant nothing had a purpose.

So I would kiss her growing belly and say, "This is our purpose. We won't be around when the stars explode and the universe becomes black. But we have a purpose together. We're meant to live and raise our son so he can experience his own life and everything wonderful that comes with it."

In the end, I was pleading with her through all these philosophical debates. Yet, she spiraled deeper and deeper, shifting from 'life has no purpose' to 'you never loved me.'

I loved her. Loved her so much that when she was gone, I didn't know if I'd go on breathing.

Sienna rubs circles over my heart as I'm failing to beat the emotion back. I just surrender and let a few tears slip out. The release steadies my voice enough to continue. "At her darkest point, she said she needed help and wanted to go to a hospital. We found one with a three-month program where they could help her with the pregnancy changes and everything else. She was only there a month and then called me to pick her up. She begged and swore she was okay and feeling stable, but I knew it wasn't a good idea. I knew, and yet…"

Sienna shifts so her cheek can press against mine, and she strokes my hair. She's crying softly as she holds me. It's a kind, comforting embrace I haven't experienced in over a decade. Haven't allowed myself to.

She already knows how the story ends, so I don't continue. But my mind does.

I remember how I brought Tiffany home from the hospital and we had one blissful week together. Something felt off, but I ignored it, thinking she only needed to adjust to being home again.

Friday of that week, I went into my office for a few hours to check on some things for NexaProtect. I can't even remember what seemed so important at the time.

It was only a few hours.

When I left that office, Tiffany was no longer in the living room watching TV. She loved her garden, so it was the first place I looked.

I found her body in the fountain in the backyard. Red flowed from her neck. Red water. Red soaking into the white baby shoes I had bought for our son. A red-stained letter accusing me of so many things—never loving her, hating our baby, wishing she was gone so I could have a better life. The letter devolved into her saying she never loved me and how she'd be a horrible mother. Then it looped to the sun exploding and everything that exists falling into nothingness.

"I want to fall into nothingness now and get it over with."

So many random, running thoughts.

Those were her last thoughts.

She died thinking that I didn't love her, telling herself that I wanted her and our son out of my life.

I have dreams about him sometimes—what kind of man he would've become. How proud I'd feel, no matter what.

I'd feel proud and happy just to have him alive.

The emotions come up stronger and I choke, covering my wet face with the crook of my elbow. "She took our son," are the last words I say about it.

Sienna cries with me, and we hold each other.

I don't sense her recoiling or wanting nothing to do with my ghosts. Just as she's done before, she gives me her presence, her understanding, her acceptance that life happens and mistakes can never be undone. Somehow, you just have to keep living.

Within my pain, for the first time, I see a way forward. It's a brush stroke. Made by Sienna.

CHAPTER 23

DECLAN

I'M ON THE COUCH TRYING to distract myself with TV, but my knee won't stop bouncing. Sienna has been in the bathroom for two hours. When she went to take a shower after lovemaking, I offered to join her. She refused, but I figured she needed a little breather after such an emotional moment together.

I know I did.

So, at first, I wasn't concerned.

Then I walked into my bedroom. It was void of her belongings; her luggage was packed and waiting in a corner.

Still, I tried to brush it off and took a shower. I changed into a fresh pair of slacks and a blue shirt. Groomed myself.

I decided that Sienna may have gotten antsy about the mess in my room and wanted to tidy up. Though I haven't told her I need to fly home tomorrow, we are initially due to leave the day after that.

She could be someone who likes to prepare for things early.

There are innocent possibilities for her suitcase to be packed.

Then a half hour passed. An hour. Ninety minutes. I had to know she was okay, so I knocked on her bathroom door a few times. Her muffled voice gave me some comfort, but the shower was still running.

Now two hours are gone, and I can still hear the distant

rush of water. I've been struggling with flashbacks of Tiffany because she used to do the same thing. Tiffany would lock herself in the bathroom for hours with the faucets running. Sometimes she was in there hurting herself, sometimes only crying.

Often, it was just a long, relaxing shower.

Nothing I've observed has indicated Sienna is a danger to herself, but given my history, I'm on edge, like I'm sparring with an opponent blindfolded. I want to give Sienna her space if that's what she needs, but it is an excessive amount of time to be in the bathroom.

And her luggage is packed.

She packed it before I returned earlier, saw her painting, made love to her.

Why is her fucking luggage packed?

My stomach lurches, so I get up and walk to the patio. I stare at the peaceful blue ocean. It does nothing for me, so I return to the couch and try to watch whatever movie is playing. Five minutes pass.

Ten.

Fifteen.

Now she's been in there for two hours and fifteen minutes.

I fling myself off the couch because I can't stand this; I have to check again.

As I'm walking into her room, the water finally turns off. My pulse races. Since I'm already nearby, I sit on the edge of the bed to wait. My knee keeps bouncing, but I'm certain I'm worrying about nothing; she was likely in there just pampering herself.

Needing distraction, I stare at the portrait resting on an easel in the corner. How could Sienna not know how incredibly talented she is? There are artists making good money who would give anything to have her perception and artistic eye. The composition of her work is flawless. The level of detail—

The bathroom door creaks open, and I turn my head. Sienna is in the doorway. On the surface, she looks the same—same blue floral dress from earlier, black hair hanging damp and heavy around her head. Same beautiful dark brown eyes and rosy skin. Her entire face is shiny and flushed, but that's likely from all the steam she trapped in the bathroom.

That steam rolls out, making the surrounding air humid and dense.

She looks the same, but something in me knows this isn't the woman who walked into the bathroom two hours and fifteen minutes ago—there are too many hard lines in her body. She's like uncompromising steel, with a gaze that could cut titanium.

When our eyes lock, she stares me down. I offer a soft smile, trying to ease the sudden tension filling the space between us. Her response is to tip her head back slightly so her eyelids close halfway, looking down at me with ice in her pupils.

What the hell happened behind that closed door?

I stand so I can move closer, but her words stop me before I even take a step.

"I'm not happy, Declan."

Every muscle stiffens, her firm tone echoing in my head. "About what?"

"Everything. This place. You." She spits out the last word.

Rhythmically, I clench my jaw, trying to work through

this situation. I'm completely sucker punched.

I replay the events of this afternoon.

When I returned to the suite, she was sad, worried that I might get hurt by my depiction in the portrait.

We made love—which I'm certain was what happened because the way she clung to me and kissed me, the way her body wrapped around mine, wasn't mere sex. Unless she's an incredible actress.

Afterward, I shared my past. She comforted me. Cried with me.

Then she disappeared into the bathroom, emerging as someone I've never met.

I shake my head like that will suddenly make the pieces of this puzzle fall into place. "What specifically has you so unhappy? Have I done something to—"

She sighs dramatically and leaves the room.

I follow.

When she reaches the kitchenette, she snatches her phone off the counter—the one I bought her—and throws it on the tile. The screen cracks, likely rendering the phone unusable.

I stare in stunned silence.

While making fists, her small frame shakes as words erupt from her throat. "I just can't do this with you any-more."

Agitation is gnawing at my insides. *What the hell is going on?* "Do what? What have I done to—"

"I really tried, Declan. I did. I *tried* to like you because at first you seemed like an okay guy. You let me come to Hawaii with you and you paid for things, and that's all very sweet but…I don't think you're that good of a man, actually. You keep telling me these awful things about your past. I mean, I feel bad about your wife and I've obviously been crying for her. And it's so tragic what happened to that innocent baby. But how can I possibly like you now that you told me all of that?" She flings a hand to motion at her bedroom, as if I don't remember where I recently spilled my guts. "I'm not, I'm not happy. I need to get away from you."

I'm in such a state of confusion that her harsh words aren't yet registering. I can only focus on the way her hand is gripping the edge of the counter like she needs stability.

Taking a breath, she pushes her shoulders back and schools her face into an angry expression. Her mannerisms are odd—strained and forced. She narrows her eyes like looking at trash someone left on the street. "I understand how your wife felt."

"What?" I say, my voice like diamond—unbreakable and sharp. Her words are hitting now—hitting places inside me I didn't know she had the capability of stabbing so brutally.

Sienna must see something in my gaze that startles her because she takes a step back. Then she whips around, talking at the wall like she can't look at me as she slices me open with each word. "Haven't you wondered what kind of influence *you* had on her mental health? Honestly, I'm still getting to know you, and this is a bombshell. How do I know you're telling the truth about what happened? Maybe she couldn't stand to be around you. It's just a lot of red flags. I think...I think there could be something about you that... that eats away at a woman until she's desperate to escape." She moves toward my bedroom, where her luggage is waiting. "I already know you have control issues. You might be a manipulator, too. Your poor"—she clears her throat, still hiding her face from me—"your poor wife. Maybe she felt suffocated and trapped, and she didn't know how to get away. You're making me…I'm feeling like that and I've only been with you a week."

I watch, having an out-of-body experience, as she enters my room and then emerges a second later with her luggage. She storms to the exit and opens the door. Then she faces me, angry tears spilling down her cheeks as she reaches a crescendo. "I can't be with a man who could've been emotionally abusing his wife." Her voice cracks and she jabs her finger in my direction. "So just stay away from me, okay? Do *not* follow me. Do not contact me." Another crack, but she pushes forward. "I want nothing more to do with your shady past and your control issues. I hate you. I fucking *hate* you, and I regret the day we met. Stay the hell away from me, you fucking monster!"

She leaves and the door clicks shut, making her absence hit like thunder.

I huff out air, my lungs stalling, and I stand in the kitchen not breathing at all. Several minutes pass and I still can't inhale. Tightness and pressure build and the world dims around the edges until I'm almost drowning in inky blackness. It's the mark on my soul that began growing the day Tiffany and our son died. I've worried that one day it would swallow me completely in a desolate, empty feeling.

In this moment, I want nothing more than to surrender and let myself get consumed.

It's where I belong. In the darkness with Tiffany, in a universe that has imploded and where all light has died. Where nothing has purpose.

Why did I stay in my office so long that day?

Why couldn't I save my wife and son?

My body finally forces me to breathe, gasping for air.

My hands claw at the kitchen counter, then I press my back against it. My legs can't support me, so I slide to the ground, making fists and shaking.

And shaking.

And shaking.

I'm back to struggling for breath until my body sucks in air again, gasping.

The door opens and Sean pokes his head in, looking alarmed. "Boss, is everything—"

"Get the fuck out!" I roar because I need to do something with these emotions.

I need the strength to dig my fingers into the marble countertop and break it into pieces, punch holes in the walls, lift the coffee table and chuck it through the nauseatingly white French doors.

Something.

Anything to relieve the bottomless, dark ache that's consuming me.

But I can't get off this floor, so I sit here like a pathetic, broken lump and let the tears fall.

Why didn't I stay with my wife that day?

CHAPTER 24

SIENNA

DECLAN IS ALL I'VE THOUGHT about these past twelve hours. After saying those cruel words to him that completely broke my soul, I left the hotel, numbly following Anthony's directions to meet a driver a few blocks away. It turned out Anthony wasn't in Hawaii, just some men he sent to 'collect' me. They picked me up and drove me to the airport while I silently wept in the back seat.

They escorted me inside. The one who reeked of cigarettes grabbed my arm forcefully and said, "Stop fucking crying. You look suspicious."

So I cleaned up in the bathroom and kept quiet until we made it onto the plane a few hours later. Once we were in the air, I put on a sleeping mask and started crying again.

I cried until my nose was too stuffed up to breathe and my eyes were swollen shut and my head throbbed with stabbing pain. Until I felt completely dehydrated and my mouth was a desert. But I didn't eat or drink. I couldn't. I wanted to cause my body so much pain and distress that I'd simply die.

How I can live with myself after those disgusting, cruel things I said to Declan?

The way he looked at me, the total devastation in his eyes—it's going to haunt me the rest of my life.

But he's safe. There's no way he'll look for me after that. *He's safe.*

We're now driving away from O'Hare International

Airport. It's around 5 AM and I'm a walking zombie from lack of sleep. Somehow, I'm still crying.

The man who smokes rolls down his passenger-side window and lights a cigarette. "God, will you shut the fuck up?" he growls over his shoulder. "You've been whimpering for nine fucking hours."

The guy driving tells him, "Chill, man."

"No. She's making me lose my damn mind."

"Hit me then," I say weakly.

He scoffs and shakes his head.

That's what I thought. They can't do a damn thing except yell and complain. If they hurt me, Anthony will hurt them. He hates people touching what he thinks belongs to him.

I close my eyes, seeing Declan's wounded, scarred expression again. It feels like my insides are bleeding. I know I had to do it, had to break his heart to save his life, but I'll never stop hating myself for what I said.

Fingering my locket, I stare out the passenger window at the streets I grew up in. A disturbing mix of nostalgia and revulsion hits me. I see the pizza place with the best meat-balls—giant ones that made eating each slice a balancing act. I used to sit in the corner booth alone until they closed because I felt more comfortable there than I did at home.

Several miles down the road, I spot the park where I did plein air paintings. They weren't good, but people always stopped to watch, looking at me like I was a real artist with some grand vision they were trying to understand. Some people asked me to paint them, but I was always too shy to accept; I didn't want them to give me money and then be disappointed by the final portrait.

That park was also where I met Anthony at age 16. A

few years later, he admitted that he'd been watching me for months before finally approaching.

My response was, "I think it's romantic that you stalked me."

What a young, naïve thing to say.

After the car turns a few corners, we pass by my high school, the one I barely graduated from. When I turned fourteen, my parents really stopped caring and barely spoke to me or noticed when I was home. They didn't even care if I went to school, leaving it up to me to decide if I wanted to go.

Before Grandpa died, he really encouraged me to get an education, so I did my best. I wasn't a good student, and I skipped a lot of classes. But I somehow turned in enough homework that I didn't completely flunk. I also lucked out by having some sympathetic teachers senior year who cut me a lot of slack.

When I turned 18 and graduated, that's when I moved in with Anthony. I started drinking more, did drugs with him. Eighteen was symbolic. I was finally an adult and felt free of my parents, even though I could've left at any time without them noticing.

And I liked being an adult in Anthony's world. He was only a year older, but that somehow made him mysterious. He also made me feel seen for the first time in my sad little existence. He was fascinated by my art when no one else cared. He was interested in my past and ambitions. And even better, he told me repeatedly that I belonged to him.

I wasn't just some mistake; I had a purpose. It was to be with him.

I felt wanted for *me*. But I was too young to understand Anthony only craved power and control. The man never understood love, only possession.

By the time I woke up and noticed the dangerous world I was in and the vanity of Anthony's attention, I was already in too deep.

The memories make my stomach churn, bile rising in my throat. Even though I haven't eaten or had water, I vomit whatever foamy liquid is in my stomach.

Cigarette Man turns to glare at me. "This is my car, you fucking—" He unbuckles himself and before I can react, his hand strikes my cheek.

My head whips to the side, hitting the window. As my ears ring, I blink through the stinging pain in my face and the throbbing in my skull. My body is shocked and shaking, but emotionally, I really don't care.

My heartbreak from leaving Declan outweighs everything.

The man who is driving grabs Cigarette Man's shoulder and shoves him back into his seat. He's a young Latino guy who looks like a newbie, his eyes always shifting around for threats. This might be his first big task.

"Chill," he says firmly. "That was stupid, and I'm going to make it clear I wasn't involved." He glances at me in the rearview mirror, fear in his eyes. "Right? I wasn't involved."

I nod. Someday, he's going to regret his decision to get involved with such dangerous men. He'll soon learn that others in Anthony's world aren't like me—others will lie and enjoy getting him in trouble.

Cigarette Man sighs and flicks his cigarette out the window. "You're cleaning it then," he tells the driver.

There wasn't much in my stomach, but I dry heave a few more times. My mind grasps for any mantra or quote to get me through this, but there's nothing.

Only silence stretching into forever.

We finally stop in front of a slim, three-story rectangular white house, and I lean forward, peering up at it. It's made of brick—colonial style with plenty of windows—and the roof is flat. It's crowded into a row of other boxy houses, only a few feet of space separating them.

The wrought-iron gate in front is just for show because anyone could hop over it—maybe that's Anthony's way of saying his enemies aren't a threat.

"Get out," the driver says. "He's waiting for you inside."

I follow directions. After I grab my luggage from the trunk, the black sedan pulls away.

My hand shakes as I stand on the sidewalk clutching my luggage handle. My breath comes in short, sharp gasps.

This is it.

Could I run?

My eyes dart around the peaceful-looking neighborhood. The street is lined with trees; it's a sunny day. Everything is radiant and beautiful, even though the house in front of me is filled with evil.

As I'm debating an exit route, knowing I wouldn't get far, the front door opens. My heart stops for a beat as Anthony appears. He stands in the doorway with that cool smirk of his that always blends his hard edges into soft shadows. It's deceptive—the man is only hard edges. His eyes fix on me. It's a look I remember—the steely focus of a predator who's finally located his prey.

Time has definitely given his body more angles. His muscles are plump and cut, a lot of ink covering his exposed forearms. And his cheeks are hollow, pulling focus to his jagged jawline and the deep grooves of his olive skin. He's always been handsome in a cruel way, but age has given him a sharpness that contrasts with his well-tailored clothes—slacks, a button down rolled to his elbows, and a black vest.

It really doesn't matter how expensive some men dress; every unspeakable thing they've done is written all over their posture.

From instinct, my eyes dart around the neighborhood again. Anthony only leans against the doorframe and crosses his arms, daring me to make a run for it. His dark eyes watch—the eyes I've painted dozens of times in dozens of paintings.

Always watching.

He knows I can't run; I know it too. He'll only go after Jada and Declan.

I take a deep, shuddering breath, squaring my shoulders. I'm going to face this. I have to be strong. Sienna is always strong.

I'm sick again, my stomach churning, as I force my legs to move. Every step feels like a mile, my feet heavy and my heart pounding. I push the squeaky gate open and let it *clang* behind me. Then I reach the bottom step. Anthony meets me there, smirking through his shadows. I glance at the gold chain around his neck, the one carrying the cross he always wears, along with something new: a gold M.

Fuck him.

His fingers brush the ends of my hair. "Black, huh? You used to have such long, beautiful blonde hair. I miss it, but I'll get used to this new look." He's about to say something else when his lips freeze. With one narrowed eye, he scans my damp eyelashes, my cheeks, my nose. Holding my chin, he makes me turn my head, revealing where some of my skin is redder than the rest. Then he grazes my forehead, finding the bump.

I wince as his touch makes the area sting.

If looks could kill, Anthony's would slaughter a hundred men.

"Who?" he bites out.

I shake my head. Cigarette Man was a jerk, but I don't want him dead. "I just…fell."

Anthony snorts. "Sure." He pulls out his phone, staring daggers at the pavement. He dials and when the call connects, he says, "Get back here."

I can only wait on the bottom step, watching some birds in a tree. Birds that are free and can fly wherever they want.

Anthony waits, too, arms crossed, eyes roaming my body.

A few minutes later, the black sedan returns and both men step out.

"Who was it, baby?" Anthony asks, sounding like he's actually a forgiving man.

I shake my head and squeeze my eyes shut. *Please, don't let him murder that man.* I don't want to be responsible for Cigarette Man losing his life. I've already been complicit in enough killings.

Holding my chin, Anthony forces me to turn my head toward the men. "Who?"

When I open my eyes, I unconsciously look at Cigarette Man. It's only a half second before I look at the ground, but that's all Anthony needs. He's good at seeing those tells in someone's body language.

"Mark. Inside," Anthony barks.

Cigarette Man, Mark, follows orders like a veteran. He doesn't shake or cower; he follows Anthony inside with a blank stare and solid shoulders.

Anthony slams the door and I flinch, fighting back tears. Something crashes inside.

I glance at the young male driver as he waits on the sidewalk. His brown skin has turned pale.

"How old are you?" I ask, my voice sounding like I'm barely clinging to consciousness.

"Eighteen."

"You're just a kid. You should run before you get—"

There's a curdling scream from inside, then another loud crash.

The young man flinches, gaping at the front door like he expects a real monster to emerge.

"You should just run," I tell him.

Peeling his eyes away from the house, he gives me a lost look. "I can't. My family needs the money."

I'm sure his family would choose his life over money. But I don't get a chance to tell him that.

The front door flings open and Mark comes stumbling out. His face is bloody, swollen, his clothes disheveled. One of his elbows is bent the wrong direction.

Holding his arm, he stumbles down the steps. "I'm sorry," he mumbles as he passes, gritting through his pain.

"No," Anthony says from the doorway, so sharp and loud that it echoes around the quiet neighborhood. "Fucking apologize correctly."

Mark turns to me, clutching his broken arm and swaying like he might pass out. He bows his head. "I'm so sorry for touching you. I shouldn't have, and it will never happen again."

"I'm sorry," I whisper to him before Anthony is beside me.

"Julio, take him to our doctor," Anthony says.

Julio hurries to help Mark into the car, then he jumps into the driver's seat and the two of them speed away.

Anthony rubs my shoulders, and I resist the urge to recoil from his bloody knuckles. "I'm so sorry about that, baby. Let's go to your room so you can rest after that long trip."

I do need to rest. I need to sleep so I can wake up and have a clear head.

I need to figure out what to do next.

Or should I just surrender?

He grabs my luggage, and I follow him inside, one painful step at a time. When the front door closes and locks behind me, I wonder when I'll see the sunlight again.

Months?

Never?

The interior of the house is everything I'd expect from a place that's probably two million—dark mahogany floors and furniture that suck all color from the room, slick white countertops, a giant fireplace and rugs and mirrors and modern opulence and wealth. It's so different from the modest penthouse Anthony used to live in. He's clearly moved up in the world.

How many years has he been out of jail, plotting for the day he'd yank me back into his world?

He rolls my luggage to the side and turns to face me as I glance at the three burly men sitting on the brown leather sectional. There's a fourth man sweeping up pieces from a shattered mirror, something Anthony must've broken with Mark's body.

This house…will it be my tomb?

No, I can't think that way.

Not yet, at least.

I can't meet Anthony's eyes, so he chuckles softly to himself, that fake softness settling into his voice. "Baby, I know it's hard to be back," he says. "So take some time to settle in. I prepared a nice room for you. It has a great view, and I stocked it with art supplies. I know how my baby loves to paint." He reaches out, his hand cupping my cheek.

A thousand needles shoot through me, and I cringe, pulling away from his touch. "Don't," I say, surprised at how firm my voice is, considering how much my throat aches from crying and puking.

Anthony doesn't listen and runs his fingers through my hair anyway, avoiding the tender spot. He chuckles again. "You always were a bitch." He slowly fists my hair, tugging until my roots ache and I make a sound. "But I wouldn't expect anything less from the woman who put me in prison."

Still fisting my hair, he leans close enough for his cologne to assault me. "A petty man would be pissed and looking for revenge. But I'm honestly proud. You're one nasty bitch, and I still get hard thinking about how you sold me out." Finally releasing my hair, he runs a thumb over my puffy cheek. "You know I love our games."

I swallow hard, forcing myself to stand my ground and not pull away again; I know my resistance only fuels him. "How did you get out? I put you in there for thirty years."

"C'mon, Magpie. You're smarter than that. I got out on good behavior." He winks.

I know he means Victor, his boss, helped him. The authorities were supposed to go after Victor too, but I guess they failed. When I made the plea deal, Victor had been showing signs of wanting to get rid of Anthony, so I thought he'd just let him rot in jail.

An ignorant miscalculation on my part.

Anthony grabs my luggage again. "Follow me. Let's get you settled."

He leads me upstairs to a guest room on the second floor. It feels more like a cell with constricting white walls and bland furniture.

"Take all the time you need," Anthony says, moving my luggage to the walk-in closet. "I'll give you space to adjust."

I know what he really means. He's giving me time to come to terms with my fate, to accept that I'm his.

I'm really trying, but it's just too hard to feel strong today. I hope he'll leave so I can crumple to the floor.

He doesn't. Instead, he walks to a pitcher of water sitting on a table by the window. After pouring a glass, he pulls a packet of pills from his pocket.

"My men told me you've been struggling," he says, stopping in front of me. "I can't have that. I need you to drink some water and take these sleeping pills so you feel better." He tries to hand me the glass and pills, but I don't move to take them. A slow grin splits his wicked expression. "You want me to force you? I don't mind, you know."

I swallow.

He inches closer, his eyes burning trails along my body. "You know, your new look is already growing on me. Cute black hair. Hateful eyes. I'd love to see what else about you is different." He rolls the pills along his fingers, pressing the edge of one against my lips. "You know, my tastes have changed since the last time we fucked. I've had time to grow up and explore. I'm a bit more…rough. So if you want me to shove these pills down your throat, I'd love to. It'll turn me on, but I don't think you're ready yet for how I like to be satisfied, are you?"

A cold jolt worms up my spine, and I bite my tongue. I

don't think he'd take me by force. He never did in the past, but I have to remember that I don't know this man anymore.

I don't know what he's grown into.

I snatch the sleeping pills and water, swallowing everything. Then I toss the glass at the wall so it shatters. I stare Anthony down, not even flinching as glass shards scatter across the wooden floorboards.

Anthony throws his head back and his laugh bounces around this confining space. Before I can flee, he sweeps me into his arms, spinning me. When I'm back on my feet, he buries his face against my neck. "Seven fucking years, Margaret. I've been waiting to see you for seven fucking years. God, you feel good. Smell good. I missed you." When he pulls back, he's grinning. His dimple is showing, and for only a second, he has the same boyish grin I remember from our youth. "Fuck, I love you. It feels so damn good to have you here." He runs a finger under my chin, tipping my head back so I'm forced to look at him through my scowl. "You'll come around, Magpie. I promise. Then it'll be just like old times." He kisses my forehead and then finally leaves.

Surprisingly, I'm not out of tears. I crawl beneath the goose down comforter and cry until the sleeping pills pull me under.

CHAPTER 25

DECLAN

THE SHARP GLOW OF THE computer screen cuts through the shadows, the only light in my otherwise dark office. I've drawn the curtains, shutting out the world and my employees, trying to lose myself in the demands of my company. But it's a futile effort, and my team has been picking up a lot of my slack lately.

Thank God I have such amazing employees; I can forgive them for whispering behind my back and giving me wary stares. They're not used to seeing me in wrinkled slacks and plain T-shirts, with a beard sprouting on my face and my hair caked with dry shampoo. It's clear something is wrong, so I understand the gossip.

If it wasn't so difficult to be alone at home with my thoughts, I wouldn't even bother coming in. Home is so tormenting that I even asked Sean to move into a guest room temporarily. He's getting paid, of course, and doesn't seem to mind since he doesn't have family. But I still feel pathetic for asking.

In the past, when I went through difficult periods, I relied on women to warm my bed and provide superficial comfort. Now I can't even fathom being with any other woman except *her*.

My thoughts always circle back to her. Sienna.

I pull up a financial report on my computer. I have to stop thinking about her. She left in a cruel way, and I can't change that.

I force myself to look at numbers. They seem low, so I grab my desk phone and buzz Davis.

"What's up?" he answers.

I rub the back of my neck, trying to focus. "I'm looking at the Q2 report. What's going on with our Executive Protection division? The numbers seem off."

"Off how?"

"Revenue is down. I thought we'd improved those numbers since last quarter."

"We did," Davis says. I hear the clack of his keyboard. "Uhh…yeah, I'm looking at the report right now. We're up five percent from projections. Not as strong as our cybersecurity growth, but still an improvement."

What is he talking about? "That's not right." I scroll through the document again, frustration mounting. "I'm looking right at it. Page twelve. The numbers are down."

There's a lot of clicking on his end. "Well, it's actually page fourteen, but I'm looking at it too. EP has shown growth."

A sinking feeling settles in my stomach. I check the header of the document and close my eyes, exhaling slowly. "Shit. It's the Q1 report."

Davis is silent for a moment, then clears his throat. "Do you want me to send over the current Q2 report?"

"No," I say, pinching the bridge of my nose. "No, I see it now in the folder. Thanks."

I hang up before he can respond and before I can feel stupider. This isn't like me. I'm usually on top of things, always three steps ahead. But lately…

I swivel my chair to face the blackout curtains and give myself a break from the computer screen. I *need* to stop lingering on a past I can't change.

It's been two weeks since Sienna stormed out of that hotel suite, since she ruthlessly stabbed every vulnerable part of me. Two weeks of replaying every moment, every conversation, trying to understand what the hell happened. One minute, I was experiencing an unparalleled high. The next…

It's still hard to understand how those words came out of those lips I had kissed so many times.

I grab a pen off my desk and start clicking it. *Click click click.*

I can't make any fucking sense of anything. Can't reconcile the woman who looked at me with such tenderness and warmth with the one who cut me to the core with her cold, empty goodbye.

The change was too sudden, too drastic. Was the entire trip a lie, then? Was every smile, every laugh, just to make me look like a fool?

I don't want to believe it. Because I've fallen for her. Deeply, irrevocably. In a way, I haven't allowed myself to fall in years, not since…

Not since Tiffany.

My thumb is aching from clicking the pen so violently, so I switch hands.

Click click click.

Sienna's gaze was…decisive, hardened.

Like she was purposefully trying to hurt me.

If I really concentrate, I can remember cracks in that icy glare. Or maybe I'm imagining it, trying to force a narrative that doesn't exist. My mind keeps trying to reconcile the moments before the bathroom and the ones after.

Before: A worried, nervous Sienna showed me the

portrait. We made love. There was no hint of bitterness, no resentment simmering beneath the surface.

After: An angry, destructive Sienna twisted a knife in me with surgical precision, finding every chink in my armor, every insecurity I thought I'd buried.

Why?

I close my eyes, dropping the pen to hold my head. I know I can't keep doing this, running in circles, but I can't shake the feeling that there's more to the story. My gut is screaming at me that something isn't right. That what she said was lies.

But is that thought only a weak attempt to comfort myself?

Was she really speaking the truth?

Could I have driven Tiffany to…

There's a sharp twist in my gut, so I push away from my desk, opening a drawer. I grab a bottle of antacids and swallow two. I finish with a shot from the whiskey bottle I keep in another drawer. I'm a horrible boss for drinking on the job, but some days I need a shot to take the edge off.

I'm clearly not good at dealing with my emotions.

Lifting my desk phone, I buzz Davis again.

"Yeah?" he answers.

"Can you come in here, please?" I swallow some water because my voice feels like rocks crashing around in my throat.

"Sure."

My office chair creaks as I lean back and wait for Davis.

The door opens, spilling light over the tile, and Davis appears, his tall frame filling the doorway. He's dressed impeccably as always, his dark hair styled and his hazel eyes sharp. But when his gaze lands on me, all of his neatness wrinkles. "What's up?"

"Come in and close the door."

"Into this vampire's den?" he tries to say lightly, but it's clear that worry is dragging his tone down. "Can I at least turn on some lights?"

"No."

"Ookay." He closes the door and fumbles through the dim light, hitting his shins on a low table. "Fuck, that'll leave a bruise," he grumbles. He finally makes it to the chair in front of my desk. Still wincing, he asks, "Are you finally going to tell me what's been going on?"

"No."

"Ookay." He crosses an ankle over his knee and waits.

I swallow more water, my voice feeling better lubricated. "I have a question for you, and I need your honest opinion. No bullshit. Don't spare my feelings. This is important, and I need the absolute truth."

He uncrosses his leg and leans forward. "Yeah. You know I always give it to you straight. What is it?"

My words are lead, filled with fragments of regret and torment that only seem to snowball the more years that pass. "Am I the reason that…Do you think being with me, or dealing with me, was what led Tiffany to—"

"No."

His firm response makes me exhale, but it doesn't erase the insecurities. "Are you certain? Maybe I put too much pressure on her. Or there's something about my personality that—"

"Stop. No, Declan. You can't blame yourself." His eyes lock with mine and that natural magnetism he has means I can't look away. "I'm absolutely certain it's nothing you did. She…Tiffany was struggling even when she was a kid. And you did more for her than I think anyone else ever did. You were supportive and kind and patient…You know, my wife still says things like, 'Declan rented out an entire restaurant for his wife on Valentine's Day, and you won't even buy me flowers!' I bought her jewelry yet somehow not having flowers"—he frowns—"Anyway…" His eyes scan my growing beard and sunken eyes and unclean hair. He scoots his chair closer to the desk. "What's going on?"

For a moment, I consider telling him everything, but as I open my mouth, the pain is too fresh for me to get the words out. But I tell him what I can. "I met someone. It didn't work out. I don't think I can talk about it yet."

"Wow," he says under his breath. "Like, someone serious? A relationship?"

I can't deal with the questions or probing, even though I appreciate him wanting to talk and let me vent. "It's hard to talk about right now, but thanks for…"

He nods, standing. "Of course. When you're ready to talk, I'm here. Just…just don't ever think of blaming yourself for Tiffany, alright? That's not even a question. Everyone knows how much you loved her. She also knew how much you loved her, no matter what her condition made her think sometimes. You founded this multi-million dollar, comprehensive security firm just for her so she'd never have to worry about money, and you did it without having a tech or business background. It was sheer willpower. I've been with you from the beginning and I still don't know how the hell you did it."

My throat is tight, so I lower my gaze.

Sensing my mood and my need to be alone again, he moves to the door. When he reaches it, he hesitates. "Hey, before I leave…Is there any action you want to take about

262 | RAINA ASH

the email?"

"What email?"

His body becomes rigid. "Oh…Uh, I thought because you were asking about Tiffany, you saw the latest email…"

I barely register his words before I'm clenching my jaw and swiveling to face my computer screen. "What did the fucking asshole send now?"

"It's not good. More of a direct threat." Davis crosses my office, moving closer to look at my screen. "It was sent to your address on the old server. Sent this morning. No one except me has seen it. I was trying to find a good time to tell you. Sorry."

My blood turns to ice as I read the subject line: *The World Should Know.*

The email itself is blank, but there's a PDF attached. I open it, scanning the details. The whiskey I swallowed starts coming back up—I'm staring at the confidential police report and medical examiner's report about Tiffany's death.

My fists clench as adrenaline surges through every cell. Davis waits, giving me time to collect my thoughts, but it's a struggle to string them together.

"Why?" is all I can manage.

Davis has worked with me long enough that he intuitively understands what I'm asking. His gaze shifts to the black curtains as his body slumps from the gravity of the email. "I honestly don't know why this person is threatening to share these records with the public. They haven't asked for money, so what do they gain from this?" His tone sounds a lot like defeat. "I think it's time we get an attorney involved. Since you didn't get those records sealed legally, if this person does expose them—"

"I'd be looking at an investigation," I say, finishing his

sentence.

"Yeah," Davis breathes.

"Fuck."

I've done nothing else illegal in my life. I just couldn't face the public knowing about my son; I didn't want Tiffany's family to go through that pain because we hadn't yet told them about the pregnancy. Tiffany had wanted to wait until she was farther along and felt more stable.

Losing their daughter was bad enough. I didn't want to throw grandson on top of that.

"Fuck," I say again to myself.

It was *one* fucking bribe to get one detective to 'lose' those reports, so he had to file new ones that didn't mention my son. At the time, it felt like a minor, inconsequential thing.

How the hell did this hacker even get the originals?

I feel a familiar tightening in my gut, the same tension I used to feel before stepping into the ring. This is a fight, and I intend to win.

Before I can think better of it, I hit reply, my fingers flying over the keys as I type out an email: **What is your end goal here?**

I hit send, my body buzzing with the need to physically face my opponent. A part of me knows I shouldn't engage, shouldn't give them the satisfaction of a response. But I want to understand. Who the fuck is this?

To my knowledge, I haven't made any enemies who hated me enough to dig into my past *this* deeply. And this person would need some serious clout and a huge vendetta to obtain these documents. Yet, no one from my boxing days was that kind of person, and the business owners I've pissed off wouldn't fight this dirty. They're all too busy with their lives and work to care.

If this person wants money, I'll gladly pay it to stop this nightmare. So why haven't they asked? If this isn't blackmail, why?

Why do this?

I'm tired of the games, tired of the cryptic emails. I want answers.

A minute passes. Then two. Just as I'm about to close the email in disgust, a new email pops up: *To make you pay. Don't touch another man's things.*

The words glare at me from the screen. Pay for what?

I start typing: *What the fuck are you—*

Davis is suddenly beside me. He touches my shoulder. "No. Stop. You might make it worse. We need to talk to our lawyers first."

Pulling my hands away from the keyboard, I lean back in my creaky chair with an exhale. "Fine. See what they have to say. Get our team to *find* this asshole."

"Okay," he says softly. He leaves, shutting the door quietly behind him.

I regret never installing a punching bag in my office because I could use one right about now. I'm debating having another shot, but that's not the right course of action. As much as I want to numb myself and escape emotionally, I need to stay clear-headed to protect my employees. If I'm exposed for bribing a detective, the company might go down with me. Shareholders are very sensitive to everything a CEO does, even if it has nothing to do with the company itself.

I grab my pen to click it again. I'll wait to see what the lawyers say, but if it comes to it, I'll step down as CEO. I won't let my company's reputation tank just because of something I did in my personal life. My existence feels unimportant at this point, so I don't care what happens to me. Maybe I'll end up in jail.

Doesn't matter; this company and its employee's livelihoods are the priority.

I only get a few moments alone to think before my secretary buzzes me. "Mr. Conte? There's someone here to see you and she's very insistent that it's, as she put it, 'insanely important to see the man in charge right this second.' I know you said not to disturb you, but she seems very on edge and I'm worried. She made a fuss with security downstairs, so I told them I would speak to her. She's still making a fuss and says she knows you and that you're expecting her. Do you know a Miss Jada Wilson?"

Jada Wilson?

I wrack my brain but come up empty. Since I don't know who she is and I have a lot of serious threats to handle, I tell my secretary, "No. Tell her I apologize, but I can't meet right now. Get her contact info and we'll—"

"Hey, stop," my secretary says, her voice muffled. "No, you can't—"

"Mr. Conte?" A new voice says quickly. "Have you seen Sienna?"

The name rings in my ears and my pulse spikes. Before I can respond, it sounds like my secretary has wrestled the phone from the woman's grasp.

"I am so sorry," my secretary says, breathless. "I've already buzzed security to—"

"No, bring her back. Please."

"Are you sure?"

"Yes. Thank you." I hang up. Then I open the curtains, the ground swaying as I squint against the blinding sun. I pace nervously for the two minutes it takes my secretary to escort the woman to my office.

After a light tapping, my secretary opens the door, her red hair frizzy from her recent scuffle. She gives me a polite nod and then frowns hard at Miss Wilson before leaving.

I don't recognize the woman, but she's average height with incredible posture. Light brown skin, blue jeans, a loose purple blouse; her braids are pulled back into a low bun.

Despite her posture and natural grace, there seems to be a gloom following her. There are puffy, purplish bags under her bloodshot eyes, and a lot of dark grooves around her mouth. She moves forward swiftly to hold out her hand. "I'm Jada."

I shake her hand. "Declan. You know Sienna?"

She looks me up and down cautiously, probably not expecting a CEO to look like such a slob. Then she hooks her thumbs around the backpack straps over her shoulders. "Yeah. I'm really sorry about this. Showing up here when you're busy. I...I just thought you might know where Sienna went? She, I think, met you a few months ago at the Fine Arts Museums Gala. She disappeared and I'm trying to find her."

My hand is shaky from my increased heart rate, but I motion to a chair. "Please, have a seat." I close the office door and then cross to my desk, sitting. "I do know Sienna, but I don't know where she is."

Jada doesn't sit, her unnaturally golden eyes—which are colored contacts—looking glassy. She drops her head. "Oh. Well, I'm sorry to bother you then. I'm just really worried about her. But I'll go." She turns toward the door. At the same second I say "Wait," she notices Sienna's color study on the wall. She rushes to it, reaching up to take the small canvas off the wall. "Why do you have this?"

When Sienna stormed out of the suite, she left behind my portrait and the small canvas with the couple and the man on top of the stairs. Maybe it was a bad idea since it's part torture, but I had to hang them up—one here, the other at home.

I like having a piece of her close, even if she destroyed me in the end.

"It seems we have a lot to tell each other, Jada." I motion at the office chair. "Please, sit." A sudden calm and stability rises inside me. I think I'm finally on the verge of getting answers and the adrenaline is clearing my head.

I wait until Jada replaces the painting, and then sits on the edge of a chair. Then I fold my hands on the desk and lean forward. "Please. Start at the beginning and tell me everything."

CHAPTER 26

SIENNA

A SOFT BREEZE CARESSES MY face as I paint near the open window. I close my eyes, and I can almost imagine myself on that patio in Hawaii, gazing out at the ocean while Declan reads a book in the living room behind me. His expression would be intense, like usual, but maybe the faintest smile would soften his face. When he'd get bored with reading, he'd come over and rest his large, warm hands on my shoulders. His woodsy scent would wrap around me, and we'd slip into some perfect, never-ending moment. Just us. Just his arms wrapped around me.

"Sienna," he'd whisper. "Princess. What is it you want? I'll give it to you."

"I just want…" I'd start, not finishing my words, because I'd turn around and kiss him.

I want you.

Forever.

A car alarm goes off somewhere in the distance, and my eyes snap open, pulling me from that fragile dream into reality. I won't let my imagination go further than a kiss; it's wrong to imagine his hands on me, considering every disgusting thing I said to him.

A tear slips down my cheek, and I catch it with my fingers. Then I examine my damp fingertips, rubbing them together until the tear dissolves. I'll give that man every single one of my tears for the rest of my life, like they're somehow penance.

What's a good quote for this situation?

Something that I saw on social media a long time ago pops into my mind. Something like: *"You love harder when you're broken—once you've been in the dark, you appreciate everything that shines."*

I like that. It's not a quote about doing anything or having a certain mindset. It's simply a fact.

I appreciate everything I shared with Declan because he does shine. Even though I tarnished what we shared in the end, when we were together, he made me shine too.

Another tear falls, but I let this one dry in the breeze. Then I glance down at my wrist where I've been covering my Phoenix tattoo with a sharpie. It's only a black square now.

I have yet to figure out any 'next steps' for this situation. I've just been going through the motions, crying over Declan, painting to distract myself, and grieving my lost life in San Fran.

I think part of me broke. Or, I've reverted back to Margaret.

Weak, pathetic Margaret.

My eyes return to the open window, and I dip my brush in some blue. I lose myself in each stroke, adding color to the feathers on a little bird in my painting. The bedroom around me contrasts with the vibrant colors blossoming on my canvas. This room has sleek lines and minimalist decor, shades of gray and white that are oppressing.

But outside, there's saturation.

There's a park in the distance, a splash of green tucked into the urban landscape. Trees sway in the gentle wind, their leaves dancing with light and shadow. I focus on the beauty beyond this prison, working more blue into my little bird.

It's ironic—now that I'm living my worst nightmare, I can only stand to paint cheerful things. I need flowers and birds and the peaceful, upscale neighborhood I see beyond my window. I've painted dark, moody macabre scenes for years, yet now I've lost the desire.

I'll admit, I was snooty before about whimsical, pastel art. I would frown at a still life and wonder what possessed someone to spend hours painting some bland little flowers or landscape. Now, I get it. Pretty paintings and happy scenes are their own form of escape. When your life is filled with so many unspeakable horrors, happy, cute images can keep you from breaking.

So, that's what I paint now—cheerful, cute things so I don't completely snap.

Anthony has kept me trapped in this bedroom for almost a month. No phone or access to the outside world. Just a TV, some books, and paint supplies. There's a 24/7 guard outside my door and under the window. And if I want to walk around the house to get a snack or change of scenery, a guard must escort me and only for a maximum of ten minutes.

It sucks, but I understand. Considering how I back-stabbed Anthony in the past—eavesdropping on his 'business' meetings and gathering sensitive information to give to the authorities—he's being extra careful. If anyone comes over to talk 'business,' the guards keep me far away from all discussions.

There are loopholes, though. My bedroom is next to the third story terrace, so I can hear conversations when people are out there. So far, it's only been guards bitching about their work.

I set my brush down, my wrist aching from painting the entire morning. I sigh at my little blue bird. Even if I hear a juicy conversation on that terrace, I don't think it'll help me get out of here.

A major difference between Sienna and Margaret is that Margaret didn't have anyone to worry about. She was alone in the world. She took a risk and exposed Anthony because the only consequence was her own life, which she didn't particularly care about.

Sienna has people Anthony will hurt.

Besides, Anthony is only one piece of a larger puzzle. Above him is Victor, a much bigger threat. The authorities were supposed to take him down along with Anthony, but Victor weaseled his way out of it. I think the only reason Victor didn't have me killed is Anthony. Anthony likely stopped him.

If I manage some miraculous escape again…I just don't know. Victor is a wildcard.

The facts glaring me in the face are part of the reason I haven't yet attempted to figure out a plan. What if there is no escape this time?

There's a knock on the door and I tense. I know it's not Anthony because he enters without knocking. Must be a guard.

"Yes?" I respond, gazing out the window and wondering if I should just jump. I'd break some bones, but if I can keep at least one leg functional, I could hobble away. I'll wait until the guard under the window is distracted and…

And then Anthony will kill Declan and Jada.

I press a palm to my chest, trying to steady myself as the guard opens the door. I don't turn around, but I hear him walk to my bed. Something that sounds like a plastic bag rustles.

"You're eating dinner with the boss tonight," is all the guard says.

He leaves and I finally look over my raised shoulder. There's a dress bag on my bed and it makes me scoff. The asshole wants me to dress up and eat dinner with him?

Well, fine.

I hope he hates what I'm going to do to that dress.

ANTHONY MAKES ME WAIT FOR half an hour at the mahogany dinner table before he appears. His guards have been standing nearby the entire time; otherwise, I would've left.

I don't stand to greet Anthony and he thankfully doesn't come closer. He just sits across the table with that amused yet venomous look of his. When he doesn't comment on my dress, I stand up to show him.

"Thanks," I say, twirling around. "It's lovely."

His eyes finally scan what I'm wearing.

Honestly, it was a beautiful dress—deep emerald, diamonds sparkling along a low-cut V, and it hugged my hips perfectly before fanning out and cascading to the floor. It was an elegant, expensive dress.

I decided to smear it with various colors of paint. I don't have any scissors in my room, but I managed to snap one of my paintbrushes in half to create a sharp point. Then I used it to help me pluck out all the diamonds and shred parts of the dress.

Unfortunately, Anthony doesn't flinch. His amused smirk only widens, and he says, "Truly, a work of art. I'm so proud of my girl for being so creative."

Making fists, I drop back into my chair.

He smiles to himself like he's pleased and then picks up his knife and fork. When he cuts into his steak, it oozes blood.

I glance down at my plate—fish and veggies—but I don't have an appetite.

Anthony says, "Tell me about your day, Magpie," as he eats and sips wine like whether or not I have dinner doesn't matter.

I scoff. "You know about my day."

"I'll tell you about mine," he says, wiping his mouth with a cloth napkin. "I had some business to take care of downtown, but I spent the entire day thinking of you. I ordered that dress last week, and I've been looking forward to seeing you in it." He grins, red wine staining his teeth. "You look beautiful. Thank you for joining me for dinner."

He's fucking insane.

I'm irritated at his indifferent attitude, so I grab my wine and swirl it, really tempted to stand up and throw it in his face. "How sweet of you," I say blandly. "I spent the day thinking about how Declan stripped me naked and fu—"

He backhands his wine glass, and it flies off the table, staining the wall red as it shatters.

I really try not to react—I try to wear an unflinching mask the way he does—but I scream. Then my heart races as I try to drink water with a shaky hand.

"Careful," Anthony bites out. He jabs his fork at my plate. "Eat your fucking food."

On instinct, I grab my fork and cram a piece of fish into my mouth. It's savory, but it feels like a boulder going down my throat when I force a swallow.

I know I should be careful, but I've been doing that for an entire month. Being back in Anthony's presence, I think I slipped into Margaret's disposition too much.

Tonight, Sienna feels more in control. Maybe it was from the act of ruining the dress, I don't know, but I want to test the boundaries—I need to know what they are.

My pulse is still racing, but I say, "You're a man of your word. You said if I did what you wanted, you wouldn't hurt Declan. So you won't. I'm free to talk about him all I want."

Anthony takes one more bite of steak, pushes his plate away, and then dabs his mouth with the napkin. His eyes are empty when they look at me, like two black marbles with only a thin border of bloodless white. "You've changed," he says. "You're rougher. Way more feisty. But I like it. When you finally settle into this life with me, when you surrender, it'll be so fucking satisfying."

He didn't give me the answer I needed, so I dig my fingers into my thighs and push where I know it'll hurt. "I already surrendered completely to him. I let him do *whatever* he wanted, and we fucked so much that I—"

His reaction isn't violent this time, but he stands. He glides to where I'm sitting, looking completely in control, like I'm a mouse caught in a trap and he's a cat ready to play. Leaning over me, he runs a finger under my jaw and grins.

"You've changed," he says again. "What makes you think I haven't? Keep talking and I just might kill that man. Then I'll shut you up." He reaches down to grab his crotch. I can't understand why, but he's half hard.

"Maybe you're into that now," he adds. "Taking it rough."

Without thinking, I spit in his face.

The gob lands on his cheek and he laughs, fucking

laughs, before yanking me from the chair. The world spins and then my back hits the wall.

Anthony presses his body into mine, his breath smelling like steak sauce and making me grimace. "Your crazy is so fucking hot," he says. He fists my hair and kisses me.

Squeezing my eyes shut, I try to think about anything except what's happening. I won't open my mouth, so the asshole bites my lip until I gasp. Before his tongue can force its way in, I manage to turn my head and break the kiss.

He only laughs more and grabs my waist.

My voice is shaky when I say, "You have changed. Looks like you're a rapist now."

That gets his attention. He inhales sharply and his entire body stills. Finally, there's a crack in his annoyingly calm, collected mask. He looks *pissed*, with nostrils flaring and eyes blazing.

I challenge him, lowering my arms, letting my body soften, opening myself up. What I'm about to do is a huge gamble because he's right—I don't know the man he is now, seven years later. This defiance could end very badly for me, but if I can figure a way out of this situation, I have to know exactly what parts of Anthony are different.

He's always been a little rough, but the Anthony of the past would've never taken me against my will or caused serious physical harm—really, the only good quality about him.

He smacks one of his palms against the wall near my head, making me flinch. "Is that what you fucking think?"

"Aren't you going to shut me up?" I snap. "Go ahead. Rape me."

His eye twitches, and I hold my breath as he stares daggers into my skull. His grip on my waist tightens uncomfortably, and I prepare myself for the worst.

He relaxes and grabs my chin, his face sliding into the illusion of control again. "Where's the fun in that? One day, you'll give yourself willingly." Shoving away from me with a groan, he turns to leave.

I clutch my chest, feeling the tears prick my eyes from that intense confrontation. As shaken as I am, this is a small win. I now have a boundary I can work with.

There's just one more thing I need to know. "How did you find me?" I ask, unable to keep my voice from wavering. "I was in WITSEC."

The few seconds it took for him to reach the dining room doorway was enough for his demeanor to completely recover. He always was good at that.

With a smugness that makes his lips curl wickedly and his eyes glint, he says, "Baby, you think the cops care about you? All it took was a few calls and one bribe to get your 'confidential' records from WITSEC. Another bribe took you out of the system. I tracked you down in Utah as soon as I got out."

I gasp. "Utah? But…"

My stomach tightens. *He was the stalker.*

He laughs. "You thought I'd be in prison longer than a year? Victor got me out. See? I care about you, baby. I've been out this entire time, but I let you enjoy your new life. Let you enjoy art school, your job at the record store, and all those other shitty places you worked. I was even rooting for you to get that art program started. Just wanted to see my girl happy."

He leaves; leaves me in a world that's suddenly spinning.

CHAPTER 27

DECLAN

HUNCHING IN MY OFFICE CHAIR, I rub my temples in a vain attempt to ease my tension headache. I'm running on two hours of sleep—all I've been able to get lately. When I have managed to rest, Sienna haunts my dreams.

Davis sits on the opposite side of my desk, the grooves in his tan forehead the deepest I've seen them. He's staring at my computer screen, where another threatening email from the hacker is displayed. We've been dealing with these fucking emails for almost a month now with no concrete way to find the asshole.

"Forensic analysis, ISP collaboration, even a damn honeypot," Davis says. "This person is good. If we find them, we should offer them a job."

I frown. "Be serious."

"I'm nothing but serious."

"You think it's a team?"

"That's the best theory we have." He flips through a folder that's open in front of him on my desk—reports and correspondence. "The emails are coming from multiple locations, bouncing through servers all over the globe. A good amount trace back to Illinois."

"Any city? County? I'd take a damn cardinal direction at this point."

Davis shakes his head, scrubbing a hand over his short-cropped hair. "Not yet. Whoever's behind this knows how to cover their tracks. Unless they slip up, or we get lucky, I'm not sure how we'll pinpoint them."

I blow out a breath, gripping a pen so tight I worry I might snap the plastic. My gaze falls on the words of the latest email. This one came with an attachment, a toxicology report that is completely fabricated.

It claims Tiffany had a lethal mix of drugs in her system, implying that what happened wasn't a suicide, that I had a hand in her death. If this fucking asshole goes public with this bullshit, well, my attorneys didn't have very encouraging words about the investigation it would open up. Then, if it went to trial, my bribe to the detective would only make me look guilty.

I read the email again, trying to keep a level head and not let rage blind me to something I might be missing: *I'm watching you. Behave and maybe no one will know you're a killer. But enjoy your other lawsuit.*

Other lawsuit? Now the hacker is talking nonsense; I don't have any lawsuits.

I feel the weight of Davis' gaze on me, the unspoken question hanging in the air. But I have no answers for him. Still no clue about who could be behind this, or why.

"I don't know what to say at this point except keep trying," I finally tell him, my voice like sandpaper. "I know using our resources for this is hurting our business with clients, so hire as many extra people as you need to carry the workload. Pay for everything out of my personal funds. I don't care at this point. I want this person found. We have to end this, if only for everyone's sanity."

He steeples his fingers, his forehead still a wrinkled mess. "Oh, I know. I want him found too. We'll keep chugging along and maybe we'll get a break."

I grunt. "And fucking soon."

Davis gathers his things and exits, leaving my office door ajar. I grab a different pen and start clicking the top with my thumb. My gaze wanders to the color study on the wall.

Jada was visibly terrified as she sat in my office a week ago—shaking as she spoke, wringing her hands, her voice cracking. She told me about a man who came to her house, assaulted her for a lock of her hair, and then threatened her unless she told him where Sienna was. He was wearing a mask, so the only thing she could tell me about him was his skin tone—his forearms were exposed—and that he was around six feet tall.

Then she showed me her last text exchange with Sienna.

Sienna sounded like a woman fleeing for her life.

Was the man in Jada's home a vengeful ex? A stalker? Or did Sienna commit a crime and piss someone off? There are a lot of possibilities, and Jada didn't have any clues; she said Sienna never wanted to talk about her past.

Whoever that man was, it's clear Sienna was in some kind of trouble. She took my invitation as a way to escape to Hawaii, and once there, it's possible her pursuer found her, since Jada gave the man my name. A few phone calls to my company would've revealed I was at a conference.

If that's true and her pursuer suddenly appeared in Hawaii, that would explain Sienna's sudden mood shift the day she stormed out.

Part of me wants to cling to that possibility, to feel relieved I did nothing wrong, that her departure was strategic. The other part of me remains cautious. Her pursuer and how she left could have nothing to do with each other;

obviously not the option I'm hoping for.

Clicking my pen, I stare at the painting and the man at the top of the stairs. Sienna said she saw him as a protector, saw me as a protector.

Now that she's gone, the question is: what am I going to do about it?

I toss the pen on my desk. Whether or not she destroyed me with her words, whether they were the truth or lies, I can't shake my feelings for her. I just need to know Sienna is safe.

Unfortunately, the private investigator I hired has hit a wall, unable to uncover much about her life before San Francisco. It's strange. There's a birth record, but nothing else. No driving permit when she turned fifteen. No school records. It's as if Sienna Bishop didn't exist before her 21st birthday.

The investigator said his gut is telling him there's been a cover-up, and I believe in trusting one's instincts.

Just how deep does this go?

He's currently trying to determine if the cover-up is legal, that she's in witness protection, or illegal, something done through the black market.

I smooth a hand over the cool surface of my wooden desk. How the fuck did I slip into a CSI episode? Several seasons of that clearly didn't prepare me enough for a real-life investigation.

I've hit a dead end. What am I supposed to do next? Where do I look?

I need to find my mystery woman. As much as I still feel the sting of her departure, there are too many open threads; my heart misses her too much. Each day that I don't know where she is gets consumed with a growing darkness, a growing heaviness. If I keep going like this, my body is going to shut down from lack of rest.

Pills don't work. Alcohol doesn't work. Nothing gets me to sleep; it's like my soul will remain restless until I find her.

If I get answers, if I can know for certain that what she said about Tiffany came from a place of fear, that she felt panicked and didn't know what else to do, I won't hesitate to forgive.

I'll fight to free her from whatever has her chained. I'll free us both.

"Declan."

Davis' voice startles me from my thoughts and I glance up. He's standing in the doorway, his face like an ashen stone mask. A man in a cheap navy suit stands behind him.

Davis moves out of the way, and the stranger approaches my desk. He extends a manila envelope. "Declan Conte?"

I nod, each one of my senses on high alert.

"You have been served." He drops the envelope on my desk, turns on his heels, and leaves.

Davis and I share a wary look. With a sinking feeling in my gut, I reach for the envelope, tearing it open with more force than necessary.

As I scan the contents, my blood runs cold. Assault charges. Filed by none other than Halliwell, the hotel CEO whose partnership I turned down.

I suppose I should be angry, disgusted, all the above, but I'm simply not. I'm too focused on trying to move pieces around in my head and fit them together. The timing is too…calculated. How did the hacker know this was coming?

Davis is now in front of me, waiting for me to speak, so I just hand him the papers so he can see for himself.

"Assault charges?" he says with wide eyes. His voice

raises, bouncing off the walls. "You didn't assault him!"

"Technically…" I start, letting the rest fall into oblivion.

Davis frowns. "Well, you barely touched him."

"It can still be seen as assault." I tap my computer screen with a finger. "But how did the hacker predict this? Someone connected to Halliwell? Or did Halliwell hire him? I didn't think he'd be so petty, but I'm not ruling it out."

Davis falls into a chair, shaking his head and slapping the lawsuit papers on my desk. "Jesus, I feel like we're on an episode of CSI."

For the first time in too long, I smirk. "I had the same thought."

"Well," Davis says, "it's accurate. I mean, what the fuck is happening?" His skull must be suddenly too heavy for his neck, because he sets his elbows on my desk and holds his head. His body folds in on itself. "This is all too much. I just want to go home and hug my wife and kids."

"Then do it. Go home."

"But—"

"Go home. Your family is important. It's the most important thing."

He stares at the papers for a moment before nodding.

As he stands, I say, "Tell everyone putting in extra hours to find the hacker that they can go home too. They'll get paid for a full day, but they all need a break. Everyone can start their weekend early."

Normally, Davis would jump on this opportunity to say something about my dating habits—some joke like I'm only trying to get to my harem sooner. But with everything that's going on, his normal lightness and humor have dimmed. It gives me a hollow ache—I can see the toll this situation is taking on him. I hope some extra time with his family helps.

With a blank face, he says, "I'll talk to HR and send out some emails." Then he's gone.

I snatch up my desk phone, my fingers jabbing the numbers. To my surprise, Halliwell answers on the first ring. But something is different. Gone is the arrogant attitude, the slimy bravado I remember.

Instead, he sounds scared.

"D-Declan," he stammers, his voice thin and reedy. "I wasn't expecting your call."

"Really?" I grit out, feeling a bit of my temper finally flaring. "You file bullshit charges against me, and you don't expect me to reach out?"

There's a beat of silence, heavy and loaded. "Why didn't you return my calls?" he finally asks. "Listen, I tried to contact you. Left you multiple voicemails. You ignored them. I didn't want this to happen."

My mind flashes back to the messages Davis relayed several weeks ago, the urgent requests that Halliwell wanted to talk. It happened while I was in Hawaii, so of course I brushed them off. I was focused on Sienna, and I thought Halliwell just wanted to schmooze me and get back in my good graces.

"I had other things on my mind," I say. "And if you didn't want this to happen, why file a lawsuit?"

"You should've taken my calls."

"Why? What did I need to know?"

"It's too late."

"It's not. We both know those charges are embellished, so I'm happy to settle the lawsuit out of court. Just name a price because I have more important things to deal with."

Halliwell lets out a shaky breath. "It's out of my hands now. I'm sorry. I can't…I can't stop it. I can't settle out of court, no matter how much you offer. If you had just answered my damn messages…"

"I'm talking to you now, so tell me."

"I'm sorry. This isn't about money." His voice drops. "My wife…It's for her safety. I'm sorry."

I hear the resignation in his voice, the fear. Like someone has him cornered. "What about your wife?"

He hangs up. When I dial him back several times, it keeps going to voicemail.

My mind is racing now, pieces of the puzzle changing shape but still not completely fitting together. Is someone threatening Halliwell's wife? Forcing him to do this lawsuit?

I'm still left with one important question: *Who?*

Who is orchestrating all of this, and why are they targeting me? It sounds crazy, but I have no other explanation—I think the hacker is trying to get to me through Halliwell.

Why?

Grabbing a stress ball, I crush it in my fist, ready to throw it against the wall because the frustration is too great. I want to rip my hair out. I don't have any enemies that would go to these insane lengths. Besides one bribe to cover up information about my son, I've done nothing else illegal. I've never taken money to throw a match, done drugs, embezzled, sexually harassed someone…I'm clean. So who, and why, and what the *fuck* is happening?

I'm a few seconds from throwing the stress ball when my personal phone vibrates in my pocket. I check the screen to find a message from Sean: ***Need to talk ASAP. Get home.***

Jesus, what now?

Me: Be there in forty minutes.

I pack up, a numbness washing over me as I'm hit with an exhaustion that creeps into my bones. Davis was right: this is too much.

CHAPTER 28

SIENNA

ANOTHER DAY OF PAINTING TO pass the time. The room is starting to overflow with canvases. For the first time I'm suffocating on my own art.

Getting off my stool near the window, I stretch my arms overhead, ready for a break. But plans change when there's a soft knock on the door, followed by, "Magpie?"

I fall back onto the stool, my stomach sinking. I don't say anything because he comes in regardless. At least he knocked this time.

The door creaks open, and there's Anthony. He's in a black suit with a red tie today, moving into my room like a tall, shadowed mass. When he smiles, the darkness that always clings to him highlights his white teeth.

"Hey, baby," he says, closing the door.

I swivel around to face my painting again. I'm still shaken from my dinner with Anthony a few days ago— shaken that he's been out there this entire time, his eyes watching, waiting.

Watching me go through school.

Watching me with my friends.

Watching everything.

I've had nightmares about trying to run away from those eyes, but every time I turn a corner, I see them.

They see me.

The more I've thought about our interaction at dinner,

the more a dark, terrible realization has taken root inside me: even if I escape this room, even if I run away again, he's going to follow.

He will always follow.

Always watch.

The only true escape from Anthony is death.

My death.

Or his.

I grab my brush with unsteady fingers and pretend to add color to a flower even though my wrist aches from the movement. Even though my insides are trembling again.

Anthony's body heat burns into my back after he stops behind me. His cologne is so strong it stings my eyes, so I rub them.

"Hmm, it's coming along," he says, studying my painting. He bends forward until his minty breath sends a chill down my spine, then he plucks the brush from my hand. He dips it in the black on my palette and then darkens my little bird's eyes, making the white highlights pop while strengthening the contrast.

I regret ever teaching Anthony to paint. He was always 'fixing' my art back in the day, and I hated him even more for doing a good job at it.

He sets the brush down and then nuzzles my neck with his cheek. "When it's finished, I want to hang it in my room, along with all your other paintings I've kept." His fingers graze my collarbone and locket. "Remember when we did those portraits of each other? Of course I saved those."
He places a kiss under my earlobe, and I shudder, feeling nauseous. He laughs. "You drew devil horns on me."

"That was right after you made me…" I don't want to say it out loud, so I stop.

288 | RAINA ASH

"Made you what?"

"The shop owner."

"Oh, yeah. I forgot about that. What a crazy night."

I want to laugh. Or sob. Just a 'crazy' night? Now I really might throw up.

That 'crazy night' was the first time I *actually* saw who Anthony was, and my youthful blind devotion to him finally cracked.

A few months after I had moved in with him, Anthony began traveling for 'business' several weeks at a time. I was lonely, so I went to the corner store every morning to talk with the sweet old man who owned it. He was kind and treated me like a daughter, something I craved. In hindsight, I told him too much about myself and my life, too much about Anthony, but I was young and still naïve to Anthony's cruel side.

I had thought Anthony was only a small-time drug dealer, not part of something...organized.

I didn't know it before the 'crazy' night, but that old man was helping Anthony with money laundering, and he kept quiet about certain deliveries made to his store. But he was resentful.

Something I told the old man gave him what Anthony called a 'bargaining chip.' The old man threatened to go to the police with the information unless Anthony cut him a new deal.

I don't know what happened between the two men, but I figured it got settled because we stopped talking about the subject. Then Anthony made me stop visiting the old man's shop. He put me a leash, controlling where I went, who I hung out with, how long I could leave the apartment. He relaxed the chains a little after a few months.

I felt suffocated, but I told myself he was only being protective. He loved me and just wanted me safe. Also, I was stupidly infatuated—what my dumb eighteen-year-old brain thought was love.

That one 'crazy' night changed everything.

I had been sleeping peacefully when Anthony shook me awake.

"Hey, Magpie, I need your help," his voice whispered in my ear.

The bedroom was dark, so I fumbled with my phone to check the time. "Now? It's midnight."

He flipped on a lamp and sat on the edge of the bed. He was in a puffy winter jacket since it was October and getting chilly outside. He stuck out his bottom lip in a pout. "Aww, baby, come on. You're gonna leave me hanging?" He started tickling my sides, waking me up fully and making me thrash the sheets around to get him to stop. Then he pinned my hands above my head and rubbed our noses together. "If you really loved me, you'd do it. Don't you love me?"

I giggled, gazing up into his dark eyes like they were actually my light. "Fine."

He kissed me. "That's my girl. Now get rid of that bad breath and put a sweater on. I'll wait outside."

He had released my hands, so I hit him with a pillow. "I don't have bad breath."

His nose scrunched as he raised a shoulder. His voice rose in pitch. "Well…"

I huffed into my hand to do a breath check. Smelled fine. "I do not," I said, chucking the pillow at him as he sauntered toward the door.

He threw his head back and laughed before leaving.

He loved teasing me.

Once I was dressed and outside, we hopped into Anthony's beat-up sedan and he drove me to a house I'd never seen. Light was shining through a living room window.

"Where are we?" I asked, shivering under my jacket and sweater because Anthony's crappy car had a broken heater.

"Jerry lives here."

Jerry was the shop owner I was forbidden from visiting. "What? Why are we here, then?"

Anthony's gaze fixated on a cat across the street, a black cat hunched under a car for warmth. Its eyes glowed like two red, reflective marbles.

"Give him some company," he said.

I should've paid more attention to the way his thin fingers strangled the steering wheel, or the way he watched that cat—not really seeing it.

But the tells in his body language, something he'd been trying to teach me, went unnoticed.

I only saw my boyfriend sitting there. After being an unwanted child, here was someone who wanted *me*, who thought *I* was important enough to help.

My grandfather was long dead, and no one else thought I had worth.

Just Anthony; he was the only person in the world who cared that I was alive.

"Why does he need company this late?" I asked through chattering teeth. "Why is he still awake?"

Anthony took off his scarf and wrapped it around my neck to help me warm up. Then he kissed me. In those early days, his kisses made any questions or doubts instantly leave my head.

He leaned across my lap to pop the door open. "He's

expecting you. Go say hi and wait for my call. I'll call you soon."

"Where are you going?"

Another kiss.

I stepped out of the car, blushing. "Fine, but this is weird."

"Thought you liked it weird?" He flashed me a stupid grin and his exceptionally straight teeth.

I laughed despite myself. "God, shut up."

He leaned over and pulled my door shut, giving me a smirk and a wink that said we'd continue the topic later.

I only felt happy.

As he drove off, I climbed the steps to the narrow house and knocked on the door. Just give the old man company? I didn't see any harm in that.

There was a loud thump inside, then Jerry yelled, "I know why you've come and I'm not going down without a fight!"

"It's Margaret," I called back. Who the hell did he think I was?

A few deadbolts unlocked, and Jerry peered through a crack in the door. Once he saw it was really me, he undid the top chain and opened it.

"Margaret?" he asked, as if he thought I was a ghost. As if a ghost had stolen his words and my name was the only one left.

My gaze fell to the gun in his hand. Anthony carried a gun, so it was something I had been around. But still... seeing Jerry clutch it with such a trembling hand made my stomach bottom out.

"E-everything okay?" I asked, eyes never leaving the gun. "Anthony wanted me to give you some company."

This old man treated me like a daughter, so I wasn't scared. Only tense. But even if you trust someone completely, when they're holding a gun, it's like they're holding pure death.

Something died in Jerry's eyes that second—a light fading to black. His leathery skin was suddenly gray and his eyes sunk to my feet. His tone was flat, like he was reading from a script. "Yes. Come in, Margaret. It's cold." He put the safety on the gun and dropped it on a side table.

I was relieved it was no longer in his shaky hands, though they kept shaking.

Nothing much happened while I stayed with him. Jerry made me some coffee because he said I looked tired. Might be a long night, he said.

I asked if something was bothering him, why he couldn't sleep, but he wouldn't answer. He said my boyfriend was nice for bringing me to see him.

"Tell him I said that, okay? You'll tell Anthony I'm grateful for your company."

I told him yes and asked about his store, but he changed the subject. He wanted to talk about his ex-wife, his daughters. He told me about having a plane ticket to visit his family for the holidays.

"Will you tell that to your boyfriend? I'd just like to visit my family for Christmas. Just let me visit them and then I'll come back, no problem. I swear."

I smiled and asked why he thought Anthony needed to know. "Just go visit your family. Anthony doesn't care."

He fell silent and turned on the TV.

Anthony finally called around two in the morning. "There's a car and driver outside. Bring Jerry with you and say I have a surprise for him at his shop."

"What—"

The call ended.

"Anthony says he has a surprise for you," I told Jerry matter-of-fact. I had no idea what was going on between the two of them, but surprises were usually good.

Jerry didn't look excited. He only got out of his chair, his knees popping, and walked to the door solemnly. Each step was like he had weights in his shoes.

I yawned. Despite the coffee, I was struggling to focus. I'd never been a late-night person, so I wanted to get done with this trip to the shop so I could go home and sleep.

Before he opened the door, Jerry grabbed the gun.

Still, I explained it away in my head—people carried concealed weapons in Chicago. Anthony did. It was late at night and parts of Chicago definitely weren't friendly. Jerry wanted to keep us safe. He was a kind, old man who I wished had been my real father. His sarcastic sense of humor and upbeat attitude also reminded me of my grandpa.

I was safe with Jerry.

We climbed in the car and the driver took us to Jerry's shop.

When we reached the door, he nudged me in front of him. "You go on, sweetheart," he said, as if still reading from a script. "Go on and say hi to your boyfriend. Tell him what I told you."

Goosebumps prickled my arms because Jerry sounded so strange, made such a strange request. Still, I walked in first.

The light immediately switched on and I gasped at the destruction around me. Aisle shelves were tipped over, broken bottles were scattered everywhere. Bags and food and liquid all mixed in a strange concoction of sweet and smoky smells.

Anthony and his friends stood in the middle of it all.

"Oh my god, what happened?" I said, trying to rush forward, but Jerry grabbed my arm. He held me in front of him.

I knew there was a gun in Jerry's shaky hand, and I saw Anthony's eyes glance at it.

"Try it," Anthony said. He tipped his chin at a man who had a gun pointed at Jerry. His voice was the hardest I'd ever heard it. "Take a chance and you'll die before your finger twitches."

My body was finally, *finally*, sensing danger, and every muscle seized up.

That wasn't Anthony. I didn't know the man in front of me—his eyes black as night, his posture relaxed yet coiled like a rattlesnake. His expression was pure hate, every line of his features unyielding and unmoving.

He didn't fit with the image of my boyfriend, who had been kissing me earlier and teasing me and flirting.

As the lightning bolt hit and I realized I didn't know anything about my boyfriend, not really, I also realized Jerry was using me as a shield. Wanted to hurt me.

I felt like the world's biggest idiot for not understanding sooner.

Jerry released me. He pushed me to the side and clicked the safety off his gun. "You tell him, Margaret. You tell him how I treated you well and I've never hurt you. Not once. How you're like family."

I didn't know what to do, so I opened my mouth.

"No, baby," Anthony said before I could speak.

The next second, one of Anthony's friends rushed Jerry from behind and grabbed his gun.

What happened then was a jumble of bodies and glass shattering and Jerry crying out for help.

I squeezed my eyes shut. How had I ended up there? How had life changed so quickly from sleeping soundly to *this*?

The worst part was that I knew Anthony did bad things. I knew he had to 'rough guys up.' He said it was just business. He said, "That's part of the game and anyone who plays understands the risks." And sometimes he came home bruised and bloody, but I had imagined fist fights between rival drug dealers, not ambushes on old men.

I knew, but I didn't want to know.

Anthony was the only person who cared for me, who treated me like someone special and gave me a place to belong, and I craved that so badly I ignored the rest.

That night, I still tried to ignore the truth, covering my face as Anthony beat that old man until he was a bloody slab of meat.

Anthony's hard voice cut through my denial, forcing me to confront what had been in front of me all along. "Margaret. Watch."

One of his friends grabbed my wrists and made me stop covering my eyes.

I watched as Anthony pounded that old man's face until he no longer had recognizable features. I watched him roll the body face down and kick the man's ribs. Spit on him. Finally, he stepped away, panting and wiping sweat from his brow. When his gaze landed on me, I screamed.

"Shh. Shh," he said, approaching.

I tried to back away, but his large friend was behind me, caging me in.

Anthony cupped my cheeks with bloody hands, and a

strangled cry tore from my throat.

"Shh, baby," he said, sounding like my boyfriend again. His gaze was tender, caring, but I still wanted to puke. "I know," he cooed. "I know that was tough, but you had to see. You need to understand our life and stop being so naïve. You can't go around blindly trusting anyone who gives you the tiniest bit of attention. You can't go telling others about us. Because it leads to this." He pointed at the motionless body. "He was screwing up my shipments and wanted to snitch. You don't want me to go to jail, do you, baby?"

I didn't respond; I didn't know how to respond because I was still coming to terms with the fact that my boyfriend was capable of such horrors.

He kissed my forehead. "Hey. Look at me." I refused, so he sighed. He lowered his hands and wiped the blood on his pants. "I'll give you some time. But honestly, don't feel too bad about the bastard. A few decades ago, he beat and raped three girls about your age."

I finally looked at him. "You're lying. He was, is…he *is* a sweet old man. He's my friend. You're lying!"

He only smirked and nodded at the man behind me. I was pulled to the car outside and then driven home.

I scrubbed myself in the shower, but never felt clean.

I never felt clean again.

Because I stayed with Anthony for three more years. I was complicit in more horrors.

I never found out if that old man lived or died, but his shop closed and never reopened.

I never found out if what Anthony said was true.

He's still behind me, hovering over me as we face the open window and my painting. I grab my paintbrush, dig it into some black and then drag it across the canvas diagonally.

Anthony tsks. "Now, why did you do that? I liked that painting."

I swivel on my stool to face him. "Did that old man die?"

He frowns, like I'm talking nonsense. "Old man?"

"From our 'crazy' night."

"Oh." He crosses his arms. "He was seventy, so he's dead by now."

I grit my teeth. "Did he die that night?"

"No."

"You're lying."

We stare at each other, and then his thin lips curl up at the corners. I can't tell if that's an admission of the truth or if he's smiling from some sexual satisfaction about getting me riled up.

He glances at his watch. "I have to go, but have dinner with me later."

"I won't be hungry."

"That wasn't a question."

I stare him down again, and he bites his bottom lip. "You're fun today," he comments before facing the door.

When he reaches for the knob, the question that's been clawing at my insides for years finally comes out, "Was it true? You told me the old man was a rapist. Was he?"

Anthony doesn't turn around, talking at the door while I study the sharp lines of his back. "It's strange how some parts of us never change," he says, his tone sounding like he's in a tunnel, echoey and distant. "We grow up, learn our lessons, but there are these stubborn, idiotic parts that just refuse to change. I thought time would've changed your idealistic view of the world, but it hasn't." He glances at me over his shoulder, his ugly smirk melting into a frown. "Why have you always had such misguided instincts? You think I'd do something disgusting like take you against your will, yet you're feeling bad about someone who would have? I protected you when no one else did." His jaw muscles flex and he tips his head back to look down at me. "I used to love your innocence, but now I find it irritating. After all these years, you still think there's good in people. But no one is good, Margaret. Some people are better at hiding it than others, but we've all done twisted shit. Even that rich asshole you're wet for."

He leaves, slamming the door.

I immediately stand and start searching the room for anything sharp. There's nothing—Anthony has my environment too controlled. He even took away that wooden paintbrush I snapped, giving me impossible-to-bend plastic ones instead.

Since I can't shred the canvas, I smear black paint all over it, not caring how it coats my clothes and drops on the floor. Then I knock the canvas over, stomp on a corner, and start bending the wooden frame. It takes a lot of effort, but I finally break it.

I toss it out the window.

The guard outside on the ground floor yelps. "What the fuck?" he calls out.

I slam the window shut, then sit on the stool and sob.

I hate him. I hate how I cared for him once. I hate myself for staying so long in the past, hoping my love would somehow change him.

I hate that he's right.

There are too many wolves in this world, and it's always the friendly ones who are the most dangerous.

I think…

I mean, I'll have to find the strength…

If I ever want to truly escape…

To truly keep Jada and Declan safe…

I have to kill the wolf.

CHAPTER 29

DECLAN

I LEAN AGAINST THE KITCHEN counter, pinching the bridge of my nose and trying to keep my mind focused while Sean recounts his conversation with Jeremy from the previous night. He spent a lot of time giving me minor details about going to the bar, ordering, what they ordered, what the server said…so far, it's a lot of pieces. He hasn't yet put it all together in a way I can wrap my head around.

He's clearly still affected by a bad hangover.

"So he's taking side jobs?" I ask.

Sean chugs the rest of his ginger tea and goes to set the mug down on my black marble countertop. It slips from his fingers partway and clunks on the marble. I frown, hoping he didn't just leave a chip.

"Uh, sorry," he mumbles, taking the mug to the sink. Then he groans and rubs his forehead, facing me. "Yeah. Jeremy is doing other gigs."

"And? Why should I care about that? You take other gigs."

"Right, but…" He pauses, looking like he's searching his brain for the right words. "He said it paid better than what you pay. He called you stingy."

I scoff. I guess he's entitled to his own opinion, but that's fucking irritating. I pay my people well, provide top-notch benefits. For Jeremy to suggest otherwise…

My jaw clenches. "Must be a good gig, considering what

I pay him."

"That's what I thought. I thought, who the fuck would pay more than Declan? I don't get why they would contact Jeremy directly and not NexaProtect."

"I can think of a reason."

Sean studies me for a moment, peering at me from under a long side-swept bang. Then understanding flashes across his face, a brow lifting. "Something illegal?"

"Normally, when you don't go through a legitimate company, you're doing something you want to keep hidden."

"Right. I didn't think much of it at the time—well, I was drunk—but the way he was talking about you, about the money...that all stuck in my head when I woke up this morning."

I grab a towel and wipe a wet spot off the counter. Yup, Sean just chipped the marble. "You think I should fire him because he might be taking illegal side jobs?" That is a reason for concern, but not something Sean had to make me rush home for.

"No, well, yeah, but it's more than that. Like I said, it's all fuzzy, but something isn't sitting right about that conversation. He said—" He rubs his forehead some more, staring at his feet. "He said something about a job under your nose and you had no idea."

My spine becomes rigid steel. "What job?"

"Didn't say. I wasn't thinking straight enough to ask. Whoever gave him that job wants him for more work. Needs more men. Something like that. It pays a fuck-ton of money, too. And he mentioned...uh, Chicago. The next job is in Chicago."

"Illinois..." I say, half-mumbling to myself.

"Uh, yeah. Chicago, Illinois."

The hair on the back of my next prickles, a rush of electricity over my skin. *Illinois.* The state where Davis traced some of those threatening emails.

Just a coincidence?

No, there have been too many coincidences lately for it all to be random. I don't yet understand how or why, but the hacker, the lawsuit, Jeremy…they seem connected.

The sooner I can figure it out, the sooner I can focus on finding Sienna. This fucking hacker situation has been too much of a distraction from that.

"Call him," I tell Sean, who is now clutching his stomach like the tea made him sick. "I need to know what job he did recently, why he thinks I'm stupid for not noticing. I also need to know who hired him, so pretend you're interested in the side work."

"Sure, but he knows I'm loyal to you. Last night, he was drunk and just running his mouth. Don't think he would've told me sober."

"Then make something up. Tell him I fired you because I caught you fucking someone in my bed."

He chokes on a laugh, then his eyes get a little shifty.

I frown. "You haven't done that, have you?"

"Uh, no, no…" His voice has a high pitch that I don't like.

I may need to burn my mattress. "Just call him, please. See what you can get."

Sean nods, already pulling out his phone. He dials Jeremy's number and puts the phone on speaker, laying it on the countertop.

"Hey, man," Jeremy answers, sounding stuffy. "Fuck. My head is still pounding from last night. Yours?"

Sean does his best to relax and act normally, his tone

friendly. "Of course, man. Appreciate you buying all my drinks. Maybe we should do it again this weekend."

Jeremy laughs. "Not if you're going to get top-shelf shots again. I said I had a *little* extra cash, not that I was rich."

Sean chuckles with him, taking the opening in the conversation. "Sorry, but you'll be buying drinks for a while. Fucking Declan fired me."

"What? No way. Why?"

"He has all these fucking rules about shit. I was getting tired of it. Don't go in certain rooms. Don't touch his food. Don't shut doors loudly. Asshole. I mean, I moved in as a favor to him and he yells at me for eating his yogurt *once*."

I frown hard at Sean, but he only shrugs a shoulder, like he's innocently just doing what I asked.

I'd argue that he's taking it a bit too far. We should have a conversation about any resentments toward me he's built over the years.

"I was pissed and wanted some payback," Sean continues, "so I may have invited a few women over when he was working late. Things got messy in Declan's bed."

I am definitely going to burn my mattress.

Jeremy is laughing hysterically now. "No fucking way. He found out?"

"He walked in."

"What, bro? Fuck, I would've loved to see the look on that asshole's face."

"It was pretty satisfying. But he kicked me out. Makes sense, but I'm out of work now."

Jeremy calms himself and says, "I can't believe he fired you after all these years, though. Glad I kept looking for other work. One year with him is enough."

"Just because I was loyal to him doesn't mean I get the

304 | RAINA ASH

same in return," Sean says.

There's a pause, then Jeremy takes the bait. I'm glad because I'm not sure how much more I can stand of Sean 'playfully' making jabs at me. I very clearly labeled that yogurt container.

Sounding edgy and hesitating around words, Jeremy asks, "You need some work?"

"Yeah, I'm pretty desperate. My savings won't last long and Declan's not going to be a reference. I'm tired of working for rich business assholes. Your guy better?"

"I was wondering if you remembered what we talked about last night."

"I won't tell anyone, but I want in. If there's an opening."

"There is. And my guy is *way* better. Pays a lot more. But you're sure? It's not what you normally do. There's a risk, so it's not like you won't be earning that bigger payday."

Sean sighs. "Honestly, I'm ready for something else. Not like I got a family to worry about, so risk isn't a problem. I just like to be prepared, so what's the job you did for your guy recently? Will it be the same work?"

My eyebrow quirks. Sean's transition into that was pretty smooth.

There's a pause, then Jeremy says, "You're really serious, though? I need to know you're really in before I tell you details, man."

"I wouldn't be calling if I wasn't. What do you want from me? I need this work, so I'm desperate."

Jeremy laughs again. "I dunno. Know that fucker's bank account?"

Sean glances at me. I'd rather not give away that information, but I have a few cards with lower limits I can risk. I feel so close to the truth that my entire body is charged.

Quickly, I pull a credit card from my wallet and hand it to Sean.

He tells Jeremy, "Bank account? No. But I swiped a card before I left. Figured I couldn't do much with it before Declan blocks transactions, but we could have a little fun if you want. I know too much shit about him, so he won't come after me."

Sean meets my gaze again and shrugs.

If anything, this conversation has enlightened me about my bodyguard. I make a mental note never to piss off Sean. He'd be a scary enemy.

"No way!" Jeremy says. "Fuck, let's do it. But alright, listen…the job I did before is different from what my guy needs now. He needs a lot of men to help transport some cargo. I can't say more than that, just 'cargo,' if you feel me."

"Sure, I got it," Sean says. I wave at him to hold on, so he says, "But, uh…"

I type a quick memo on my phone, then show Sean the screen.

"But what?" Jeremy asks.

Sean's eyes scan what I want him to ask. "Uh, well, last night you said the guy is in Chicago. So the job is there?"

"Yeah."

"Why doesn't he find guys near him? Why take us?"

"Hah, we must think alike. I asked the same thing. The guy said his city is full of backstabbers. Too many men who work for his enemies. He always hires guys from different states who don't care about Chicago politics and just want to make some easy cash."

Sean and I share a look. This situation keeps getting more and more layered. The guy sounds like a crime boss, so I'm wondering what he could possibly have against me.

Why the hacking?

"Makes sense," Sean says.

"Oh, and we'll have some heavy weapons on us in case shit goes down. You have good aim?"

"I was in the Marines."

"Oh, right," Jeremy says. "Cool. Let's meet and we can talk about it. I'll tell you more about the guy. Don't want to say too much over the phone."

"I got it. I'm curious...how long will I be there?"

"Probably a few weeks. Maybe a month. But my guy will give us housing, food, women"—he laughs—"*everything*, man. It's risky work, but it's worth it."

I can sense Jeremy is ready to hang up without giving up the information I really need, so I motion at Sean to keep him talking.

"Hey, thanks for bringing me in," Sean says. He glances at the new memo I typed on my phone. "Uh...yeah, so I really appreciate this. What was the job you did for the guy recently?"

I grimace—he asked that too directly.

Thankfully, Jeremy doesn't notice. "Eh, nothing that exciting. When we were in Hawaii, he wanted me to look the other way so he could deliver something to that woman. You remember? That day I walked in that room service cart myself."

My breath stills.

"Deliver what?" Sean asks, his tone upbeat but his expression heavy.

"A note I think. I didn't ask for details. He offered me money, said he wanted the woman Declan was fucking, so I helped. Sorry I had to deceive you, too, man. That's why I told you I checked the food and wouldn't let you look under the cover. Hope you understand."

Sean looks sick again, his skin turning pale, but to his credit, his tone is friendly and unaffected. "Hey, it's a job. I don't care. Why do you think he wanted her?"

Jeremy laughs. "Dunno. He seemed like a vengeful ex to me, but maybe she fucked him over or something. I haven't met the guy paying me yet. The one who wanted her. But I'll meet him in Chicago."

"Cool," Sean says. "Well, I have to go, but let's meet tonight. Text me later. We'll use Declan's card."

"Sounds good, man. See you then."

The call ends and silence fills the kitchen.

My mind is anything but quiet. In fact, there's so much in my head that I can't even form full thoughts.

Sienna's ex?

Chicago.

Ex is…behind emails.

Sienna's there? Chicago?

Crime boss.

Underneath it all is the loud roar of the only thing helping me keep myself together: Sienna lied.

That day in Hawaii when she was suddenly acting strange and then stormed out, she needed an excuse to leave.

Because her ex threatened her with some note, kidnapped her.

She lied.

And I couldn't be fucking happier.

As I lean hard against the kitchen counter for support, Sean finally breaks the silence. He's clutching his stomach, hovering near the sink. "I…I'm sorry. Why didn't I check the platter?"

I try to touch his shoulder, but he jerks away.

"No, don't tell me some bullshit," he growls. "Don't tell me that I didn't know Jeremy was deceiving me, or that it was an oversight, because those things shouldn't fucking happen." He hunches over the sink, dry heaving. "Why do I keep…fucking up when it counts most?"

"I'm not blaming you for this," I tell him, though I know he's blaming himself.

He's the best bodyguard I've ever met, but when I hired him, there was a chunk of time left off his resume. He told me he took a sabbatical for a year, so I left it at that. Since then, I've witnessed how hard he is on himself, even for minor miscalculations. My gut tells me something happened during that year. Something that shook him badly.

I touch his shoulder, refusing to let him shake me off this time. "Jeremy had a job, too, and he's the one who failed. Sienna's ex sounds like the kind of man who would've found another way, even if you had discovered the note."

He turns on the faucet to splash water on his face. "I should've looked. I should've done my job. She'd be safe if I had." He straightens, giving me a strained look, like he's fighting against the urge to dry heave again. "We have to go to the police."

"And tell them what, exactly? What's your evidence? You heard a wild story from a drunk coworker? You don't even know the location of this job in Chicago."

"Okay, so I meet Jeremy tonight, get the address, then we go to the cops. Your woman was kidnapped, and it's my fault. I have to—"

"The police won't do anything without some proof. And you're talking across state lines. Besides, when I get to Chicago and find the man terrorizing her, I might just murder him."

Sean stares at me like I spoke in tongues. "You can't confront this person yourself."

"Why the hell not?" As soon as I ask, I know it's a stupid question. I'm not some vigilante, and this man could actually be a crime boss. But I've had an adrenaline spike and I'm ready to climb onto my private jet right now in search of justice.

He better not have hurt Sienna.

Sean is thankfully being the rational one. "The man sounds dangerous," he says, pressing two fingers against his temple like his headache just got worse. "He likely has connections. We don't know anything about him. Jeremy said he was moving cargo, so what if he's cartel?" He sizes me up. "You've never even held a gun, yet you want to go confront a criminal?"

"Isn't that why I have you? You're ex-military."

Sean won't stop shaking his head, and I can only wonder what he's telling himself. Probably worrying about more mistakes. But I trust him.

Finally, he sighs. "What are you suggesting?"

"We just need to bring Sienna home, then we can go to the police. Meet with Jeremy tonight, get more details, and then we'll think of a plan."

"This is insane."

"Probably."

"And it sounds like going down this path means I'll be flying to Chicago and joining this...gang."

"Only until we get Sienna."

Sean crosses his arms and stares at the tile, suddenly looking like he aged five years, his body limp and skin sallow.

"It's your choice," I add. "You certainly didn't sign up for this, and I won't fire you if you say no. I know this is a big ask, and it puts your life in danger. No amount of money can compensate for that, but it goes without saying that you'll get a huge bonus."

"But you'd still go? Alone?"

"Yes."

Turning my back on this isn't an option. I won't stop, won't rest, until she's safe. Until she's back where she belongs.

With me.

She's done something—opened me up, exposed me. She's given me the courage to move away from the tragedy of my past and let myself find happiness again.

I'm her protector, after all; the man at the top of the stairs.

I'm ready to give my life to be that man for her.

Sean finally groans and then straightens, shoving a hand through his hair, which pushes his black bangs away and gives me a rare glimpse of his entire face.

There's a scar on his upper forehead. Why have I never noticed that?

"Even if you didn't pay me," he says through tight lips, "I'm not letting you do this alone. You'll just get yourself killed, then I'll be out an employer. I kind of like my benefits."

I lay a hand on his shoulder, squeezing. "I appreciate this. Name a price and it's yours."

With a laugh, he blurts out, "Five million and a yacht."

"Done."

He gapes at me, his jaw going slack. I don't know why he thought I wasn't serious—I'm a man of my word.

His face contorts, and he curses under his breath.
"Should've asked for more. I don't even want a yacht…"
After a beat, he gives me a grave look, nods his head, and
then goes off to prepare for his meeting with Jeremy later.

I walk to the living room and stare at Sienna's perfect
portrait of me, which now hangs prominently above my
couch.

I'll fight for her.

I'll bring her home.

Or I'll die trying.

CHAPTER 30

SIENNA

I'VE BEEN IN THIS ROOM too many days, refusing to leave and forcing Anthony or the guards to bring me food. Thankfully, he's stopped demanding I have dinner with him, and he's backed off a little.

I'm relieved; I need time to myself to think.

Could I really kill him?

I haven't even gotten to the part where I try to figure out how—How would I do it? When? Is there a way to stop Victor from coming after me?—because I'm stuck on the beginning question: Can I?

Meaning, do I have it in me to take a life?

As Margaret, I would've never gone that far. Sienna is supposed to be better than her, yet now I'm considering…?

I can't even figure out a quote to help me figure things out; there's nothing.

I need a break from this room, a break from my thoughts. I should go to the kitchen for a snack and give myself a few minutes to walk through the house, to dull the hard edges, to numb the constant ache.

I open my bedroom door. As expected, there's a guard sitting in the hallway, staring at his phone. His bored eyes lift when I appear.

"I want to go to the kitchen," I say, my voice as still as a poisoned pond that no animals dare approach. Being flat and emotionless is the only way to survive in this stupid house.

He nods, pocketing his phone and escorting me down the hallway. When I turn toward the living room, the normal route to the stairs leading up to the kitchen, he touches my elbow.

"Business meeting," he says gruffly, guiding me through a detour. Outside, there's a tiny patio with a staircase that connects to the third-story terrace. From there, an outside door connects to the kitchen.

I don't know why this house is such a maze; I wonder if Anthony actually designed it himself. If so, I'm sure he had some strategy in mind for enemies. Secret rooms and hidden hallways or whatever.

Sounds like him.

No doubt, he's sitting around in the living room right now with his 'associates,' talking about drug smuggling or human trafficking or whatever he's up to nowadays. I do my best not to think about it.

As we step outside and climb the stairs to the terrace, I breathe in the fresh air, letting it fill my lungs. Letting the afternoon sun warm my skin. Getting out of the room is making me feel better, and it is a beautiful day.

We reach the top step, and the day suddenly becomes dark. Every cell in my body ceases functioning.

He's here.

Near the railing.

Victor.

Anthony's boss. I've only seen him a few times in my life, but he's a man who sparks an instant terror, even if you know nothing about him. It's the cut of his cheekbones, or the cut of his shoulders, or just the overpowering energy he emits. It must be the fear a rabbit feels when it sees the glowing, hungry eyes of a predator.

He's standing at the edge of the terrace in a white suit, his gaze distant, his face carved from stone. He's not a big man; he's actually just a few inches taller than me. But he doesn't need to be tall and bulky—he has the aura of a viper always poised to strike. I've seen men who were well above six feet cower before this man.

When he hears footsteps, he angles his head slightly. Our eyes meet, a glimmer of recognition passing between us as my legs wobble. I wonder if he's killed a man simply by staring him down with those soulless eyes.

He says one word to me that cuts like glass: "You."

I scurry back down the stairs, the guard following. I don't need to eat; I'd rather get back to my room and lock myself in forever.

The guard stays in the hallway as I enter my bedroom and slam the door, locking it and checking a few times to make sure it's secure. It's a false sense of safety, but it's all I have and it's what I need.

You.

My spine suddenly feels fragile under the weight of the panic gripping me; I might snap at any moment. It sounded like he wasn't expecting to see me. He knows everything I did—knows I'm a snitch—so I have been wondering why he let Anthony bring me here.

Unless he didn't know.

I collapse on the edge of my bed, running sweaty palms along my black leggings as the cold realization hits.

Anthony is hiding me from Victor.

Or was.

It all makes sense now. Anthony probably didn't come after me as soon as he got out of prison because he had to wait for the right time. He's clearly been moving up in the world, gaining wealth, status, connections. He had to wait until he thought he could sneak me past Victor, or until he thought he could handle Victor's wrath about the situation.

Now the secret is out, and I don't know what that means.

Sucking on my bottom lip, I finger my locket. Victor isn't forgiving. I imagine he'd want to punish me, sell me to some person who will lock me in a room and use me as a sex doll.

The thought is sickening.

My only comfort is knowing that Anthony would wage war before letting me get sold to the highest bidder. Literally.

He's a sick, twisted bastard who gets rough sometimes, but he's never assaulted me. After testing his boundaries, I'm confident he'd never kill me or want me dead. He would fight Victor to keep me safe.

So, if I somehow find the courage to kill Anthony now...I'm even more fucked.

I wilt onto the bed, falling deeper into a bottomless hole. Is there no escape?

Turning onto my side, I pull a small journal from my nightstand and run my hand over the cool surface. I'm doing my best to fight, but every day feels like I'm closer and closer to getting crushed by the darkness thickening around me.

Now I have to rely on Anthony for protection? When he's the one holding me captive...

What a fucked up life.

I might be getting punished by the Universe for my crimes. I thought that sending Anthony to jail and having the authorities say, "You're good to go. Here's a new identity," was me facing justice and redemption.

I forgot about karma. It's a much bigger bitch than I imagined.

First, I get a taste of a good life in San Fran, only for it to be ripped away without warning. Then I meet the man of my dreams—caring, patient, devoted—only for us to be doomed to be apart. Now I'm forced to rely on my enemy because there's a much bigger threat.

I'm just so tired.

I slip a folded paper from my journal and open it. For the first time in days, I'm able to smile, a tiny light still flickering in my chest.

The paper is a sketch I drew of Declan, a copy of the selfie he sent me the day I left Hawaii. I knew I couldn't bring that phone with me, so I saved the image to the cloud. I also knew Anthony wouldn't let me access the Internet for a very long time, so I simply drew a copy of the selfie as quickly as I could, capturing as many details as possible.

A graphite version of Declan smiles at me from the slip of paper, his eyes crinkling at the edges, hair messy after a night of fucking. Guilt eats at me every time I look at this sketch, but I tell it to just please let me have *this*. I only need a few minutes to feel the warmth that man gave me, to think of how peaceful I felt in his arms.

It's helping me survive until I figure a way out.

So many pictures of this beautiful man now fill my sketchbook. Him sitting on the couch, laying on a bed, stepping out of the shower with his hair all sexy and wet, his muscles flexing as he hits a punching bag...I've been capturing every memory of him I can. And I've hidden some of the drawings around the room in case Anthony ever looks at my sketchbook and throws a fit.

My greatest comfort, though, is knowing that there's

still the actual picture of Declan waiting for me in the cloud. I may have broken his heart and ruined any chance of him ever speaking to me again, but I still have that one perfect picture. Someday, I'll be able to see it again. Something worth fighting for.

I press the drawing to my chest, apologizing for the thousandth time about what I said. After crying into my pillow, I take a nap, images of Declan's pained, broken gaze filling my nightmares.

I WAKE WITH A JOLT from the sound of glass shattering outside. Rubbing sleep from my eyes and trying to get my heart out of my throat, I hurry to the window. I hear familiar voices floating down from the terrace.

"You're refusing?" Victor says in that cold, collected way of his. Even so, there's a slow, simmering anger behind every word.

I hear glass shards scraping against something, like someone is kicking them out of the way. "She won't be a problem," Anthony bites back. "It's handled."

"I cleaned up your mess *once*, but you clearly didn't learn your lesson. That woman cannot be trusted, so take care of her." There's a pause, then a stifled groan. Did Victor grab Anthony? "If you don't," Victor spits, "then whatever happens to you isn't my problem. Dig your own grave if you like, but I won't be rescuing you again."

I press fingers to my lips, unable to even gasp. So…if I did something to Anthony, does that mean Victor would leave me alone? As long as I don't do anything against Victor, maybe—

There's a loud smack, skin hitting skin, then the sliding door opens, presumably Victor leaving.

Anthony cusses then someone else, probably one of his men, says, "What are we doing, boss? I can take care of her right now."

My heart leaps higher in my throat.

"Margaret stays," Anthony yells, and it sounds like he smacks his hand against the railing. "Do not fucking touch her. No one touches her! End of discussion."

"Okay, boss. Okay."

Anthony sighs heavily. "Are those fucking documents finished? And the PR release?"

"Uh…which documents, boss?"

"The fucking reports Emerson was making." There's a pause, like his guy might be looking confused. "About Tiffany Conte? Toxicology?"

"Oh, right. Thought you wanted something about the actress."

Anthony sighs again and more glass is kicked around. "No, that woman is a future problem and not entirely mine to deal with. Right now, I want the rich bastard who touched my woman to get fucked by every news outlet in America."

"They should be ready by the end of the week."

"Good. Fuck, I need a drink." Glass crunches. "And clean this shit up." The sliding door opens and closes.

I stumble away from my window, knocking my easel and paints over. They scatter on the floor, but I just kick them aside.

What is Anthony doing to Declan?

I hurry to my bedroom door and unlock it. "I need Anthony," I tell the guard sitting outside.

He doesn't look up from his phone. "There's a meeting

right—"

"I need to see him. You want me to scream and piss off Victor?"

The guard rolls his neck, looking like he's not having a good day. After typing out a message on his phone, he says, "There."

I pace in the hallway until Anthony appears a few minutes later. He's scowling, but there's a hint of concern.

"What?" he asks when he's close, scanning me to see if I have an injury.

My eyes fixate on the redness of his right cheek and the slight purple along the bone.

Victor struck him.

"What?" Anthony asks again, harder this time.

"Uh…" I move into the bedroom, shutting the door after he follows. I'm simply too exhausted from this entire day that I don't have the energy to approach this carefully. Maybe I should try to soften him up, get him in a relaxed mood, but my anxiety is making me irrational.

"You said you wouldn't hurt Declan," I blurt out.

His eyes narrow and then dart to the open window. He runs a hand through his dark hair, looking too weathered and old for a 29-year-old. Dark grooves cut the skin around his eyes and his gaze is sunken. "So, you're being a nosey bitch?"

"You said if I came with you, that you wouldn't hurt Declan."

"People change."

"You've never broken your word."

He huffs out a laugh, then steps closer. His eyes close and he sighs. "Baby, I said he'd *live*. I didn't say anything about making him deal with consequences. He touched something that belongs to me, so I'm going to ruin his life. But he'll live. That was my only agreement."

My voice wavers when I ask, "How? What are you doing?"

He smirks like he's feeling satisfied with himself, like he's so genius for whatever he's planning. "You thought that man didn't have his own secrets? He's a criminal, like the rest of us."

I shake my head; it doesn't matter if I know what he's planning. I just need to stop him. "What do you want? To leave Declan alone, what do you want?"

He scans my body, taking in the curves he can see from my tight leggings and sleeveless top. "I've already got you, so I can't say there's anything else I need." He steps close enough for me to smell the cigar smoke on his breath. His smirk fades in an instant, replaced by heavy brows that are like cuts on his face. He grabs my arm and I yelp. "If you're going to offer to fuck me to save that man, don't. Sex isn't a currency." His brows soften just a few centimeters and his long lashes flutter. A vulnerability. But it's quickly smothered by sharpness. "The day I fuck you is the day you give your-self willingly and remember how good we are together."

Our perception of 'good' must be worlds apart.

Bile rises in my throat because I think I know what will convince Anthony to leave Declan alone—the one thing Anthony has always sought.

God, I don't want to say this, but...it's for Declan. All I want is for Declan to be safe, no matter what happens to me. I force the words out. "I'll...I'll marry you. I'll become your wife, and you'll have all of me forever."

He releases my arm and his mouth falls open. "Today?"

I swallow a protest. "Today. Bring me the papers and I'll

sign them. We can have a ceremony later if you want."

"Fuck," he mutters.

My words must've flipped a switch because his demeanor is completely different—shining eyes, straight spine. A boyish grin. He grabs my waist and rolls his growing hardness against me to show how much the idea excites him. He opens his mouth to say something, but then kisses me instead.

I inhale sharply through my nose, my lips sealed shut. Then I think of why I need to do this, for the man I really love, and I force my mouth open, letting Anthony deepen the kiss with tongue. He tastes like cigars and whiskey and… a past I really want to leave behind.

My death.

Or his.

Maybe marrying him can serve two purposes.

He pulls away, pressing his forehead to mine and cradling my face. "Fuck, baby. I don't think I have time to get the papers today, but I will before I head out of town next week. We'll sign the paperwork, but let's put the ceremony off for a few months. Once you're ready for the wedding night, we'll start planning, okay? I want you to have the time you need to feel comfortable."

His voice has softened so much I feel like Margaret again, listening to her boyfriend say caring things. I don't like the contrast. Sometimes, I wish people were only black and white, especially someone as twisted as Anthony.

But he's not pure evil, no one is. We all have grays that exist between right and wrong. Right now, Anthony is reminding me of the charming, lovesick boy he was when we first met, not the ruthless killer who hunted me down and took away my life.

I suppose he's both.

I suppose I'm half Margaret, half Sienna. Half needy and half strong.

Am I half a killer too?

"Okay," I say, lowering my gaze.

"Damn, waiting this long…it'll be like popping your cherry all over again on our wedding night. You remember our first time?"

I try not to. I need to get him focused on the main issue, so I say, "If I marry you, will you promise to stop whatever you're planning?"

The shining parts of him immediately dim, a frown making him gloomy. "No, baby, I can't do that. But I promise not to hurt him physically."

"Please," I whisper, touching his chest and willing my body to move closer to his. "I'm yours. I'll be your wife soon. Isn't that what matters? He didn't know I was yours. I never told him, so it's not his fault. You should be mad at me. Please." I touch his red cheek carefully with a shaky hand, forcing out more words I don't want to say. "You're my"—I swallow bile and clear my throat—"husband. He's…just in the past and not important."

Anthony groans and cups my hand, pressing it against his bruise; I know it must hurt. "Damn, stop begging. You're turning me on too much." His jaw flexes and then he relents with a sigh. "Fine. I'll go easier on him, but he's getting *some* consequences."

I nod, knowing this small victory is all I'm getting right now. I'll work on softening him more later. Hopefully, I'll get him to let go of his revenge scheme completely.

Declan has been through enough.

I want Anthony to leave, but there's one more thing on

my mind. "Is Victor going to…will he…"

Without hesitation, Anthony cradles my face, forcing me to meet his gaze. "No, baby. I promise. I brought you here. I'll keep you safe." He kisses my forehead. "I love you. You know that. I'd die before I let him hurt you."

I exhale, hating that I have to rely on him, at least for now. He's obsessive and cruel and manipulative…but his feelings for me have always been absolute, even though he doesn't understand real love. His parents are probably to blame for that; either way, his affection comes from a place of possession and power games, not genuine care.

Doesn't matter. Right now, I only need him to keep me safe from a bigger monster and to leave Declan and my friends alone.

And when the timing is right, I'll…

I'll…

Walk him to his deathbed? Do I have that in me?

He wipes a tear from my cheek. "Shh, baby, it's okay."

Why am I crying? I hate this man. I hate how he fucked up my life, stalked me, made everything a nightmare.

And yet…I've never been cut out for his world. I've played along, but I've never fit. I don't know if I can really kill him. Taking a life is such a heavy burden, even if it's the only way I can save myself.

If only I'd never met him.

He kisses my forehead again. "Take it easy the rest of the day. I'll send more art supplies, baby. If I'm here in the morning, have breakfast with me."

It's not a question, but I nod.

He leaves the room.

I return to my bed to clutch a drawing of Declan.

Please let Anthony keep his word.

CHAPTER 31

SIENNA

I STAND IN FRONT OF my dresser, gripping the expensive mahogany. The marriage document sits on top, one edge crinkled. Anthony didn't waste time getting it.

But I've been wasting time and not signing it.

Once I do, once this document gets filed, I'll be Anthony's wife. The weight of that fact has been pressing down on me, suffocating me. I have to do it to protect Declan, and it'll help me get Anthony to trust me someday and let down his guard...but this is permanent. Whatever happens, he'll be a fixed smudge on my life. There will be an official record of us together. He won't just be an ex, he'll be an ex-husband.

The only true escape is death.

I turn away from the dresser. I need another break from this room, and some heavy emotional eating. Thankfully, Victor left a few days ago, so I won't be seeing that terrifying face again.

I open my bedroom door and the guard in the hallway escorts me to the kitchen. Cold seeps into my feet from the tile as I rummage through the pantry. Soon, my arms are overflowing with bags of chips, cookies, and a box of Twinkies.

I'm about to leave the kitchen when a burst of laughter from the outside terrace catches my attention. I glance out the kitchen window and my heart plummets.

There, on the terrace, is Sean, smiling and chatting with

Anthony's men like they're old buddies.

Well, at least now I know he was the bribed bodyguard. I was really hoping it was the other guy, because I kind of liked Sean.

My guard is ready to escort me back to my room through the house, but I move out the terrace door too fast for him to stop me. The men outside all pause to look my way. Sean gives me a cool glance.

I tip my chin at him, spit out the word, "Asshole," then throw the box of Twinkies at his head.

He catches it, one-handed, with a cocky smirk. He says something too low for me to hear, and the guys around him crack up.

"Alright, come on," my guard says, touching my arm lightly to guide me down the outside stairs that lead to the second floor.

Once I'm back in my room, I slam the door and shove a cookie into my mouth. The chocolate isn't doing its job to make me feel better, so I shove another one in, almost choking. Finally, I flop on the bed.

No one can be trusted, can they?

Sean was supposed to be Declan's bodyguard, yet Anthony bought him off, no problem.

Everyone is like that, just waiting to stab you in the back. Hurt you. Throw you in the trash.

I grip my locket. Well, not Grandpa. And not Jada. Or Declan.

My heart knows that. I don't care what Anthony says about him doing his own twisted shit because I've done much worse. If I don't believe that at least a few people in the world have good intentions, is there a point to living?

I have to believe that Declan always had good intentions.

I let out a groan, which might be a half-sob since my insides are crumbling, and shove one more cookie into my stupid face. Then I grab my sketchbook and start drawing butterflies in a cheery meadow.

A few hours pass, and I'm lost in a haze of half-hearted attempts at sketching when there's a knock at my door. Anthony walks in before I can tell him to enter, like always.

He looks dressed to kill, literally. His gray suit probably has a lot of weapons hidden underneath. "Hey, Magpie," he says, stuffing his hands in his pockets like he doesn't have a care in the world. "Need anything?"

"No, thanks," I respond, not looking at him and focusing instead on the mushroom I'm drawing. I'm giving it evil, beady eyes.

He saunters over to the dresser and glances at the license. "Come here."

My heart lurches, but I close my sketchbook and walk across the room. Resisting won't help anything right now.

He pulls out a pen and offers it to me. "Thought you decided to be a good girl. If you're going back on your word, maybe I'll—"

I snatch the pen, hovering it over the flimsy paper that has the power to completely change someone's life. I stare at him until he peaks an eyebrow.

"Promise you'll leave Declan alone," I say. "Whatever you're planning, just stop all of it."

He growls, his fingernails scraping over the dresser top as he slowly makes a fist. "You're about to become *my* wife, yet you're still—"

"Your wife," I echo, dropping the pen so I can spread my palms over his chest. After all, Anthony is the one who taught Margaret how to manipulate people. It's a skill I need to perfect again. My body softens into him. "I'll be your wife, not his. He's in the past, so I don't want to think about him anymore. We can let it go. Move on." I caress his cheek, reminding myself it's for a purpose. "I want it all to be forgotten so we can focus on us." My thumb trails his bottom lip. "Don't you want it to be just us?"

His hungry eyes almost make me shove him away. But I stand firm. This is for a purpose.

His fist relaxes, and he glances at the marriage license. "This fucking weak spot for you…fine. I won't do anything unless he provokes me."

"Provokes you? What—"

"Just a saying. I gave you my word, now will you sign the goddamn paper?"

I grab the pen and sign 'Sienna Bishop.'

I drop the pen like it's burning me.

Done.

There's no going back now.

A wide grin splits his sharp features. "Damn, you're really my wife."

He sweeps me into a strong embrace and nips my earlobe. He's already hard, pressing it against me. I try not to let my internal grimace show.

"Feels so good to call you Mrs. Russo," he whispers.

I want to gag but manage to stop myself. No matter what he calls me, in my heart I'm Mrs. Conte.

Mrs. Declan Conte.

Sienna Conte.

Has a wonderful sound to it.

Thinking of that, I'm able to smile at Anthony, so he smiles back, his dark eyes actually reflecting light. But my smile was a mistake, because the next second he kisses me.

It'll be suspicious if I pull away, so I let him, making myself numb, counting the seconds until he stops, then I move out of his embrace as much as he'll let me and hug myself.

"You sure you're good?" he asks, glancing at my easel by the open window. "Don't need anything?"

"I'm good for now."

He rests his hands on my hips, his fingers caressing the skin above my leggings' waistband. "Well, baby, I'm heading out for work. Just wanted to say goodbye. It's a big job for Victor, so I'll be gone a few weeks. Don't miss me too much." He kisses my cheek while lowering his hands to grab my ass. He tips his chin at the dresser. "Just leave that there. I don't have time to file it now, but I will as soon as I get back. Then we'll go ring shopping." Snaking his hand between my shoulder blades, he wraps my hair around his fist, yanking so my head snaps back. He licks up the middle of my throat, the most vulnerable part. "Sound good, Mrs. Russo?"

"Yes," I whisper, wincing at the sharp sting in my scalp.

He releases my hair. "I'm happy to see you're settling in, baby. I'll miss you, but I'll be back as soon as I can. Promise." He kisses me again before leaving.

Once the door closes, I wipe my mouth, then my hand shoots to the dresser. I feel like collapsing. But I won't. I'll force myself to keep standing.

I've finally thought of the right quote to get me through this, one by Roosevelt: *"Don't foul, don't flinch—hit the line hard."*

Declan is safe, so now I just need to figure out the right opportunity to save myself.

When I do, I won't flinch.

I wait an hour and then have my guard take me to the kitchen again, grabbing the dinner Anthony left for me in the fridge. I'm not hungry. I just want to scope out the situation. The house is completely empty, save for my single guard.

I glance at him. He's a giant, close to seven feet and built like a horse, so I'm guessing Anthony doesn't expect me to fight him for my freedom. It's clear I would lose, but Anthony's not worried I might try to mind fuck him? Sneak off when the guy takes a nap?

That's right...what about sleep? This guy has to sleep eventually, so who will watch me then?

I think signing that paper helped Anthony trust me a little, but not enough to leave me so unguarded. It's odd that Anthony only left one guy. Is this some strange test?

I decide to ignore it. Anthony probably has guards keeping watch outside, and someone will probably come by to relieve this one. Knowing Anthony, he has some kind of safeguard to make sure I don't escape. Simply running from him again isn't my plan, anyway. I'm just happy to have some space; maybe I can actually watch TV in the living room.

And, with Anthony gone, I don't have to worry about him entering my room at random times.

After I return to my bedroom and set the dinner plate down, I pull out my sketches of Declan, spreading them around the room. I have about fifty of them so far, so I scatter them everywhere I can. His smile, his eyes, the way he looked at me like I was precious...every place I glance now, that's what I see.

I trace my finger over one of the drawings, a lump forming in my throat. Whatever he's up to now, I just want him to find happiness. I hope he pushed me from his memories and is moving on. I'll never move on from him, from us, but he needs to. He needs to find a wonderful woman who will treat him with all the love and respect in the world. He deserves so much.

Blinking back tears, I flick on the TV, surrounded by images of my lost love.

CHAPTER 32

DECLAN

I PULL THE CURTAIN BACK, peering through the grimy motel window. The sky is still dark, but there's a light gray along the horizon. Sun will rise soon.

Sean was supposed to be back by now.

I release the curtain and return to pacing. I've been up for hours, creating a path in the worn carpet like a caged animal, my mind racing with best- and worst-case scenarios.

Best-case: Sean and I pull this off. We drive to the house a few miles away, the one owned by Sienna's ex, Anthony Russo, rescue Sienna, and get the fuck out of this city.

Worst-case: I get killed. Or Sean does. But considering how trained Sean is, I think he's going to make it.

Actually, that's not right. The worst-case scenario is that Sienna gets killed, something I'll do everything in my power to prevent. What happens to me is irrelevant; she needs to be safe and away from that criminal.

A rhythmic knock echoes through the tiny room—two quick taps, a pause, then two more. I exhale from the sound of Sean's signal. I'm at the door in an instant. A quick look through the peephole confirms that it's him, so I unlatch the door.

His expression is grim as he slips inside, his eyes darting around the room before settling on me. But he doesn't yet speak, only exhales and sits on the edge of a twin bed. He looks exhausted, hunching forward and staring at the floor like he needs a moment.

I doubt we really have any moments to rest, but I give him some time. I prop my hip against the motel dresser and cross my arms, waiting.

When a few minutes have passed, I finally speak up. "You okay?"

My words snap him back to this room, and he rubs his forehead. "Memories from my time in the Marines. I'm okay." His eyes are haunted, but he stands and walks to the closet.

"Is there an opening for us to do this?" I ask.

He pulls two bulletproof vests from the closet, setting them on one of the twin beds. "I think so. Russo got on a plane out of town. The rest of us were in a caravan transporting something. They wouldn't tell me what it is because I'm just the 'hired muscle.' Honestly, I don't want to know. I don't want to know about any of this. We need to get Sienna and leave this because—" He shakes his head, grabbing the gun case from the closet and setting it on the dresser. "We're in over our heads. Even regular cops would be in over their heads. This is FBI level shit, something you do with a large task force behind you. I want nothing to fucking do with this."

"Then I'll give you an out. You've already helped me get this far. If the house has less guards, I can sneak in—"

"I'm not leaving." He shoots me a look of disbelief, as if appalled I would even suggest it. Then he jams a magazine into the gun. "I don't know how many men are left at the house because they ushered me and Jeremy into our own car pretty quick. Regardless, you'll get yourself killed alone."

"Thanks for the vote of confidence."

He hands me a bulletproof vest. "You're welcome."

I put it on, feeling completely out of my element, and yet strangely calm. The insane thing I'm about to do doesn't even register; my entire focus is on getting to Sienna. Somehow, I'll deal with everything as it comes, in the moment, hoping my boxing skills will do me some kind of good. No matter what, I'm getting to her. I'm getting her out.

"You said Jeremy was in a car with you?"

Sean is adjusting his vest. "He was driving."

"How did you get back here?"

"I took care of him."

I pause what I'm doing to stare at the bodyguard I thought I knew. He said that too casually, with ice in the words.

When he notices I've become still, he stops to glance at me. "He's not dead. Unfortunately."

"You sure?"

His light chuckle breaks the tension. "I knocked him out, but yeah, he's alive. He's on the side of the road with no cell phone. He'll be fine." Sean fastens his gun into a holster and smirks to himself. He flashes his bruised knuckles. "Felt good to punch him. I did it more than necessary."

"Wish I could have."

He grabs some extra bullet magazines, switching topics. "If they haven't yet realized one car in the caravan is missing, they will soon. We have a window, but it's a small one."

"Understood."

Both of us put on jackets to conceal our vests so we don't stand out.

He pulls a second gun from the case and hands it to me. "You okay to use this?"

I nod because I have no choice; the men at the house will be armed. "I had a great teacher," I say, referencing the crash course he gave me at the shooting range recently.

Sean's eyes only become vacant and he glances at himself in the cracked dresser mirror. I wonder what he's seeing.

I'm seeing glimpses of the Marine he must've been, and it's an awe-inspiring, though intimidating, sight. It's also a shock to my psyche because this is a side of him I've never seen—his movements are precise, skilled, fast. He's no longer the bodyguard who sits around casually reading while hyper-aware of threats. His body is actively coiled, ready to attack or defend without hesitation or doubts.

I'd go into that house by myself to save Sienna, but thank God I have Sean.

"You're getting ten million," I tell him.

He pulls his gaze away from his reflection and stalks to the door. "I don't care about the money. Don't pay me a dime. It's my fault—"

"It's not your fault."

He glares at me. "It's *my* fault she got kidnapped, and I'm fixing it. Let's go."

For the first time in my life, I say, "Yes, boss," and follow him out.

IT'S A FEW HOURS after sunrise as we sit in the SUV parked across from Anthony Russo's house. It's a rectangular white brick building, flat roof. There's a flimsy wrought-iron gate in front, and the house is sandwiched between other similar structures, with only a few feet separating each property.

Sean's been scanning the place with binoculars for the

past hour, just observing. We didn't have time to discuss a concrete plan—an oversight I normally wouldn't go along with—but he's been at the house for a week, getting what information he could. He also sent me information on the security devices that Russo uses. In a stroke of luck, he uses NexaProtect. The account isn't under his name, but Sean sent me the serial numbers of his devices and, sure enough, the alarm system for this house is from my company. I disabled them in a way that hopefully wouldn't alert Russo.

Now, it's just a matter of getting past his guards. Sean assured me he has some ideas about how to do that. I trust him.

"Seems to be only that one guy outside," he says. "As far as I can tell. Haven't seen others. No movement inside through the windows. It's not ideal to be doing this in daylight."

I stare at the large man who's been standing outside the front door. "How should we enter?"

"If that guy doesn't move, I don't know. Might have to enter someone else's backyard and work our way to Russo's back patio. There's a second-story window that's usually open. If all else fails, we might find a way—"

Without warning, the man out front checks his phone and then turns to walk around the side of the house.

"Or we follow that guy now and take him out," Sean says quickly, dropping the binoculars. He checks the tranquilizer needles in his pocket, then nods at me. "Ready?"

I don't speak; I get out of the SUV.

My heart rate spikes, adrenaline flooding my system. We walk across the street, trying to look casual, then we slip down the narrow path beside the house.

At a corner, Sean signals for me to wait. I hang back,

watching in awe as he vaults over the shallow, wrought-iron fence around the back patio. He disappears. I hear some grunts and shoes scuffling across concrete. I glance around the corner in time to see Sean take down the much larger man with a move so fast I barely follow it. A quick jab with the syringe, and the guard goes limp.

Sean's breath comes in heavy pants as he shoves hair from his face, remaining squatted next to the guard to observe him for a moment. Then he searches the man's pockets. When he pulls out keys, he grins at me.

Sean waves me over, and I quietly follow him to the back door. Passing by the unconscious man, I'm struck by the surreal nature of this moment. I'm about to break into a criminal's house, armed and wearing a bulletproof vest. It's something out of a movie, not the life of a tech CEO.

But then I think of Sienna, trapped somewhere inside, and my resolve hardens. This is real. This is necessary. And I'll do whatever it takes to get her out safely.

This is for the woman I love; I'd do anything for her.

Sean sticks a key in the lock but pauses.

"What is it?" I whisper.

He pulls the key out and turns the knob. "It's unlocked."

"A lazy guard?"

"I don't know. Something feels off, but we don't have much time so…" He makes eye contact and I wonder if his pulse is pounding as much as mine.

Probably not; he was trained for intense situations like this.

"I'm ready," I whisper, checking the gun on my hip.

There's no time for worry or hesitation. I know Russo isn't a stupid man; he likely knows Sean is gone. He'll know who came for Sienna.

Fuck him.

I'll deal with him when the time comes; he'll get pay-back for kidnapping Sienna and trying to ruin my company.

I'll deal with him.

Right now, Sienna is my entire focus.

Sean turns the knob, and the door slowly opens into darkness.

I let it embrace me.

Soon, Sienna will be in my arms again, and I'm never letting go.

CHAPTER 33

SIENNA

MORNING COMES AND I DECIDE to paint next to the window again. I wanted to watch a movie on the couch, but the guard said I'm still not allowed to leave my room, so no living room time for me. Jerk. I'm dealing with the disappointment by painting the gray storm clouds I can see billowing along the horizon.

Mindlessly, I'm twirling my locket with one hand, painting with the other, when there's a loud crash in the hallway. I startle so much I drop my paintbrush. Did that giant outside my door fall and break a vase?

I wait, frozen on my stool, straining to hear.

There's another loud crash and I'm off the stool. Muffled, deep voices punch through the hallway, along with scattered, loud footsteps. It sounds like people are fighting.

My mouth becomes sandpaper—what if it's Victor?

What if he sent Anthony away on purpose just so he could come for me? Give me my punishment?

I glance at the window; my only escape.

The people in the hallway slam into the door, and I yelp.

I press my shaky fingers to my forehead. *Okay, I need to figure this out quick.*

There are three options: fight, give up, take my chances with the window.

Shoving my easel out of the way, I look over the windowsill at the ground below.

God, that's a long drop. But…I could probably survive the fall. Maybe only break a few bones.

Maybe.

Fuck.

There's another loud bang on my door and my eyes dart around the room, looking for any kind of weapon. I grab the metal easel and collapse it. It's awkward, but if I swing it right, I might stun any attacker long enough to escape out the door.

If there's only one of them.

My heart is pounding so loud in my head, it's the only thing I can hear as I watch the doorknob slowly turn.

I've decided on a plan of action: wait to see. If I'm outnumbered or if it's Victor himself, I take my chances jumping out the window. If it's only one guy, I'll fight.

Giving up isn't an option because I've already made it this far, survived this long.

Victor can try to capture me, but I'm going down swinging.

Tears are pooling in my eyes, but I blink them away—I need to keep my vision sharp, my mind focused. But I can feel despair creeping in; when I woke up a few hours ago, I didn't expect this day could be my last.

I didn't get to see Declan's selfie one last time.

Life is so incredibly cruel.

Well, if I don't survive this, then I'll finally see Grandpa again. I've missed him so much.

Gripping the collapsed easel, I widen my stance and wait as the door slowly creaks open.

One heartbeat.

Two.

I drop the easel, covering my mouth with both hands. Declan is standing in the open doorway trying to catch his breath.

Am I dreaming?

I'm fucking dreaming.

My vision blurs as I take in the trickle of blood down the side of his head, his disheveled T-shirt, his brooding intensity that looks stronger than ever—eyes focused, face like stone, but with a slightly quirked eyebrow. Sean is behind him in the hallway, pointing a gun at the unconscious guard.

Declan takes a step toward me.

I inch back, my heartbeat overwhelming my senses.

He takes another step; I move even closer to the window. His eyes dart around the room at all of my sketches, then messy lines crease his brows and he returns to staring at me, his breath steadier now.

Another step.

I don't understand how he's here, *why* he's here.

Did I hurt him so badly he decided to come after me, just like Anthony? Or Victor?

Does he want revenge?

I can't possibly believe he'd be here for any other reason.

"Sienna..." he says, inching closer.

I continue my slow movement backward until my ass bumps the windowsill. I glance over my shoulder at the ground below.

God, even if he's here to rescue me, I don't know how I can possibly face him. How could I ever make amends for what I said?

I lean back into the open window.

He's in front of me suddenly and grabs my arm. "What

are you doing? Are you insane?"

I lower my head and sob, not wanting to look at him. The cracked pieces inside me I've been trying to patch with slivers of hope, over and over, all suddenly shatter. "You're the…insane…one. You can't…can't be here. Anthony will… kill you. Why would you—"

He pulls me into his chest, enveloping me in his arms and familiar woodsy scent. "I found you."

I've heard those words before from a violent man whose only focus was winning—I've always been his trophy, his prize.

But Declan sounds relieved. Grateful.

I completely crumble as I cling to his shirt, soaking the fabric with a flood of tears.

What is wrong with this man?

I broke his heart, ran to keep him safe, and he just… follows me?

I'm near hyperventilating as I choke out words through my cracked voice. "I said…so many…awful things. Why are you…? You can't…You have to…leave before—"

Declan cradles my face in hands that are large and warm and gentle, forcing my puffy eyes to look up at him. My face is swollen, and snot is running free, but he doesn't seem to care about my appearance.

"Did you mean it?" he asks.

"W-what?"

"Did you mean what you said? In Hawaii. Tell me the truth."

I bite back a sob. "No, of course not. He…would've killed you…if I didn't—"

He pulls me against him, smoothing a hand over my hair. "Then I don't remember what you're talking about."

My knees almost buckle, but I find the strength to push hard against his chest. To get him away from me. He's too strong, though, and won't budge.

I swallow and sniff until I'm contained enough to speak clearer. "You don't know what you're saying," I grit out, struggling to keep my voice steady and functioning. "Stop it. I'm not…not a good person. Sienna isn't…I used to be Margaret. And—"

He kisses me. I'm a sloppy, rambling mess with so many bleeding edges, yet this insane man kisses me.

I kiss him back, pulling on his shirt so hard the threads in the collar pop.

I've missed him so much, my heart never stopped aching.

But I quickly come to my senses and turn my head.

"Stop," I say with more power. "Just stop. You're not listening. I was born Margaret Diane Ariti. I've hurt people. I was with Anthony. I did things for him. I was complicit in so many terrible things. The only reason I never went to jail was because I was offered a plea deal…but that doesn't change what I did. You don't want someone like me."

Even with the truth out, Declan never looks away. His lips never twitch down and his eyes don't narrow or widen or do anything except gaze at me like I'm the only thing precious in this world.

Cupping my face, he wipes tears away with his thumbs. "Sienna, you can tell me all about your past later. Right now, we need to go."

"I'm a criminal and you're ignoring that?"

"I'm not ignoring it, but I understand that willfully hurting someone is different from being coerced or feeling like your own life was threatened. Once I learned the name of your ex, my private investigator did some digging. You turned yourself into the authorities and they absolved you. I'm guessing your ex used manipulation and threats to put you in a position where you felt you had no choice but to do what he said, correct?"

I wipe under my nose and shake my head. "That doesn't matter."

"Yes, it does."

Fresh tears are filling my eyes. "I should've said no. I—"

"Your past changes nothing for me," Declan says, his voice like a soft golden ray filling me with light. "I want all of you. Your past. Your damage. Margaret. Sienna. I need every damn part. I've felt like a new man since we met. You've only shown me understanding and acceptance of everything I carry. I'm here to do the same for you. Whatever you do or don't do, I just need to be by your side. That's enough." His vibrant blue irises hold mine captive, and I want to be held there forever. "I only need to be deserving of you, offer you safety. When we first met, I told you I was a possessive man. You're mine. Tell me you see that."

I'm so close to giving in, but the burden of past experiences still has a fortress around my heart. "Are you a wolf?" I whisper.

He studies me for a moment, his eyes searching mine, before he says, "If, by 'wolf,' you mean someone who will do anything to protect their chosen mate, then yes. I'm a wolf."

I have no arguments, no more defenses, because why had that never occurred to me? There are so many wolves in the world, but not all of them are pure predators.

Wolves can be loyal, nurturing, and protective.

Fresh tears fall as I nod. "I want to be yours. I've always just wanted to belong. And I see it; I belong with you."

His mouth claims mine, and we cling to each other, this suffocating room and the entire world fading away.

"I love you," he whispers, before deepening the kiss.

I long to say it back, to speak what's already in my heart, but I don't get the chance.

We've both shut out the world too fiercely.

There's a muted pop.

Declan cries out and staggers away from me, reaching for his pant leg that's quickly darkening with blood.

There's a bullet hole in his calf.

CHAPTER 34

SIENNA

MY EYES FALL ON ANTHONY as he looms in the doorway, pointing a gun with a silencer on it. Sean is collapsed behind him on top of the guard.

My first reaction—besides my chest caving in with pure terror—is to dart in front of Declan, putting myself in the path of any more bullets. Declan tries to resist and push me behind him, so I say firmly, "No. He wouldn't shoot me."

Anthony dips a shoulder and lowers the gun. "My wife is good at thinking on her feet. Guess that's why I married her."

"Wife?" Declan says, like he just tasted something bitter.

Anthony walks to the dresser and picks up the marriage license. He tucks it into his jacket, turning his lazy gaze at Declan. He's the epitome of calm, an immovable tree in a hurricane, but I know him; anger is boiling just under the surface like a volcano about to erupt.

"Thought I told you not to touch what's fucking *mine*."

Declan scoffs, his demeanor just as calm and simmering as Anthony. "I've been wondering," he says, "what the emails have been about. Seems it's just a child throwing a tantrum."

I'm not sure what he's talking about, but I keep myself in front of him when he tries to get around me again. "No," I whisper. Then I tremble.

God, why can't I be collected and confident like these two? They're the ones about to kill each other, yet I'm the one falling to pieces?

Anthony laughs and checks the magazine in his gun. Clicking it back into place, he says, "After I kill you, I'll have fun ruining your company. First, everyone will think you're a psychopath who murdered his family. I'll throw in some embezzlement, make it look like you committed suicide, then the new CEO of your company will be my next target. I won't stop until NexaProtect no longer exists." He grins like a kid on Christmas morning. "Just like you."

As I watch these two men snarl at each other, something suddenly clicks in my head. "Y-you didn't have a job from Victor," I say to Anthony.

"Oh, I did, baby," he says. "But when Declan's other bodyguard showed up, I gave my men the wrong date. I had a feeling your White Knight would be coming. Think I'd miss that? It wasn't hard to switch my security system to his company, so I'd know exactly when he was coming."

Declan growls beside me.

"Then it was just a matter of setting the trap and waiting to pounce," Anthony continues. His icy gaze falls on me. "And the shit you've been trying to pull...Honestly, Margaret, I thought I taught you to play people better than that. It's clear from your body language you don't want to move on and 'focus on us.' But you'll get there. You're my wife." He waves the gun. "Now get out of the way, baby. Don't want blood on that beautiful face."

Anthony makes me feel foolish because he always seems to be one step ahead. But fuck him. I back up into Declan, spreading my arms out and trying to put as much of my body in front of him as I can. I even stand on my tiptoes, trying to get closer to Declan's height.

"Last chance," Anthony says, pointing the gun at Declan's head, which is towering over mine. If he wasn't so tall, it'd be easier to shield him. Anthony clicks his tongue. "You know I'm an excellent shot. I could've killed him earlier when he had his tongue down your fucking throat, but call me sentimental. I like to look a man in the eyes when I send him to hell."

What happens next is so fast, I don't have time to react.

Declan shoves me to the side, ducks out of the gun's path, and rushes Anthony.

As I'm stumbling toward my bed, Anthony fires. The bullet zips into the wall, and Declan's shoulder rams into Anthony's chest.

Both men tumble, crashing into the dresser. They exchange blows, grunting and grappling and flinging fists. I can barely tell what's happening, but then Declan wrestles Anthony to the floor. He tries to pull out a gun, but Anthony wrestles it away and it slides into the hallway. Declan punches him in the jaw before Anthony twists out of his grasp and hits Declan in the stomach.

Declan groans.

Then I see it: Anthony's gun.

It's on the floor a few feet away from me.

I've never been good with a gun, but I've used one a few times at a gun range.

What if I hit Declan?

The men are still on the floor, grappling, and Anthony gets a hand behind his back. He yanks a knife from his belt, slashes at Declan's throat, but Declan catches his wrist.

Anthony yanks free and stabs the knife in Declan's thigh, the same leg with the bullet wound.

There must be a lot of adrenaline coursing through Declan's veins because he only grunts and tries to strangle Anthony, pinning him to the floor and digging his hands into Anthony's throat.

It's clear Declan is stronger, and a great fighter, but Anthony is calculated. I've seen him take down men twice as big as Declan, and he always seems to have an unlimited supply of weapons hidden on his body.

I glance at the gun again since Anthony is completely distracted and not paying attention to me.

Maybe I'll fail. I might hit the wall. Or Declan.

God, I don't want to hit Declan.

But I can either let others control my fate, or I can take a chance.

Take control and save myself.

Stop the wolf once and for all.

Do I have the strength to do that?

My entire life, I've been focused on escape—escape from my parents, escape from my pain, escape from Anthony, from my past, my failures, my insecurities.

I'm just so fucking tired of running, hiding, fearing for my life and sanity. Tired of being caged and treated like Anthony's property when I don't want to be his.

If I don't end this now, he'll follow me.

He'll watch me for the rest of my life.

I need this all to end.

I'm so tired...

As the two men struggle to their feet, still grappling and locked in battle, I lunge for the gun. Neither of them notices. Declan gets an opening and punches Anthony in the jaw. Anthony stumbles back a few inches, putting space between him and Declan.

I don't blink.

I fire.

Anthony sucks in a sharp breath and groans. He stumbles back a few more steps, touching his side where blood is flowing from the bullet wound. His eyes dart to mine, his face swollen and his cheeks beginning to purple from Declan's punches.

For only a second, his skin seems to become translucent, showing me all the tiny capillaries underneath, all the cells and veins and muscle and bones that weave together to give him life—that underneath the violence and obsession and cruelty, he's just a lost little boy wanting to be seen. Understood.

But it's gone before I can even really see it.

He groans again, smirking like he still has the upper hand. "You fucking bitch." He falls against the wall next to the door and slides down, his breaths coming in sharp, ragged bursts.

Declan limps to me as fast as he can. His face is also swollen and bruised. He looks me over for any injuries. "Are you okay?"

I nod, but my hand is shaking so badly I'm about to drop the gun. He takes it from me, puts the safety on, and then tucks it in his belt.

I glance down at his bloody leg and the knife handle jutting from his thigh. I reach a shaky hand toward it, but he stops me.

"Leave it," he says, wincing and hissing from the pain of shifting his weight. He bites out, "It's probably halting the blood loss."

Barely aware of what I'm doing because waves of tremors keep coursing through me, I move to my closet and grab a few thin dresses. Then I tear off strips of fabric to use as a tourniquet for his injured leg.

"Thank you," Declan says, but I shake my head.

I should be thanking him, not the other way around.

Once I'm done tying the fabric as tight as I can, I glance at Anthony. His gaze is unfocused, but he seems to be watching me. For the first time in years, I see the shadow of that young, sweet teenage boy who approached me one day in the park. I had been crying silently, pretending I was sketching.

He didn't seem uncomfortable about being near a girl who was sobbing; he just sat down on the grass and crossed his willowy legs. Then he didn't say anything for a while—didn't ask what was wrong or try to comfort me. Just sat and gave me company, watching my hand as I sketched.

I was sobbing too much to care that some strange boy was lingering around.

Finally, he asked, "Who should I beat up?"

That startled me enough to stop crying. I sniffed and wiped my face with my shirt collar. "What?"

"The person who made you cry. I'll beat them up for you."

I gave him a tiny smile. "My parents. You going to beat them up?"

He leaned back, resting his palms on the grass behind him. "Hmm, sure, I can do that. But afterwards, will you help beat up mine?"

I laughed.

It was the first time my heart did a little flip for someone.

Declan touches my shoulder and I flinch. "We need to go," he says.

I nod as I continue to stare at Anthony. Blood soaks his shirt. Blood pooling around him on the floor.

"Go where?" I ask softly. "I'm worried about Anthony's boss, Victor. He might try to find me."

"Naw," Anthony gurgles. He spits blood from his mouth, then grins with red teeth. "Naw, my old man doesn't give a shit this time."

My mouth falls open because it feels like a lightning bolt just struck me. "He's your father?"

"You didn't figure that out by now? I'm the bastard son he never wanted. Why'd you think I understood you so well?" He runs a bloody hand through his hair, like he's still trying to look cool despite the injuries. "I got him to leave you alone for what you did before. He'll honor that. But he made it clear he doesn't care this time. You haven't done anything recent to him, and if I die, he'll be happy. It's what he's always wanted. Less for him to deal with." He coughs. "You know…think you just freed me."

Declan nudges me toward the door. "We should really go."

I nod again. Years of Anthony's behavior make more sense now, though it's still not an excuse for what he did.

Part of Margaret still feels bad for him, getting stuck with a father like Victor.

I wish things could've ended differently for both of us.

Hooking Declan's arm over my shoulders so I can help support him as he limps, I take a few steps toward the door.

We pass by Anthony, and he grabs my wrist. "Wait, baby. Just another minute. I want to look at you…another minute. You're so beautiful."

I don't owe him anything, but Margaret waits.

"Did you forget what you told me?" he asks, holding

my wrist loosely, as if it's taking all of his energy to keep talking. "Remember that day? When we met. You had the prettiest golden hair, but you looked like...like some badass rocker chick. And...and you told me you'd hang out with me if I bought you dinner and we could talk about...about beating up your parents." A corner of his mouth lifts, his eyes crinkling. "You chickened out at the last minute. Never did get to beat those bastards. But baby..." His head lolls down for a moment and he groans.

When he looks back up, his normally olive skin is pale and blue. "Baby, later that day...you said, 'I'm just looking for where I belong. Everyone has to belong somewhere.' And I said, 'You belong with me.' I said that, day one, and you thought it was a pickup line. But that was always the truth." He touches his chest. "Here. You belonged here. You just needed to stay with me...I needed...What I never said...I was looking for someone to love. I wanted to be needed like that. Be important to somebody. Why wouldn't you accept it? Just wanted to love you. I love you, Magpie. I always... The only times in my life I haven't felt alone were with you." He releases my wrist.

A tear rolls down my cheek. "Why couldn't you just let me go?" I ask. "Then you wouldn't be like this."

"You don't abandon the things you love."

Things. Like I'm a possession, not a person.

"I don't think you know what real love is."

He rests his head on the wall. "Maybe you're right." Then, with a limp, shaky hand, he reaches into his jacket for the marriage license. "But I'll prove it." He tries to tear it, but his grip is too weak.

I reach down and do it for him. The pieces fall to the floor beside him, soaking up his blood.

"See, baby? Love you. This asshole better appreciate… appreciate this gift I'm giving him…" His eyes close. His chest is still rising and falling with breath, but I don't know if he's aware of anything anymore.

I finally step into the hallway with Declan.

Goodbye, Anthony.

Declan tries to use his good leg to bend down and check on Sean, but he's struggling.

"No, I'll do it," I say, helping him lean against the wall. "Sean was with you all along?"

"Yeah," Declan says through a groan, pain heavy in his voice. "I wouldn't have made it this far without him. I owe him my life."

Bending, I press my fingers to Sean's neck. He has a weak pulse. I check him over: he doesn't have any bullet wounds, but there's a big welt on his head, probably where Anthony struck him. I shake him as hard as I can. Thankfully, he wakes up.

He's very out of it, but I help him to his feet. The three of us hobble down the hallway, and I try to support Declan's weight as much as I can as he limps along.

Once we're outside, we get some very concerned stares from a few passersby.

"That's ours," Declan says, gesturing at a black SUV parked across the street.

Sean and I are helping Declan into the back when a loud boom rattles my senses.

I gasp as Sean yanks me into his chest, covering me and spinning me away from the explosion. I peek over his shoulder to see flames shooting from the top of Anthony's house.

"Why would he—" I cry out. "Why not just call an

ambulance to—"

"I don't know," Declan says, taking my hand. "I don't know."

Shedding a few tears, I return my focus to getting Declan and Sean to the hospital; Anthony made his choice. I can't linger on it.

I try to walk to the driver's side, but Sean stops me.

"I'll drive," he says weakly.

Wiping my damp cheeks, I give him a firm look. "No. You could have a concussion. I don't know why men are so stubborn, but get in the passenger side."

His gaze challenges me for a second before his body hunches and he follows my command. I think I hear Declan chuckle.

Once we're all fastened in, I put the car in gear and pull away from the curb. I glance at the flames spreading over Anthony's house; they're so large I swear I can feel the heat. In the rearview mirror, I watch for as long as I can, until I turn a corner and can no longer see the building.

After that, every few seconds, I glance at the dark plumes of smoke lingering in the sky.

This time, they won't follow me.

They'll fade.

Finally, they'll fade.

EPILOGUE

SIENNA

ONE YEAR LATER

I'M STANDING AT THE EDGE of the world. Well, on The Cliffs of Moher in Ireland. A gradient of muted blues stretches out below and above, the ocean blending with the gray sky. The wind whips through my newly dyed crimson hair, and I can taste the salty tang of the Atlantic on my tongue. I close my eyes and stretch out my arms.

Feels like I'm flying.

Free.

Declan's warm, familiar arms wrap around my waist, and he rumbles in my ear. "It's endless."

"It's beautiful."

"Is this a place you'd like to stay for a while? Or should we pick our next destination?"

I consider the question, my hand unconsciously reaching for the locket around my neck. Inside, nestled next to the picture of my grandfather, is a photo of Declan. He had the whole thing cleaned and restored for me, erasing the tarnish and any lingering bits of charcoal dust. It's now shining like new and bursting with so much love.

"I think we can stay here longer. Explore some of the history." I tip my head back and his comforting lips press against my forehead. "There's a cute bed-and-breakfast in Doolin."

"Whatever you like. I'm just along for the ride."

I snuggle back against him, holding onto his forearms as we gaze at the ocean together. We're completely warm inside our bubble despite the biting wind.

This past year, he's told me that a lot: "Whatever you like."

I felt guilty at first because he gave up so much to live this nomadic lifestyle with me.

He stepped down as CEO of NexaProtect, handing the reins over to his VP, Davis. Thankfully, the lawsuit against him got dropped, so he sold his house, cut ties with his old life, and now devotes himself entirely to supporting my dreams and goals.

I struggled for months to accept that, until one day, he finally sat me down in a hotel room and asked, "Sienna, why are you so against giving me what I want?"

"What *you* want?" I responded. "The scales are completely tipped toward me now. It feels like I'm being selfish because you pay for all our travel, everything I need. I get every bit of your attention. I worry I'm taking away your life. Don't you want to, I don't know, work on your boxing career again?"

He laughed, an abundance of new laugh lines surrounding his smile. "Boxing? First of all, I'm too old to start that again. And second, there's nothing wrong with wanting to devote myself entirely to you. That's a decision I made. You didn't force me into this. I've accomplished a lot in my life. I've won matches against top opponents. I built a successful company. I've supported charities and done volunteer work in different countries, which I continue to do. And now my life is with you." He pressed my palm over his heart and grinned—so wide and so vibrant. "I'm fucking happy. And life is too short and too precious for me not to spend every goddamn minute with you I can. Do whatever you like; I only ask that you let me follow. I only care about being with you for as long as you'll have me."

I was so moved that I asked if he'd follow me to Vegas.

We eloped the next day in a tiny white chapel lined with flowers.

Jada was *pissed* that she wasn't there, so we had an extremely small beach ceremony for our friends the following month. It was on a San Francisco shoreline with a view of the Golden Gate Bridge during sunset. It was a perfect day.

Sean even attended, after months of keeping to himself.

Declan told me he feels responsible for what happened in Hawaii, even though I don't blame him for anything. He tried to quit working for NexaProtect's Executive Protection branch, but Declan wouldn't let him. He gave him a huge amount of money for helping with my rescue and told Sean, "You're on leave. Take as long as you want, but you're not quitting."

Sean was grumbly but agreed. He's been really distant, though. We call him every month to check in, but he still seems…torn up.

I worry about him and hope he's okay.

But, after getting married, Declan and I have been traveling, leaving our footprints in different U.S. cities and around the globe.

We're exploring. The world is too big and too beautiful to be tethered to just one spot, and I get restless when I feel stuck somewhere. I prefer to keep moving.

"Oh, I almost forgot," Declan says, pulling out his phone. He shows me the screen. "As requested, two front row tickets to Jada's opening night show in two months."

"She's going to be so amazing," I say.

I'm so happy for her—she finally landed a spot in a Broadway touring company. She doesn't expect me there on opening night, so I want to surprise her with a dozen red roses.

I turn to face Declan. He opens the front of his large wool trench coat and swallows me in the fabric. "I'd like to stop by the office next month," I say. "Let's stay here for a few weeks, drive around, and then I should do some responsible adult stuff."

"Of course," he says. He lifts my hand to kiss the inside of my wrist, right below my Phoenix tattoo, where there's a date inked in my skin: our wedding anniversary. So I'll always know where I belong.

Pressing my cheek against his left pectoral, where he has a matching tattoo, I close my eyes. I try not to think about everything waiting for me at my office in San Francisco. With Declan's help, I finally established my art program under NexaProtect's umbrella. It's starting to take root and grow, spreading through word of mouth. Some teenagers and young adults are even beginning to visit weekly, either for one of the free art classes or just for open studios. There are also a few rooms where anyone in crisis can stay overnight and get help with finding resources for their situation.

NexaProtect and the non-profit employees have done a lot of the heavy lifting, but I still help to manage it remotely, helping with expansion efforts, always staying behind the scenes and stopping into the office every other month. I also like to teach some of the watercolor classes.

The role fits perfectly with my new lifestyle and the artwork I continue to make, because I've discovered that I prefer to work incognito. Using various pseudonyms, I've been getting my pieces into galleries across the U.S. A few savvy art collectors have connected the dots, realizing that the paintings were all done by the same artist. They've started rumors about who the mysterious artist might be.

I kind of love it.

Overall, life is better than I ever could have hoped. I only wish…

Declan lifts my chin to kiss me. I fall into the moment with him, savoring his warm lips when the rest of my face is so cold. Then I turn toward the ocean again.

Anthony.

I only wish things had ended differently for Anthony.

Underneath it all, he was just a broken little boy, searching for something he had yet to find.

Even after a year, the memory of that day still haunts me. Two bodies were found in the rubble of Anthony's burned house, but both were so badly blackened that neither was officially identified. One is presumed to be Anthony, the other a guard, but a part of me still wonders…

No. He's dead.

I need to stop wondering and let his memory rest.

Still, his memory reminds me why I want to keep growing my art program, spreading it to more cities. When he was young, if he'd had a place to go or had someone who cared about the living hell I'm sure Victor put him through…maybe his life would've been different. He would've been different.

I want to give that hope to other teens in trouble.

Shaking my head, I push the thoughts away, turning my focus back to my husband, to this beautiful moment.

I rest the back of my head on his chest. "You know, you don't always have to agree with me. You can say, 'Screw Ireland. Let's go to Paris.' I want to accommodate you too."

He wraps his muscular arms around me again, securing me against his torso with one hand. The other hand pushes down the front of my jeans.

I gasp and glance around. I don't see anyone, but I still feel scandalous about him teasing me like this in public.

"I have plenty of demands," he says against my ear. "You know that. If you think my dirty princess doesn't have to get on her knees whenever I command it, you're very mistaken."

I squirm against him. "Fine. So you want me on my knees, getting arrested for public indecency."

He chuckles. "I doubt that. No one else is here. But no…you'll be doing everything I want once we get to the bed-and-breakfast."

"Then let's go."

He pulls his hand from my pants, sucking on his fingers before holding me again. "Not yet. I want to watch the sunrise with you."

As I stand here, wrapped in my husband's arms, watching the sun rise on a new day, I think about Margaret. She'll always be a part of my past, but she no longer defines me. Even Sienna doesn't define me.

I'm just…an artist, an idealist, a survivor. Someone with the freedom to change into newer, stronger versions of herself whenever she's ready. Because I've learned that holding on to hope is so much better than drowning in despair.

That running toward my future is better than running from my past.

That life is a continual work in progress, with all its imperfections and happy accidents, its light and shadow.

That's what makes it my greatest masterpiece.

AUTHOR'S NOTE

Thank you for reading! I hope this book was an enjoyable emotional rollercoaster :) And FYI: this series is just getting started. The next book, *Ugly Beautiful Scars*, will explore Sean's story. But I'm getting ahead of myself...

For a while now, I've been wanting to write a main character who was an artist. Why? Well, before I became a romance author, I actually earned a Fine Arts degree. I grew up writing and making art, so as a teen, I was torn about which one to focus on. I started with both writing and art classes, but ultimately decided to focus on art (that worked out well, didn't it??).

While I ultimately got a writing job right after graduation, that artistic background has never really left. Now, it comes out mostly in my book covers, photography, and the occasional painting.

That's why I was happy infuse some of my artistic side into Sienna.

My art school experience was pretty chill. Think less 'tortured artist' and more 'let's experiment and have fun!' I focused on conceptual art—the kind that makes your relatives go "...but is a giant blue circle hanging from a banana taped to the ceiling REALLY art?"

Even though my experience was good, I've heard plenty of horror stories about harsher art schools. The pressure, the soul-crushing critiques, the competitive atmosphere that can make you question why the hell you're there.

As I wrote Sienna, I thought about those more disheart-

ening art experiences. Unlike me, Sienna is all about traditional art forms—watercolors, paint on canvas, etc. Her art
school experience was also the complete opposite of mine.

Writing Sienna's journey got me thinking about the different paths we take in pursuing our passions. Sometimes it's
easy, sometimes it's like trying to talk while you're drowning.

And that's where *Beautiful Damage* really started to
take shape. Pursuing our passions isn't just about the act
itself. It's about what drives us, what we're running from, and
what we're running towards.

One of the main themes in this book is escape, and I
had fun showing how each character was seeking/expressing
it.

For Sienna, her art was an escape. A way to reinvent
herself and run from a past that haunted her. But the bad
thing about running all the time...no matter how far you
escape, your demons always seem to find you.

Declan was also trying to escape his past, only he did
it by burying himself in work and keeping everyone at a
distance. Then he met Sienna and escape became more
difficult; she made him face his wounds.

And Anthony, well, he couldn't escape, even if he had
wanted to in his heart.

These characters explore how we often try to outrun
our problems, our fears, our very selves. But the way to
really move forward is standing still long enough to confront
what's chasing us.

I've certainly had my moments of wanting to escape!
Whether it's spending a night reading a book when I should
be sleeping, losing myself in making miniatures (my new
obsession), or yes, fantasizing about running off to a tropical
island. But escape can only last so long and eventually I have

to come back to the real world and *deal.*

So…I hope you loved this book as much as I loved writing it. And I hope you're ready for more! There are more books coming as Sean and other characters struggle with our big baddie, Victor.

A few quick things before you go:

Would you like a bonus scenes of Declan and Sienna's wedding (and wedding night)? Look for the QR code and web address in a few pages.

Also, the series will continue in *Ugly Beautiful Scars,* which is Sean and Londyn's story. Sign up to my newsletter or follow me on Amazon for updates!

Do you like book playlists? If you missed it, there's a QR code before the first chapter that will take you to the soundtrack I created for the series.

If you enjoyed this book, you can make an *enormous* difference by leaving a review! Reviews mean so much in an author's life because they're the reason a reader gives an author a chance. As an indie author, I don't have the power of a big publisher, but I have something better: YOU!

It would mean so much if you took just a few minutes to leave a review on Amazon or Goodreads. Even one sentence makes a big difference, and can help others discover this book.

Until next time,

Raina Ash

Review on
Goodreads

Review on
Amazon

BONUS SCENE

Whether you're new to my romance world or a longtime fan, let's stay in touch! In my newsletter, I share behind-the-scenes looks, sneak peeks, bonus stories, comedy routines... Okay, not comedy routines. But I promise you'll be entertained. If you like cats, well, hold on to your sexy heels! Because I share plenty of cute cat pics.

As a special thank you for joining my newsletter, you'll get **an exclusive bonus scenes:**

•*Married in Vegas*—Declan follows Sienna to Vegas to elope. During the wedding night, the question is: Will Declan want to 'ruin' the wedding dress?

To get the bonus scenes, visit:

romancebyraina.com/beautiful-D-bonus45

ABOUT THE AUTHOR

Raina Ash is an Amazon Charts bestselling author, and her book *Love & Panic* was a 2023 Best Book Awards finalist. She writes stories about healing love—stories that are emotional, funny, and uplifting. Expect complex, resilient women, passion that's off the charts, neurodiverse characters, and protective men you can't help but crush on.

Raina is a mental health advocate and lives in Arizona with two cats, a bearded man, and several plants she struggles to keep alive. She enjoys quiet moments, video games, and sushi. Lots of sushi.

romancebyraina.com
@romancebyraina

Made in the USA
Las Vegas, NV
02 April 2025

20427008R00213